EIGHT DOGS FLYING

Samantha and Dr. Augustin enter the high-stakes, low-life world of greyhound racing—to chase down a clever killer . . .

COPY CAT CRIMES

A basket of wet, undernourished kittens turns up at the back door of Dr. Augustin's clinic—on the very same morning that one of his clients turns up dead in a nearby canal . . .

BEWARE SLEEPING DOGS

A series of unexplained illnesses in Dr. Augustin's canine patients has Samantha puzzled. But her discovery of a body in the woods is even more disturbing—and leaves her with plenty of questions to sort out . . .

Praise for the Samantha Holt series by Karen Ann Wilson:

"Engaging . . . delightful!" —Melissa Cleary, author of *Murder Most Beastly*

"An interesting setting and entertaining characters that will pique jaded mystery readers' attention." —*Gothic Journal*

MORE MYSTERIES FROM THE
BERKLEY PUBLISHING GROUP . . .

DOG LOVERS' MYSTERIES STARRING HOLLY WINTER: With her Alaskan malamute Rowdy, Holly dogs the trails of dangerous criminals. "A gifted and original writer." —Carolyn G. Hart

by Susan Conant

A NEW LEASH ON DEATH	A BITE OF DEATH
DEAD AND DOGGONE	PAWS BEFORE DYING

DOG LOVERS' MYSTERIES STARRING JACKIE WALSH: She's starting a new life with her son and an ex-police dog named Jake . . . teaching film classes and solving crimes!

by Melissa Cleary

A TAIL OF TWO MURDERS	FIRST PEDIGREE MURDER	THE MALTESE PUPPY
DOG COLLAR CRIME	SKULL AND DOG BONES	MURDER MOST BEASTLY
HOUNDED TO DEATH	DEAD AND BURIED	

CHARLOTTE GRAHAM MYSTERIES: She's an actress with a flair for dramatics— and an eye for detection. "You'll get hooked on Charlotte Graham!" —*Rave Reviews*

by Stefanie Matteson

MURDER AT THE SPA	MURDER ON THE SILK ROAD	MURDER AMONG THE ANGELS
MURDER AT TEATIME	MURDER AT THE FALLS	
MURDER ON THE CLIFF	MURDER ON HIGH	

PEACHES DANN MYSTERIES: Peaches has never had a very good memory. But she's learned to cope with it over the years . . . Fortunately, though, when it comes to murder, this absentminded amateur sleuth doesn't forgive and forget!

by Elizabeth Daniels Squire

WHO KILLED WHAT'S-HER-NAME?	REMEMBER THE ALIBI
MEMORY CAN BE MURDER	

HEMLOCK FALLS MYSTERIES: The Quilliam sisters combine their culinary and business skills to run an inn in upstate New York. But when it comes to murder, their talent for detection takes over . . .

by Claudia Bishop

A TASTE FOR MURDER	A DASH OF DEATH
A PINCH OF POISON	

SAMANTHA HOLT MYSTERIES: Dogs, cats, and crooks are all part of a day's work for this veterinary technician . . . "Delightful!" —Melissa Cleary

by Karen Ann Wilson

EIGHT DOGS FLYING	COPY CAT CRIMES
BEWARE SLEEPING DOGS	

BEWARE SLEEPING DOGS

KAREN ANN WILSON

BERKLEY PRIME CRIME, NEW YORK

BEWARE SLEEPING DOGS

A Berkley Prime Crime Book / published by arrangement with the author

PRINTING HISTORY
Berkley Prime Crime edition / June 1996

The Putnam Berkley World Wide Web site address is
http://www.berkley.com

ISBN: 0-425-15337-1

Berkley Prime Crime Books are published
by The Berkley Publishing Group,
200 Madison Avenue, New York, NY 10016.
The name BERKLEY PRIME CRIME and the BERKLEY PRIME CRIME
design are trademarks belonging to Berkley Publishing Corporation.

PRINTED IN THE UNITED STATES OF AMERICA

10 9 8 7 6 5 4 3 2 1

For Jefferson H.

ACKNOWLEDGMENTS

•

I would like to acknowledge the technical assistance of the following people: Timothy A. Whitfield, Forensic Science Section, Pinellas County Sheriff's Office, Clearwater; Alvin Dale, DVM, Lake Seminole Animal Hospital, Seminole; Roy Finley, MD, St. Petersburg; Mark Petrie, Materials Tester, Engineering Department, City of Clearwater; Michael Link, Stormwater Utility Manager, Engineering Department, City of St. Petersburg; Thomas Sheehan, Ph.D., Gainesville; Wayne Benedict, Millwork and Design, Seminole. Any errors are entirely my own.

As always, I want to thank my father, Donald F. Wilson, for his helpful suggestions. Special thanks go to the entire Benedict family: Wayne, Debbie, Amy, and Joy, and to Anneliece Coates. I would also like to express my appreciation to George, Ardyce, and Stephanie Matzke. I want to acknowledge the continued support of my agent, Robin Rue, and my editor, Ginjer Buchanan. And, of course, I want to thank my husband, Robert A. Knight.

BEWARE
SLEEPING
DOGS

CHAPTER 1

•

Tuesday, October 5

The fire started just before dawn and, backlit by the rising sun, was visible all the way across town. I couldn't hear the fire trucks, as I jogged along the causeway, but I could see the smoke. It rose straight up in a narrow column, hit some invisible high pressure zone aloft, and flattened out in both directions. It looked like a giant parasol mushroom. And I could smell it—wet, charred paper, slightly pungent, a little musty, with faint chemical overtones. Like the smell on Christmas morning up north when I was a child. The unmistakable aroma of wrapping paper, ribbon, and cellophane burning in people's fireplaces. Back then, nobody thought about dioxin, or phosgene gas, or candy cane-colored carcinogens floating up their chimneys in the wake of Santa's sleigh. These days, Santa would be wise to wear protective clothing.

When I got back to my apartment, I turned on the TV. But Charlie and Joan were talking about the latest advances in plastic surgery, so I hurried into the shower. The local news had just started when I finished drying my hair. I went into the kitchen and fixed myself a bowl of raisin bran. Then I carried it and a cup of coffee into the living room and sat down in my recliner.

Almost immediately, my cats, Tina and Miss Priss, took up positions on either side of me and began tracking the flight path of my spoon. I tried to ignore them.

"Laurel and Osceola avenues are blocked off from Main Street to South Lincoln," the news anchor, a petite blonde with a slight overbite, was saying. "Traffic is being rerouted down Tenth Avenue. Fire officials are asking all City employees who work at the Municipal Technical Services Building to report to City Hall instead, and the public is requested to avoid the downtown area this morning unless absolutely necessary."

The young woman's horsey smile suddenly was replaced by the sweaty frown of Brightwater Beach's fire chief who, complete with helmet and faint smudges of soot on his nose and left cheek, was obviously directing his troops from the front line.

As he talked, the camera panned the scene behind him. The Municipal Technical Services Building, an old brick structure dating back to the mid-fifties, when they built things to last, was still standing. But most of the windows on the third and fourth floors had been reduced to gaping holes, through which thick grey smoke billowed. Two ladder trucks were backed up to the building, and firemen were busy pumping water through the fourth-floor windows and onto the roof, what there was left of it. Smoke had begun to pour through that, as well.

The fire chief wasn't adding anything to what the news anchor had already said, except that the early hour had prevented any loss of life or serious injury, so I switched off the TV. I couldn't afford to be late. Cynthia Caswell, our receptionist, was having her teeth cleaned and wouldn't be in until sometime after nine. According to the surgical and appointment schedule posted each day, we had two spays and a neuter that morning. As usual, the clients had been instructed to drop their pets off before 8:30.

On my way down the stairs, I passed my next-door neighbor, Jeffrey Gamble. He is twenty-five, adorable, one hundred thirty pounds, and all legs. He runs marathons and waits tables at a local eatery. We are close, in a platonic sort of way. I was surprised to see him up before ten. But he'd evidently been running, because he was sweating profusely.

The weather in October over much of central and south Florida is still summerlike. It is difficult to tell when fall actually arrives here, but by mid-December, most of the maples and bald cypress and sweetgums have begun to turn. It is not even close to the beauty of New England or the Smokies, but if you look for it, you can see it. Occasionally, we just skip fall altogether. You wake up one morning to the high thirties, and a few days later all the leaves go from green to brown and drop off. Then the temperature rises again to the mid-seventies. I really am surprised the birds and the bees know what time of year it is, but they always seem to.

"You're up early," I said to Jeffrey.

He paused on the step below me. "They want me to work two shifts today. I figured I'd be too tired after waiting tables for ten hours to run, so I'm out this morning. But God, it's hot. And that smoke from downtown is nasty. Must be a doozy of a fire." He wiped sweat from his forehead with a handkerchief. Then he looked me over. Suddenly his blue eyes twinkled. "I hope you ran this morning. You need to stay in shape, Samantha. You're not getting any younger, you know."

I aimed a fist at him in mock anger, and grinning, he backed down one step.

"I'll bet you expected me to forget that your birthday is coming up," he added. "Well, I didn't. But I promise not to get you any over-the-hill stuff."

"I am not 'over-the-hill,' Jeffrey. Thirty-three is not *old*."

"Okay, okay." He stuck a finger in my ribs as he trotted past me up the stairs. He leaned over and took his key out of the pouch on his shoe. "Then again, a little wrinkle cream might not hurt." He blew me a kiss and hurried into his apartment, before I could retaliate.

"Terrific," I groaned. "And I can probably expect the same kind of 'humor' at work, too."

Feeling every bit over-the-hill, I trudged the rest of the way down the stairs and across the parking lot to my car.

Cynthia's Buick was parked in its usual spot when I arrived at the clinic.

"I thought you had a dental appointment," I said to Cynthia's back.

She was in the storage closet behind her desk, shoving boxes of cat food and flea shampoo around. Apparently, she hadn't heard me, because she jumped and put her hand over her heart when she turned around and saw me standing in the doorway.

"Don't *do* that!" she shouted.

"Do what?"

"Sneak up on people like that. It could give someone a heart attack."

She leaned over and, huffing loudly, dragged a cardboard carton past me to her desk. The carton had "Decorations" written on its top and side in large black letters. Then she sat down and took a couple of deep breaths.

Cynthia is an overweight sixty-year-old divorcee who still thinks that only horses sweat and the quickest way to a man's heart is through his stomach. Needless to say, she is a terrific cook, which is probably why Dr. Augustin hired her, although she certainly is efficient enough. She is a lot like my mother, and I let her treat me like the daughter she never had. It is a workable arrangement, except when it comes to men. Cynthia is determined to marry me off and acts like time is of the essence in that regard. I am still recovering from a one-sided relationship back home in Connecticut and have no intention of making the same mistake twice. Not in this lifetime, anyway.

"I thought you had a dental appointment," I repeated.

"I did. But the police and the fire department have everything blocked off downtown. I couldn't get anywhere close to the Union Bank building. That's where my dentist has his office." She began opening the carton. "On the news, they said the entire upper two floors of the Municipal Technical Services Building are gone. What a shame." She shook her head, then pulled out a large orange paper jack-o'-lantern and smoothed down a dog-eared edge.

"Look on the bright side," I said. "Dr. Augustin should be tickled to death. Now the city staff won't be able to refute his arguments at the commission meetings. Not with all their records burned to a crisp."

Cynthia looked at her watch, then through the tinted plate-glass wall that fronts the clinic. "Speaking of his majesty," she said, "don't you think you should get busy? He'll be here any minute."

"I suppose," I said, sighing.

I picked up my purse and lunch bag and started for the hall, just as Dr. Augustin's Jeep pulled into the parking lot. I turned around and watched him get out. He was wearing his usual—hiking boots, jeans, and a cotton shirt. This one was pale green. His shoulder-length hair was still wet. It glistened and sparkled in the sun like rough-cut obsidian.

"Well?" Cynthia said. She stared at me, her lips drawn together, the fingers of her right hand drumming the surface of her desk.

I grinned sheepishly and took off for the lab.

I was escorting our last appointment of the morning—a male black Labrador retriever with an ear infection—into an exam room when I saw a white county van pull up and stop by the front door. I paused at the reception desk and watched as John Deland, one of the county's Animal Control officers, got out. He went around to the rear of the van and removed a large dog carrier.

I looked at Cynthia. "Teddy is a recheck," I said, holding up the Labrador's file. "If John has something that can't wait, go ahead and put him in the treatment room. Tell him Dr. Augustin will be along shortly." Then I quickly ushered Teddy and his owner into Room 2.

Teddy's mistress, Katrina Treckle, was a fifty-something widow with a penchant for black clothing and handmade silver jewelry. She had very long, prematurely white hair that she obviously spent considerable time braiding and arranging in a neat coil on the back of her head. I could only remember seeing her hair down on one occasion, when she'd rushed Teddy to the clinic late on a Friday evening, after he'd tried to swallow a chicken bone thrown over the fence by a malicious neighbor. I couldn't imagine then, and still can't, why anyone would want to have that much hair in Florida, where nothing seems to dry completely on its own. But Mrs. Treckle always looked cool and fresh as a daisy. In fact, I was amazed at how cool she appeared, both inwardly and outwardly. She always sat very straight and still in the reception room, her eyes aimed at some imaginary spot on the wall across from her. And she had a perpetual half smile on her face, almost condescending, but not actually offensive. Her whole demeanor was regal, poised, and self-assured. She had no discernible accent, but I periodically wondered if she was some reincarnated Russian czarina.

What she needs, I thought, as she settled herself in the room's only chair, is a borzoi, not a black Lab, although Teddy's color certainly goes well with her normal attire. According to Cynthia, the woman's husband had been dead for over fifteen years. Her apparent desire to remain in mourning for the rest of her life was unquestionably romantic, but a bit overdone by my way of thinking.

By the time Dr. Augustin came in the exam room, I had managed, unaided, to lift Teddy onto the exam table and now stood next to him with my hand on his collar. Katrina remained seated.

"Good morning Mrs. Treckle—Katrina," said Dr. Augustin, smiling.

Katrina dipped her head in a sort of nod, but otherwise did not change her expression. "Good morning," she replied.

If Dr. Augustin was offended by Mrs. Treckle's lack of awe at his broad shoulders and nicely fitting jeans, he did not show it. He took the otoscope off its charger and examined Teddy's ear. "Looks real fine," he said. He removed the plastic speculum and tossed it on the counter. Then he snapped the otoscope back on the charger and picked up the small squeeze bottle of drying agent I had put out for him.

"If Teddy decides to go for another swim, Mrs. Treckle, squirt a little of this in each ear."

He took the cap off the bottle and filled Teddy's left ear canal. Then, before he could swab the ear out completely, Teddy shook his head. The dog's ears and jowls flapped noisily, and a shower of tiny ethylene glycol droplets spewed forth, coating the table and adjacent linoleum floor.

"I recommend you do this outside," Dr. Augustin said, "for obvious reasons."

He tore a paper towel from the roll over the sink and wiped Teddy's ear and neck, then lifted the dog off the table. I snapped Teddy's leash to his collar and handed it and the bottle to Mrs. Treckle.

Katrina stood up, took the leash and bottle, and started for the door. Then she stopped and turned around. Dr. Augustin was writing something in Teddy's record. When he looked up, she broadened her half smile just a bit and extended her hand.

"Thank you, Dr. Augustin," she said. "Teddy thanks you, as well."

Dr. Augustin shook her hand, using both of his and taking a little longer than necessary. I could tell he was giving her his best hypnotic stare, the one most women find totally disarming.

"No problem," he said. "Glad we could help."

I watched Katrina's face and was positive she blushed. The pink color that suffused her cheeks was very faint, but I hadn't imagined it.

Dr. Augustin had seen it, too, because he glanced over at me with that nauseating smirk he always gets when he knows he has won over another rare recalcitrant female. The tougher the contest, the more nauseating the smirk. I pretended not to notice. It didn't fool him, though, and he winked at me as he exited the room.

I carried Teddy's file up to the reception room and handed

it to Cynthia. Katrina, pen poised over her checkbook, waited as Cynthia began to punch Dr. Augustin's charges into the computer. Suddenly she pulled her eyebrows together and pursed her lips, producing a landscape of ripples and wrinkles that hadn't been there before. The action was so synchronized, it was like her face was a piece of fabric some playful cat had snagged.

At first, I assumed she had spotted the preserved dog heart Dr. Augustin insists on keeping in the reception room to remind clients to put their dogs on heartworm prevention. The heart belonged to a golden retriever who died from heartworm disease. It is a gross, pale pinkish-tan and has long, thin white strands sticking out of it. To make matters worse, it is floating in a glass, fluid-filled womb that has Hellmann's Mayonnaise printed on the lid.

But Katrina wasn't looking at the dog heart. She was staring at the candy dish next to it. The dish, a miniature black ceramic cauldron, was filled with candy corn. At its base, it was attached to a ceramic witch—one of those humorous Disney-type creations, complete with warty chin and hooked nose. I started to say something like "Please, just ignore the jar and help yourself to some candy," but her expression stopped me. Then she shook her head slowly, relaxed her face, and went back to her check writing.

I smiled at the man who was waiting to pay for a refill prescription and left without telling Katrina good-bye.

Dr. Augustin and John Deland were in the treatment room, examining a recumbent mixed-breed dog the size of a chow. In fact, it looked a little like a chow. It had the furry, lionlike head and fluffy tail of a chow, but its body was too long and lean, and it was a brindle black and tan, rather than the usual solid color.

"What's wrong with her?" I asked. I went over to the exam table and looked down at the dog. She was breathing, but that's about all she was doing.

John shook his head. "We think someone may have poisoned her. She's from that pack of wild dogs up in the Carriage Hill area that's been eluding us for, what, three years now? I guess one or two of the residents finally decided to take matters into their own hands." He shook his head. "We found another one yesterday, but it was already dead. I was able to catch this one, because she was staggering around like a drunk and didn't see me."

Dr. Augustin handed me two blood collection tubes, each containing a small quantity of blood. "Have Tracey do a CBC right away and a cross-match with that donor blood we have left over from last week," he said. "And send out serum for a chemical profile." He looked down at the dog. "She's so anemic and dehydrated, I was lucky to get anything out of those veins, so don't waste any." He squeezed her abdomen. "We might be able to get a urine sample, too, but I doubt it."

I was surprised he hadn't euthanized the dog already. Unless Animal Control finds a license on an injured dog or cat or is fairly certain it is someone's pet, they aren't willing to let it suffer indefinitely or to spend public money to fix it up. And Dr. Augustin, who volunteers his services doing spays and neuters for cost, isn't inclined to spend his own money, either, particularly if the animal isn't a good candidate for adoption.

"I guess if you're going to do a transfusion," I said, "it means you're not going to euthanize her."

Dr. Augustin shrugged. "I'd like to find out what's making her sick, first. It'll help John locate the person or persons responsible. Hopefully before they kill again. Before they get someone's pet. Or a kid."

Tracey Nevins, our laboratory technician, was at the sink in the lab, cleaning microscope slides. "Too bad about that dog," she said over her shoulder. "It probably pooped in some rich guy's yard."

Tracey is twenty-two, an ovo-lacto vegetarian who spends most of her free time oogling the drummer in a local rock band, a group called "Death Watch." Other than that, she is a fairly levelheaded and astute kid. Best of all, she likes pizza—sans pepperoni, of course—and doesn't let Dr. Augustin get under her skin, something I have so far been unsuccessful at.

I labeled the tubes, put them in the rack, and wrote the required tests down in the logbook. "John said she's part of that pack up in the Carriage Hill subdivision he and the rest of Animal Control have been trying to catch for a couple of years."

"Pack?" asked Tracey. She dried her hands on a paper towel. Then she took one of the blood tubes out of the rack and studied it. "Not good," she mumbled, mostly to herself.

"There are about two dozen strays in the pack now, according to John. They're organized, with a leader—a female, if you can believe that—who keeps them together and well fed and away from the traps Animal Control sets. Actually, most of us who don't live in Carriage Hill think it's kind of funny, all those supposedly dumb animals running circles around a bunch of humans who are determined to catch them. But I guess if you live up there, it isn't so humorous."

Tracey took a container of hematocrit tubes out of the cabinet over the microscope. "No, I guess not. Still, poisoning them surely isn't the answer."

I turned to go, then stopped. A large paper cutout of a black cat, its back arched and its tail puffed out, was pinned to the hall bulletin board opposite the door to the lab. The inscription, in squiggly black lettering over the cat's head, was "Happy Halloween." Cynthia had obviously been hard at work, getting us "in the spirit." And it was only the beginning of October. I turned around.

"You don't suppose these poisonings are some sick kid's Halloween prank, do you?" I asked Tracey.

She shook her head. "They only do that to black cats. Besides, it's way too early for tricks or treats."

But I wasn't so sure. Kmart already had their Christmas decorations up.

CHAPTER 2

•

Wednesday, October 6

I had the day off, so I stayed in bed until Tina and Priss weren't happy to just sit and stare at me. Their stereo purring and gentle tapping on my face with their front paws (one cat on each side, like altar boys) finally was more than I could handle. I dreaded the end of the month and the end of daylight saving time. It would mean being awakened an hour earlier. At least until I got them back on schedule. My mother had given me one of those self-feeders for Christmas, in the hopes that my cats would eat whenever they were hungry and leave me alone. Unfortunately, Priss cleaned the whole thing out the first day.

I did my three miles, scanned the paper, and ate breakfast. Then I headed for the laundromat around the corner to wash some clothes. I was halfway across the parking lot in front of my building when Michael Halsey's BMW pulled up and stopped.

Michael lowered his window and smiled out at me. "Greetings," he said, his words nearly drowned out by the car's CD player. His selection that morning was a contemporary piece with lots of brass. He reached over and turned the volume down. "Thought I'd drop by and see what you had on tap for this evening."

He was wearing his charcoal suit, white Oxford shirt, and nice conservative tie. The maroon one with diagonal grey

11

stripes. If he'd been thirty instead of fifty, he could have posed for some yuppie magazine ad. I can picture him on Wall Street, buying and selling corporate stock and living with his lovely wife and their 2.4 children in a three-thousand-square-foot apartment on the Upper East Side, or wherever people like that live in New York.

But Michael Halsey is a widower who, for whatever reason, has elected to live in Brightwater Beach, Florida. And as an assistant editor for the local paper is earning an order of magnitude less than he would wheeling and dealing at the Stock Exchange. Which raises the question of how a glorified newspaper reporter can afford the lifestlye that Michael enjoys, including frequent trips to the Caribbean on his forty-foot Chris Craft, called the *Serendipity*. Despite subtle probing, to date I haven't gotten a satisfactory explanation out of him.

"Why?" I asked, putting down my laundry basket. "What did you have in mind?"

"I'm doing a feature on that high-voltage power-line project the electric company is proposing. The public hearing is tonight. It should be pretty entertaining. I guess you've read about it in the paper."

"Not really," I said. "I haven't had time lately to read more than the front page." I grinned. "And the comics. I usually rely on Cynthia to keep me up-to-date on things of interest in the area. I'm surprised she hasn't mentioned it."

"*I'm* surprised Dr. Augustin hasn't said something. This is right up his alley. Nice and controversial."

"If you're inviting me to tag along, I accept," I said. It was the first time he had asked me to go with him on an assignment.

"Great! I'll be over about five-thirty with dinner. Chinese okay?"

"Sure," I said.

He winked, closed his window, and pulled away.

I watched his car disappear around the corner. Then I

picked up my laundry basket and continued my trek to the laundromat.

I first met Michael in February, when he came to the clinic seeking information about Dr. Augustin's ex-wife, Rachel. Actually, he wanted to know about one of Rachel's greyhounds, who had viciously attacked a little girl for no apparent reason.

At that time, Dr. Augustin considered journalists only a step or two up the evolutionary ladder from slime molds, doubtless the result of being misquoted by them on several occasions. So, he wasn't thrilled to find I had agreed to go out with Mr. Halsey. Eventually, however, he came to tolerate Michael. Particularly when he found out how helpful reporters can be at digging up information not readily available to the average citizen.

Michael doesn't seem to mind helping Dr. Augustin out, either; however, I suspect he is doing it more for me than for my boss. When you get right down to it, I think Michael would do anything for me, even something a little unethical. And therein lies my dilemma. Michael is fun to look at and be with, knows which fork to use, and isn't instantly transformed into an octopus the minute we are alone. Cynthia loves him (what mother wouldn't?) and pulls out the latest issue of *Bride* magazine every time he comes in the clinic. But although I like Michael a great deal and enjoy his company, I don't love him. Getting involved with him outside of the occasional date would only mean heartache for us both, eventually. There was no question about that. So why was I continuing to lead him on? Selfishness? Did I enjoy being wined and dined and treated like a lady more than I cared to admit? Or was I too much of a coward to look him in the eye and tell him I didn't think there was much future in our relationship?

I mulled all of this over through two loads of wash but found no answers spinning around in the dryer with my underwear. All I succeeded in doing that morning was make myself angry, so at ten, I dumped my laundry on the sofa, put on my swimsuit, and headed for the beach.

At 5:30 on the dot, Michael arrived carrying a large paper sack and two foam cups filled with hot tea. We went into my kitchen and I began unloading the sack.

"No chopsticks?" I asked, laughing.

"They intimidate you, remember?"

"I thought you were going to teach me how to use them," I said, laying silverware and plates out on my dining table.

Michael opened the carry-out boxes and stuck a spoon in each one. "No time," he said. "The hearing starts at six-thirty." He pulled my chair out for me.

"So," I began, peering in the first container, "tell me about this power-line controversy."

He sat down next to me and opened his tea. "The hearing is actually to discuss an Army Corps of Engineers dredge and fill permit," he said. "The electric company has applied to fill part of a small freshwater marsh at one end of their proposed transmission corridor. It runs diagonally across the northeast corner of the City. Most of it is in the County, but the marsh is within the city limits. That's why the Corps is holding the hearing in Brightwater Beach instead of in Tampa."

"And the environmentalists are fighting it, right?" I tasted a little of the Mongolian beef to see how spicy it was. I like Szechzuan, but it is prudent to be forewarned.

"Sort of," said Michael. "Although, to their credit, the company has made a lot of changes to their original plan in an effort to satisfy the concerns of the environmental people. The legitimate ones, that is."

"There are illegitimate environmentalists?" I asked, laughing.

He frowned. "I suspect that a large number of those opposed to the project don't give a damn about the fish and wildlife aspects." He spooned out a serving of curried chicken, his favorite. "Have you ever heard of EMFs?"

"I seem to recall something about EMFs and electric blankets. That there were supposed to be health problems associated with using them, especially if the person is pregnant."

Michael chewed for a moment, then swallowed. He took a sip of tea. "Actually, 'EMF,' or 'electromagnetic field,' is an abbreviation for two different but related things, according to my source at the power company."

He waved his fork at me and took on a very professional air as he spoke. I tried to imagine him teaching my physics class. Maybe I would have learned more if he had. At least going to class would have been tolerable if we'd had Michael to look at instead of Dr. Otis, a skeleton of a man with an equally lively personality.

"There are 'electric fields,' " he was saying, "created by the electric charges in the wires that carry electricity to and from an outlet and in any electric appliance plugged into one of those outlets, whether or not the appliance is operating. And there are 'magnetic fields,' created by the movement of those charges through the wires when the current is flowing. Unlike an electric field, you can only have a magnetic field when the appliance is drawing current." He sipped his tea.

"So these EMFs are all around us, wherever there are electrical charges—in buildings, our cars, lightning, even our own bodies, I suppose," I said, looking suspiciously at my microwave oven.

"Exactly." He scooped out the rest of the Mongolian beef. "So far, no one has been able to prove with certainty that EMFs, such as those created by overhead power lines, cause any health problems. Of course, that hasn't stopped people from blaming them for a variety of ills, ranging from depression and headaches to cancer and birth defects."

"So the controversy over the proposed power-line thing is a health issue, rather than a dredge and fill issue, right?" I asked.

"A little of both, actually. However, since the Corps of Engineers is only interested in the impact of construction on the wetlands, several of the more crafty opponents of the project are claiming the marsh is the reason the permit should be denied. In any case, tonight's public hearing should prove interesting."

He looked at his watch, then reached into the paper sack. "Almost time to go," he said. He took out a small bag containing two fortune cookies and handed one of them to me. "These things have sample Lotto numbers printed on them now. Did you know that? You can gamble and have your fortune told all at the same time."

He snapped his cookie in two and pulled out the little strip of paper baked inside. " 'You will take a trip to a faraway land.' Sounds promising. What does yours say?" He smiled benignly.

I cracked open my cookie and withdrew the paper strip. It read, "Love is a fortune worth waiting for." I swallowed.

"Well, what's the good word?"

I balled up the paper and tossed it into the empty Mongolian beef carton. " 'Love of money is the root of all evil,' " I said, not looking at him. "I guess that means I shouldn't buy a Lotto ticket this week."

Michael got up and began cleaning the table. "Hmmm," he mumbled.

CHAPTER 3

•

On the way to the city's new Civic Center auditorium, Michael took me on a quick tour of Carriage Hill, New York developer Alan Greiner's latest planned community for the upwardly mobile. While Michael described the four- and five-bedroom model homes with their vaulted ceilings, wet bars, and computerized security systems (and names like Mt. Vernon and Monticello), I couldn't help remembering Dr. Augustin's version of the place. According to him, what had once been an enormous pine forest, cool and green, was now a desert of shifting sand and relentless sun, broken up by an ever-expanding network of asphalt and concrete. Thirsty imported landscaping with little or no wildlife value had replaced the native vegetation. I had to admit, the hiss and spit of Rain Birds, clearly in defiance of the area's sprinkling restrictions, was hard to ignore. Like the highly publicized water shortage was just so much propaganda.

According to the billboards on U.S. 19, the homes in Carriage Hill started at $300,000. It's pretty obvious why John Deland's feral dogs have taken up residence here, I thought, as we passed a Stuffed Mushroom catering truck. When you can eat like these folks do, why settle for bologna and hot dogs? The pack leader undoubtedly knows the garbage collection schedule and sends her followers out the night before pickup to graze on leftover veal piccatta and mussels marinara.

Except for praising Mr. Greiner's accomplishments, Michael said little. He had slipped a recording of Handel's *Water Music* into the car's CD player before we left, and we listened to it during most of the half-hour trip. Michael concentrated on the rush-hour traffic, and I spent too much time pondering the significance of my fortune cookie.

We arrived at the Civic Center at 6:30. The parking lot was full, so Michael let me out at the door and told me the seats reserved for the press probably would be marked accordingly. Then he took off to find a parking space in one of the overflow lots down the street.

I ducked into the ladies room. Women of all shapes and sizes (and all tax brackets, by the look of their outfits and jewelry) were lined up to use the toilets. It was apparent that they envisioned a long and arduous battle that evening and wanted to be in top form. It was all I could do to squeeze my hands through the crush at the sink and briefly run water over them. Forget the soap. Up and down the line, women were shadow boxing in front of the mirror, brandishing brushes, cans of hair spray, and lipstick like medieval weapons. Others were busy tugging on various pieces of their attire, as if arranging suits of mail.

Several of the women had large buttons prominently displayed on their persons that read SAY NO TO OVERHEAD POWER LINES. I refrained from commenting, although even I, a complete novice on the subject of electric power transmission, knew that the cost of burying the huge lines everyone was so worried about had to be astronomical. And I wondered who these ladies thought would end up paying to bury the lines, if, indeed, they *could* be buried.

As we left the rest room and headed for the auditorium, one of the button women, a plump but attractive brunette somewhere around forty, wearing white sandals and a plain cotton dress the color of Granny Smith apples, was talking about the power company's lawyer, one Martin Walker. To hear her tell it, Mr. Walker routinely stole candy from children and drop-kicked cats and dogs for sport. Instead of some smooth-talking corporate executive, I half expected to see Darth Vader sitting in the audience, surrounded by a horde of storm troopers.

The woman spoke with such conviction and eloquence, I found myself, with no facts whatever, prepared to fight the power-line project tooth and nail. If Dr. Augustin ever decides to run for public office, I thought, he would be wise to hire this lady as his campaign manager. I smiled at her, then stopped just inside the double doors to look for Michael.

Nearly every seat in the spacious auditorium was occupied, or would be once the contingent from the ladies' room located their significant others. The noise level wasn't too bad, however, owing to the building's fancy acoustics, and I was able to eavesdrop on a few of the many conversations under way at the back of the room. Three men to my right were discussing their children's soccer coach, using terms not suitable for young listeners. Apparently, their team wasn't having a good season, and Coach Marshall was obviously to blame. They were trying to decide what to do about the guy. I got the distinct impression that lynching was not out of the question.

Another little group, a few feet to my left, was discussing the hearing. They had chosen a spokesperson to represent them that evening and were waiting for him (or her) to arrive. Darth Vader's name surfaced, again, complete with expletives. I smiled. There really isn't a whole lot of difference between these two groups, I thought. It is simply a matter of priorities.

Several people with battery packs strapped around their waists stood along the right wall, amid a jumble of TV cameras, cables, and other miscellaneous equipment. They looked bored. One of them was drinking a Coke just a couple of feet from a large NO FOOD OR DRINK IN AUDITORIUM sign. Another was talking to a woman perched precariously on the arm of a chair midway up the aisle. She was obviously a member of the press, because she had a microphone in her lap. I started wending my way slowly toward her.

There wasn't anyone obviously in charge at the front of the room. The stage was empty, except for two eight-foot tables, each with four chairs set up behind it. The tables were covered with dark green tablecloths and had a microphone positioned between each pair of chairs. Someone had printed something with a black Magic Marker on eight oblong pieces of white posterboard and then had propped the pieces up at regular intervals along the tables. The printing was too small to make out. A pitcher of water and several glasses sat at the far end of the table to my left. The pitcher was sweating and had soaked the tablecloth so thoroughly, the piece of posterboard nearest it was beginning to wilt.

"Samantha, what are you doing here?" I heard a familiar voice directly behind me ask.

I stopped and looked over my shoulder. I spied Dr. Augustin sitting on the aisle next to Bill O'Shea, a mutual friend and owner of the Paper Moon, a popular beach bar near the clinic.

"I came with Michael," I said, looking around. "Now I've lost him. You wouldn't happen to know where the press section is, would you?"

Dr. Augustin grinned. "Is this Mr. Halsey's idea of a fun date?"

Bill smiled and looked away.

I ignored the crack. "So how come you haven't been ranting and raving about this power-line thing back at the clinic?"

He sat up. "I do not 'rant and rave,' Samantha," he said indignantly.

It was my turn to grin. "Sure you don't."

"In any case, I haven't formed an opinion on this project yet," he said. "One way or the other."

Before I could express my disbelief at this, someone began testing the PA system.

"Later," I said, and continued down the aisle.

Michael snagged me as I was about to ask the woman with the microphone if she was in the section reserved for the press.

"Up here," he whispered and led me to the front row.

We sat down in two chairs evidently saved for us by a man with a *Times* ID badge clipped to his shirt pocket. The man was in his thirties, skinny as a rail, and had obviously suffered from a very severe case of acne as a teenager, because his face looked like the surface of the moon.

"This is Chip Reason," said Michael. "From our Tampa office. Chip, this is Samantha Holt."

Chip and I shook hands. His expression was one of curiosity mingled with mild amusement.

"I'm very happy to meet you," he said, smiling. He let go of my hand but continued to evaluate me, his eyes moving over my body like I was a piece of microfiche.

Suddenly I felt sorry for Michael. I had always wondered why he never invited me to office parties or functions. I had never met a single person Michael worked with or any of his friends outside the office, assuming he had any friends other than Cynthia and me. We never seemed to run into anyone Michael knew, even though we ate out regularly and frequented local nightclubs and, lately, the ballet and the theater. I was convinced Michael felt embarrassed about dating someone seventeen years his junior, although he never showed it. Not to me, anyway.

Of course, there was always Mary, Michael's wife, dead for over two years but clearly not content to rest in peace. There were actually times when I thought I could feel her presence, wedged like an invisible doorstop between Michael and me. She refused to let Michael alone and was forever trying to get his attention. Like Patrick Swayze trying to communicate with Demi Moore in the movie *Ghost*. Who was I supposed to be? Whoopi Goldberg?

The PA system coughed a couple of times, and the TV people suddenly woke up. Then four men, one of them in uniform, and two women stepped up onto the stage and walked across to the tables. They seemed momentarily confused. One of the women pointed to the posterboard nameplates, and then all six of them played musical chairs for several seconds, until everyone was finally where he or she was supposed to be. Two of the chairs remained empty.

The man in uniform blew on his microphone, then in a very official voice asked everyone to please find a seat so they could get started. He waited a minute, then introduced himself as Major Samuel Hall, Deputy District Engineer for the U.S. Army Corps of Engineers. Then he introduced his companions, a lawyer—one of the women—and three regulatory agents. The sixth member of the panel, also a woman, was the Corps' chief public affairs officer. She was black and extremely attractive. She was also at least six feet tall and towered over the major, who was seated next to her. Even the lawyer, a middle-aged, slightly overweight woman dressed in a somber grey and black shirtwaist and also sitting next to the major, was taller than he was. Despite his uniform, dutifully adorned with evidence of past accomplishments, the man looked like a toy soldier in the company of Amazons.

"This hearing," Major Hall informed us, "is being recorded by a court reporter, seated to my right."

He pointed down toward the front of the audience. I could just make out a young woman pecking away at one of those strange machines you see in lawyer movies.

Major Hall sat ramrod-straight in his chair, one hand over the other in front of him, cleared his throat, and began to outline the procedures for conducting the hearing. He told us how long each person could speak and in what order, how he sincerely hoped everyone would refrain from applauding (he did not say they should refrain from booing), and how there would be no cross-examination, as this was not an adjudicatory hearing.

I noticed the TV people were napping again, presumably dreaming about the vacations they would take with all their overtime pay. I started to ask Michael how long he planned to tough it out, but decided to wait awhile. At least until people began to yawn, which seemed imminent at the rate we were progressing.

The major followed all of this with a lengthy and boring

monologue, during which time I caught the words "dredge and fill," "wetlands," "water quality," "energy needs," and "the needs and welfare of the people." "Food and fiber production" and "mineral needs" also were mentioned, although I had no idea why. Was the power company planning to diversify? The "needs and welfare of the people" caused a slight buzzing sound to start up behind me. One of the TV guys obviously heard it, too, because he hoisted his camera up onto his shoulder and flipped on the zillion-watt light positioned like a giant eye above the lens, and began to pan the room. The buzzing died down almost immediately. The cameraman turned off the light.

When he had finished with the formalities, the major introduced the applicant's representative, a thin, pale, rather nerdy-looking man, dressed in a short-sleeved white shirt and skinny brown tie. I expected him to be wearing flood pants and white socks, as well, but was disappointed. He did have a calculator and two mechanical pencils sticking out of his breast pocket, however.

He walked to the front of the room, just below the stage, where a lectern, complete with reading light and microphone, had been set up facing the audience.

No one behind me made a sound, but I felt the animosity grow more palpable with every collective breath the audience took. I wondered if the guys at the electric company had drawn straws for this assignment. And now the winners (because this man was certainly the loser) were safe at home drinking a cold one in memory of their fallen comrade.

The man opened a file folder and positioned it in front of him on the lectern. Then he loosened his tie, drew in a deep breath, and began to speak. Amazingly, he had a strong, authoritative voice and obviously knew his subject. He briefly outlined the proposed project, including the need for it and the various safeguards that would be in place during construction to protect the wetlands and any eagle's nest that might be present on or adjacent to the site. He ignored the rumblings of the audience when he got to the part about "minimal permanent impact to the natural environment." He simply raised his voice and continued on.

When the engineer had finished, the major, who had been studying his posterboard nameplate, snapped to attention.

"Thank you, Mr. Bishop," he said.

He smiled blandly, then whispered something to the lawyer. She, in turn, pointed to the lectern. One of the regulatory chaps nodded and got up. He went across the stage and down the steps. Someone from the audience joined him, and together they shoved the lectern around, until it was facing the stage.

"And now, is there any local elected official here, tonight," the major asked, "who would like to make a statement?" He nodded toward the back of the room. "All right. But please remember to keep your comments to five minutes or less."

A tall, wiry, deeply tanned gentleman dressed in a long-sleeved, pale blue, snap-front shirt and bolo approached the lectern. He was wearing cowboy boots. Black, with two-inch heels. He was about to face the stage, but apparently remembered the TV cameras. He smiled in their direction. Then he turned around.

"Thank you, Major Hall, for allowing me this opportunity to speak."

His voice was deep and resonant, and he spoke slowly, with a practiced folksy twang that Dr. Augustin calls "southern snake oil salesman."

"For those of you who don't know me, and I think most of you already do, my name is Lester Jordan. I'm chairman of the County Commission. Now, I've lived in this neck of the woods all my life and I know a thing or two about this fine city. I care deeply about its residents, especially the children." His drawl deepened. Just a good neighbor chatting with his friends.

The cameramen obviously weren't prepared. The guy who had been first to record the audience while the power company rep was talking made an end run around the rest of

the news pack and stopped at the corner of the stage. He
aimed his camera at Mr. Jordan and turned on the light. The
room vanished in a flood of white light.

"Hey, turn that damned thing off," I heard someone yell.
Mercifully, the cameraman did as he was asked.

I blinked a couple of times, then watched as Mr. Jordan
pulled several folded-up sheets of paper out of his back
pocket. He unfolded them, held the bunch at arm's length,
and squinted. Then he took a pair of reading glasses out of
his breast pocket. He put them on and studied the top sheet
of paper again, this time at a more comfortable distance.

"I have here with me a resolution pertaining to this project passed just last week by the commission, and I'd like to
read it into the record, if that's okay."

Without waiting to see if it was and undoubtedly with no
regard for the five-minute time limit, Mr. Jordan began to
read, his voice tremulous, with all the passion and theatrics
of a career politician intent on the presidency.

The resolution was filled with so many whereases and be-
it-thats, I soon lost track and interest. My eyes and mind
began to wander, and I longed for an earthquake or level-
four hurricane or, at the very least, the sound of the fire
alarm. A power outage would be nice, I thought. Appropriate, too. Or a bolt of lightning through the PA system. I
could tell a lot of other people shared my sentiments, because seats all around me started to squeak, and the rear
doors opened and closed several times in quick succes-
sion—a whap-whap sound.

Michael was writing in his notebook. I leaned over and
whispered to him. "How long do you think this guy is going
to talk?" I crossed and uncrossed my legs, in an effort to get
some blood into them.

Michael smiled and shook his head. "Hard to say. He can
get pretty bombastic at times. Shouldn't be long, though, or
the major will have to intervene."

But the major was asleep. He was bent over his notepad,
and his hand held a ballpoint like he was busy taking notes,

but his head kept getting lower and lower. I felt myself willing him to wake up. I wasn't so much concerned about saving the man almost certain embarrassment should he fall facedown on the table, as I was about my own welfare. If Major Hall didn't wake up in time, who would stop Mr. Jordan from rambling on forever?

I thought about Dr. Augustin. He and Bill are probably back there having a great old time discussing football or the benefits of red meat, I told myself. Ten rows from the front you could do that and not appear rude. I looked at Michael, again. He seemed quite content to sit essentially motionless and work on his story. Why weren't his legs cramping up? Mine certainly were. I crossed and uncrossed them. I needed a drink of water to dilute the soy sauce from dinner, but I wasn't about to give Dr. Augustin another opportunity to make some snappy remark about my date. Even if it *was* boring. I opened my purse and began fishing around for a stick of gum.

Suddenly I heard Mr. Jordan pause. Then he said, very dramatically, " 'Now, therefore, be it resolved that the Board of County Commissioners has deemed Peninsular Power Corporation's proposed power-line corridor to be contrary to the public interest and requests that the U.S. Army Corps of Engineers deny said company's Section 404 dredge and fill permit application, until such time as a full Environmental Impact Statement can be prepared on the proposed project and analyzed by the appropriate agencies.' "

The lawyer nudged Major Hall, and his head popped up and bobbled a bit, like one of those inflatable clowns, and then he sat up nice and straight and smiled.

"Thank you, Mr. Jordan," he said. He looked at his watch, then at a thick stack of 3x5 cards handed to him by his chief of public affairs. "Our next speaker is Mr. Daniel Kenney." He looked up. "Is Mr. Kenney here?" His face fell. "All right then, but *please* keep your comments to five minutes or less. We want to give everyone here a chance to speak,

and there are quite a few people who have filled out cards."
He held up the stack as if to emphasize his point.

Mr. Jordan smiled down at the news media on the front
row, then proceeded up the aisle toward the back of the
room. He had a rocking, slightly bowlegged gait that I imagined came from years of sitting on a horse. Either that or
walking to and fro on the deck of a ship. Or else he hadn't
drunk enough milk as a child.

"What does Mr. Jordan do, aside from run the county?" I
asked Michael, as a balding, middle-aged man with a faint
beer belly stepped up to the lectern. He was wearing one of
the SAY NO TO OVERHEAD POWER LINES buttons.

"He's a rancher," whispered Michael. "Very successful,
too, I understand. Raises Brangus cattle, mostly, although I
hear he has a sizable portion of his land in sod. There's apparently a lot of money to be made in sod around here. And
he dabbles in real estate."

The man with the pot gut cleared his throat. "Thank you.
My name is Daniel Kenney. My wife, Carol, and my three
children and I live in Maraldee Manor, which is located
about five miles from here, as the crow flies."

He placed both hands on the lectern, apparently for support. Clearly, he was nervous. The top of his head gleamed
with sweat.

"I've come here tonight to tell you about my son. About
Joey." His voice broke slightly. "Joey is only ten, Major, and
he has acute lymphoblastic leukemia. I don't know if you
are familiar with this disease, and I pray to God you never
have to be, because no one should have to learn about it
firsthand like my wife and I have."

He stopped, took a handkerchief out of his back pocket,
and wiped his face and the top of his head. "Right now our
Joey is in Tampa receiving treatment, which is no fun for
him, let me tell you. I won't go into the details, because I
only have a few minutes here, but I must tell you that Joey
isn't alone. There have been three other little boys that I
know of in Maraldee Manor and one little girl who have

been diagnosed with cancer within the past two years. According to Joey's doctors, this is above the national average."

He wiped his face again. All of the people on the stage were paying attention. Not rapt attention, mind you, but they weren't sleeping or doodling or whispering to each other. The lawyer looked particularly attentive. I wondered if it was a conditioned response to the word "doctor."

"The reason I mention Joey and his friends to you is we have one of those power-line corridors running along the back of our property. It is a 230,000 volt line. What the power company is proposing here tonight is a 500,000 volt line, which is over twice what we have."

He paused and gripped the sides of the lectern. "Major Hall, I am sure you are aware of the studies done with EMFs—electromagnetic fields. There is a lot of disagreement about the health effects of those EMFs, I'll admit. Now I am certainly not a scientist or a doctor, but I am a father, and I know that my son and his little friends are sick. And all the doctors over there in Tampa can say is it is simply a coincidence that so many kids in our neighborhood have cancer. Well, I'm not so sure."

The major looked at his watch and then at the stack of 3x5 cards. Kenney got the message.

"So I am begging you, Major Hall, for the sake of all those precious children who might come to live near this proposed corridor, don't grant this permit. Until there is absolutely no question about the safety of overhead power lines, don't let the power company put another life at risk." He wiped his face and stuffed the handkerchief back into his pocket. "Thank you, Major, for listening."

Mr. Kenney turned around, and not surprisingly, the audience began to applaud, softly at first, then louder and louder. Several people stood up and clapped and cheered as Kenney walked slowly up the aisle. The TV cameras followed his progress, their lights reflecting off Kenney's bald pate, creating a halo around his head and shoulders.

Suddenly the woman in the apple-green dress, tears flowing down her face, stepped out in front of Mr. Kenney, and the two embraced. The TV people loved it. They filled the aisle, cameramen jostling for position, newscasters stepping all over each other in their haste to be first to ask the grief-stricken couple what it felt like to have a son on death's doorstep. People all along the aisle reached out to touch Mrs. Kenney, like her tears were not human tears at all but, rather, those of some plaster of paris Madonna.

I looked up at the major. He was trying, unsuccessfully, to regain control. He tapped on the microphone several times with his ballpoint. He even shouted for people to please sit, but no one was listening. Finally, he called a ten-minute recess, then disappeared behind the curtain at the back of the stage. The lawyer and the public affairs chief hurried after him.

CHAPTER 4

•

I went outside and sat by the fountain in front of the Civic Center. Because of the ongoing drought and the political implications of ignoring it, water had yet to spew forth from the two dozen fancy nozzles at the base of the fountain or fill the aquamarine-colored pond shaped like a dolphin. The city uses reclaimed water on its golf courses and parkways, but there is something unappetizing about eating one's lunch next to a pool of treated sewage. Never mind the fact that these days it is cleaner than most rain puddles.

Michael had gone to use his car phone, since the two pay phones in the building were occupied. I secretly hoped some problem had developed back at the newspaper that would necessitate his immediate return. I had never acquired a taste for soap operas, and now the thought of sitting through this one for three or four more hours was making me ill.

"Enjoying yourself?" It was Dr. Augustin. He walked around the fountain and sat down next to me.

"Not really," I admitted. "I can't understand how reporters do it. I mean, sit around for hours listening to people ramble."

"It does take a certain degree of patience."

I laughed. "Then how do *you* manage to sit through those boring commission meetings every month?"

"Anticipation," he said.

"Of what, pray tell."

"Of a good knock-down-drag-out fight. Some of those boring meetings can get pretty bloody."

I saw his watch glow briefly. He stood up.

"Why don't you join Bill and me later? We're going to that new pub down the road. The one that supposedly stocks over a hundred and fifty varieties of imported beer."

The offer was appealing. "I don't know," I said. "Michael . . ."

"Bring Mr. Halsey along, Samantha. I promise to behave myself."

I couldn't see his face clearly. He sounded sincere.

"Maybe," I said. "I'll ask."

He touched me lightly on the shoulder. "Okay. See you later, then." He headed back toward the auditorium.

Michael came across the grass. "It never ceases to amaze me that we actually produce a paper each night," he said. He sounded angry.

"What's the problem?"

"Oh, nothing new. The left and right hands not communicating."

We got to the door in time to hear Major Hall ask for quiet. The crowd hadn't thinned out much, so it took us a while to reach the front row. Chip smiled up at me from his seat. He still looked amused.

"Our next speaker is Justin Blaize," said Major Hall.

The major looked considerably more alert than he had earlier. I noticed he and the lawyer and two of the regulatory guys had jumbo McDonald's coffee cups in front of them, despite the NO FOOD OR DRINK sign.

The major continued. "I must remind the audience to *please* refrain from any type of outburst that might delay these proceedings," he said. "I don't know about you folks, but I'd like to get out of here before the sun comes up."

A few people chuckled. I heard one of the TV people mumble, "Fat chance."

The major leaned into his microphone. "If you please!"

Just then, a tall blond man in an exquisitely tailored suit came down the aisle and stepped up to the lectern. Everything about the guy screamed "Money!" From the rear, he could have passed for my ex-fiancé back in Connecticut. The resemblance was striking, and I felt myself tense up. It doesn't matter what this guy says, I thought, I wouldn't trust him with my dirty laundry.

"Major, my name is Justin Blaize," said the man. He even sounded a little like David. "I live in Carriage Hill and have come here tonight to voice my opposition to this proposed transmission corridor. I sympathize with Mr. Kenney and his wife, but since the issue at hand is an application to dredge and fill, I will confine my remarks to the impact this project will have on the natural environment."

"That is commendable, Mr. Blaize," said the major.

Justin Blaize was no dummy. I'd have to give him credit. He knew the right buttons to push.

"An acquaintance of mine at the University of South Florida has compiled a list of all the animal species the Fish and Wildlife people consider endangered or threatened that are known or expected to frequent the site." He took a sheet of paper out of his jacket pocket. "I would like to have this list entered into the record."

He walked up to the stage, and one of the regulatory men came around from behind the table and took the sheet of paper from him. Then Mr. Blaize went back to the lectern. From the front, he didn't look anything like David. His heart-shaped face was uniformly pink, and at first I thought he was an albino. But his hair wasn't white, just very light blond, and he had blue eyes. At least I thought they were blue. They were so pale, it was like I could see clear through his head to the stage beyond.

"Major Hall," he continued, "the site in question is still, for the most part, in a natural state, with few disturbed areas. According to my expert, it supports the kind of plant communities necessary for the survival of the animals listed on that sheet. All of those communities are dependent on the natural fluctuations in the water table, already under severe stress from our ongoing drought.

"Dredging and filling activities here in Florida have a history of upsetting the delicate balance between surface waters and our drinking water supply, the Floridan Aquifer, as I am certain you are aware. Until recently, the Corps of Engineers brought about much of those impacts."

Mr. Blaize paused just long enough for a cloud to settle over the stage. The public affairs chief leaned forward and was about to grab the microphone, when Blaize continued, right on cue.

"Fortunately, the Corps has come to realize the importance of protecting our natural resources and is making great strides in this area. These public hearings are only one example of their commitment to the environment."

I decided that Justin Blaize was a lawyer, undoubtedly a trial lawyer, and a good one at that. He had prepared his case, practiced his opening remarks, and had the jury eating out of his hand even before the evidence had been presented. Whatever he said after his little "commitment to the environment" spiel was irrelevant. The public affairs chief and the major were smiling; the regulatory guys were completely at ease. Only the lawyer seemed edgy. It takes one to know one, I thought, and she knows Mr. Blaize is quickly forcing them into a corner, politically speaking. Grant the permit, and they look like the old Corps. Deny it, and the power company will blame the government for all future blackouts, no matter what the cause.

"It is this commitment to the environment," Blaize said, "that we, here tonight, are counting on, Major. You must deny this dredge and fill permit until an Environmental Impact Statement has been filed and evaluated. I feel certain that such an EIS will clearly demonstrate the harm this project will have on our wetlands."

He glanced down at his watch, as if he had just crossed the finish line in a road race and wanted to record his time. "Thank you for allowing me this chance to speak."

Major Hall smiled. "Thank *you,* Mr. Blaize," he said, picking up one of his 3x5 cards.

Justin Blaize turned around and started up the aisle. He was smiling. Several people nodded at him. I leaned over and tapped Michael on the arm.

"Have you ever run into this Blaize guy before?" I whispered.

Michael nodded. "He's a contractor," he whispered. "Sewer and water installations, drainage. Does quite a bit of work for the City. He's very successful. I'm told he has a law degree, but only practiced briefly."

The major rapped on his microphone with his ballpoint a couple of times, even though the audience was behaving itself.

"Our next speaker is Bruce—"

Major Hall was interrupted by a loud crashing noise and the muffled sound of masculine voices hurling invectives. The disturbance apparently was just outside the rear doors to the auditorium.

Suddenly the doors flew open, and a woman burst in.

"There's been an accident!" she screamed. "Is there a doctor here? We need a doctor!" She was holding both hands together under her chin, as though in prayer.

The promise of blood and gore created an immediate log-jam at the doors, as dozens of excitement-starved people tried to exit the auditorium simultaneously. Eventually, however, the crowd gained control of itself and allowed three men and a woman, presumably doctors, to leave.

I sat down and looked at the major. He and his public affairs chief were conferring. The rest of his entourage was watching the rear of the auditorium. No one seemed terribly concerned, as if used to disturbances of this magnitude.

With all the TV cameras scattered about, lights bouncing off walls, and people tripping over cables and extension cords, I felt like I was on the set of some action movie. Any second, the director would scream "Cut!" and everyone would stop and sit down.

Apparently, the major planned to continue the hearing whether or not the action stopped. Undaunted, he held up his 3x5 card and leaned into his microphone. "Our next speaker is Bruce Biddings," he said quite loudly. He smiled at what was left of the audience. "Is Mr. Biddings here?"

He waited a few seconds, then pitched the card onto the table and took another card off the stack. His smile had grown wider. "Is Mr. Westphall here?"

Michael appeared at the end of the row and walked across to his seat. "Chip has gone outside to see what happened," he said, sitting down. "Apparently, there was a fight, and one of the participants did not fare too well."

"Is Mr. Lyons here?" It was the major. He was grinning now, flinging cards willy-nilly, obviously overjoyed by the prospect of an early adjournment.

Michael looked at his watch. "Let's get a cup of coffee at the Hyatt," he said, "and then I'll take you home. This hearing is over for all intents and purposes. And I need to get back to the office."

I thought about Dr. Augustin and the one hundred-fifty varieties of imported beer, and about my vow to never drink coffee at night.

"Sure," I said, a tad unenthusiastically. "A cup of coffee would be nice."

CHAPTER 5

•

Thursday, October 7

When I got to the clinic, Cynthia was putting the finishing touches on our door decorations—a wreath made of corn husks and dried baby calico corn on the cob.

"Nice," I said.

She stood back and admired her work. "Dr. Augustin wouldn't let me put up my decoupage witch. He said we shouldn't encourage the *Children of the Corn* mentality that seems to be so prevalent these days. That television already gives them enough ideas." She shook her head and frowned. "When *I* was a child, parents never worried about their kids getting sick ideas from TV."

"When you were a child, there wasn't any TV."

She fluttered a hand in the air, as if to indicate this fact did not in any way diminish her point.

We went into the reception room, and I helped her put the decorations box back on its shelf in the supply closet. Then I started toward Dr. Augustin's office.

"I wouldn't go in there if I were you," warned Cynthia, her voice low.

I stopped and jerked my hand back, as if the doorknob was electrically charged. "Why not?"

Cynthia's eyes darted from the door in question to the hallway. "This is not turning out to be one of his better days," she said softly. "That dog John Deland brought in died sometime last night. And the fire chief was wrong about no one being killed in that fire Tuesday."

I stared at her.

"They found a body on the third floor. It was that Environmental Management friend of Dr. Augustin's. 'Jack' something." She began leafing through the newspaper that was scattered across her desk. "Here it is. 'Jack Lanier, age thirty-eight. Married with two children.' " She sat down. "What a shame. The police are looking into his death and the fire as 'suspicious.' "

"Why on earth would Jack want to burn down the Municipal Technical Services Building?" I asked, not really expecting an answer.

"He wouldn't," said Dr. Augustin from the hallway. He obviously hadn't been in his office.

"I'm sorry about your friend," I said.

Dr. Augustin leaned against the door frame and proceeded to dry his hands on a paper towel. "He was really only an acquaintance. I didn't know him very well. But he was a good man. Honest, which is more than I can say for most of the government people I've met recently." He walked over to Cynthia's desk and tossed the paper towel into her trash can.

"Anyway," he continued, "I seriously doubt Jack started that fire. Unless it was an accident."

The phone rang. Cynthia quickly gathered the newspaper together and stuffed it into a lower desk drawer. Then she picked up the phone.

Dr. Augustin went into his office. "That chow mix—the one John brought us—died last night," he said. "Which was to be expected, I guess, considering the condition of her bone marrow." He sat down at his desk and picked up a copy of a lab analysis report. "Animal Control understandably won't authorize a thorough toxicology screen, because of the cost, but it's pretty obvious she was slowly being poisoned. I can't think what else might cause her to develop aplastic anemia as well as screw up her liver enzymes. She either got into something or someone is systematically getting rid of a neighborhood nuisance."

He put the report in a manila folder and dropped it into his top drawer. Then he leaned back in his chair.

"You should have gone with us last night," he said.

I knew he was staring at me with his laser eyes. I pretended to read a few of the titles on his bookshelf. "Michael had to get back to the office," I said. "Some kind of problem withe the local section of the paper." I quickly changed the subject. "Did you hang around long enough to find out what the fight was all about?"

"No, but scuttlebutt has it the guy who got beat up was one of the landowners who have agreed to give the power company easements for that transmission corridor. The guy who did the beating was Mr. Kenney. The one with the sick kid."

"I'm surprised," I said. "He didn't look like the barroom brawling type."

"True," said Dr. Augustin, "but we don't know what the victim looked like. Could have been the guy was a wimp."

He got up. "What are you doing this weekend, Samantha? Say, Sunday afternoon." He took his exam jacket off its hanger and put it on.

I hesitated. Alarms were going off in my head. "I hadn't thought about it," I said. "Why?" The question was a reflex. I really didn't want to know.

"The commission has put that dredge and fill permit—in fact the entire matter of the five-hundred-KV line—on its agenda for Thursday. Better late than never, I guess. Anyway, I need to go out there and take a look around before then." He smiled, and his eyes flared up. "I thought you might enjoy a little hike in the woods. The exercise would do you good. As we get older, it takes more time and effort to keep in shape, you know." The smile had turned into a grin.

I frowned. "Don't start with me about my age," I snapped and marched out of his office. I could hear him chuckling.

• • •

September and October tend to be slow months, mostly because the new school year takes up a lot of people's time, at least those people with children. And most of the snowbirds haven't arrived yet. They want to enjoy the fall colors before making their annual winter pilgrimage to Florida, where they'll complain about the heat to the locals and brag about it to their northern friends and relatives. There are a few regular clients, however, who keep us occupied. One of them is Glynnis Winter.

Mrs. Winter is a well-bred, well-shod, and extremely well-preserved forty-seven-year-old widow with the hots for Dr. Augustin. Her Maltese, Frosty, is a canine hypochondriac of sorts, an unwilling participant in Glynnis Winter's constant quest for entertainment. Frosty suffers from a plethora of skin and digestive disorders, some real and some only figments of Glynnis's imagination.

That day it was Frosty's skin, evidently. When Cynthia called me to the front, I found Glynnis sitting ever so primly in one of the reception-room chairs, Frosty in her lap, as usual shaking and panting like one of those battery-operated massage pillows. He seemed to be exceptionally nervous, however, even for him. In between shaking and quaking, he gnawed viciously on one or the other of his front feet, as if they were blood-sucking vermin he was trying to dislodge. He'd been doing it for some time, too, because his saliva had turned his soft white hair a pale cinnamon color.

"Good afternoon, Mrs. Winter," I said, smiling. I took Frosty's file from Cynthia and waited while Glynnis gathered together her purse and her dog and stood up.

She was wearing an orange, red, and yellow tie-dyed broomstick skirt, which I thought extremely appropriate, considering the season. Her peasant blouse (which no peasant could afford) was white. It made the skin on her arms look like German chocolate.

I feel certain everything about Glynnis—from her auburn hair and vivid green eyes to her perfect teeth and blemish-free tan—is artificially enhanced. If you have enough money, man-made can sometimes be better than the real thing. In Glynnis's case, the result of all her primping and pampering is truly breathtaking. That day, so was her perfume.

"Poison," said Cynthia quietly, as I was about to follow Glynnis and Frosty into Room 1.

I stopped in the reception-room doorway and turned around. "What?"

Cynthia nodded her head in Mrs. Winter's direction. "Her perfume. It's Poison. I noticed you sniffing that cloud around her."

I grimaced. "Whatever it is, it's making my eyes water." I paused and stared at Frosty's record. "I wonder if that's what is making Frosty chew on his feet."

Cynthia shook her head. "I always knew Glynnis Winter would be the death of that poor dog."

It turned out to be the new carpeting in Glynnis Winter's Gulf-view condominium. "Contact dermatitis" they call it. She told Dr. Augustin "her baby" started itching and chewing right after the carpets were installed.

"I thought perhaps he didn't approve of the color," she said, smiling playfully.

Dr. Augustin laughed, dutifully, all the while eyeing me, as I stood behind Mrs. Winter with my finger down my throat.

The solution was to have the carpets professionally cleaned, according to Dr. Augustin. He recommended an environment friendly, hypoallergenic product that wouldn't add insult to injury.

Mrs. Winter was beside herself with gratitude. I thought Dr. Augustin was going to choke to death on the Poison when she came close enough to him to offer him her hand. For a second I thought she was going to offer him more than that. And for a second I wished she had, just to see Dr. Augustin's reaction.

• • •

Promptly at 5:30 Dr. Augustin left for the day. Once a week, usually on Tuesday or Thursday, he and a friend, Dale Weisop, eat dinner with Bill O'Shea at the Paper Moon. Then the three of them go watch Dale's twelve-year-old daughter, Amy, play soccer.

Which leaves me to do evening treatments and secure everything. Since Tracey is dating Frank Jennings, our kennel manager/rock musician, I cannot count on her to hang around and help. Frank has to get home and change from his kennel attire—jeans with the knees torn out and a grubby T-shirt—to his stage attire—jeans with the knees torn out and a grubby T-shirt—and usually takes off about 4:30. Tracey leaves as soon thereafter as possible so she can join her beloved. The life of a groupie can indeed be hectic.

I was in the treatment room when the phone rang. I ignored it. Cynthia turns on the answering machine at five, so she can fight with the computer over the day's total. I was surprised when she called me on the intercom.

"It's Richard Westphall," she said testily. "Something about his shepherd. I guess you'd better take it."

I groaned. Why hadn't the machine been on to instruct Mr. Westphall to take his dog to the Emergency Clinic?

"Hello?" I said into the hall extension. "This is Samantha Holt. What seems to be the problem, Mr. Westphall?"

"Princess is acting very peculiarly, Miss Holt. Almost like she's going into labor. But she isn't due for another two weeks."

I could hear the panic in his voice. Mr. Westphall wasn't the type to overreact.

"What exactly is she doing?" I asked.

Mr. Westphall paused. "She won't eat. And she keeps going under my son's bed. Gets right up against the wall, like she does during a thunderstorm."

Cynthia came down the hall and handed me the shepherd's file.

"Have you taken her temperature?" I asked. "Does she have a fever? Or is her temperature below normal?"

I could tell he had put his hand over the mouthpiece. I heard muffled conversation. Then he was back.

"My wife says Princess doesn't feel hot. We haven't taken her temperature."

"Does she have any discharge that you can see?"

"No." Again, he said something to his wife that I couldn't hear. "Darlene says the puppies haven't been moving around like they were earlier in the week. At least she hasn't noticed them moving."

"Can you hang on a minute, Mr. Westphall?" I asked the man. He agreed, and I pushed the HOLD button.

I chewed on my lower lip and argued silently with myself. If I tell Mr. Westphall to watch the dog and take her to the Emergency Clinic if she gets any worse or if going there would make the Westphalls feel better, Dr. Augustin will say I should have called him at the Paper Moon. If, on the other hand, I call Dr. Augustin, he undoubtedly will tell me I should have sent Mr. Westphall to the Emergency Clinic. Let Dr. Wilson handle it.

I opened Princess's file. The Westphalls had recently bought a ranchette clear across town. They continued to bring Princess to Dr. Augustin, but it was approaching a thirty-minute drive. The Emergency Clinic, although not convenient either, would be closer.

I pushed the button for Line 1. "Mr. Westphall? I'm going to attempt to reach Dr. Augustin. Then he can phone you and decide what should be done, if anything. If I can't get him, I'll call you back and you can take Princess to the Emergency Clinic. Dr. Wilson is an excellent veterinarian and a personal friend of Dr. Augustin's."

Mr. Westphall sounded relieved. "Thank you, Miss Holt. I'll wait until I hear from you or Dr. Augustin." He hung up.

I took the file back to Cynthia's desk and looked up the number for the Paper Moon.

"This is probably a mistake," I told Cynthia, "but I'm going to do it anyway."

I used Cynthia's phone to punch in the number for the Moon. After what seemed like an eternity, the bartender answered. I had to shout to be heard over the music playing in the background. It was Jimmy Buffet's "Cheeseburger in Paradise." Dr. Augustin is obviously still there, I thought, and feeding the jukebox.

"Yes, Samantha, what is it?" he growled after a couple of minutes. Jimmy Buffet had been replaced by John Lennon.

"I'm sorry to bother you," I said, "but I felt sure you would want me to get in touch with you on this one." Then I told him about Princess Westphall.

I waited for him to yell at me, but he didn't.

"If I remember correctly," he said, "Westphall lives someplace up near the Northeast Recreation Complex. I'm headed that way, so I'll drop in and check on the dog myself. What's their number?"

I gave it to him.

"Thanks, Sam," he said, and hung up.

I breathed a giant sigh of relief and quickly turned on the answering machine.

CHAPTER 6

•

Friday, October 8

Princess was in a bottom cage in Isolation when I got to the clinic at 7:30. Hastily scrawled on the cage card, in Dr. Augustin's handwriting, was "Westphall, Princess. Observation."

I peered through the bars at her. "Princess, honey, how are you feeling?"

The dog was lying flat on her stomach with her head down between her front paws. She rolled her eyes up at me and thumped her tail, but otherwise did not move. There was a trace of blood on the newspapers beneath her rack.

I searched around for the Westphall file, spotted it on the counter, and picked it up. The last entry was "Five puppies stillborn, 2:50 A.M. Three females, two males. No apparent external deformities."

I looked back at Princess. She was obviously depressed. I dumped the file in the basket on the counter and left to put on the coffee.

Mr. Westphall came by at 1:30. I put him in an exam room and closed the door. Then I went to tell Dr. Augustin. He was in his office eating a submarine sandwich.

"Where did you get that?" I asked, pointing to the sandwich. The room smelled like a luncheonette in Ybor City, Tampa's Latin quarter.

"The Publix Deli. It's not bad for supermarket food. You want half?" He took a noisy bite. Tiny crumbs floated onto the desktop.

I shook my head. "Thanks, but I've already eaten." My stomach wasn't convinced, however. Fat-free cottage cheese and sliced peaches just can't compare with a full day's allotment of fat grams and calories nestled inside a crusty Cuban roll. "Mr. Westphall is waiting in Room One," I said, my mouth watering.

Dr. Augustin wrapped up the remainder of his sandwich, put it back in its little bag, and finished his Coke. He got up, threw the empty can in the wastepaper basket next to his desk, then paused and retrieved it.

"Why can't Frank sort through the trash for this recycle stuff?" he said, handing me the can. He frowned. "Since this was your idea, maybe *you* should be separating the garbage." He didn't wait for me to reply, but marched through the lab and across the hall.

Mr. Westphall was seated in a chair in the corner of the room, his head in his hands. "It's not just the money," he was saying, "although I'll probably have to fork over a stud fee, now that there isn't going to be any pick of the litter."

He straightened up. He looked like his dog—tired and depressed. "I feel sorry for Princess. She is going to be all right, isn't she?"

Dr. Augustin leaned his elbows on the exam table. He was starting to look a little ragged. I wasn't sure when he had finally gotten to bed, Thursday night, but it had to have been late. I am always impressed by how little sleep Dr. Augustin requires, but even *he* has his limits.

"We'll know more this evening," he said, "when we get the results of her blood chemistry back. She's a little anemic, but there isn't any evidence of an infection." He took a deep breath. "You realize, we may never find out what caused this. Viruses, bacteria, genetic problems, all can lead to fetal death. Princess is young, and she's never had any difficulty carrying her pups to term that I know of." He paused and looked down at Westphall. "What about the male? Is this her first litter by him?"

Westphall shook his head. "No, the second. Last year's pups were his. You said they were top-notch. Really large and healthy." His tone had an edge to it. Like he might somehow be blaming Dr. Augustin for Princess's misfortune.

Dr. Augustin picked up the Westphall file and flipped through it. "According to my notes, here, both Princess and the male tested negative for brucellosis last year." He looked up. "You said you hadn't noticed any vaginal discharge. How about sneezing or watery eyes?"

Again, Mr. Westphall shook his head. "Not that I can remember."

"Any chance Princess got into something out in the garage or in the yard? Do you let her run loose in the woods?"

Mr. Westphall stared at the wallpaper. He ran his hand along his jaw. Then he got up and came over to the exam table.

"Three or four times a week, Darlene, Timmy, and I take Princess and the horses and ride along that transmission corridor. There's a trail that parallels the corridor for a mile or so, and nearly everyone at our barn uses it. We always thought it was a nice, safe place. You know, away from traffic." His eyes grew very large, and his voice trembled slightly. "Oh, my God," he said suddenly. "You don't think those power lines had anything to do with this, do you? I mean, Darlene is expecting in May." He looked briefly at the floor. "Her pregnancy caught us by surprise. You see, Timmy is adopted and . . . Anyway, she doesn't ride anymore, but she did for the first month or so. You don't think . . . ?" His mouth remained open.

Dr. Augustin put his hand on Westphall's arm. "Take it easy, Dick," he said gently. "I'm sure those power lines are in no way involved."

Westphall seemed to relax a little. He closed his mouth

and went back to his chair. I saw Dr. Augustin look at his watch, and I glanced down at mine. It was 2:10. A little earlier, I'd heard Cynthia put our first client of the afternoon in Room 2. Any minute I expected her to rap on the door to Room 1 and tell me they were waiting.

"I was at the Civic Center Wednesday," said Mr. Westphall, who wasn't wearing a watch. "At the public hearing for that proposed power line. I saw Miss Holt there." He smiled at me.

"Before all the commotion started, I was going to make a statement in opposition." He smiled. "I'm sort of an unofficial spokesman for the local Horseman's Association.

"Anyway, the power company wants to keep horseback riders out of their corridors. They say people have been using their towers for target practice. That it costs them time and money to keep replacing the insulators. Well, nobody in the Horseman's Association is responsible for damaging anything, I can assure you. That shark, Walker—their *lawyer*—has threatened to send the cops out after anyone they catch riding inside the corridor." He shook his head.

"If they put fences and gates up along that new corridor, folks up that way won't have anyplace left to ride. With all the development going on, our greenspace has shrunk down to practically nothing. Darlene and I moved up there to get away from all the congestion and people."

He looked first at me, then at Dr. Augustin. "So you see, I always thought it was a land issue. A dredge and fill thing. Until now, I never really believed all that snapping and crackling coming from those lines could make people sick."

"That snapping is from electricity arcing around the insulators," said Dr. Augustin. "It's harmless. And no one has proven any connection between high-voltage power lines and disease. Not yet, at any rate."

I thought I detected a hint of doubt in his voice, but it could have been my imagination.

Dr. Augustin began easing himself in the direction of the exam-room door. "Why don't you go in and visit with

Princess for a little while, Dick?" he said. "Samantha and I
need to start seeing our afternoon clients."

As if to emphasize Dr. Augustin's point, I opened the
door. I made certain I was smiling.

Mr. Westphall jumped to his feet. "I'm sorry, Doc, I
didn't realize it was so late. I called in sick this morning and
I've kind of lost track of the time." He sidled past me and
stepped into the hallway.

Dr. Augustin followed him. "I'll phone you this evening,
Dick," he said. "Try not to worry about Princess."

They shook hands, and Dr. Augustin went into Room 2.
When he opened the door, I could see our two o'clock appointment—a young woman with a hyperactive golden retriever puppy and two elementary-age children. All three
youngsters looked like they could use a dose of Ritalin.

"Over here," I said to Mr. Westphall and ushered him into
Isolation.

After opening the door to Princess's cage and positioning
a stool next to it for Mr. Westphall to sit on, I excused myself and hurried out to help Dr. Augustin. From every countertop and corner in the clinic, electricity pulsed through
instruments and assorted appliances like arterial blood
through some gigantic alien monster.

Michael Halsey came to the clinic at 5:50. He and Cynthia were sitting behind her desk, obviously discussing
something of great import, when I entered the reception
room.

"Hi," I said cheerily.

They both glanced over at me, stopped talking, and
straightened up in their chairs. I felt like an eighth-grade
homeroom teacher who'd just caught two of my students
passing notes back and forth, instead of doing their algebra.

"Samantha!" Michael exclaimed, getting up and button-
ing his suit jacket. "You look lovely, as usual." He smiled
broadly.

I didn't say anything. I was perspiring heavily, and my

face and arms were covered with dog hair. To make matters worse, my pale blue uniform top had a large reddish wet spot on it, where I had attempted to remove a bloodstain. Lovely I was not, and I knew it.

Michael cleared his throat. "I have a small favor to ask of you, Samantha," he said.

I walked over to Cynthia's desk and scooped up a handful of candy corn. I had to fortify myself for this one. "And what's that?" I asked, dropping a couple of the concentrated sugar kernels in my mouth.

"At seven this evening, I'm flying up to D.C. for the weekend. To a conference. It was a last-minute thing, and now I need someone to look after Randy and Katie."

"I'd be happy to, Michael." I looked at the clock over Cynthia's desk. "I'm going to be here for at least another hour, if you want to drop them off."

"I was hoping to leave them at home. I'm sure they'll be happier there, don't you agree?" He never paused. "How much of an inconvenience would it be for you to go by my condo and feed them a couple of times each day and change their kitty pan?" He reached into his pocket and pulled out a set of keys.

I felt a twinge of irritation. At least he could wait until I said "Yes," I thought. But I smiled, anyway. It was hard to stay mad at Michael.

"Sure," I said. "It's no trouble at all."

Michael removed a key from the ring and handed it to me. "Their food is in the refrigerator, already mixed up, and their litter pan is where it always is—in the guest bathroom."

I took the key. Cynthia, ever ready to help fuel my relationship with Michael, handed me an empty key ring. It had a little ID tag attached to it on which she had written "Mike's Condo."

"I really appreciate this, Samantha," Michael said. "My return flight lands in Tampa at seven-thirty Sunday evening."

"How do I get your key back to you?" I asked, holding it up.

"You keep it," he said. "I have another one." He winked at Cynthia.

"Hmm," I mumbled, my irritation growing. I put the key in my pocket. "I've really got to get back to work. Have a nice trip." I started toward the hall.

"I'm staying at the Hilton," Michael said. "The number is by the phone. Please feel free to call me."

I stopped and turned around. "Okay, but I'm sure I won't need to. Everything will be fine. Don't worry."

I waved a hand at him and quickly left for the treatment room, all the while wondering what Michael and Cynthia had been plotting.

CHAPTER 7

•

I drove to the Marina Towers as soon as I finished up at the clinic. I had been to Michael's place many times, but never alone, and my desire to rummage around his condominium was like a hard-to-reach itch. The thought that I might finally satisfy my curiosity about the man had me practically panting with anticipation. Whatever guilt this little expedition generates, I said to myself as I turned onto Gulf Drive, I will have to deal with later.

Michael lives on the tenth floor in a corner unit overlooking the marina. He can see his boat from the living room. Half the building is unoccupied at one time or another, while residents cruise about in their yachts. As a result, security is tight. The property is surrounded by an eight-foot brick wall topped with metal spikes, which add another foot or so. A guard is posted at the gate. Once you get past him, you still need a key to enter the building's ground floor. Without one, you must press a button, identify yourself, and wait for somebody upstairs to release the lock on the front door.

Fortunately, Chuck, the guard, knew me and waved me through without the slightest hesitation. Little did he know I was about to commit burglary of a sort.

I let myself in, took the elevator to the tenth floor, and walked to the end of the hall. On my way, I passed three people, none of whom said a word to me. One, an elderly

woman in her seventies with a toy poodle, presumably was
returning from taking her dog for a walk.

The woman was dressed in a floral print housecoat and
pearls. The pearls looked real. She had bloodred lips and
small circles of rouge on her otherwise colorless cheeks. Her
hair was jet-black and arranged in tiny tight curls all over
her head, as if she'd taken the bobby pins out but hadn't gotten around to brushing it. She reminded me of a shriveled-
up Kewpie doll. She wouldn't look at me. I still had my
uniform on and still had a few dog hairs on my arms. I
guessed she was not the type to discuss the weather with
"the help." Her dog, however, sniffed longingly at my uniform pants. I was afraid he might lift his leg and was greatly
relieved when they exited the elevator on the third floor.

The other two residents were men who'd obviously just
gotten off work and were only interested in what would undoubtedly be the first of several martinis. It *was* Friday, after
all, and worrying about one's millions all week can be ex-
hausting.

I unlocked Michael's door and went inside. The kittens
were curled up on opposite ends of the sofa. They looked at
me and yawned, but didn't seem eager to lead me into the
kitchen. Michael had apparently fed them before he left.
Good, I said to myself. That gives me more time to browse.

I scratched Katie's head, then picked Randy up, and
walked over to the window. Randy began to purr and knead
my shoulder and drool. I was happy to see the kittens were
starting to gain weight and grow. They'd been strays, abandoned at less than six weeks of age under the strangest of
circumstances. And they both had been born with cleft
palates and should have died, except Dr. Augustin decided
they deserved a chance. Besides, they had aided him in his
quest to catch a murderer, and that obviously counted for
something.

Anyway, after the kittens' birth defects were repaired, it
became my job to find them homes. So I talked Michael into
adopting them. Actually, it didn't take much to convince

him. I knew he was lonely, and until he could secure permanent human companionship (me, if Cynthia had anything
to do with it), he was willing to settle for a pet.

With Randy perched on my shoulder sounding like a tiny
aquarium pump, I gazed down at the acre or so of boats
moored in nice straight rows to a skeleton of floating docks.
As far as the eye could see, masts and outriggers rocked
gently back and forth in time to the rhythm of the tides and
the wind. I wondered how much money that acre represented.

I spotted Michael's forty-footer, small next to its yacht-
sized neighbors, but certainly not a dingy. The *Serendipity*
had probably set Michael back a couple of hundred thou-
sand, at least. And again, I wondered where Michael's
money came from.

I turned around. Katie was on the floor scratching the corner of the sofa. I clapped my hands together and shouted,
"No!" Randy dug his claws into my neck. Katie ignored me
and continued to exercise her toenails on the pale blue,
knobby-weave upholstery.

I put Randy on the floor. Suddenly he arched his back,
bounced sideways across the room like a crab, and threw
himself at Katie. The two of them thrashed about for a few
seconds, then took off for the bedroom, with Katie in the
lead. It was great fun, evidently, because a second or two
later, Randy came flying out, with Katie only a few paces
behind him. They raced around the room, up over the coffee
table, and back into the bedroom.

I picked up a brass coaster that had been hurled to the
floor and put it back on the coffee table. If Michael's expensive apartment survived the next six or eight months, it
would be a miracle. The eggshell walls, genuine Oriental
rugs, and contemporary furniture—a mixture of Italian
leather, solid cherry wood, and expensive fabric—looked as
though no one had ever touched them, as if everything
(minus the kittens) was for display purposes only. Framed
watercolors depicting sailing craft of one type or another

added to the model home appearance. Even the trash can
next to one of the armchairs was empty and squeaky clean
on the inside.

Michael is neat to a fault. When he cooks—wonderful
pasta dishes and omelets—he cleans up as he goes. At the
end of the meal, we have only our plates to contend with. I
am a sharp contrast. On those rare evenings when I have
company over for dinner, I usually leave my sink full and let
my cats take care of the dishes during the night. I chuckled.
That litter pan in Michael's guest bathroom must drive him
crazy, I thought.

I went into the master bedroom. The look was country
French, clearly feminine, and not something Michael would
have selected for himself. Here were the remnants of his life
with Mary, from the dusty rose and evergreen floral print
comforter on the king-sized poster bed to the dressing table,
with its delicate needlepoint-cushioned stool.

I sat down in front of the dressing table and stared at myself in the mirror. I tried to imagine, as I had on numerous
occasions, what Mary had looked like. Was she tall and
blond, like me, or petite with dark hair and eyes, the great-
great-granddaughter of some Spanish nobleman? And where
were the pictures? Everyone had pictures.

I began opening drawers, gently prying into Michael's
personal life. I thought about Dr. Augustin, who actually enjoyed snooping, or so it seemed. "Well, *I* don't enjoy this,"
I said aloud. "Not one bit."

I was beginning to perspire, despite the rather chilly
seventy-four degrees Michael maintained throughout his
condo. And I had the feeling someone was watching me. I
glanced up, nervously. In the dressing-table mirror, I could
see Randy and Katie sitting motionless at the foot of the bed
like stuffed toys. They were staring at me.

"And don't either of you breathe a word to Michael about
this," I said sternly, "do you understand me?"

Randy yawned.

I was about to give the search up when I spotted a small

picture frame lying facedown in the lower right-hand drawer. I pulled it out, then held my breath as I turned it over.

The photo was taken on Michael's boat or, at least, on someone's boat. I couldn't see the name. Michael, dressed like a participant in the America's Cup, had his arm around an attractive, fortyish woman wearing shorts and a baggy white shirt tied up in front so that her navel showed. She was tall and blond and deeply tanned. But other than that, she didn't resemble me at all. She was a lot thinner for one thing.

Standing in front of Michael and the woman, who I assumed was his late wife, Mary, was a boy of nine or ten. He was thin, an awkward, gangly sort of cute, with light brown hair and an impish smile. He really didn't look anything like Michael. Or Mary, for that matter.

The idea that Michael might have children had never occurred to me. Most parents would be more than happy to tell you about their kids. Show you pictures. Bore you to death with details about their academic or athletic prowess.

I slid the cardboard support out of the picture frame and looked at the back of the photograph. Someone had written "Michael, Mary, and Kevin" and the date in the upper left corner.

Suddenly it hit me that perhaps Kevin, too, had died, and Michael couldn't talk about the boy, because it hurt too much. That I had, in fact, *two* ghosts to contend with, not just one.

I looked at Randy and Katie, still watching me with that inscrutable intensity cats are famous for, and once again, I wondered if there really was such a thing as reincarnation.

"What are *you* looking at?" I asked the kittens.

Katie's tail swished violently, but her eyes never left my face.

I reassembled the picture frame and returned it to the drawer, facedown. Then I closed the drawer. I was about to get up and check the contents of Michael's desk when the phone rang. The noise sent both cats under the bed and caused my heart to slam up against my sternum. I took a couple of deep breaths and stood up. The ringing stopped abruptly, and I heard Michael's machine click on. I went into the living room and sat down on the sofa.

The beep at the end of the announcement sounded, and then I heard a woman's voice. She was obviously upset.

"Michael! Where the hell are you? It's eight-thirty! I've been trying to reach you all day. I need to talk to you about Kevin. It's important. Phone me as soon as you get in. Please!" The line went dead.

My hands and feet were like ice. I listened as the machine rewound the announcement. Then I got up, grabbed my purse from the coffee table, and left. I didn't even tell the cats good-bye.

CHAPTER 8

•

Saturday, October 9

I kept pretty much to myself all morning, blaming my mood on a sinus headache. A lot of fall-blooming trees and flowers were keeping the pollen count up, so Tracey and Dr. Augustin fell for it. Cynthia, on the other hand, knew I was ticked off about something. She'd look questioningly at me every time I came into the reception room. But she never said a word. She didn't have to. She knew I'd come clean eventually.

At noon, after Dr. Augustin and Tracey left for lunch, I marched up front and plopped into one of the reception-room chairs. Charlie and Pearl, the clinic's feline mascots, were perched on opposite ends of the reception desk, staring at Cynthia. They looked like mismatched bookends. Charlie is black as night and a touch overweight, owing to the fact that he steals food whenever he can, which is often, since he has learned how to open all but the intensive-care cages with his paw. Pearl, on the other hand, is nearly pure white, slender, and not nearly as resourceful as Charlie, although lately she has taken to knocking small objects off the shelves in the supply closet and hiding them under the refrigerator. I think she enjoys watching us fish them out with a yardstick.

Cynthia gazed at me over the top of her computer screen. "Let's have it, Samantha," she said. "What's the problem?"

I stared out of the window at a flock of seagulls standing in a line on the roof of the building across from the clinic. One of them floated down and plucked a scrap of food from off the roadway, narrowly avoiding a car. The rest of the group waited until he was back on the roof before attacking him. He dropped his prize and took off.

Suddenly I felt a terrible hurt—an emotional pain worse than any physical pain I could remember experiencing. Like the pain I had felt on my wedding day, when David failed to show up at the church. Men seem determined to disappoint me one way or the other, I thought. Directly or indirectly. And then I remembered the time the lead female role in my school's annual play went to Julie Travis, instead of to me. I was thirteen. Sensitive, impressionable. And too tall, they said. Three inches taller than the lead male. That simply wouldn't do. So, although I was better for the part than Julie, and prettier, I had to settle for the role of the grandmother.

I felt my eyes start to burn, and I blinked several times and swallowed hard in an effort to keep tears from forming.

"Samantha?"

"I don't like being lied to," I said through clenched teeth. "And I don't like being taken advantage of." I shifted my gaze to Cynthia. "This is all your fault, you know. I should have trusted my instincts and told Mr. Halsey—your Mr. Halsey—thanks, but no thanks."

Cynthia pushed the computer screen around, so she could see me better. "What on earth are you talking about?"

"Michael isn't a widower," I said. "Mary is still alive. For all I know, they're still married." I took great pleasure in seeing Cynthia's face blanche and her mouth open slightly.

"And he has a son," I continued, rubbing it in gleefully. "Kevin. I saw a photo of the happy little threesome when I went to Mr. Halsey's condo last night. He'd hidden the picture in a drawer in his bedroom, but I found it."

I was on a roll. I smiled sadistically at Cynthia. "And Mary phoned while I was there. The machine was on, but I heard the message. She wanted Michael to call her. She said

it was about Kevin." No wonder the bastard never introduced me to any of his buddies at work, I thought angrily.
Now I know why Chip grinned at me the way he did.

Cynthia got up from her desk and came across the room.
She sat down next to me. "What were you doing searching
around in Mike's bedroom?" she asked. She had that
parental "you should be ashamed of yourself" expression on
her face.

I stared at her. "You're actually siding with him. I can't
believe it! The guy's a two-timing . . ."

"Samantha, honey," Cynthia said gently, but firmly.
"Calm yourself. I'm sure there's a perfectly reasonable explanation for all this."

"Right," I said. I chewed viciously on the inside of my
lower lip, until I tasted blood.

"Why don't you ask Michael about the phone call?" she
said. "He can't blame you for overhearing it. You don't have
to tell him about the picture." She put her hand on my arm.

I got up. "I most certainly will not! I'll continue feeding
his cats until tomorrow, but that's it. I'm finished with all the
excuses and lies. I'm finished with men. Period."

I opened the front door and took off across the parking
lot. I was going to McDonald's. I intended to eat a Big Mac
and a large order of fries. Maybe follow them up with a
chocolate shake.

After lunch, I tried to keep clear of Cynthia. We were
booked solid all afternoon, so it wasn't difficult.

Mr. Westphall came for Princess at 2:30. I put him in a
room and went for his dog. When I got back, Dr. Augustin
was there talking to Mr. Westphall about Princess's test results, which hadn't come back until that morning.

Westphall gave his dog a hug and took her leash from me.
"She certainly looks better than she did the other night," he
said. "Is there anything special I should do?"

"Samantha will get you a bottle of vitamin supplements
with iron," said Dr. Augustin. "Just follow the directions

on the label. The anemia worries me a little. As I told you, her liver enzymes were essentially within normal limits, but I have no explanation for the anemia. I'll want to see her in a month for another blood count. And let's not breed her again for a while."

Westphall nodded. "And I think we'll stay away from those power lines," he said. "Until Darlene and I are satisfied they don't pose any danger. Especially to Timmy and Darlene's baby."

He started to leave, then turned around. "Are you going to the commission meeting Thursday?" he asked Dr. Augustin. "The Horseman's Association wants me to speak, and I'd appreciate your support, Doc. Maybe you could tell them about Princess."

His hand strayed down to Princess's head. The dog looked up at him and wagged her tail. She really did look like her old self.

Dr. Augustin closed the Westphall file and stuck his pen in his shirt pocket. Then he glanced over at Mr. Westphall. His voice was pleasant enough, but he wasn't smiling.

"If I *do* say anything Thursday, it will be after I've taken a look at that marsh and the rest of the land Peninsular Power intends to put that line across. I'm not qualified to talk about the effects of EMFs on the public health, assuming there are any effects."

"But Princess . . ." began Mr. Westphall.

Dr. Augustin squeezed his right hand into a fist, then opened it, a sure sign his blood pressure was on the rise. He took a deep breath and let it out slowly.

"I've already told you, Dick, I don't know what caused Princess to abort those puppies. Or what's causing her anemia. I wish I did. I'm not even sure the two things are related."

Mr. Westphall continued to scratch Princess's head. Then he nodded and stuck out his right hand. "You're right. Sorry. And thanks for helping out the other night."

"No problem," said Dr. Augustin. He shook Westphall's

hand. "If all goes well, we won't have to see Princess for a month or so."

I walked Mr. Westphall and his dog up to the reception room. While Cynthia totaled up the charges, I grabbed a bottle of liquid vitamins from out of the supply closet behind Cynthia's desk and wrote the date and Princess's name on the label.

"This should last you a good month," I said, handing the bottle to Mr. Westphall.

He smiled sheepishly. "I hope Dr. Augustin isn't PO'd at me for that power-line thing," he said.

"He's not." I lowered my voice. "And don't give up on him. He's planning to check out the site this weekend. Then he'll probably make some kind of statement Thursday night. He always does, you know, if it's something he believes in or is dead-set against. You might get support out of him yet." I winked.

Mr. Westphall nodded. He was about to say something when our next client came through the door with a cat carrier in each hand, and I left to clean the exam room.

At five, John Deland presented us with another victim of the mysterious "Carriage Hill-itis," as Dr. Augustin had started calling it.

"This one's considerably more alert than the last one," John said, putting the carrier on the treatment-room table. He was wearing leather gloves.

Cautiously I peered into the carrier. A tan, hairy face with large, liquid brown eyes stared back at me. I noticed the dog was moving its head back and forth. It reminded me of those plastic dogs you see occasionally in the rear windows of people's cars. The kind with the head that bobs drunkenly to and fro. I had to concentrate to keep from rocking my head in unison with the dog's.

Suddenly a faint rumble started in the animal's throat, and then it slowly opened its mouth and curled its lips back from its teeth. The rumble became a full-fledged snarl. I'd obviously gotten a little too close.

"Stand back, Samantha," said Dr. Augustin from the treatment-room doorway. He walked over to the cabinet by the refrigerator and opened it. "The last thing I need around here is my technician foaming at the mouth." He took out a blue nylon muzzle and a pair of heavy leather gloves and came over to the table. He put the gloves on.

John opened the carrier and upended it. The dog, a buff-colored terrier mix, tumbled forward onto the table. Dr. Augustin pinned it down while John slipped the muzzle on and secured it. The dog was so busy trying to gain its balance on the slick metal tabletop, it didn't even notice the muzzle until it was in place.

Dr. Augustin took off his gloves and reached for the stethoscope hanging on the wall. "Is this one of your pack dogs or somebody's pet?" he asked John.

The three of us watched the little dog stagger around on the table, then collapse. His head continued to nod back and forth, and he was trembling. He was also panting heavily. His skin had an odd odor to it.

"No tag or tattoo," said John, taking off his gloves and putting them on the counter. "I haven't seen him before. Of course, it's hard to tell if his fear of people is because he's feral or because he's sick."

"He smells awful," I said, wrinkling my nose.

John nodded. "It's a strange odor, that's for sure. Probably from digging in garbage cans."

"It's not from garbage," said Dr. Augustin. "At least not from your typical spoiled meat and day-old bread."

He went to the table and very slowly extended his hand to the dog's back. The animal flinched but made no attempt to get away. Then Dr. Augustin ran his hand down the animal's hind legs.

"It's from some kind of chemical. Cleaning fluid, maybe." He smelled his hand. "Seems to be confined to his legs and feet." He placed the stethoscope against the dog's chest and listened.

Suddenly the dog began to seizure. Dr. Augustin abandoned his stethoscope and grabbed the bottle of Valium from off the shelf. I got a syringe out of the drawer, tore it out of its package, and handed it to Dr. Augustin. He drew up some of the Valium and, with John's help, managed to inject a portion of it into one of the dog's veins.

Almost immediately, the animal stopped his shaking and jerking. He slumped onto the table and closed his eyes.

"That's what he was doing when we found him," said John. "Only this episode was worse."

Dr. Augustin resumed his examination. After a couple of minutes, he stepped back and folded his arms over his chest. "We'll start him on IV fluids to help his kidneys flush out whatever is in his system. I'd like to do an ECG. And we'll take some blood. He doesn't appear anemic, at least not as anemic as the one you brought us Tuesday."

"I'm going to have a hard time justifying anything heroic, you realize," said John, picking up the carrier and his gloves. "I really think the political types running Animal Control are tickled to death these Carriage Hill strays are biting the big one. Takes the pressure off."

Dr. Augustin continued to watch the little dog. He didn't say anything.

John started for the door. "You do what you think is best, Lou. I sure as hell don't want any of those animal rights types accusing the department of condoning poison. You'd think these poor dogs were wolves out to get somebody's sheep or cattle instead of their garbage. Come to think of it, wolves deserve better."

He left. Dr. Augustin drew a blood sample from the dog and gave it to Tracey. Then he carried the animal into the surgery, and while I hooked it up to the ECG machine, he washed his hands.

"We're still on for tomorrow afternoon, aren't we? Or do you have a hot date with Mr. Wonderful?"

I switched on the machine. "No, no date," I said softly. I knew he was baiting me, but under the circumstances, defending Michael was the last thing I wanted to do.

He turned around and stared at me, his eyes dark and piercing. Sometimes I think he can read minds with those eyes.

He grinned. "Fine," he said. "I'll pick you up at two."

CHAPTER 9

•

Sunday, October 10

I got up at eight, threw a pair of shorts on over my bathing suit, and drove to Michael's. If I had to baby-sit for him, at least I could take advantage of the pool behind his building.

Randy and Katie were waiting at the door, looking very lovey-dovey, even for them. Allowing for the fact that they were hungry, I concluded some type of mischief had occurred somewhere. A roll of toilet paper unwound, a flower arrangement disassembled. Unlike dogs, cats do not hang their heads in shame, do not get that subservient "I'm sorry I ate your shoes" (or, more likely, "I'm sorry for whatever I did to make you angry") expression dogs can get. Cats are too self-centered. However, they are not entirely without morals. They are also far from stupid. So, instead of acting guilty and accepting their fate, they try to divert your attention with a lot of loud purring.

I decided to let Michael take care of whatever small disaster had occurred. It would do him good.

The kittens followed me into the kitchen and ran figure-eights in and out of my legs, while I prepared their breakfast. I hadn't intended to search the rest of Michael's condo for fear of what I might find (lacy underwear, whips and chains), but curiosity got the better of me. I began opening cabinets and drawers in the kitchen, looking for God knows what. I even rummaged through his small walk-in pantry.

All I found of interest was a seafood cookbook entitled *From Hook to Table.* An inscription on the inside cover said, "To Michael from Jim and Melissa. Many happy returns." It was dated May 5, 1975.

I scooped out the litter pan, refilled the kittens' water dish, and made sure the front door was locked. Then I went downstairs, got my towel out of my car, and walked around to the back of the building.

Because it was Sunday and still early, I hadn't expected to find anyone at the pool. However, a woman somewhere in her sixties, wearing a white bathing cap and a royal-blue swimsuit, was doing slow but steady laps. Another woman, about the same age, wearing a terry-cloth robe and sunglasses, was reading. She evidently had already been in the water, because her hair was wet. I could see the straps of a dark green bathing suit peeking out from under the robe. A glass of what looked like iced tea sat on the table next to her chair.

Two balding, grey-haired men, possibly the women's husbands, were in the shallow end of the pool, talking. They both looked up and watched me as I came across the pool deck.

I put my purse and towel on a vacant recliner and took off my shorts. Then I went over to the shower and rinsed off. The men continued to watch me. I noticed the woman in the robe was watching me, as well, although it was hard to be sure, because of the sunglasses.

For a moment I thought maybe I'd only imagined slipping on my bathing suit. That I was actually stark naked. I did a quick check of my attire.

"Come on in, the water's terrific!" shouted one of the men. He waved at me.

I smiled and walked around to the shallow end. Upon closer inspection, I realized the men were pushing eighty, instead of seventy. Although they were nicely tanned and not the least bit overweight, their skin lay in wrinkled layers around their necks and on their arms, seeming to drip off of them like varnish off old wood.

I slid into the water. It was brisk, and I gave a little involuntary gasp, which appeared to amuse the two men.

"Good for the ole ticker," said the taller man, thumping his chest. "Nothing like a little jump-start in the A.M., I always say." He grinned suggestively. He was wearing an expensive gold diver's watch and a large diamond ring. In the sun they blinked like aircraft warning beacons. "You're new here, aren't you?"

Before I could respond, I heard a lounge chair creak behind me, followed by a noisy splash. I turned my head.

The two women were cutting through the water like a couple of sharks homing in on a piece of fresh-cut bait. When they reached us, they took up positions next to their (I presumed) spouses. The one with the sunglasses hadn't taken them off. I get very nervous when I can't see someone's eyes. Particularly when that someone might not have my best interests at heart.

"I'm pet-sitting for a friend," I said. "Michael Halsey. Tenth floor."

The shorter of the two men smiled. "You must be Samantha," he said. "Mike mentioned you'd be stopping by to feed his cats."

"Are you the 'girl' Mr. Halsey has been seeing?" asked the sunglasses. Like she'd left out the word "call," just to be polite.

"I don't believe I caught your name," I said to her.

The tall man—her husband, apparently—stuck out his hand. "I'm Harry Tilley," he said. "And this is my wife, Jane." He gave her a dirty look.

I shook Mr. Tilley's hand, but Mrs. Tilley refrained, despite her husband's glare.

"I'm George Lasko," said the short man. He turned to the woman with the bathing cap. "And this is Sophie."

Sophie hesitated, as if not wanting to offend her buddy, Jane. In the end, marital vows won out, and she smiled and offered me her hand. "Nice to meet you," she said. She was having to stand on her tippy toes to keep from drowning, even in the shallow end.

Both Sophie and George had slight foreign accents. Sophie's was more pronounced than his.

"How do you do?" I said, shaking Sophie's hand. Then I looked back at Mr. Tilley. "Have you known Michael long?" I asked him.

He shrugged. "We speak occasionally, but I don't really *know* him. Mike keeps to himself pretty much. Jane and I run into him down at the dock. We talk about boats and fishing." He paused. "Mike's only been here a couple of years. Moved in right after his wife, Mary, died. He's from New York originally. But, then, you already know that." He smiled.

"Mary's son, Kevin, spent last summer down here," said Jane. "I expected him to come again this year, but of course, Mr. Halsey's been pretty busy lately, hasn't he?"

I wanted to reach up and yank the sunglasses from her face, just so I could verify what I'd already decided. That her eyes were the color of stagnant pond scum.

"Yes, he has," I said. "He's an assistant editor at the *Times,* now, and that keeps him pretty busy." I knew Jane hadn't been referring to Michael's job, and it was gratifying to see her scowl.

"I simply cannot understand why he would want to sell his business and move out of New York," she said.

Mr. Tilley glanced over at his wife with a somewhat less than loving expression. "No," he said, "you wouldn't."

Jane drew her mouth up into a little pout. Sophie and George exchanged nervous glances.

The water was a bit chilly for just standing around, and Mrs. Tilley certainly wasn't adding any warmth to the party. I was starting to shiver, and goose bumps were popping up everywhere. I needed to go home and take a nice hot shower. Besides, I figured I wasn't going to discover anything more about Michael, without letting on how little I knew. And I wasn't about to give Jane the satisfaction.

"I really should be going," I said, trying to keep my teeth from chattering. "It was *very* nice to meet you," I added, looking directly at Mr. Tilley and smiling flirtatiously.

"Yes, indeed it was, Miss . . ." said Harry, taking my hand in his.

I got the distinct impression he was shopping. "Holt," I said, not doing a very good job of hiding my amusement. He was old enough to be my grandfather. "Samantha Holt."

Harry let go of my hand. I knew Jane would give him hell later, and I sort of felt sorry for him, but it was fun being a teensy bit wicked.

George and Sophie smiled, and then all five of us climbed out of the water. I literally ran to the opposite end of the pool. I slipped on my sandals, grabbed my towel and the rest of my stuff, and dashed through the gate to the parking lot, before Jane's icy stare could further my case of frostbite.

"Okay," I said aloud as I drove back to my apartment. "So maybe Mary *is* dead. And Kevin is living with relatives. Jane did say he was *Mary*'s son, not *their* son." I chewed on the inside of my cheek. "Still, Michael should have told me about the boy. Not telling the whole truth is tantamount to lying, isn't it? And why hasn't he told me about his business back in New York?"

I had to slow down as I approached the First Baptist Church of Brightwater Beach. A police officer was directing traffic into the church parking lot. He smiled at me and waved me on.

Okay, I thought, so maybe I should have asked. Maybe I was wrong about Michael. And I could almost hear Cynthia saying "I told you so."

CHAPTER 10

•

By 1:45 the temperature had climbed to eighty degrees. I stood on the landing, waiting for Dr. Augustin, and watched the steady stream of cars flowing up and down Gulf Drive. The locals were obviously taking advantage of the lull between the summer tourists and the snowbirds. A faint breeze out of the west carried an odor of coconut oil and the sound of rock music all the way across the island to my apartment building. I could almost taste the beer and jalapeño poppers down at Woody's. It was Jeffrey's turn to buy. Of course, it had been Jeffrey's turn to buy our last three trips to Woody's.

Dr. Augustin rounded the corner at 2:05 and pulled into the parking lot. I locked my door and went down the steps.

"Beautiful day for a hike in the woods, don't you think?" he asked as I got into the Jeep.

"Actually, I was thinking it was a nice day for the beach," I said.

He started across the causeway. "Don't be such a putz, Samantha. Think of this as a learning experience. A chance to become more familiar with the flora and fauna of west central Florida."

I didn't say anything. My life was a mess . . . well, my love life at any rate—and he was taking me into the swamp to study snakes and spiders. Neat.

70

We cruised through town, drove past the new performing arts center in Pine Bluffs and the Summerland Greyhound Track, then turned north onto Bayside Boulevard. Traffic was unusually light, particularly for a Sunday, and we made pretty good time. Then Dr. Augustin left the main thorough-fare and started down a little county road called Possum Flats Lane, and we had to creep along to avoid getting beat to death by all the potholes.

"Where do they come up with these names?" I asked. "Possum Flats Lane, Moccasin Wallow Road, Cooter Trail? I mean, really."

"They were given those names eons ago," said Dr. Augustin, "by the early settlers. It's easier to remember a road if you name it after some distinctive feature of the area."

I couldn't tell if he was teasing me or not. His sunglasses hid his eyes.

"Maybe you upper-crust types would prefer Avalon Way or Royal Court?" he said. "In fact, I think there's an Avalon Drive in the Carriage Hill subdivision." He laughed. "Of course, Dog Pack Run would be more appropriate." He had his left arm resting on the open window, and he drummed his fingers lightly on the roof. He was in an unusually good mood.

"Do you know where we're going, exactly?" I asked. My mood, on the other hand, was deteriorating rapidly.

"More or less," he said. "This road gives out somewhere due east of Carriage Hill. We'll have to play it by ear after that. Peninsular Power has probably cut a few temporary roads in for their survey crews. I'm hoping to locate one of them, but we may have to hoof it at least part of the way." He looked down at my feet. "I hope those shoes are sturdy."

Lovely, I thought. I could be basking in the sun right about now, drinking a Foster's.

Dr. Augustin wasn't kidding. Possum Flats Lane ended, rather abruptly, at a creek that looked like it might have been spawned in early June and had recently reached the toddler stage. Unfortunately, the water was cloudy, and it was difficult to gauge its depth. On the far side, I could see a sort of two-rut dirt road that wandered off into a tangle of undergrowth.

"What do you suggest we do now?" I asked, fearful he might actually say "hike." I'm certainly not opposed to exercise, but I prefer to do it out in the open, where I can see what I'm getting myself into. And what is about to get me.

He didn't answer. Instead, he threw the Jeep into reverse and slowly backed up. Then he stopped and peered out of the window.

I looked over his shoulder. Two short wooden stakes with pieces of fluorescent pink plastic tape tied to them had been stuck in the ground by the edge of the road. The letters PPC-Bal were written in black on the stakes. Between them, the grass and weeds were matted down, as if a vehicle had recently traveled that way.

"I suggest we try this route," said Dr. Augustin.

He eased the Jeep through the stakes. The ground was extremely uneven, and the Jeep's tires fell into one hole after another, which wasn't doing my neck any good. We surprised several rabbits and a covey of quail. The rabbits darted first one way and then another before finally escaping into the brush. I could smell something burning.

"Grass on the exhaust manifold," said Dr. Augustin. "Not to worry."

But I could just see us starting a forest fire, with roast bunny and quail the end result.

After what seemed like a mile of bronc riding, we came to a barbed-wire fence that looked new. Fresh dirt was piled up around the fence posts. A large sign on the fence said PRIVATE PROPERTY. NO TRESPASSING.

"This is the end of the line, I guess," said Dr. Augustin.

He turned off the engine and got out of the Jeep. Then he shut his door. Obviously he hadn't meant for me to take him literally, because he looked across the seat at me and said, "Well?"

I opened my door into a bunch of palmettos. Something scurried off into the shadows, and I hesitated.

"What are you waiting for, Samantha, an invitation?" He frowned, then went around to the back of the Jeep. He opened the hatch and took out an old blanket and a machete.

I slammed the door and tried to ignore the rustling noises as I squeezed past the stiff palmetto fronds. I stopped at the NO TRESPASSING sign. Dr. Augustin walked up and flipped the blanket over the top wire of the fence. "Private Property" clearly meant nothing to him.

"Climb over," he commanded. He pulled down on the blanket.

"You're kidding, right?" I asked, staring at the waist-high wire, its barbs glistening in the sun like shark's teeth.

"Just lean on the fence post, put your foot on the bottom wire, and hop over." He patted the post to our left. "And be quick about it. My arm is getting tired."

I tested the bottom wire with my shoe. It wobbled back and forth. I glared at Dr. Augustin, then grabbed the fence post with both hands and stepped up. It was like I imagined a high-wire artist must feel the first time out, but after swaying a bit, I managed to get myself over the top wire without tearing anything.

Dr. Augustin tossed the machete over, then vaulted the fence easily. He picked up the machete.

"I don't suppose the NO TRESPASSING sign applies to us," I said.

Dr. Augustin ignored me. He took off into the palmettos. I hurried after him, silently praying that whatever snakes he scared up would bite him instead of me, being as he was in the lead.

A narrow path appeared suddenly to our right, and Dr. Augustin turned down it. We couldn't see the fence or the Jeep anymore. I cleared my throat.

"You know how to get back here, right?" I asked. Then, before he could make some snappy remark, I added, "Of course you do. What a silly question."

Dr. Augustin looked back at me. "Weren't you ever a Girl Scout?"

"We sold cookies," I said.

The path we were on turned left into a large, and for the most part, barren sandy area dominated by short scrubby trees and bushes and masses of purple, yellow, and white wildflowers. I was surprised. October seemed like a strange time for so many flowers. And everywhere, butterflies danced from one plant to another, occasionally pausing in midflight to spar with a passing cousin.

Being a relatively recent transplant to the Sunshine State, I was understandably ignorant of the local "flora and fauna," as Dr. Augustin put it. But I was up on the basics. Palmetto, cabbage palm, live oak, and bald cypress. Monarch, sulfur, and swallowtail butterflies. And I had finally learned the difference between a sandpiper and a plover. I hadn't done much bird-watching back home. David's idea of a nature hike was venturing into the rough in search of his golf ball.

Dr. Augustin, in contrast, looked like he had been born with a compass in one hand and a machete in the other. He also had apparently been born with wings on his feet, because all of a sudden, he disappeared. I stopped.

"Over here, Samantha."

I walked around a large clump of stunted live oak. He was pointing down at the ground.

"Gopher tortoise burrow," he said.

A hole about a foot wide and bordered by an apron of well-packed sand plunged downward.

"This guy and the species he shares his burrow with might actually make it if the power company doesn't trample them to death during construction."

I spotted a thin, tall plant with an upright spike of tiny purple flowers. Three monarch butterflies were crawling around in the blooms. One of the monarchs had a small yellow object on its lower wing. "What is that?" I asked.

"Blazing star," said Dr. Augustin. "And a monarch with a wing tag."

"Tag?" I asked.

"Somebody's probably studying them again. Their winter

home in Mexico is being destroyed, which isn't surprising. Progress marches on."

And so did we.

The sun was intense, and the breeze I have come to expect out on the island was noticeably absent. Tiny heat waves rose up from the sand like steam. I pushed the bangs off my forehead and drew in a deep breath. The air smelled of toasted pine and bayberry candles. Sort of Christmasy.

Suddenly Dr. Augustin stopped and looked around. "We're too far south," he said. "That marsh is more to the northeast, if I remember the topo map correctly." He pointed in front of us and to the right. "That way."

We left the trail and started back through the palmettos. I could see a wooded area ahead, and pretty soon the palmettos thinned out, and we entered an oak hammock. The dappled sunlight and damp earth floor of the hammock combined to lower the temperature several degrees. It was pleasant. I wanted to sit down among the ferns, lean against one of the massive oaks, and enjoy the birds, most of whom I could hear but not see. Tiny little birds that twittered and warbled all around us. Probably screaming out a warning to the rest of the forest's inhabitants.

Dr. Augustin obviously had other ideas, however. So we pressed on and soon located two more survey markers.

"All of this will go," he said. "Some of these trees are in excess of a hundred years old." He touched the bark on a nearby specimen. Then he pointed to a small bush with shiny green leaves and bloodred berries. "Coastal wild coffee," he said. "Good wildlife value. There should be some beauty berry around here, too. Although by now the birds and raccoons have probably stripped it bare."

We continued walking. After a while the oak hammock merged with a thicket of willow and through that I could see cattails growing in full sun.

Dr. Augustin walked to the edge of the willow. "I think we've found our marsh," he said. "Be careful where you step."

I froze, visions of water moccasins and alligators dancing in my head. Dr. Augustin disappeared into the willows. A moment later I heard him calling me.

"What do you mean, 'be careful where I step'?" I asked, still motionless.

I heard some light thrashing, and Dr. Augustin reappeared.

"The gators hide in the saw grass with their mouths open," he said, "waiting for something to wander by."

I smacked a mosquito and stared at him.

"I'm kidding, Samantha. I just don't want you to fall in the drink. It's hard to tell where solid ground ends and water begins around here." He parted the willows and swept his hand down and forward, like a guy inviting his date into a fancy restaurant. I thought about the spider and the fly as I walked cautiously past him.

"Also," he added, "you're less likely to get snake bit." He chuckled, then put his hand into the small of my back and shoved me forward.

The willows and sawgrass were hiding a lovely round pond, half-covered with vegetation. A couple of small black water birds paddled along the far shore. When they spotted us, they began to make high-pitched clacking noises.

"Moorhens," said Dr. Augustin.

Yellow sulfur butterflies and a variety of sparrow-sized birds, most of them drab olive-brown, darted in and out of the willows. An occasional frog chirped from somewhere out in the pond.

"The power company is going to fill this in?" I asked.

"If they get a permit, they will. In the great scheme of things, this marsh probably doesn't matter. That hammock back there probably doesn't either. But added to all the other freshwater marshland and hardwood hammocks destroyed in the name of progress, they become significant." He dipped the blade of the machete into the water. Tiny round leaflike plants clung to the metal. "At what point is enough enough?"

"Can't they move the corridor?" I asked. "At least away from this area?"

"If they had access to another strip of property, I'm sure they would. If only to avoid the dredge and fill aspect. But that wouldn't ensure the preservation of this pond. The guy who owns the land, or his children, could turn around and sell it to someone else who wants to develop it."

I smacked another mosquito, and Dr. Augustin looked at his watch.

"Let's go," he said.

We went around to the opposite side of the pond, so Dr. Augustin could see how extensive the marsh really was, and soon ran into a wide, well-worn trail, with evidence that horses and four-wheel drive vehicles frequented it.

Dr. Augustin looked up and down the trail, then up at the sky. "This seems to run north and south. It probably comes out on Possum Flats Lane. We must have missed the entrance. Let's go down it, shall we?"

I felt better being on a path that allowed me to see where I was going. I also felt better knowing somebody would eventually come by and rescue me, if need be. Dr. Augustin's trail blazing was fun to a point, but we had definitely reached that point some time earlier.

The sun was finally low enough in the sky to occasionally be obscured by the trees along the trail, and I realized I was getting chilly. And I needed to pee.

"Can we stop for a minute?" I asked. "I have to . . ." I pointed to the trees off to our left.

"Certainly, Samantha," said Dr. Augustin, "be my guest. Just watch where you . . ."

"I know. Watch where I put my feet."

I took off in search of a suitable clump of trees. I did my business, then headed west toward the sun, which should have put me back on the trail, eventually, but it didn't. I stopped. How could I get lost? I asked myself. I haven't gone anywhere to speak of.

"Dr. Augustin?" I called, reluctantly.

"Over here, Samantha." His grin was evident from his tone.

I walked in the direction of his voice and came out on the trail. It had taken a sharp dogleg to the west.

"Samantha?"

I jogged north toward the bend. Another mosquito nailed me. I was busy swatting at it, not watching where I put my feet, and stumbled over something lying in the weeds at the edge of the trail. I fell, scraping my palm on some loose rock. As I was straightening up, a terrible odor of decomposing animal matter nearly overcame me. I held my breath and pushed the weeds aside with my foot.

I expected to find a dead dog or a deer with buckshot in its chest. But it was the incredible Hulk—a swollen, billious green former human male. I guessed it was a male from his work clothes and the length of his hair. It could have been a female. It could have been an alien invader for that matter.

I jumped back about the time Dr. Augustin came around the bend. He looked first at me, then at the clump of weeds.

"Samantha?"

I didn't need to say anything, because the smell clearly hit him like the blast from an oven, and he covered his mouth and nose with his free hand. With the tip of the machete, he carefully parted the weeds.

It was then that I noticed the guy's face, what hadn't sloughed off. A dark, blackish symbol—a five-pointed star inside a circle—had been carved into the man's forehead. It was like a brand. Or a warning.

Without thinking further, I started to run.

CHAPTER 11

•

Dr. Augustin caught up with me and grabbed my arm. I was breathing hard, harder than I should have been for the distance I'd covered, and probably would have run out of steam a bit farther down the trail, anyway.

"I'm sorry about that, Samantha," he told me, nodding his head in the direction of the body. "This was supposed to have been a pleasant little stroll in the woods."

Had I been able to talk at that point, I'd have told him none of our extracurricular sorties were ever little *or* pleasant.

We walked south for a couple of minutes, while I took lots of deep breaths and concentrated on slowing my heart rate. Dr. Augustin kept looking at me like I might expire right there in front of him. Presumably he was concerned about my health and not how he was going to explain being in the company of two corpses.

He stopped. "You're bleeding," he said. It was a statement of fact. Nothing more.

He took hold of my right hand and examined it. Blood and dirt had mixed together across my palm to form a nice clot over the scrape. It didn't really hurt, but I suspected it would as soon as the shock wore off.

"I'll live," I said.

Dr. Augustin let go of my hand. "We should contact the police. I need to figure out where we are, so I can give them directions to the body. I'm fairly certain this trail intersects Possum Flats Lane, not too far from where we took off. We probably drove right by the junction." He turned back toward the bend in the trail. "There's a fence back there that runs east and west. If we follow it, I guarantee we'll find the Jeep."

"I'm not going near that body again," I said flatly. Actually, it wasn't the body that terrified me. Granted, it was gross and disgusting and smelled worse than anything I'd ever experienced at the clinic. And the body *was* a person, not the remains of some poor dog or cat. But I could stand to be around it for a short time, if only to locate the fence and, ultimately, my ticket home. No, it was the carving on the guy's forehead that sent me flying down that path. Some deep-seated and totally irrational fear of the "dark side." It didn't matter that I had no idea what the carving actually represented or why the dead man was wearing it. It *looked* evil, all black and oozy and that was enough.

Dr. Augustin eyed me for a moment, and I geared myself up for a fight.

"All right," he said. "We'll take the trail. It shouldn't be too far. Maybe a mile."

But it was closer to two miles by the time we reached Possum Flats Lane. My hand was throbbing and my mouth felt like I'd eaten an entire jar of grade-school paste. And we weren't even to the Jeep yet.

"No wonder I missed this when we came by here earlier," said Dr. Augustin. "It looks like a private drive."

A large metal gate was closed across the intersection of the trail and the road. A heavy padlock secured it. Dr. Augustin climbed over the gate, then helped me over. We stood on the shoulder of the road and studied the area. Dried horse droppings, multiple tire tracks, and a small metal sign on the gate proclaiming the trail to be the property of the Northside Horseman's Association left little doubt as to the trail's users.

"I wonder who has the key," I said, fingering the padlock.

"I suspect there are a number of keys to that lock. Obviously, a lot of people routinely use this trail. Which means the body was dumped there, probably late last night. Otherwise, somebody would have called the cops by now. You don't ride by a smell like that without investigating it."

I frowned. Speak for yourself, I thought.

We walked up Possum Flats Lane to the survey markers and then over the chuckholes and rabbit warrens to the Jeep. The whole time, Dr. Augustin rattled on about the importance of sandhills in the recharge of our drinking water supply, and the role of marshes in the purification of stormwater runoff. For good measure, he threw in a recitation about the migratory habits of the northern water thrush, probably just to impress me. I began to feel sorry for the city commissioners. I figured he was preparing his remarks for Thursday's meeting. I knew he had no intention of being labeled a tree-hugger and wanted some good, practical reasons for protecting the areas. After all, what self-respecting community leader could oppose protection of our drinking water supply?

Dr. Augustin unlocked the Jeep and got in. He picked up his cellular phone. "You wouldn't happen to know that detective's number would you? Sergeant Robinson?"

I shook my head, surprised he didn't already have the number programmed into the phone. He punched in "911" and, after several minutes involving multiple transfers, finally reached Sergeant Robinson. The detective agreed to meet us at the Horseman's Association gate.

Dr. Augustin took the blanket off the fence and put it in the back of the Jeep. He opened a red and white cooler and took out two Cokes, one of which he handed to me. Then he pulled out his medical bag.

"You might as well scrub that hand while we wait," he said. He gave me a bottle of Betadine soap and a couple of sterile gauze pads. He was clean out of sympathy.

After I'd washed my palm thoroughly, wincing and groaning the whole time, while Dr. Augustin gave me his

"God, what a sissy" look, we got in the Jeep and drove back to the trail entrance.

"What was that thing on the corpse's forehead," Dr. Augustin asked. "A pentagram?" Apparently, he was unable to stay away from the subject any longer. He had done well to go half an hour.

"A five-pointed star in a circle? I guess." I drank my Coke and stared out the window. Who cares, anyway? Let the cops figure it out. Then I sighed and thought, I should be so lucky.

Robinson and company arrived at 4:30. A patrol car, a Crime Scene Investigations van, and two additional unmarked vehicles squeezed in along the shoulder on either side of the gate.

Detective Sergeant Robinson, wearing a wrinkled navy suit, blue and white striped shirt, and navy tie, pulled loose, stepped out of one of the unmarked cars and came over to the Jeep.

"Afternoon, folks," he said. He looked like he'd been up all night.

Dr. Augustin climbed out, and the two men shook hands.

"The guy is a little over a mile and a half up the trail," said Dr. Augustin, "in some weeds on the west side. Just before the dogleg. You can't miss it. He's pretty ripe."

Robinson smiled at me through the open driver's side window. "I understand you stumbled across the body," he said. "Literally." Then he looked at my hand, stained yellow by the Betadine and streaked with red. His smile vanished. "Are you okay?"

At least somebody cared. I nodded. "It's nothing, really. A couple of scratches." I was silently praying Dr. Augustin would not feel compelled to "help" the detective gather clues and such. I wanted to go home. There was a beer with my name on it waiting in my refrigerator. Maybe more than one.

Sergeant Robinson and Dr. Augustin went over to the detective's car. Robinson got out a notepad and, while Dr. Augustin talked, using both his mouth and his hands, took notes. Dr. Augustin looked like he was giving a lecture. And I was relatively certain the topic wasn't the demise of the gopher tortoise.

A uniformed officer took bolt cutters out of the Crime Scene van and broke through the padlock, then opened the gate. The van proceeded slowly up the trail, followed by one of the unmarked cars. Sergant Robinson and Dr. Augustin shook hands again. Then the detective got in his car and drove through the gate. The patrol car and one uniformed officer remained behind, presumably to keep the hordes of onlookers at bay.

Dr. Augustin climbed in the Jeep, and started the engine. He backed out onto Possum Flats Lane but, as I feared, did not head east. He turned up the trail after Sergeant Robinson. To my dismay, the patrolman ignored us.

"What are you doing?" I asked. "Trust me, they can find that decomposing corpse all by themselves."

Dr. Augustin grinned. "I'm sure they can. But I'd like to know what else they find. Clues, Samantha. Aren't you the least bit curious about who the guy was or why someone would dump him out here? Or about that pentagram on his forehead?"

"No." Of course, I was curious. But for all I knew, the person or persons who'd done the man in were back home preparing straw effigies of me and Dr. Augustin.

"Where's your sense of adventure?" he asked.

I held up my wounded paw. "I've had enough adventure for one day, thank you very much." Then I began digging in my purse for some aspirin.

The parade of police cars had come to a halt several yards down from the bend in the trail. The Crime Scene boys were donning jumpsuits, rubber gloves, and masks. One of the men was stringing up yellow tape. It extended across the trail and into the woods.

"I can't imagine the cops wanting us here, adding to the confusion," I said.

Dr. Augustin pulled off the trail just shy of the tape barrier and parked. "You're going to have to show them where you fell, Samantha," he said quietly. "So your blood, and so forth don't 'add to the confusion.' " He wouldn't look at me.

"I'm not going near that body."

We sat in silence and watched the police work. One of the men had some kind of high-tech light and was shining it slowly over the ground. Whenever he found something of interest, he'd place a small plastic sign with a number on it by the spot, then move on.

Detective Robinson came over to the Jeep. "Ms. Holt," he said, "approximately where did you fall? Can you tell me, without having to walk around over there?"

He was such a nice man. "I really don't remember," I said. "Not exactly. I know I tripped over the body, and scraped my palm on the dirt and gravel that covers the trail. So it was probably a few feet farther up."

"That helps," said Robinson. "Thanks." He went back to the Crime Scene van.

I could tell Dr. Augustin wanted to get out and prowl around. Fortunately, he had better sense.

"I guess we should go, shouldn't we?" he asked.

"Yes, we should."

He started the engine. Sergeant Robinson looked over at us and waved, which made it pretty clear he didn't need us anymore. Reluctantly, Dr. Augustin made a wide turn and headed down the trail toward the road. You'd have thought he was leaving the love of his life behind, never to see her again, which suited me just fine.

"What are you going to say at the commission meeting Thursday?" I asked, once we were safely back on Bayside Boulevard.

"What?"

"You know, about the transmission corridor site."

Dr. Augustin thought for a few seconds. "I'm going to suggest the power company consider using that horse trail. It isn't wide enough, of course, but the land to the east of it appears to have been previously disturbed. It's overgrown with Brazilian pepper, among other things. If they stay to the east of the trail, they'll avoid the marsh entirely. And that sandhill."

"Don't you think their planning people have already considered that land and, for whatever reason, eliminated it?"

He rubbed the steering wheel with his right palm. "No doubt they have. I'm hoping by bringing it up Thursday, someone at Peninsular Power will have to tell us *why* they've eliminated it."

I felt a stab of pain in my right arm. Somebody was sticking pins in my little straw look-alike.

CHAPTER 12

•

Monday, October 11

The blood had run in small rivulets down the front of the
door, here and there touching Cynthia's wreath, forming tiny
puddles under the corncobs, then overflowing. It had begun
to dry and thicken, but was still moist enough to smear if
you put a little muscle into it. I knew it was blood from the
smell. Chicken blood. At least I hoped it wasn't human. I
stared at my fingers, then wiped them on the dew-soaked
grass, suddenly afraid I might catch something.

The pentagram was upside-down, like the one cut into the
dead man's forehead. I wanted to pick up the hose and blast
it off the door, but I was certain Dr. Augustin would want to
see it first.

So this is what it feels like to be the neighborhood pariah,
I thought, as I let myself into the clinic, careful not to brush
against the blood. Why had that reporter put our names in
the paper? Why couldn't he have just said that two hikers
found the body? It was as if Dr. Augustin and I had gone into
the woods for some kind of nefarious activity. At least whoever did this didn't put a cross up in the front yard and set it
on fire.

And then I remembered that the article hadn't mentioned
the pentagram. Because the police didn't want that bit of information known, according to Dr. Augustin. So, I asked
myself, how come the person who did this knew about it?

Suddenly an image of half-crazed devil-worshipers dancing around a fire, their bodies smeared with the blood of some recent sacrifice, popped into my head. In the absence of a suitable virgin, they would use a black cat, I theorized, and then I thought about Charlie and panicked. With my purse still slung over my shoulder, I raced down the hall to the kennel.

Charlie had his face and chest pressed against the bars of his cage door and his paw was fruitlessly pushing up on the latch. When he realized someone was watching him, he sat back and began to meow his indignity at having been locked up for over twelve hours. Fortunately, Frank had remembered to padlock the cat's cage, and for once, I wanted to kiss him for it. Had Charlie been out and visible through the front wall of the clinic . . . I hated to think.

"Samantha!" Cynthia's voice was only faintly audible over all the barking and whining.

I took my keys out of my pocket and unlocked Charlie's cage, wincing slightly at the pain in my hand and wrist. I had barely gotten the door open when Charlie hopped to the floor and slithered out of the kennel and down the hall, his belly hugging the linoleum like a dust mop. Then I reached up to let Pearl out. Pearl, the antithesis of Charlie, not only in appearance but in personality, was crouched in the back of her cage. She had no head or legs. All I could see was a round, smudged white ball with two large blue disks staring out at me. It was pretty obvious she did not intend to venture forth, but I opened her cage anyway, in case she changed her mind.

"Samantha! Did you see what someone did to our door?" Cynthia stood in the kennel doorway, her hands on her hips.

It was a rhetorical question, I knew, since I'd obviously come in that way.

"Whoever it was deserves a good spanking," she said, as if this was only a child's prank and not the work of some deviant adult mind. "They've probably ruined my door decoration." She paused. "Shouldn't we wash it off before the clients start arriving?"

"Wait until Dr. Augustin gets here," I said.

Just then, Frank came in the back door, followed by Tracey. They both looked at Cynthia and me, grinned sheepishly, and headed for the lab and a much needed cup of coffee, if I was reading the circles under their eyes correctly.

"It's not made yet," I hollered after them.

Cynthia and I went up to the reception room. Charlie was sitting on Cynthia's desk, staring at the front door. His tail ws twitching violently. I reached out to pet him, and he growled, then jumped off the desk and ran into Dr. Augustin's office.

Cynthia watched him disappear around the corner. "I wonder what's gotten into him."

"Bad vibes," I said. "Probably knows Dr. Augustin is going to pitch a fit over the door."

Cynthia sat down at her desk. "He isn't going to be very pleased about this, either," she said, holding up the local section of the paper. The headline read MAN'S BODY FOUND NEAR CARRIAGE HILL. "Too bad Michael wasn't here to do the article. This Paul Richardson made it sound like you and Dr. Augustin were up to no good out there in those woods." She looked at me, a quizzical expression on her face. "Just exactly what *were* you doing, anyway?"

"Looking that proposed transmission corridor over before Thursday's commission meeting."

Cynthia hadn't been very subtle when she'd mentioned Michael, but she did have a point. He would have done a better job of reporting the facts, and we probably could have persuaded him to leave out our names.

I was about to go start treatments, when Dr. Augustin drove up. I watched him get out of his Jeep and walk across the parking lot. When he saw the door, he stopped and stared at it. Then he came inside, eyebrows drawn together, lips a hard, thin line. He looked like some great bird of prey, ready to dive down on an unsuspecting rodent. Without thinking, I stepped behind Cynthia's desk.

"Samantha!" he snapped. "Get Peter Robinson on the phone." He went into his office.

Almost immediately, Charlie shot out, as if propelled by the blast from a cannon. He paused only long enough to negotiate the turn into the storage closet behind Cynthia's desk. I heard him scramble up to his favorite hiding place atop the mountain of dog food bags.

Dr. Augustin reappeared in the doorway. "And put that cat in his cage. Use the padlock. I don't want him loose in the clinic until after Halloween." He hesitated, and his eyes darted over to Cynthia, then back to me. "And take down that black cat, jack-o'-lantern thing from the bulletin board. In fact, get rid of all this Halloween nonsense." He went into his office and slammed the door. I heard his chair creak.

"Call Sergeant Robinson, would you?" I asked Cynthia. "His number is in the computer."

As I was about to leave, I saw Mrs. O'Hara drive up and get out of her car. Her pug, Chester, was scheduled to be neutered that morning. But Chester never made it inside. Mrs. O'Hara took one look at the front door, crossed herself (and Chester), and got back in the car. She sped off like Marley's ghost was after her, leaving a thin trail of rubber on the roadway.

"I guess our appointment schedule is going to be a little light this morning," I said. "At least until we wash the door."

With that, Cynthia picked up the phone and started dialing the police station.

Michael Halsey beat the cops to the clinic by twenty minutes. Over the intercom, Cynthia announced his arrival. I told her I'd be up as soon as I could. That I was still doing treatments. In all honesty, I wasn't ready to face him. The fact that he had no idea I had found the picture or overheard the phone call made little difference. He would know something was wrong, and I didn't feel like explaining to him why I was snooping around in his condo and falsely accusing him of adultery.

I managed to stay in the kennel just long enough for him to leave. When I finally finished medicating everyone who needed it and a few who didn't (they got vitamins), I went up to the reception room.

"Mike will be back this afternoon," said Cynthia as Peter Robinson pulled into the parking lot. He had someone with him.

"Did you say anything?" I asked her. "I mean about the picture or the phone call?"

"I certainly did not," she said indignantly. "After all, it isn't any of my business, now is it?" She wouldn't look at me.

Yeah, right, I thought.

I told Dr. Augustin the cops had arrived and went to clean the surgery. Not that it needed cleaning. So far, we'd had three cancellations, and the morning wasn't over yet.

When I finished, I wandered into the lab for a cup of coffee. With no surgery patients to do blood work on, Tracey had gone back to the kennel to help her dearly beloved.

"Please don't take this as an insult, Dr. Augustin," I heard Robinson say, "but for people who heal warm, furry creatures for a living, you and Miss Holt appear to have an affinity for murder and mayhem. Or is that just my imagination?"

"We do seem to stumble onto more than our share of dead bodies, don't we?" said Dr. Augustin, rather jovially.

I choked, then stepped into the doorway. Robinson was sitting in the chair next to Dr. Augustin's desk. He seemed relaxed, as did Dr. Augustin, who was leaning comfortably back in his own chair, his hands clasped loosely in his lap. They both looked up at me.

"Come in, Samantha," said Dr. Augustin. He indicated the daybed.

My my, I thought. Aren't we chummy. Especially considering we've lost several hundred dollars' worth of business so far today. He ought to be fuming mad, not acting like Mr. Rogers and everything was right in the neighborhood.

I went over and sat down.

Robinson smiled. "Greetings, Miss Holt. You appear to have recovered nicely from your little experience yesterday. I guess finding Trexler's body the way you did would be quite a shock even for the best of us."

"Trexler?" I asked.

"William 'Billy' Trexler," said Robinson. "Age thirty-five. Worked for Peninsular Power as a surveyor. He was single—divorced—and had taken a few days off, so no one missed him. Who killed him and how his body got to the site are still unknown.

"The ME estimates he was killed a week or so ago. Shot in the back at close range. He ws dumped on that trail Saturday night or Sunday morning. The body is in pretty good shape, considering. Possibly he was buried for a while or stored somewhere. Someplace cool and dry." He paused. "There were wood shavings on his hair and clothes. Maybe from a hastily constructed coffin. We're sending a sample to the forensic botanist we employ from time to time. He'll tell us what kind of wood it was, which should help."

"What about the symbol on his forehead?" asked Dr. Augustin.

"The results of the autopsy aren't official yet," said the detective, "but we do know it was made recently, Probably after he was dumped."

"Why the delay, do you suppose?"

"Now that is a puzzle," said the detective. "My guess is those Wiccans up there in Carriage Hill found the body and decided to take advantage of it. Left the power company a message. That symbol was a pentacle."

"I don't understand," I said. "Who or what are 'Wiccans.' "

"Witches," said Robinson. "Wicca is a form of religion."

"You mean like Satanism?" asked Dr. Augustin.

The detective shook his head. "No, no, nothing like that. Wiccans don't worship the devil, apparently. As I understand it, they base their religious beliefs on pre-Christian folklore and pagan rituals that center around nature and Mother Earth. They're supposed to be a peaceful group. A lot of upper middle-class feminists and environmentalists here in the U.S. are Wiccans, it turns out." He leaned back in his chair and loosened his tie.

I heard a cabinet door slam shut and saw Dr. Augustin look toward the lab. He nodded to me and then in the direction of the noise. I got up and quietly closed the lab door, then went back to the daybed.

"Why would these Wiccans want to carve a pentagram—pentacle into some dead guy's forehead," I asked. "More importantly, why would they want to paint one on the clinic's front door?"

"I figure it's a warning," said Robinson. " The Carriage Hill area is known to have a sizable Wiccan population. I'm told they hold meetings and carry out ceremonies in the woods up there, although I don't know that for a fact. Anyway, I presume they don't want that power line to disturb the ecosystem or whatever. And they probably don't want a lot of construction traffic interfering with their religious activities, either. They're preying on people's superstitions."

"It could be that someone is trying to make us think it was the Wiccans who killed Mr. Trexler," said Dr. Augustin. "And decorated my door."

Robinson nodded. "There is that, of course."

Dr. Augustin shifted in his chair. "Have you found out anything about that fire in the Technical Services Building? Or about Jack Lanier's death?"

Robinson looked over at me and smiled. It was almost like he'd been waiting for Dr. Augustin to ask about Lanier. That he was amazed it had taken as long as it had for Dr. Augustin to bring up the subject.

"Just curious, you understand," said Dr. Augustin innocently. Well, maybe not exactly innocently.

"You and Lanier were friendly, weren't you?" asked the detective. He was still smiling. "I remember seeing you together at a couple of commission meetings. When they were arguing about that sewage treatment plant."

"You've got a good memory, Sergeant," said Dr. Augustin.

"It's part of my job description." He paused, as if considering the consequences of telling us what the *Times* people obviously hadn't discovered yet.

"Lanier was shot in the head with a thirty-caliber rifle. Possibly a Winchester thirty-thirty. Execution style—very close range. But not in the Technical Services Building. His body was moved there from the municipal parking garage shortly after he died. We found the bullet and traces of his blood in the garage, although someone went to great lengths to clean the place up. It had to have been messy. The fire at the Technical Services Building was set, presumably to cover up the murder. They tried to make it look accidental, but the arson people found evidence of a flammable solvent."

"Did they carve a pentacle in his forehead?" I asked.

"Hard to say. Half his face was blown away. What was left was badly charred."

I swallowed.

"Is there a connection between Lanier's death and that of this surveyor, Trexler?" asked Dr. Augustin. "You said Jack was shot with a thirty-caliber rifle. What about the gun that killed Trexler?"

Robinson shrugged. "We haven't recovered the bullet that killed him, but after examining the wound, the ME said it could have been from a thirty-caliber weapon. Hopefully, we'll know more later this week." He smiled. "A lot of people up in that part of the county have rifles. For deer hunting, mainly. Or target practice. And they look impressive on the gun rack of a Chevy pickup."

At that moment Robinson's companion tapped on Dr. Augustin's door. Then he opened it and stuck his head in.

"Sarge, they want us back at the station," he said.

He was cute, with short brown hair and rosy cheeks on a youthful, open face. He smiled at me, and I felt myself blush.

"I hope you don't mind," he said, "but I figured you'd want that door washed as soon as the Crime Scene guys were finished, so I helped myself to your hose." His eyes were violet.

"I appreciate that," I said. "Business has been a little slow this morning because of that door."

Robinson stood up. "I guess I can trust you to keep all of this under your hats." He looked first at Dr. Augustin, then at me.

Dr. Augustin walked him to the door. "Absolutely," he said. "And thanks for sharing what you know with us, Sergeant."

"It's Peter," Robinson said. "I've run into you so many times over the last few months, I feel like we should be on a first-name basis, don't you?" He held out his hand.

Dr. Augustin shook it. "Call me Lou, then."

Robinson paused. "I'm probably wasting my breath," he said from the doorway. "But try to stay away from this. Really." He lowered his voice. "A lot of people—very powerful people— are involved in that transmission corridor issue. It wouldn't surprise me one bit if somebody else gets hurt before this thing plays itself out. I'd hate to think you or Miss Holt were that somebody."

He looked hard at Dr. Augustin, presumably saw that his words had fallen on deaf ears, and shrugged. He looked back at me, still seated on the daybed, and smiled. It was clearly a smile of condolence. Then he went out into the reception room. I heard Cynthia tell him good-bye.

Dr. Augustin walked over to the closet and took out his exam jacket. "Our ten-thirty is here," he said. He slipped the jacket on and buttoned it.

"Why do you think Sergeant Robinson is confiding in us?" I asked, getting up. "That can't be accepted police procedure, can it?"

"Robinson is nobody's fool," he said. "I imagine he feels we can be useful to him."

I thought about this as we headed for the exam room and

Mrs. Whittle's Jack Russell terrier, Libby. It's more likely, I told myself, that Robinson figures if he gives Dr. Augustin a little information, maybe he'll be happy to stop snooping around. Of course, in reality, all the detective has accomplished is to whet Dr. Augustin's appetite.

"You know, I've seen that pentacle symbol before," I said. "Recently."

Dr. Augustin looked at me. "Oh?"

"Yes. Mrs. Treckle wears one around her neck."

"Well now, how fortunate for us," Dr. Augustin said, smiling.

"Fortunate?" I asked, suddenly sorry I'd opened my mouth. "What do you mean, 'fortunate'?"

But he was already fawning over Libby and exuding charm and testosterone solely for Mrs. Whittle's benefit. Libby would have been happier had she been left at home.

CHAPTER 13

•

Michael never came by the clinic. Tracey volunteered to close up, so I left promptly at 5:30, just in case he was late. Cynthia was still acting indignant. In her eyes, Michael could do no wrong.

Jeffrey opened his door when I reached the landing outside my apartment. "Hi," he said.

"Hi, back." I took my key out of my purse. "What's up?" I could hear my cats making plaintive noises on the other side of the door.

"Not much."

Jeffrey was hiding something, that was pretty obvious. I unlocked my door, then looked back at him. "Okay, out with it," I said.

He held one finger up, then dashed into his apartment. A second later, he reappeared holding a huge vase filled with roses. Red as the blood on the clinic's front door.

"The delivery guy from the florist's almost dropped these coming up the stairs," he said.

He followed me into my apartment and put the vase on the kitchen counter, careful to make a lot of impressive grunting sounds. He opened my refrigerator, took out a beer, and popped the top.

"I assume they're from Michael," he said. "Nobody else could afford them."

"I suppose," I replied. Jeffrey picked right up on my lack of enthusiasm. "Uh-oh, has Michael been a bad boy?" He took a long swig of beer.

I didn't say anything. I poured food into the two cat dishes next to the dishwasher.

"Hey, if it isn't any of my business, just say so," he said, burping.

"It isn't."

Jeffrey and I don't have a lot of secrets, so I knew he was probably hurt. But I also knew he'd get over it. And anyway, how could I tell him what was bothering me when I wasn't sure myself?

"I'm sorry," I said. "I just don't want to talk about it right now."

Jeffrey smiled his wonderful smile. "Hey, that's cool." He started for the door. "I've got stuff to do, anyway." He held up his beer can. "Thanks for the brew. See ya."

He went out and closed the door behind him, leaving me to watch my cats gorge themselves and wonder why I felt like I had the lead role in *Jane Eyre*.

At 8:30 the doorbell rang. I was sitting in front of the TV eating my version of comfort food—a grilled cheese sandwich and a bowl of Campbell's tomato soup. My hair was wet, and I was dressed in my robe. Reluctantly I got up, put my tray on the dining table, and went to the door, knowing full well who it was.

"I hope you don't mind me dropping in like this, unannounced," he said. "But I was tied up all afternoon." He glanced over my shoulder. "I've only got a few minutes . . ."

I opened the door, and he came inside, smelling like an herb garden. Why does he have to be so handsome and so damned polite? I asked myself. And why doesn't he ever spill anything on his tie?

"Thanks for the roses, Michael," I said, closing the door. "But they weren't necessary."

The card had read, "We love you, Samantha. From Randy and Katie." It wasn't difficult to read between the lines.

"Oh, but they were," he said. "Where else can I get a pet-sitter on such short notice?"

He went over to the sofa and sat down. He looked tired.

"Did you have a nice trip?" I asked. I sat down in the recliner, rather than on the sofa, a move that did not go unnoticed by Michael.

"Not really. The seminar was boring, and the couple in the room next to mine were on their honeymoon. I didn't get a lot of sleep." A faint grin crossed his face. Then he frowned. "I have to go to New York, Samantha. On . . . a personal matter." He took a deep breath. "I'm not sure how long I'll be gone."

"Who is Kevin?" I asked suddenly. The question was as much a surprise to me as it obviously was to Michael. "I overheard that message on your recorder. Whoever that was called while I was checking on your cats."

"Mary's son," he said quietly, after several seconds. "By her first husband. He was a Navy pilot, killed in a training mission when Kevin was an infant. Now the boy lives with my sister-in-law, Dorothy. She's divorced with two children of her own, and Kevin has become something of a problem. Apparently, he's been skipping school and stealing. She says she can't deal with it anymore." He rubbed his eyes and leaned his head back against the sofa cushion.

"I'm sorry, Michael," I said. But I stayed on the recliner.

He looked over at me. "For what? For being curious? I should have told you about Kevin before. By choice, I support the boy financially, but I never legally adopted him. Mary wanted him to keep his father's name. So Dorothy got custody when Mary passed away." He drifted off for a moment, then shook his head. "Big mistake, but what could I do?"

He looked at his watch. "The reason I came by was to tell you I'll be dropping the kittens off at the clinic in the morning. I could be gone for as long as a week. Maybe more.

Whatever it takes. I'm going to suggest Kevin be enrolled in a private boarding school. He needs to get away from Dorothy."

He got up and headed for the door, then turned around. "Take care of yourself, Samantha," he said. He started to say something else, but evidently changed his mind.

"Let me know where you're staying," I said, "in case I need to get in touch with you. Besides, I'm sure you'll want to know how the kittens are doing." I was still sitting down.

"I will," he said. "First chance I get, I'll call." He opened the door.

Suddenly I jumped up and ran across the room. He caught me in his arms and pressed me close, so close I had trouble breathing. Then he kissed me. It was achingly tender and tantalizingly controlled. He wanted me to remember it.

"I love you, Samantha," he said. "Don't you ever forget that."

I thought I saw a faint glistening in his eyes, but before I could be certain, he was out on the landing and headed for the stairs.

"Good-bye, Michael," I said after him.

He waved a hand at me but didn't look back.

I closed the door and turned around in time to see Miss Priss drag the rest of my grilled cheese sandwich off my plate. The tomato soup was history.

CHAPTER 14

•

Tuesday, October 12

The little terrier mix was recovering nicely. After a couple of days, it became clear the dog was someone's pet. He wagged his tail and "smiled" every time anybody came into Isolation.

"Let's move him to the kennel," said Dr. Augustin. He put his stethoscope back on its peg by the door. "I don't want to send him to Animal Control just yet, but there's no reason to keep him in here any longer." He rubbed the little dog's ears.

"I had Cynthia check the Lost and Found section of the paper, I said. "Nothing."

Dr. Augustin shrugged and headed for the hallway. Then he stopped and turned around. "I'm going to watch Dale's daughter play soccer tonight," he said. "At the Northeast Recreation Complex. It's time I checked out the climate up there, anyway. See what's cooking in regard to that transmission corridor. I'm sure a lot of the kids in Daniel Kenney's neighborhood frequent the rec center. Maybe some of them are on the local soccer team." He hesitated. "Want to come along? You might overhear something that could be useful. Besides, I don't want you to get too lonely, what with Mr. Halsey gone and everything." He leaned against the door frame and smiled benignly.

"Okay," I said, feeling like an alcoholic who'd fallen off the wagon. Why couldn't I learn to "Just say no"?

• • •

We didn't leave the clinic until six, so instead of a nice leisurely supper at the Paper Moon, I had to endure a fast-food hamburger on the run. How Dr. Augustin manages to eat and drive at the same time without wearing at least some of his food on his T-shirt is a puzzlement. There was enough mayonnaise on my Whopper to make a gallon of potato salad. It took three napkins and a lot of manual dexterity on my part to eat it without making a mess. When I was finished, I felt like a blimp.

The lights around the soccer field made the night sky glow like a big city off in the distance. When we arrived, the game was under way. There were several cars parked on the grass along Sloan Avenue. A sheriff's car was among them, so rather than waste time driving around in what was undoubtedly a full parking lot, Dr. Augustin decided to risk pulling in behind the deputy.

A cheer went up suddenly, followed by a voice on the PA system announcing a goal for the Eagles, the team Dale's daughter played on. The score, according to the announcer, was Eagles one, Marauders zip.

"Way to go, Eagles," said Dr. Augustin heartily.

Bill O'Shea was waiting for us at the gate. "Missed you guys at the Moon," he said, politely omitting any savory details about the meal. "Nice of you to tag along, Samantha." He pointed to the bleachers. "Sixth row, midway."

As expected, the bleachers were packed. We climbed the center stairs to row six and stopped in front of several well-dressed women seated on a folded stadium blanket. One of the women smiled up at Dr. Augustin.

"Lou," she gushed. "I was afraid you weren't going to make it." She flashed her porcelain crowns at him. "Stephanie would have been disappointed." From the glow on her face, I gathered Stephanie wasn't the only one who'd have been disappointed.

The woman had red hair cut short and freckles unencumbered by makeup. Her eyes were green. Like the rest of the

women on the right half of row six, she was in her late thirties to early forties and dressed conservatively. Her midcalf
denim skirt and hand-knit sweater looked expensive but
pointedly casual.

Dr. Augustin laughed. "I thought I made her nervous."

There was a lot of polite clapping, mostly from our area
of the bleachers.

"Side out, Eagles," said the announcer.

I glanced down at the field. A referee stood by the side-
line holding his hand up. He looked like a giant six-year-old
pre-school boy in his regulation black shirt, shorts, and knee
socks. Beside him, a girl in green and white with a pert
ponytail and precocious breasts was holding the ball. She
spotted a teammate and pitched the ball onto the field in the
girl's direction. Unfortunately, a player in red beat her to it.
She swooped down on the ball like a hawk and deftly dribbled it toward the left goal.

"Get the lead out, Susan," screamed one of the women
sitting on the stadium blanket.

"Come *on,* Kelly!" shouted someone above us. "Move
up!"

Bill O'Shea continued across the row and sat down next
to Dale Weisop.

"Have a seat, Samantha," said Bill, patting the bench.

I sat down. Dr. Augustin stepped in front of me and Bill
and took a seat next to Weisop.

"So, how's Amy doing?" he asked Dale.

"She won't stay on her line," said Weisop. "She's lucky
their first two shots at goal were wide."

The red Marauders were older and taller than the green
and white Eagles. And faster. They kept up with the ball and,
as a consequence, snagged it repeatedly from their opponents. Apparently, at that point, the only thing standing between the red team and a tying goal was Dale Weisop's
daughter. I looked to my left. Amy stood in the penalty area,
just over the crease, and danced lightly from one foot to the
other, as the ball slowly moved in her direction.

Then, amid much cheering and clapping from our side of the stands, one of the Eagles commandeered the ball and passed it to a teammate, number twenty. She started back toward the opposite end of the field.

"Thattagirl, Stephanie," cried Dale.

Number twenty had long red hair pulled back in a ponytail. She was agile and quick, clearly one of the Eagles' best players, and fended off multiple attacks from the opposition, as she neared the right goal.

The cheering and clapping grew louder. Unfortunately, the celebration was a bit premature. A girl in red zoomed up, stuck her foot out, and tripped Stephanie. She snagged the ball and started back toward the Eagles' goal. The referee stood stock-still, hands on hips, watching.

"What?" screamed the group on row six. "Are you blind?"

The vast majority of the crowd was in support of the home team. They began chanting, "Go, go, go . . ." while stomping their feet on the metal bleachers. I figured it was an effort to drown out the cries of protest from the Eagles' supporters.

The red team was nearing the Eagles' goal. Amy stepped over the crease and ventured into the penalty area.

"No, no! Get back!" her father yelled.

She couldn't hear him because of the noise, and even if she had, it would have been too late. One of the Marauders kicked the ball behind Amy and across the goal line, tying the score. The stadium rocked.

"I've told her over and over," said Dale, "you can't leave your line like that, or they'll nail you. She won't listen."

"She's thirteen years old, Dale," said Bill. "Give the kid a break."

Weisop shook his head. "She knows better."

It was halftime. The two teams ambled over to their respective benches. Amy trailed the group by a good distance, head down, feet dragging the turf. I felt sorry for her. Goalies catch all the flack when the team loses, but the forwards get all the credit when the team wins.

Dr. Augustin stood up and walked behind Bill and me toward the end of the row.

"How about some hot chocolate?" Dale asked me.

Dr. Augustin was talking to Stephanie's mother.

"No thanks," I said. I got up. "But I would like to visit the rest room."

Dale pointed to a building behind the bleachers, and I started across the row for the aisle. When I reached Dr. Augustin and Stephanie's mother, I paused. Dr. Augustin looked at me and smiled.

"Sam," he said, "this is Melody Harding. Mel, this is my able assistant, Samantha Holt."

We shook hands. Hers, I noticed, were as cold as a corpse's. The look she gave me wasn't a lot warmer.

"Melody works at City Hall," said Dr. Augustin. "Records Department."

"Lou certainly keeps me busy," Melody said. She was gazing at him the way most of our female clients do, like he was God's gift to women and small animals. Except she wasn't one of our clients, which made me wonder what he had done to deserve such admiration.

Dr. Augustin seemed torn between Melody's fawning and a group of men who'd gathered at the foot of the stairs. Several of them looked familiar, and then I remembered seeing them at the public hearing. They'd been orchestrating a lynching of their daughters' soccer coach.

"Listen, Mel," said Dr. Augustin, "I'll be back in a few minutes."

He went down the stairs, before she could protest. I smiled at Melody, although it was a waste of time, then followed Dr. Augustin down the stairs. He was slouched against the bleachers support wall, near the men, but facing the concession area, as if waiting for someone to return with his hot dog. I winked at him, then walked across the grass to the rest rooms.

There was a line, of course. I stepped behind a woman with a young child in tow. The little girl looked pretty desperate. She was standing with her knees together, and she kept glancing fearfully up at her mother. The mother seemed unconcerned.

Most of the women were Melody's age, and most of them were wearing jeans and sweaters or sweatshirts. There was a lot of chatter going on. For some inexplicable reason, women treat lavatory stalls like confessionals. I only hoped one or two of them had something juicy to confess.

I spotted Mrs. Kenney near the front of the line. Or rather, I heard her. She was arguing with a woman in the end stall.

"I can't believe you said that, Marge!" Mrs. Kenney spouted. "After all we've been through with Joey."

A toilet flushed and pretty soon the middle stall door opened. A woman with a little boy of about three or four emerged.

"I, for one, am looking forward to that power line," said the woman. She guided her son over to the row of sinks along the left wall.

Mrs. Kenney whirled around. "What!?" she screamed.

It was Kenney's turn to use one of the toilets, but she wasn't paying attention. So the woman with the little girl, like a mall shopper in search of an empty parking space, dashed around Mrs. Kenney into the stall and shut the door.

Mrs. Kenney appeared less concerned about the condition of her bladder than about the audacity of some people. When Marge came out of her stall, she and Mrs. Kenney moved over to the sinks. I took Marge's place and shut the door.

"You want that monstrosity to vilify your neighborhood, too?" asked Mrs. Kenney. Like the transmission towers were a string of prostitutes.

"What I want," said the lady with the little boy, "is to not have to endure any more rolling blackouts that always seem to happen when I am entertaining. Anyway, that power-line corridor will be over two miles away."

"Carol, honey," said another woman, who I took to be Marge, "you don't know for a fact that power line had anything to do with Joey's illness. Besides, like I've been trying to tell you, when we bought our houses, those transmission towers were already there. It isn't like they secretly sprang up overnight."

Suddenly a loud knock on the door to my stall woke me up.

"Are you okay?"

I flushed the toilet and slowly opened the door. "Sorry," I said to the line of women waiting.

"We should use the men's room," said a twenty-something female near the end. "There's never anyone waiting there."

She had copper-colored hair and black eyeliner so thick I could easily have mistaken her face for a Halloween mask. She was smoking a cigarette. I wondered if she was a student who'd flunked a couple of years or, Heaven forbid, one of the mothers.

Mrs. Kenney, Marge, and the woman with the little boy were gone. I washed my hands and went outside in search of Dr. Augustin. He was up in the bleachers talking to Ms. Harding.

Melody's smile reversed itself when she saw me at the top of the stairs. Her comrades-in-arms looked like a circle of wagons ready to fend off the enemy, so I continued across the row to my seat.

"Nachos?" Dale asked, holding out a paper bowl of flaccid tortilla chips topped with some kind of orange glue.

"No, thanks," I said quickly, then watched in horror as Dale pulled a chip free and stuck it in his mouth. I turned away.

The second half of the soccer game had started. During the break, someone had evidently threatened the Eagles with Sunday morning practice sessions, because they were playing more aggressively than they had in the first half. The ball was moving slowly but surely toward the Marauders' goal, with most of the green and white players keeping up. A couple of girls lagged behind, however, which prompted the woman on row six to yell, rather loudly, "Get a move on, Susan!"

The girl in question looked the bleachers and frowned. "Shut up, Mother!" she screamed.

Several people, including the players on the Marauders' bench, laughed. The Eagles' coach looked eagerly at his watch.

Near the goal line, Stephanie took charge and worked the ball past the Marauders' goalie and into the net. Everyone on our side of the stadium screamed and clapped, while the locals sat glumly staring at the time clock.

"Stephanie's hot tonight," said Bill.

"She certainly is," said Dale, winking. He caught me looking at him and blushed.

The Marauders made several aborted attempts to tie up the game. When the two-minute period ended, the Eagles remained on top, two to one.

The four of us made our way down the stairs, thankfully avoiding Melody who, along with her chums, had vanished. Of course, had I been Susan's mother, I wouldn't have wanted to hang around, either.

There was a crush at the exit, as players and parents joined together for the trip home. I got separated from Dr. Augustin and wound up behind County Commission Chairman Les Jordan. He was wearing his cowboy boots and a cowboy hat, and I'd have known him anywhere. He had his arm around one of the Marauders. A woman about my age was with them, and I decided she was Jordan's daughter or daughter-in-law. The kid had to be his granddaughter.

They were discussing various options for a late supper. When Jordan suggested The Stadium, a local sports bar that catered to the area's soccer clubs, his granddaughter objected.

"Absolutely *everyone*'s going to the rec center," she whined. "Marybeth's mom is having a barbecue in the picnic area. It's Marybeth's birthday. You wouldn't want me to, like, be a no-show, would you?" She was pulling out all the steps in her grandparent buttering-up armament. "Pleeeze!"

She hung on his arm and leaned her body against his. If she had been a little older, the action might have been misinterpreted by the people around them. I noticed the girl's mother, if she was her mother, had nothing to say about the matter, and Jordan didn't seem inclined to ask for her opinion. He was staring at someone in line just ahead of us. I looked. It was Daniel Kenney and his wife.

"I don't think so, Lucy," Jordan said, finally. "I think we'll go to The Stadium."

Lucy immediately let go of Jordan's arm and switched into her petulant teenager mode. Any minute, the tears would start. I knew that from personal experience. But somehow I also knew they wouldn't have the desired effect. Les Jordan, for whatever reason, did not want to go to that picnic.

The crowd began to move, and I met up with Dr. Augustin at the Jeep. When we had made it through the bottleneck at County Road 12 and North Lincoln Street, I told Dr. Augustin about the arugment between Mrs. Kenney and the woman with the little boy.

"I guess there's a lot of disagreement about that powerline project, isn't there?" I asked. "Neighbor against neighbor. That sort of thing. I saw Les Jordan as we were leaving. I got the distinct impression he doesn't care for the Kenneys." I waited for him to say something. When he didn't, I added, "What did you learn from that group of men outside the concession area?"

"The Marauders' coach is a jackass," he said. His voice lacked enthusiasm.

"That's it?"

He looked over at me. "I want you to visit Katrina Treckle," he said. "Find out about the Wiccans up near Carriage Hill. See if Mrs. Treckle can shed any light on who might have put that pentacle on our door."

"And just how am I supposed to go about that?" I asked. It was dark in the Jeep, but I felt him glower anyway.

"You drive over there to her house and exercise your vocal cords, Samantha. I mean, how difficult could it be?"

There were a dozen things I wanted to say to him at that moment, any one of which could have gotten me fired. More to the point, however, was the fact that I knew nothing short of resigning would get me out of visiting Katrina Treckle. So I kept my mouth shut and thought about all the different ways you could murder someone, if you were so inclined.

CHAPTER 15

•

Thursday, October 14

Dr. Augustin was after me all day to carry out his little witch hunt. At a quarter past four, I couldn't stand it anymore and called Katrina. I didn't lie and tell her I wanted to check Teddy's ear or that I was selling Avon and thought she could use a little color in her life. Somehow I knew she wouldn't believe me. So I took the easy way out. I told her the truth. Fortunately, Dr. Augustin wasn't around to hear me. He'd have been disappointed, I'm sure.

I need to talk to you, Mrs. Treckle," I said. "I promise it won't take long. It's a . . . personal matter."

She didn't say anything right away, and I thought we'd been disconnected. Then I heard Teddy bark.

"I should be home all evening, Miss Holt," Katrina said, finally. "I'll be waiting for you. It's the grey house on the corner. The one with the picket fence."

I told her I'd be there around 7:30. Then I asked about Teddy, just so she'd know I was basically a good person.

"Teddy is fine, Miss Holt," she said. Her solicitous smile came over the phone line clear as a bell. "See you at seven-thirty." Then she hung up, not out of rudeness, I realized. There just wasn't any point in continuing the conversation. It was like she already knew what I wanted.

•　•　•

The Treckles lived in a quiet, middle-class residential area a couple of miles to the east of Paradise Cay. The kind of place where garbage cans must be kept out of sight except on pickup days, and the mailboxes are painted to match the houses. Most of the residents are retired from Michigan or New York and spend a good percentage of their waking hours gardening. However, instead of tomatoes or green peppers, a lot of northern transplants seem to prefer exotic fruit trees and flowering shrubs from Malaysia. As a result, the air always smells like lavender gumdrops.

Katrina's house was a modest little two-story wood-frame with a detached garage and so many trees in the front—oak mostly—that the grass there was sparse to nonexistent. As I went through the gate and up the walk to the porch, I could hear water dripping somewhere. It was like being in the woods.

I rang the bell. Teddy barked a couple of times. Then the door opened.

"Hello, Miss Holt," said Katrina. She stepped aside, and I walked into the foyer. The dripping sound grew louder.

Katrina was dressed in a caftan—black, with fine white stitching on the sleeves and around the yoke. Her hair was long and tied in back with a trailing black scarf. She had on her silver pentacle necklace. Tiny pentacle earrings dangled from her earlobes. She smelled like Yardley soap. And she was barefoot.

"I want to thank you for seeing me on such short notice," I began, "and without knowing the purpose of my visit."

"You told me it was a personal matter."

"Yes," I said, feeling increasingly guilty. Religion is always a personal matter, isn't it?

I followed her down a long hallway, past the kitchen, and into a large, high-ceilinged great room that seemed even larger, because a set of French doors had been opened wide onto a converted screened porch. Movable glass panels covered the screens, and the ceramic tile in the great room continued uninterrupted all the way to the back door.

Katrina, her smile fixed on her face like a paralytic spasm, indicated a rattan sofa to my right. Teddy was lying next to the sofa. He wagged his tail when I looked his way.

"Please, Miss Holt," Katrina said, "do have a seat. I've made us some herbal tea. I'll just get it." She hesitated a fraction of a second, then left for the kitchen, her shadowy caftan billowing out behind her.

If Katrina's front yard had seemed like the deep woods, her porch was like a tropical rain forest. She even had an Amazon parrot. It sat on a wooden perch suspended from the ceiling and stared at me.

"Ack!" it said suddenly. It fluffed out its feathers and shook, then began rummaging around in its food cup.

The wall to my left, directly across from the rattan sofa, was the source of the dripping sound. It was made to resemble a rocky cliff. Ferns grew out of every little crack and crevasse, and moss, like the mold that covers stuff left too long in the refrigerator, made the rocks look furry. Down the center of the cliff flowed a steady stream of water. It came from a slit in one of the rocks near the ceiling, then gently dripped and cascaded over the mossy surfaces to collect in a rocky, dished-out area just above the floor. I couldn't hear a pump running, but I knew there had to be one somewhere behind the wall.

Three skylights in the great room obviously provided sufficient illumination during the day to support the cliff-dwelling ferns and the dozens of flowering plants Katrina had scattered around the room. They hung from brackets mounted on the walls and sat on plant stands and on the flat surfaces of her furniture. She had gasneriads and African violets and lady slippers.

Orchids hung near the waterfall, their white roots dangling beneath them, thriving in the greenhouselike environment. Masses of orange, red, and dark maroon flowers, like molten lava, seemed to erupt from the face of the cliff. I put my hand out to touch one of them, and the parrot shrieked.

"Kill the messenger!" he said, which made absolutely no

sense to me, but I took my hand away, just in case the bird knew something I didn't.

"Off with 'er 'ed!"

The bird was becoming increasingly agitated for some reason, so I went back through the French doors to the great room.

"Ack! Kill the messenger!"

Teddy got up and followed me, his ears back, his tail between his legs.

The great room, with it's porch add-on, apparently was Katrina's private little world, where I imagined she spent much of her time. And there was plenty to occupy her. I didn't see a television, but she had two large, floor-to-ceiling bookcases filled with a variety of books and magazines. Most of the titles dealt with history and ancient civilizations. There were a few texts on Native American Indians, and I spotted *Silent Spring* and *Cadillac Desert,* along with several gardening books. *Home Orchid Growing.*

She had quite a collection of novels, none of them what I would consider out in left field. And I was a little disappointed. I had expected, at the very least, to find a few Stephen Kings. *The Stand,* perhaps. Or *Needful Things.*

A huge aquarium, resplendent with tropical fish and live plants, was wedged between the bookcases. In the center of the room, a rocker and love seat, both upholstered in dark green chintz, and a coffee table and two end tables were arranged in an informal grouping. The rocker had a matching footstool. Some type of needlework project lay on it.

To the left of the rocker was a fireplace. I walked over and studied the objects lined up on the mantel. Candles of varying sizes, some in pewter candlesticks, some freestanding, were clustered on either side of a pewter goblet. A small wooden stick, like a twig from a tree, carefully stripped of its bark and polished to a high gloss, lay next to the goblet. And next to that a pentacle carved out of wood hung on a little stand.

I stared at the pentacle and felt a shiver move up my back. This is an altar, I thought. Clearly an altar. But who or what does Katrina worship?

"You had a question you wanted to ask me, Miss Holt?"

I whirled around and grabbed the edge of the mantel, knocking over one of the candles. Katrina stood by the coffee table, holding a pewter tray. She leaned over and placed the tray on the table. She had to push aside a couple of African violets to make room. Then she straightened up and looked at me. Her smile had faded just a little, but she still looked annoyingly composed.

"Question?" I asked. I was anything but composed, and I knew my face was a mirror of how I felt. I turned quickly away from her and picked up the candle. Then I squeezed my eyes shut for a second, took a nice deep breath, and turned back around.

"You came here to ask me something," said Katrina. "So ask."

She sat down on the love seat and picked up a white china teapot. Teddy walked over to the rocker and stretched out on the floor next to the footstool.

"Off with 'er 'ed," screamed the parrot.

Katrina looked over at the bird. "Hush, Henry!" she said. She poured tea into a large china teacup. The liquid was a rich reddish color. "You must excuse Henry. His previous owner had a rather warped sense of humor." She poured tea into a second cup. "Won't you join me, Miss Holt?" She pointed to the love seat.

I walked across the room and sat down next to her. "He's a beautiful bird," I said. "In fact, this whole room is beautiful. The plants, the aquarium . . ."

Katrina handed me a cup of tea. The aroma was pleasantly fruity. Like raspberries.

"The question, Miss Holt . . . ?"

I tried the tea. It wasn't raspberry, but cranberry. And surprisingly sweet. "Yes," I said. "I was curious about your jewelry. It's handmade, isn't it?" I had no idea why I was beating around the bush. The woman obviously knew my real reason for being there. I wasn't sure how, but she definitely knew. "Actually, I wanted to ask you about the pentacle. Are you familiar with Wicca?"

Katrina sipped her tea and gazed at me over the cup. Her eyes weren't the same color. One was green and the other was hazel. I hadn't noticed that before.

"Come now, Miss Holt. Is that the only reason you're here?"

I didn't know what she was driving at, so I kept quiet.

She put her teacup back on the tray. "The earth is like an aquarium, Miss Holt. Self-contained and in perfect harmony, it can go on forever. But man is destroying the balance. He is greedy and self-absorbed. He has forgotten about harmony, about the delicate balance between the forces of nature and all living things."

She ran a slim finger along the arm of the love seat. "He kills off the insects and wonders where the birds have gone. He sucks up all the freshwater and asks why the Everglades are dying. He cuts all the trees down and covers the earth with asphalt and can't understand why it's so hot. And he spews poison into the air and wants to know why his children are sick."

She picked up the teapot and pointed to my cup. "I hope you like the tea, Miss Holt. I hope it isn't too sweet. I make it myself from fresh herbs and fruit."

I was beginning to relax. I held out my cup. "Yes," I said, "it's delicious." I tried to remember my conversation with Dr. Augustin. What he had wanted me to ask her.

"It hasn't always been that way," Katrina continued. "And it isn't too late to regain the balance. But first, we must learn to put our trust in nature." She fingered an earring.

I leaned back and listened to the dripping. It seemed to echo off the walls and ceiling—a musical tinkling sound that had a certain hypnotic quality about it.

"Wicca is an ancient pagan religion, Miss Holt," said Katrina. "The word itself is old English for 'witch.' And not the warty-nosed, broom-toting Hollywood witches, either. We don't dance naked around fires or sacrifice animals or brew potions from bat's wings." Her voice had a snap to it that hinted at great anger carefully controlled.

"Long before Christianity and Satan and devil-worship, witches were wise old women who had a special gift—the power to heal. Heal, Miss Holt. But man has a habit of getting rid of the things he doesn't understand. Things he fears. Or he blames them for all the misfortunes that befall him. Floods, droughts, death. To make him feel less impotent, I suppose."

I had a sneaking suspicion that her reference to "man" was more than generic.

"So you can understand why those of us who believe in the power of nature, who worship the forces that hold the earth in balance, wouldn't want to call attention to ourselves. Too many bad connotations about plagues and stillborn children and dairy cattle drying up."

And about being burned at the stake, I'll bet. "But with all the people concerned about the environment," I said aloud, "I should think Wicca would be attracting quite a following."

Katrina nodded. "Sadly, though, we Wiccans must continue to practice our beliefs in the privacy of our homes. Traditional religions do not possess much flexibility or tolerance, Miss Holt. It is rather ironic, don't you think, that devout Christians seem to exhibit the most un-Christian behavior when confronted with someone who doesn't happen to share their beliefs?"

She got up and walked over to the aquarium. "New covens are forming all the time," she said. She picked up a container of fish food and sprinkled a tiny bit into the tank. "Rich, poor, men, women—Wiccans all share a common bond, Miss Holt. A desire to heal the planet and its inhabitants. To bring things back into balance."

I watched fish appear suddenly out of the feathery green plants growing up from rocks arranged across the bottom.

They darted back and forth near the surface sucking up the tiny flakes of food.

"Are there any Wiccans up near Carriage Hill?" I asked. "I noticed quite a few environmentally inclined people at the public hearing for that transmission corridor. I wonder if any of them are Wiccans." I played with the handle on my teacup, took a sip of tea, then put my cup and saucer back on the tray. I glanced over at Teddy, who was asleep, but out of the corner of my eye I watched Katrina.

She put the fish food back on the shelf and went over to the rocker. She sat down and looked at me. "I am told a new coven has formed in that part of the county. It wouldn't be unusual for them to peacefully oppose destruction of our environment."

Her ever-present smile was making me nervous. It was time to go.

"Why don't we talk about *you,* Miss Holt?" Katrina said. "Isn't there a question you would like to ask me? A question you've been seeking an answer to for some time now? About a gentleman friend, perhaps?"

I stared at her. This witch thing is getting a bit farfetched, I said to myself. We've suddenly progressed (or digressed) from cleaning up the planet to palm-reading.

"I don't know what you mean," I told her.

"Everyone who comes here is seeking advice of one kind or another," she said. She picked up a deck of cards from the end table between the rocker and the love seat. "Shall I read the Tarot for you?" She began shuffling the cards.

I had never had my fortune told. I only read the horoscope in the newspaper when I am manning the front desk for Cynthia and have nothing better to do. Until that moment, I didn't believe in such things. But Katrina was not a con artist or a senile old woman or a fruitcake in need of psychiatric help. At least she didn't act like it. In fact, she seemed intelligent and amazingly well balanced, despite the Wicca thing. Or possibly because of it, although my traditional God-fearing background was interfering with my attempt to analyze her rationally. In any case, it was hard to discount the fact that I *did* have a question about my future. And it did involve a gentleman friend.

Katrina cradled the deck of cards in her left hand and leaned slightly forward. Her green eye twinkled. "Certainly you, Miss Holt, aren't afraid of what the Tarot might tell you."

I picked up my empty cup, then put it down again. "No, of course not," I said. "It's just that . . ."

"That you don't believe in such things, is that it?"

"Well, I guess so. When you get right down to it."

"Then you shouldn't mind humoring a lonely old widow," she said. She smiled her smile.

The parrot began tapping the corner of his food dish with his beak. It sounded like someone knocking at the door.

"Come in!" said the bird.

I moved around in the love seat. I felt stiff, and I was beginning to get sleepy. Had Katrina drugged me with her herbs and whatnot?

"All right," I said. "I'd be happy if you would read the cards for me." I stiffled a yawn.

Katrina cleared off the end table of its gesneriad and *National Geographic*s. Then she cut the deck of cards into three piles. With her left hand, she reassembled the deck. Then she shuffled and cut the cards again, once more making three piles and once more reassembling them with her left hand. The third time she cut the deck, she selected the middle stack. With her right hand, she pushed aside the remaining cards.

"I will do the Celtic Cross for you," she said, shuffling the stack. "It is the most complete system."

She began laying out the cards. I watched her hands, the way she touched the cards, almost lovingly, the way she paused after each card placement, as if the remaining cards needed time to arrange themselves properly. If it had been someone else, someone whose front window had a giant pink neon hand in it, I could have laughed over the ritual.

But I didn't feel like laughing. I found myself, as ridiculous as I knew it was, fearing the cards.

Katrina was apparently finished. There were ten cards on the table, neatly arranged in four rows of varying lengths. One of the cards was covering a second card.

"The first card," she began, "is your current situation. It is the card all other cards relate to." She extracted the bottom card of the two that were touching and turned it over.

Because I was viewing the cards upside-down, I saw the Hanged Man as if he were standing, rather than hanging. His head was shaved, his eyes were closed. He looked dead. And I felt a twinge of panic. This is not an auspicious beginning, I told myself.

"The Hanged Man does not mean death, Miss Holt," said Katrina quickly. She was studying my face. "It means that your life, currently, is at a stalemate. The Hanged Man is, for all intents and purposes, stuck in a rut." She paused, letting her words take effect. "Does this apply to you, Miss Holt?"

Of course it does, I thought. I am constantly running around in circles trying to get away from Michael, yet trying to stay close to him. I can't stand the thought that he might move back to New York and give up on me and fearful that he won't. "Yes," I said simply.

Katrina turned over the card that had been on top of the first card. "The Knight of Swords," she said. She placed the card next to the Hanged Man. "The Knight of Swords represents someone close to you who has power over your thoughts and actions. The way you approach life. He is both intelligent and passionate. Thoughts and ideas come to him with lightning speed. His body, intellect, and spirit are in perfect balance."

The Knight was dressed in iridescent green armor and sat on a magnificent horse. He carried a sword in each hand and for some reason, the swords, rather than Katrina's description, made me think of Dr. Augustin.

"Is there someone in your life right now who has a strong influence over you?" Katrina asked. "Because you must de-

cide if you want to continue allowing that person to domi-
nate your thinking."

I didn't say anything, and Katrina turned over the third
card.

"The Seven of Disks," said Katrina. "Failure." She
touched the card with her right index finger. "You are afraid
of failing, Miss Holt. Something in your past, perhaps a person, has filled you with a sense of defeat. It is hindering your
forward progress." She looked at me. Then she reached for
the fourth card.

I wanted to grab her hand to stop her. Tell her I had to go
home. It was late. I had a headache. I'd left the oven on. But
I just sat there, masochistically waiting for the next chapter
in my rather uninspiring life's story.

But Katrina looked almost relieved when she turned the
card over. She smiled. "Ah," she said. "The Two of Cups.
Love."

I stared at the card, bending my head slightly so I could
view the two fishes right-side-up. Their bodies were en-
twined suggestively. Two goblets overflowed with what appeared to be water.

"You are looking for love," Katrina said. "It hasn't happened yet, but your inner self is clearly receptive."

Possibly, I thought, but like in the song, was I looking for
it in all the wrong places?

Katrina flipped over card number five without glancing at
it first, buoyed, presumably, by the love card. Her smile
faded.

"The Five of Cups," she said. "Disappointment." She
aimed her odd eyes at me. "Someone has caused you great
disappointment in the past, and it is affecting the way you
view your life. This ties in, you see, with the fear of failure."

"I was engaged once," I said, out of the blue. "To a very
self-centered man. He dumped me for another woman the
day we were to be married." I hadn't intended to tell her
anything about myself, certainly nothing personal. But she

had a certain quality about her that encouraged confession. "It kind of changes the way one views men." I clamped my mouth closed to avoid having anything else slip out unintentionally.

Katrina nodded. Her smile was gone, and without it she looked older. "The past," she said, "is a terrible burden. For all of us. But is *is* the past, and we should leave it there. Learn from it and move ahead."

I got the feeling she was talking about herself, as well as about me. She closed her eyes and shook both hands briefly, as if to cleanse them. Then she picked up the next card.

My head was swimming. The dripping waterfall was beginning to sound like a torrential downpour. Then I heard thunder and realized it was raining. Teddy got up and dashed out of the room. The parrot ruffled his head feathers. I tried to concentrate on what Katrina was saying. She was picking up card number six. Or was it seven?

"This is you, Miss Holt," she said, with a slight lilt to her voice. "The Princess of Swords. You are a fighter. You have the ability to cut out everything negative that stands in your way. You simply need a little guidance. A little encouragement."

She reached across the table and touched my hand. Then she turned over card number eight.

"The Prince of Wands," she said. "There is great energy in this card. The Prince of Wands is creative and resourceful. Full of love and strength. This is a good card, Miss Holt. The Prince of Wands can help you conquer your fears, if you let him."

Him, I thought. Was this Michael? It couldn't be Dr. Augustin. Where were the lightning bolts and ominous dark clouds?

Katrina was staring at me. Two cards remained on the table. I hadn't worn a watch, but it felt like I had been in Katrina's house for an eternity. I couldn't remember what I'd had for supper, but whatever it had been was burning a hole in my stomach. Maybe I had forgotten to eat dinner in

my haste to oblige Dr. Augustin. I looked at the teapot.
What had really been in that tea? Some new designer drug?
That might explain my light-headedness and general confu-
sion.

Katrina shrugged and reached for card number nine.
"This image represents your hopes and fears for the future,
Miss Holt," she said. She flipped the card over and clapped
her hands together. "You see? I was right! You *are* seeking
love."

The image depicted on the card needed no explanation. A
man and a woman were being joined in holy matrimony by
some huge gnomelike creature completely encased in a robe
of sorts. The man was dark and the woman fair. Opposites,
like night and day. Good and evil. The word "Lovers" was
written beneath them.

"Hopes and *fears,* Mrs. Treckle," I said. "Hopes and
fears."

She tilted her head to one side and studied me. I started to
ask her why she seemed so determined for me to fall in love.
Had Cynthia put a bug in her ear? I wanted to tell her there
was a far sight more to life than marriage and babies. She
had obviously stacked the deck. There could be no other explanation. And then I remembered how diligently she had
shuffled and cut the cards.

Katrina sighed and reached for the tenth and final card.
"This last image," she said, her voice filled with optimism,
"is the result of your struggle to overcome failure and
disappointment." She picked up the card and looked at it.
Her expression was unremarkable, but her eyes darted
my way very briefly. Then she put the card faceup on the
table.

I don't know what I was expecting. After the Prince of
Wands and the Lovers, I was losing interest in the Tarot. I
didn't know if there was a Baby or Conception card. That
certainly seemed like the next logical step. But I definitely
wasn't prepared for the skeleton with its scythe and the word

"Death" across the bottom of the card. Upside-down, it still read Death.

I uttered a sharp gasp of surprise. Henry, who'd been napping throughout most of the Tarot, suddenly flapped his wings and shrieked, "Off with 'er'ed!"

CHAPTER 16

•

Friday, October 15

Dr. Augustin stuck his face into the lab and smiled. "Good morning, ladies," he said. Then he went back into his office and closed the door.

I looked at Tracey and shook my head. Either he hadn't made it to the commission meeting or the commissioners had asked for his advice and taken it, which was highly unlikely.

"I think I prefer him the other way," said Tracey, turning off the centrifuge. "You know, grouchy. When he's in a good mood, I worry." She looked over her shoulder at me. "It usually means he's up to something, doesn't it?" Tracey was a fast learner.

"Usually," I said. "A good mystery, preferably accompanied by a dead body or two, does tend to lift his spirits." I put the bottle of prednisone back on the shelf. I didn't tell her I thought there was more to this particular good mood than simply another opportunity to outshine the police.

"Tracey, have you ever had your fortune told?" I asked suddenly.

She took the cover off the centrifuge and turned around. "You mean like at the Medieval Faire? With Tarot cards and women dressed like gypsies?"

The way she rolled her eyes and waved her free hand in the air, as if over some invisible crystal ball, I knew her opinion of fortune-tellers and horoscopes without asking. A week earlier I'd have agreed with her.

"I guess," I said.

Tracey put the cover on the counter and plucked the hematocrit tube out of the centrifuge. She held it up to the light and squinted at it.

"I couldn't see spending ten bucks," she said, "to find out I was going to meet a handsome stranger. I mean, how ambiguous can you get with that one?" She laughed. "Why do you ask?"

"Because I had mine told last night for free by one of our clients." I opened the refrigerator and began searching through the contents of the door.

"So what did the cards say? That you were going to receive a sum of money? Pretty safe bet, considering nearly everyone gets paid at least twice a month."

"It wasn't anything like that," I told her. "Really. At least not like a horoscope. It was like, 'here is the past'—that part was right on track, trust me—'and here is the future.' But that's where it got confusing." I took an insulin syringe out of the drawer. "Apparently I've come to a fork in the road, and I have to choose which path to take. It was very disconcerting, in addition to being confusing."

Tracey sat down on her stool and smiled at me. There clearly was a lot more to Tracey than her veggie burgers and choice of musicians implied.

"Everyone has to make a decision sometime," she said, "about what they want the rest of their life to be like." The smile flickered. "Sometimes we make the wrong choices. But we can always start over, can't we?"

I was about to tell her I couldn't spend my whole life "starting over," when Dr. Augustin appeared in the doorway.

"Don't you think we should get going, Samantha?" he asked, his tone pleasant enough. But his smile was forced. "It's eight-thirty, and we have a full schedule." He didn't wait for an answer, but headed for the surgery.

I looked down at the vial of insulin. Tracey slid off her stool and came across the room.

"That's for Mugsy, isn't it?" she asked me. When I nodded, she said, "I'll give it to him. You go ahead."

"Thanks, Tracey. I owe you one." I took a last swig of coffee and raced off down the hall. Not only am I constantly starting over, I thought, but I'm constantly trying to catch up, as well.

Our first "customer," as Dr. Augustin sometimes calls his spay/neuter patients, was a ten-month-old female Siberian husky by the name of White Fang.

"What do they call her, 'Fang,' or 'Whitey'?" I asked Dr. Augustin as I finished prepping the dog's belly.

"Beats me," he said. He was at the sink, scrubbing. "I'm pretty sure the Rhinehold children named her. I wonder how many Chewbaccas the *Star Wars* movie spawned." He chuckled through his mask. Of course, 'Chewy' isn't such a bad name for a puppy, is it?"

I opened his gown pack for him, and he took out the sterile hand towel and began drying his hands.

"Did anything interesting happen at the commission meeting last night?" I asked.

He slipped his gown on and turned around so I could tie it closed. "Mr. and Mrs. Kenney were there, with their faithful. That was to be expected. And Justin Blaize—God, what a name." He pulled a glove on. "Westphall, of course. But I'm happy to report he kept his mouth shut about Princess. Stuck to his script. You know—the impact of the project on the horse people up there."

I opened the spay pack and Dr. Augustin laid out his instruments. Then I watched as he arranged the drape over the dog's belly.

"What was the vote?" I asked, not really caring. I felt oddly detached, like a part of me—the part that mattered—was someplace else tending to business. That the *real* me would show up sooner or later to claim my body double.

"Samantha?"

He was staring at me over his mask, his eyes trying to see inside my head. Only it wasn't *my* head, and there was nothing to see.

I realized he was holding his scalpel up in the air, and I glanced at it. No blade. I drew in a quick breath, went around to the cabinet, and got out a blade pack. Then I peeled it open, and Dr. Augustin pulled the blade out.

"Sorry," I said.

He continued to stare at me for a couple of seconds with his onyx eyes, which always manages to rattle me, and then he went about snapping the blade onto the end of the handle.

"Was there ever any question about how those idiots would vote?" he asked, apparently not interested in pursuing my current state of mind. "With half of Carriage Hill there and most of Brightwater Beach's future tax revenue, what could they really do, anyway, but vote to oppose the corridor? Even after I brought up the possibility of moving it east—that would save the marsh and increase the distance between the houses in Carriage Hill and the power lines. Of course the power company spokesman had no idea why they hadn't elected to go that way in the first place."

He was having trouble closing one of his hemostats. He grew impatient, flung it toward the sink, and missed. It hit the floor and bounced against my foot. I left it there. So much for another piece of surgical equipment, I thought. If it wasn't defective before, it certainly is now.

"Those rich bastards in Carriage Hill and Fox Meadows," continued Dr. Augustin, "with their damned electric meters whizzing away have no right to complain about the power company needing a new transmission corridor. Even *if* another piece of Florida's environment bites the dust in the process. Their NIMBY complex really burns me."

"NIMBY?"

He looked up. "Come on, Samantha. You know—'Not in my backyard.' "

"Oh, right," I said.

I turned up the volume on the cardiac monitor, not because I couldn't hear it well enough already, but because I wanted something repetitive to focus on. I kept seeing the Tarot cards, the skeleton with its scythe seemingly aimed at the Lovers. And the Prince of Wands. Who was that? Michael? So close to my card, the Princess of Swords. Were Michael and I the Lovers?

Instead of helping me, Katrina had only added to my confusion. I don't know any more now than I did before I went to see her, I told myself. Or do I?

I took a couple of deep breaths and rolled my head around on my shoulders to release some of the tension I felt in my neck. This whole fortune-telling thing is a bunch of hooey, anyway, I thought.

Dr. Augustin was talking again. "Justin Blaize and his plant community studies . . ." he said. "Now that's a real crock." He threw the spay hook on the instrument table with such force, a hemostat bounced onto the floor. "Carriage Hill has destroyed more sensitive ecosystems than that transmission corridor could ever hope to. And to top it all off, Mr. Blaize makes his living raping the environment."

He was starting to perspire, and the veins in his neck were protruding. But his hands were steady, his fingers manipulating tissues and suture material with unerring precision.

Dr. Augustin is like a brontosaurus, I thought, with unexpected amusement. He has one brain that runs his mouth and another that operates the rest of him.

" 'By God, I've got mine,' " he was saying, " 'to hell with you.' "

I kept my mouth shut, partly because I was afraid he might transfer his hostility to me and partly because he was right. I'd lived with or dated entirely too many Justin Blaizes in my thirty-two years (was it really almost thirty-three?) not to know what they were like.

Suddenly I heard Dr. Augustin clear his throat. I looked down. He had finished closing the incision, taken off his gloves and gown, and was staring at me again. I could feel the hairs on the back of my neck twitching.

"Samantha," he said, as patiently as was possible for him, "what's wrong with you this morning? You act like you're a million miles away."

I leaned over and retrieved the hemostat. Then I pretended to check the anesthesia machine, even though I'd at least had the presence of mind to keep tabs on it during my musings. I'm sure Whitey appreciated that fact.

"Well?"

"The Prince of Swords," I said, not looking at him.

"What?"

"That's the card Katrina said represented you. At least I think it's you."

"Katrina?"

"Katrina Treckle. The woman with the black Lab. The one who wears that pentacle around her neck."

"I know who she is, Samantha. I just didn't know you were on a first-name basis with her." His patience was evaporating rapidly. "And what in God's name is this Prince of Swords? I sent you to the woman's house to find out if she was one of those Wiccans. Did you even bring up the subject?"

His neck was pulsing again.

"I did," I said. "And she is."

The husky had started to gnaw on her endotracheal tube, so I pulled it out. Then Dr. Augustin carefully lifted her off the table and carried her to the foam pad we have on the floor for large dogs—ones who don't need special care and wouldn't be comfortable in a recovery cage. In a short while, she would be sufficiently awake to take back to her run in the kennel.

I put the instruments in the sink. Then I gathered up the soiled drapes and Dr. Augustin's gloves and gown.

Dr. Augustin stroked the husky's head, then stood up. He came over to the table and picked up the few remaining bits of debris and threw them in the garbage.

"Tell me about it," he said. "Your visit." He leaned against the counter and watched me clean the table. "What did you find out?" His tone was almost apologetic.

"The detective was right," I said. "According to Mrs. Treckle, Wiccans are a peaceful group. And very private. They believe it is wrong to do harm, particularly to the environment, but to people, as well, I gather. I don't think they would do anything so public as defile our door, and I'm convinced they wouldn't kill anybody, dogs included."

Dr. Augustin went over to the sink and began washing his hands.

"They aren't Satanists," I continued, "because Wicca is a pagan religion that started long before Christianity. They do call themselves witches, but they don't cast 'spells,' at least not like the 'spells' Hollywood dreams up. They pray to Mother Earth, I guess, or the earth goddess, or whatever, in an effort to make the world a better place. More harmonious, as Mrs. Treckle put it."

Dr. Augustin looked at me over his shoulder. "So you don't think there's some group of these Wiccans practicing their beliefs out in the woods next to Carriage Hill, where the power company wants to put that transmission corridor?"

"No," I said. "Mrs. Treckle told me there's a newly formed 'coven' up in that part of town, but they do their things indoors. She said she wouldn't be surprised if they are opposed to the transmission corridor from an environmental standpoint, just like Justin Blaize supposedly is, but they aren't going to kill anybody over it. At least that's the impression I got."

We were ready for the next spay, so while Dr. Augustin scrubbed, I went into the kennel to get the animal. Tracey was helping Frank bathe an Old English sheepdog. All three of them were covered in shampoo. Frank was blowing handfuls of lather at Tracey, and she was laughing. The dog obviously was enjoying the whole thing immensely, and although Dr. Augustin would say they were acting unprofessional and wasting time, I hated to spoil their fun.

I felt a sudden pang of jealousy. To be twenty-one again, like Tracey, and concerned only with the moment had to be better than worrying all the time about making the right choices.

I got the little poodle out of her cage and went back into the surgery.

"So," said Dr. Augustin, after the dog was asleep and I'd hooked her up to an IV and the heart monitor, "what's this Prince of Swords you were telling me about?"

"Katrina reads Tarot cards," I said, a little reluctantly. "She did a reading for me."

Dr. Augustin chuckled. "You mean like at the Medieval Faire, with those women who dress like gypsies and wear a ring on every finger?" He lowered his voice an octave or so and took on an exaggerated accent. " 'You will meet a handsome stranger.' " He paused, and I knew he was grinning under his mask. "You mean like that?"

CHAPTER 17

•

Saturday, October 16

Vivian Porter put the cat carrier on the exam table. "You must think I'm trying to kill poor Harvey," she said, looking at me and then at the black and white face peering out from the back of the carrier. "First I hit him with my car, then I almost poison him."

She was perspiring lightly. Tiny beads of sweat clung to the fine hairs on her upper lip, giving the impression of a silver mustache. She was wearing a flowered shirtwaist that did not suit her. The flowers—giant dahlias—only added thickness to Mrs. Porter's already "mature" figure. She looked like a huge piece of upholstered furniture. And I wasn't used to seeing her in heels. She was more the "sensible" shoes type.

"I am painting my kitchen cabinets, Miss Holt, because I've grown tired of all that natural wood. Pine is so pretty when it's new, but it has darkened with age. White enamel should brighten the place up, don't you think?" She hesitated, apparently realizing she had digressed, then continued.

"Anyway, Harvey jumped up on the counter when I wasn't looking and stuck his paw in the paint can." She frowned. "Before I could grab him, he'd flung paint everywhere. What a mess." She waggled a finger at Harvey. "You were a very naughty boy," she told the cat.

Harvey flattened his ears and snarled at her.

I opened the carrier and pulled the animal, hissing and growling, onto the exam table. Harvey was definitely a survivor. In addition to everything else, he had managed to avoid being eaten by Mrs. Porter's Doberman, Dresden.

"And what did you use to clean his feet?" I could smell whatever it was. The cat reeked.

"Paint thinner," Mrs. Porter said. "And when I tried to give him a bath, he acted like a wild animal. Shrieked as though I were torturing him, then ran off. Now he won't eat. I'm afraid the paint thinner has made him sick."

I wrote all of this down in Harvey's file, then took his temperature. Although he continued to growl and hiss, he made no attempt to bite me. Harvey was a lot of hot air. But it seemed to work pretty well with Dresden.

"His temperature is normal, Mrs. Porter," I said after a couple of minutes.

I had to let go of the cat in order to reach the paper towel dispenser. Harvey saw his chance and retreated back into the carrier. The growling ceased.

"Dr. Augustin will be right in," I told Mrs. Porter. I tried not to grin, but the bouquet across her bodice made it seem like her very bosom was about to burst into bloom. I went out into the hall and quickly closed the door.

Harvey's tongue had sores on it from the paint thinner, which was why he had stopped eating. Although he wasn't actually sick, it had seemed that way to Mrs. Porter. Needless to say, she was relieved she hadn't poisoned the animal. But she wasn't thrilled to find that Harvey would never submit to a bath the way Dresden did.

"Domestic cats do not like water," said Dr. Augustin as he administered a healthy dose of tranquilizer to Harvey, so that Frank could bathe him. "They are descended from wild cats who lived in the more arid regions of Africa." He paused. "I guess that's why God gave them such efficient tongues."

Mrs. Porter, the widow of an Episcopal minister, nodded vigorously.

Dr. Augustin was doing an admirable job of ignoring the dahlias. He was busy writing in Harvey's file. His notes were beginning to resemble a novella, in length at least.

We were waiting for Harvey to settle down before handing him over to Frank. He was still growling, but he seemed to have lost some of his enthusiasm. When Harvey growls, it sounds like a swarm of bees, particularly appropriate, I thought, in light of Mrs. Porter's attire.

"Oh, gracious, just look at the time," said Mrs. Porter suddenly. "I'm due at the Biltmore at noon, and I simply cannot be late." She picked up her purse and started for the door. It wasn't clear if her tardiness would create some kind of social faux pas, or it would mean she might miss out on the shrimp cocktail. "I'll be back for Harvey at five o'clock," she said. She held out her hand. "Thank you so much, Dr. Augustin."

Dr. Augustin had to look at her then, and a smile spread over his face that Mrs. Porter evidently interpreted as a gesture of friendship, because she smiled back.

"See you at five," I said hastily and ushered her out before Dr. Augustin's eyes could give him away.

During lunch, I went back to the kennel to check on Randy and Katie. The kittens were together in a large top cage two doors down from Pearl. I had given them a small rubber ball to play with, and Randy was trying to push it through the bars on their door.

Dr. Augustin came in and stood next to me. He was watching John Deland's terrier. The dog was in a cage immediately below Randy and Katie.

"I've decided that odor of cleaning fluid we smelled on this little guy when John first brought him in," he said, "wasn't cleaning fluid at all."

I looked at him.

"It was paint thinner. Just like the stuff Vivian used on Harvey."

"Maybe someone illegally threw a container of paint thinner in the garbage," I said. "Those new homes up in Carriage Hill probably have a ton of paint and other chemicals lying around. Maybe that's what John's feral dogs ran across.

Randy finally managed to push the ball out of the cage. I caught it. The kitten watched me and waited, his pupils dilated in anticipation.

"A run-in with paint thinner may be what brought about this dog's neurological disturbance, but aplastic anemia generally is from chronic exposure, not a onetime acute situation."

I opened Randy's cage and tossed in the ball.

"Still," Dr. Augustin continued, "I'm positive there's a connection between this dog and the chow mix who died. Just don't ask me why or what that connection is." He turned to go, then stopped. "What are you doing after work?" he asked.

"Before I answer that," I said cautiously, "what exactly did you have in mind?" I may not be as quick a study as Tracey, but I'm not a total idiot.

Dr. Augustin grinned and aimed his laser eyes at me. "Goodness, Samantha, aren't we the suspicious one?"

"Lately, I've had plenty of reason to be," I said.

He ignored the remark. "I was going to invite you to a rodeo."

"A rodeo?"

He leaned against the door frame and studied his nails. "Well, not exactly a rodeo, per se. A team penning competition. And there's supposed to be barrel racing, according to Dick Westphall. He mentioned it to me Thursday at the commission meeting. Gave us an open invitation to drop by and observe." He looked up. "I thought you'd enjoy it. I know Mr. Halsey is out of town . . ."

Still suspicious, I turned back to the kittens. "All right," I said, finally. "But promise me this has nothing to do with murder and mayhem, as that detective put it. Promise you won't get me killed or make me look at any more dead bodies."

"I promise I won't get you killed," he said, laughing. He sounded like Boris Karloff.

CHAPTER 18

•

Dr. Augustin took the "scenic" route. Of course, his definition of "scenic" and the one used by the AAA people aren't necessarily the same.

After stopping briefly at a Burger King for a satisfying meal of fat and cholesterol, we turned onto Sloan Avenue and cruised through the original downtown Brightwater Beach, the part of the city not mentioned in the Chamber of Commerce's tourist guide.

Abandoned warehouses and dilapidated stores, like the wrecks in an auto salvage yard, their hearts and other internal organs ripped out, stand around waiting for time to reduce them to compost. If I ignore the desolation and rust, I can almost picture Model T's and horse-drawn wagons moving up and down the streets. And shopkeepers setting out their wares. Now about the only businesses still thriving in this section of the city are pawnshops and crack houses. Even the hookers have gone in search of greener pastures.

On the outskirts of this topographical blemish is Brightwater Beach's largest public housing project. Except for the children and the occasional geranium struggling to survive, it looks like a continuation of old downtown, with few trees, little grass, and apparently no routine maintenance. Broken windows are covered with duct tape or plywood, and graf-

fiti is only painted over by city workers if an elected official
is blasphemed.

"Couldn't the housing authority have selected a more attractive place for this project?" I asked as Dr. Augustin
slowed the Jeep to the required thirty miles per hour. "The
residents might feel inclined to take better care of the place."

"Vacant land is too valuable, Samantha," said Dr. Augustin, swerving around an unsupervised toddler riding his
tricycle in the middle of the road. "You don't think the City
is about to build a housing project on land that could be used
for a library or museum, do you? Something the *taxpayers*
would appreciate? Besides, put it next door to the average
residential community, like Maraldee Manor or, God forbid,
Carriage Hill, and the people there would scream bloody
murder."

"As in NIMBY?" I asked.

"Exactly."

"So, why are we here, anyway?"

I was getting nervous. A group of ten or twelve teenaged
boys standing just ahead of us on the sidewalk had spotted
the Jeep. Two of the boys stepped out onto the road. Dr. Augustin gave them a wide berth.

"Because that police substation the commission voted
down in February was mentioned Thursday as a possible
agenda item for the next commission meeting. I wanted to
take another look."

A shiny black sedan, a dead ringer for the Batmobile, suddenly careened around the corner, missed hitting us by a
couple of feet, then slammed on the brakes. In the side mirror, I watched it come to a stop next to the teenagers.

"Well, even if there wasn't a drug problem here," I said,
watching a transaction of some kind taking place behind us,
"the children need the cops just to keep them from getting
run over. You know, teach them to stay out of the road or, at
least, look both ways."

As if to emphasize my point, a little girl, barefoot and
clutching what appeared to be a Popsicle, ran in front of us.

A large, skinny brown dog was right behind her. Dr. Augustin hit the brakes, swore, then didn't say anything else until we were safely out of the project. Then he speeded up.

"I doubt the commission will authorize a new substation," he said, " just so a bunch of poor kids can live long enough to get thrown in jail. But it's a good point, Samantha, and worth a try." He glanced over at me and winked. "Every once in a while you come up with a useful suggestion."

There wasn't anything convenient to throw at him, so I pouted instead. Out of the corner of my eye, I could see the smirk on his face broaden.

A mile up Sloan Avenue, and the barren soil and decay of old downtown and its immediate surroundings suddenly vanished, only to be replaced by a vast expanse of lush green sod, in the center of which stood the Northeast Recreation Complex. The white and blue building, practically a palace after what we'd just passed, was surrounded by live oak and watermelon red and pink crepe myrtles, still in bloom despite the lateness of the season.

Some indoor activity was obviously under way, because the parking lot was full. I noticed the cars looked a little expensive for the residents of the project.

"Cynthia contends that putting this ritzy recreation center way out here was some kind of mistake," I said as we drove past the complex's huge stormwater retention pond.

Picnic tables were strategically positioned amid clusters of bald cypress and river birch, beckoning families to lunch in the shade. I wondered if anyone had ever used them for what they were originally intended.

"They should have built it nearer the beach, so the city's 'taxpayers' wouldn't have to drive so far."

"Actually," said Dr. Augustin, "it belongs right where it is, although I will have to admit, it's a little out of character for the City to exhibit such foresight and planning."

We drove past the high school immediately north of the recreation complex, then took a right onto a smooth four-lane expanse of asphalt that, a few years earlier, was nothing more than a two-lane shortcut through the woods on the way to nowhere.

"It was only a matter of time," Dr. Augustin continued, "before developers began carving up this area of the county. The fact that the City anticipated it and annexed the land, then drew up the plans for the Recreation Complex before the widening of this road was even started amazes me."

What amazed me was how Dr. Augustin found the time to keep up with local goings-on. Of course, a good bit of what he knew he gleaned from the biweekly commission meetings or the newspaper. But what about the rest of it? Did he learn about day-to-day activities from Melody What's-Her-Name? I had never overheard him talking to her on the phone, at least I didn't think I had. Were they dating? And why hadn't Cynthia mentioned her to me?

We passed the drive into Carriage Hill. The sprinklers were going again, watering the oasis around the pristine stone and brass entrance sign. The sun, now low in the sky, cast a lovely golden wash over the pines along the subdivision's eastern border. Gold. Now there's an appropriate color for Carriage Hill, I thought. And huge ugly metal transmission towers, although not nearly as close to the development as the existing towers behind Maraldee Manor, nevertheless aren't going to do much for Mr. Blaize's property value, now are they?

"I guess this proposed transmission corridor thing is more a matter of money to the people in Carriage Hill than one of health effects, isn't it?" I asked. "I mean, when you're talking about half a million bucks, even a ten percent loss in resale value is pretty significant, wouldn't you agree?"

Dr. Augustin laughed and looked over at me. "Why, Samantha, you aren't implying that someone of Mr. Blaize's caliber might resort to violence to save fifty grand, are you?"

"Well, it is a possibility."

"It certainly is," he said, turning his attention back to the road. "A strong possibility." He rolled the palm of his left hand over the steering wheel.

We drove by Maraldee Manor. The paint on the entrance sign was beginning to fade. I looked west. Silhouetted by the sun, the transmission towers loomed out of the woods like giant Erector Set robots. I thought about the Kenney family.

Apparently thinking along the same line, Dr. Augustin continued," Of course, it's also a strong possibility that someone thinks their kid got sick because of those power lines, no matter how improbable that might be."

"Hmm," I mumbled. I still wasn't willing to believe that Mr. Kenney or one of his neighbors was a cold-blooded killer. Punching a guy in the face at a public hearing was one thing. But premeditated *murder?* No, I would rather find that Justin Blaize was our man. For whatever reason. *Him* I could hate.

Neither of us said anything for several minutes. I wanted to enjoy the evening, not think about death, although it seemed to be everywhere lately, even in my own immediate future if Katrina was right. Of course, she did say the Death card didn't have to mean physical death. It could mean some kind of change or transformation. This question is, I asked myself, am I the one doing the transforming? And if so, are we talking phoenix, rising from the ashes, or some hairy dog that howls at the moon?

I touched the cool glass of the passenger window with my fingertips and tried to concentrate on the scenery. North of Maraldee Manor, the flood of new subdivisions and shopping centers had, for the time being at least, subsided. The marshland and pine flatwoods, with their beauty berry and wild coffee, and the little white farmhouses, made me think of *The Yearling*. This is the *real* Florida, I told myself. The Florida Marjorie Keenan Rawlings knew. Before air conditioning and pesticides and the Army Corps of Engineers made paradise more acceptable, more like the paradise on TV, where no one sweats, and there aren't any bugs. Fantasy

Land. But signs here and there along the highway proclaiming ACREAGE FOR SALE and the current crop of survey markers hinted at the future. And it sure wasn't anything like *Cross Creek*.

Dr. Augustin slowed down and began peering to our right. Suddenly he pulled off the road and stopped next to an open gate. A modest sign nailed to the fence read LAZY J RANCH. LES JORDAN, OWNER. BRANGUS AND LONGHORNS. STALLS FOR RENT. Underneath that was a smaller sign that said LJ SOD COMPANY. It gave a telephone number.

"This must be the place," said Dr. Augustin. "Hang on."

We rattled over a bunch of cattle bars, then bumped our way down a winding washboard road, before entering a large grassy field. An arena, complete with bleachers, a barn, and several other outbuildings, took up most of the left half of the field. Scattered around the open area to our right was a diverse and colorful collection of horse trailers and pickup trucks.

Everywhere, horses, most of them already saddled, stood patiently, tied to trailers or the arena railing. A few were being ridden. I noticed several of the riders were children. They trotted and cantered up and down the narrow spaces between trailers, laughing and chasing each other, their mounts apparently used to being treated like bumper cars. And there were numerous dogs, too, mostly Labradors and various herding breeds, running and playing together or sitting obediently in the backs of pickups, watching the action.

Dr. Augustin made his way slowly around the arena to the back of the bleachers and parked between a hunter-green Dodge Caravan and a trailerless pickup truck fitted with an aluminum camper top. The license tag on the van was "West 2."

Dr. Augustin turned off the ignition. Over the PA system I could hear a man with a voice like a tight rubber band singing something about love in the back of a pickup truck.

"Westphall said he'd probably be in the announcer's booth." Dr. Augustin pointed toward a covered platform at the top of the bleachers. "I'll start there. You get us a couple of seats."

He climbed out of the Jeep and headed for the bleachers. I watched him go. I couldn't decide if it was the waning light playing tricks on me, or if he had suddenly developed a bowlegged swagger, in keeping with the occasion. I chuckled. It was only a matter of time before he started smoking one of those carved pipes and carrying a magnifying glass.

A woman replaced the man with the rubber-band larynx. She was a lot better, in my opinion. Her song was about falling out of love, and her voice, two-stepping softly over the PA system, had me tapping my leg in time to it. She was just finishing up when Westphall's voice informed the crowd that the cloverleaf barrels would start momentarily.

"You peewees out there please proceed to the gate," he said over the PA system. "And all you team penners, please remember to register your team's name when you pay your fee. Penning entries close at seven-thirty sharp!"

I got out of the car and wandered around to the front of the bleachers, then made my way up to the second row. Several people smiled at me and nodded. They seemed like a friendly bunch. I smiled back. I noticed most of them, including the women, wore cowboy hats and boots and T-shirts advertising such popular products as chewing tobacco and equine worming paste.

Suddenly four banks of floodlights clunked noisily on, turning dusk into day, and a small cheer went up from the riders gathered at the near end of the arena. I was nearly blinded by the dazzle of belt buckles big enough to intercept satellite transmissions. On the opposite end of the arena, three oil drums painted white and arranged in an arrowhead formation burst into view as if ignited.

"Our first entry this evening," said Mr. Westphall's disembodied voice, "Is little Robin Smith riding Chief. Robin is a second-grader at Pine Bluffs Elementary."

Several people one row up cheered and clapped when an attractive little paint trotted into the arena. Westphall hadn't been exaggerating when he used the term "peewee." Robin Smith was tiny, so tiny, in fact, that her stirrups were up as far as they could go. And although she wore spurs on her doll-sized boots, she wasn't about to do any harm to her horse with them. Her saddle pad, maybe.

A man at the rail wearing a headset nodded to the girl, and she prodded her horse and yelled loudly. The animal got the message, evidently, because he leaped into the air and hit the ground at a dead run. The child, reins in her left hand, grabbed the saddle horn with her right, as the paint rounded the left-hand oil drum. Then he headed for the right drum with Robin kicking and bouncing up and down and yelling. She was perilously close to falling off, I thought, as Chief rounded the second drum, and her hat tumbled to the ground. But she stayed in the saddle and urged her horse on to the final drum, which he took a little wide. Then Robin went into her frenzied kicking and yelling routine. Chief flew across the finish line, which I took to be the area in front of the man with the headset, because at that point he punched a stopwatch and said something into his mouthpiece. He was obviously hooked up to the announcer's booth.

"Twenty-two-seventy," said Mr. Westphall. "Good job, Robin. Let's hear it for Robin Smith, ladies and gentlemen!"

The crowd cheered wildly, while a second child, this one an inch or so taller than Robin, entered the arena. Her mount was a little chestnut mare with a white face.

"Miss Holt?"

I looked up. The light from the arena was behind the man standing next to me, so I couldn't see his face clearly. His voice was sort of familiar, though.

"Remember me?" he asked. "Detective Hummer. Tom Hummer."

I stared at him, squinting.

"I cleaned off your door Monday." He shook his head. "Come to think of it, Sergeant Robinson never did introduce us. May I?" He sat down.

"Oh, yes," I said. "The pentacle."

He'd been wearing a suit and tie and had looked a lot younger then. In his jeans and black Horseman's Association T-shirt, he looked about twenty-eight or twenty-nine. The one thing I did remember about him were his lavender eyes. The floodlights weren't doing them justice.

"So what do you think?" he asked, smiling. "I take it you haven't been to one of these things before. Are you enjoying yourself?"

I glanced self-consciously down at my pale blue pullover sweater and white sneakers and laughed. "Is it that obvious?"

He looked embarrassed. "No, really. What I meant was, I haven't seen you here before."

Suddenly the crowd gasped in unison, then groaned, and I looked toward the arena. The little girl's horse had apparently collided with one of the barrels, which was on its side, slowly rolling away. The child sat in the dirt on her duff, crying.

Several people ran out into the arena. A couple of them went after the girl's horse, who seemed confused. She was attempting to exit the arena on the side opposite the gate. The rest of the group went to check on the girl.

"Yes," I said, "I am. Enjoying myself, that is."

The child appeared to be all right, and everyone clapped as she and her horse were led from the arena.

"Next up is Susan Ferenzi, on Danforth's Dandy," said Mr. Westphall.

This caused Detective Hummer to turn his head, and together we watched as an extremely attractive (and extremely thin) brunette rode out on an equally winsome bay gelding. Ms. Ferenzi appeared to be in her early twenties and reminded me of Tracey, whose desert southwest getup—the one she'd worn on her interview with Dr. Augustin—would have been perfect for the event. Ms. Ferenzi had topped off hers with a creamy white cowboy hat.

The man with the stopwatch gave the woman a nod, and

she and her horse sprang into action. I had to admit, they were pretty remarkable. Except for the little clouds of dust accompanying each turn around the barrels, Danforth's Dandy appeared to float over the ground. And Ms. Ferenzi's hat never wobbled.

"Sixteen-eighty-five," announced Mr. Westphall as the pair crossed the finish line. The crowd went wild.

I looked over at Tom. His tongue was practically dragging on the bleachers. He did manage to pull himself together, however, and smile at me.

"Would you like something to drink?" he asked. "A cup of coffee or a Coke?" He looked at his watch. "There are two more entries in the barrels and then it'll take a while for them to get ready for the team penning." He pointed toward the arena. "You know, bring in the steers and set up the pen."

I glanced at the announcer's booth, but couldn't see who was inside it. "I came here with Dr. Augustin," I said. "He went to find Dick Westphall. I probably ought to wait for them."

Tom got up and put his hand under my elbow. "Come on," he said, pulling me to my feet. "Dick won't be free for another fifteen minutes, at least. Plenty of time. Besides, I want to show you around the place, since you've never been here before. By the way, have you ridden much?"

Now that we were face-to-face, I could see his eyes more clearly. They were a darker version of Jeffrey's eyes. And I couldn't imagine him investigating murders or associating with drug pushers or rapists. He had such a pleasant, open way about him. Like Jeffrey, only a little older and wiser, but without the cynicism that comes with age and dealing with the general public, if Dr. Augustin was any indication.

"I used to," I said, "up north. Of course, I'm certain we never had this much fun."

Tom laughed. "Well, then," he said, "all the more reason to show you around."

I hesitated for a couple of seconds, then shrugged. "Sure," I said, "why not?"

We made our way across and down the bleachers as another rider successfully negotiated the barrels and exited the arena. She was taller and heavier than Ms. Ferenzi, and her horse was slower. I heard Mr. Westphall announce a time of nineteen-forty, two and a half seconds off the time of Danforth's Dandy. But the crowd cheered enthusiastically anyway, and I wondered if the snooty show-jumping bunch I'd hung around with back in Connecticut would have been so gracious. Probably not.

It was crowded behind the bleachers. People, horses, and several dogs attracted by the odor of grilling hamburgers made navigating the area between the Port-O-Lets and the mobile concession stand difficult. But Tom and I finally got our drinks and struck out for the barn. On the way, we passed a T-shirt vendor selling his wares out of what looked like a modified "roach coach." One item caught my eye—three cowboys herding a steer into a tiny corral. The animal had a wide plastic band around his neck that bore a large number "5." The caption was TEAM PENNING.

I pointed to the T-shirt. "So what exactly is Team Penning?"

Tom smiled. I'd obviously hit on a favorite topic.

"A bunch of ranch hands out in California started it about forty years ago," he said. "For fun, I guess. Like bull riding. Anyway, they decided to see who was the fastest at cutting a certain number of steers out of a large herd and driving them through a gate."

He finished his Coke, quickly crushed the can, then folded the two ends together. The action appeared to be essentially unconscious and not some pointed display of masculine prowess, as it would have been for Dr. Augustin. I waited for him to toss the compacted can into a nearby trash container, but he slid it into his back pocket.

"The sport eventually evolved into a team effort," he continued. "Three riders are given two minutes to separate and pen three like-numbered steers out of a group of about thirty animals. There are a few special rules, like you can't have

more than four steers across the starting line at one time, and
you can't touch the steers—that's to keep them from being
injured." He grinned. "Rodeo events have come a long way
since animal rights and such."

"I'm happy to hear it," I said.

"I figured."

He guided me around a water trough, where three horses
were drinking. Their riders—young, buxom women—
laughed and giggled. One of them looked our way and
touched her neighbor's leg with the toe of her boot.

"Hi, Tom," she crooned. This started another wave of giggling.

"Hi, Patty," he called over his shoulder. Then he picked
up the pace considerably. I had to hustle to keep from being
left behind. "The Dream Team," he said to me, once we
were out of earshot.

"I beg your pardon."

"That's the name of their team. Patty, Jodie, and Teri. All
three of them are 'hot to trot,' if you'll excuse the vernacu-
lar."

He was blushing. Even in the dim light, I could see the
color creep up his neck and spread across his cheeks.

"So," I said quickly, "how long have you been with the
police department?"

We were nearing the barn, which was actually a series of
stalls and feed rooms joined together under a common roof.
The place was well lighted. I could see people moving
about, caring for their horses, cleaning stalls. Several outbuildings apparently were doing double duty as tack rooms
and storage for miscellaneous equipment. One of them contained a riding mower and a small front-end loader, in addition to saddles and other riding paraphernalia.

"Six years," he said. He stopped at one of the stalls. A
nameplate on the door said CHEROKEE. OWNER: TOM HUM-
MER. "This is my horse," he said. He clucked his tongue, and
a nice-looking sorrel stuck his head over the door. Tom
rubbed the animal's neck.

"Aren't you riding tonight?" I asked. "I would have thought you'd be out there in the thick of it."

He smiled. "Ordinarily I would, but Cherokee has a sore shoulder. I thought he could use the rest. These Saturday night affairs are just for fun and practice, anyway. No sense in risking permanent damage."

I heard a new voice over the loudspeaker announce that team penning was about to begin. Tom gave his horse one last rub, and we started back toward the arena. As we were leaving the barn, I noticed the name on the end stall—MISTY MORNING. OWNER: AMANDA BLAIZE.

"Is she any relation to Justin Blaize?" I asked, pointing to the nameplate.

Tom nodded. "His daughter. She's ten. You missed her. She rode earlier." He looked at me a little quizzically. "Now don't tell me the Blaize family treks all the way across the county to your clinic."

"No," I said. "I saw him at the public hearing the Army Corps of Engineers had for that electric transmission corridor. He spoke against the project. And very convincingly, I might add."

Tom rolled his eyes, and for a minute I thought he was going to say something unflattering about Justin Blaize. I was wrong.

"That stupid corridor is tearing this community apart," he said, his voice husky. "We've practically got a range war on our hands, for God's sake. I wish the power company would give it up and find someplace else for that high-voltage line." He took a deep breath.

"They've got their hotshot experts and their overpriced lawyers and ad people pulling the wool over the government's eyes. You watch—the Corps will approve that dredge and fill permit. Just as sure as we're standing here talking."

"You'd rather it was someone else's problem, is that it?" I asked. I sounded like Dr. Augustin. But I really didn't have an opinion one way or the other about the power line, except that I knew its construction was inevitable. Just as sure as we were standing there talking.

Tom frowned. "I guess that *is* what I'm saying, isn't it?" He started walking again. "Let's talk about something else."

We got to the arena and went up into the bleachers. Dr. Augustin and Mr. Westphall were sitting in the middle of the third row. Dr. Augustin looked at Tom, then at me, and grinned. I tried not to let it annoy me, but was unsuccessful. I sat down next to Mr. Westphall.

"I'm going down to see if they need me to man the gate," said Tom. "Dick can explain the penning procedure to you." He winked at Mr. Westphall.

"Thanks for the Coke," I said, holding up my can.

"Sure. Next time you can buy."

He hurried off, pausing to speak to a man on the first row.

Dr. Augustin simply could not leave it alone. "Now what would Mr. Halsey say if he knew you were chasing around after a police detective?" he asked, eyes gleaming.

"I was not *chasing* after him," I hissed. "He came up to me and offered to show me around. That's all! Besides, I don't really care what Mr. Halsey thinks!"

Dr. Augustin looked bemused. Mr. Westphall, on the other hand, looked like someone who had suddenly found himself in the midst of a gang war.

"Uh . . ." he began.

A female voice interrupted our little exchange. "Rough Riders, you're up," she said. "Dream Team on deck."

I glanced down at the arena. The barrels were gone. About midway along the right-hand side of the arena several sections of fence made of welded metal pipe had been hooked together to form a mini-corral. On the side facing the bleachers, one section was angled open.

"Rough Riders," said the announcer, "your number is four!"

At that moment, three riders—one adult woman and two small boys somewhere around six or seven—raced their horses across the imaginary starting line toward a group of yearling steers huddled together at the far end of the arena. Each of the steers was wearing a large numbered neck band.

The woman reached the herd first and cut out a steer bearing the number "4." Then she and her horse began to work the steer away from the rest of the herd and down the arena toward the pen.

"Johnny!" she yelled at one of the boys. "Get in the hole!"

The child urged his horse slowly into the narrow space between the arena fence and the pen, and stopped. Meanwhile, the woman carefully drove the steer just past the pen and began forcing the animal toward the arena fence.

"Chip!" she yelled at the second boy. "Get the wing."

The boy seemed momentarily deaf and began to follow the woman.

"On the wing, on the wing!" she screamed.

He finally heard her, evidently, and positioned his horse just off the open section of the pen, which I presumed was "the wing" or door. The woman urged the steer toward the pen opening. At first the animal resisted and tried to escape down the alley between the pen and the fence. But the first boy was holding his position, blocking the way. The steer then headed for the second child. The woman spurred her horse and managed to reach the wing before the steer. At that point, the opening in the pen must have looked pretty inviting, because the steer ran inside. The woman raised her hand high in the air, and the man with the stopwatch said something into his mouthpiece.

"One-forty-two," said the announcer. "Good job, Rough Riders."

The crowd cheered, and the two little boys looked victorious as they trotted out of the arena. Their female companion looked exhausted. She smiled weakly at someone on the first row and shrugged.

Dr. Augustin glanced over at me. "So," he began, "what did you and the detective talk about?"

Mr. Westphall looked a little pale, as if he sensed more sniper fire about to occur. He stood up. "I've got to check on

Darlene." He looked up at the announcer's booth and squinted. "See if she needs any help up there. I'll catch you guys later." He excused himself, stepped in front of me, and hurried across the row and down the steps.

Dr. Augustin smiled innocently.

"He told me that power-line corridor is creating a range war of sorts up here," I said. "I guess he knows it's necessary. He just wishes it would go somewhere else."

Dr. Augustin wasn't listening. Something or someone had caught his attention. I turned my head and followed his gaze. Two rows down, Dick Westphall and a tall man who looked vaguely familiar, even from the back, were having a rather heated discussion. Westphall looked extremely angry. "If looks could kill" angry. I couldn't see the other man's face, but his cowboy hat was distinctive.

"That's Les Jordan," whispered Dr. Augustin. "Now what has he done to piss Dick off? I wonder."

We watched the two men for a minute or so. Then, as the Dream Team entered the arena, Mr. Jordan got up and left. Mr. Westphall crushed his apparently empty Coke can and threw it at Jordan. It ricocheted off the edge of the bleachers and clattered to the ground.

CHAPTER 19

•

"Dick is head of the Horseman's Association," I said. "Maybe it was business. Something to do with using Jordan's land for the rodeo."

The Dream Team was having a bad day. They looked like the three blind mice scurrying about. Steers were everywhere. I hadn't heard what the team's number was, but it didn't matter. The number didn't go as high as thirteen.

"Time!" said the announcer. "Please bunch your cattle."

The girls weren't even managing that very well, and a male rider entered the arena to help them out. He quickly and efficiently gathered the herd together, while the girls rode about giggling and laughing, their boobs bouncing merrily up and down, to the obvious delight of Dr. Augustin and several other male spectators. One of the girls lost her hat. A boy by the rail dashed in and retrieved it, and the Dream Team finally exited the arena.

"Thank you, ladies," said the announcer, her voice almost emotional with relief.

"Maybe," said Dr. Augustin, once his view of the buxom lassies was obstructed by the bleachers. "Maybe not."

"Too bad we weren't one row closer," I said.

We watched two more teams, neither of which managed to pen any steers, although the team dubbed Too Bucking Bad came pretty close.

"Shall we go?" asked Dr. Augustin as the steers were being bunched up for the next trio.

"I guess," I said. I was a little put out that Dr. Augustin could withstand the boredom of a lengthy commission meeting or public hearing but wasn't willing to sit through even half of the team penning competition. I could have insisted, but I knew he would squirm around in his seat and act miserable, so what was the point?

On the way to the Jeep, I made a quick detour into one of the Port-O-Lets. When I came out, Dr. Augustin was standing by the Dumpster, which was full to overflowing with tree branches, empty feed bags, and foam cups. He was prodding something on the ground with his boot.

"Take a look at this," he told me.

I walked slowly over to the Dumpster and looked down. A dead yellow Labrador retriever lay in the debris. It looked as if someone had tried to stuff it into one of the feed bags.

The animal was filthy. Its feet were covered with some kind of black goo, and its head and shoulders were caked with mud. It had been dead for some time.

"Poor guy," I said.

"They probably ran across him when they were mowing the field," said Dr. Augustin. "Or else it was someone's yard dog, and they didn't feel like going to the trouble of burying it. My guess is he's been dead a week or so. Maybe more."

"That's disgusting," I said. "Leaving him here in the garbage." The smell was unbelievable.

"Not everyone looks at dogs the way you and I do, Samantha." He turned around. "Let's go."

We dodged a couple of horses on their way to the water trough and a group of little girls chasing a dog. The animal had a red second-place ribbon in its mouth. One of the girls was Robin Smith, from the barrel racing event. Dr. Augustin reached out and grabbed the dog. He pried the ribbon from its mouth and handed it to the girl. She mumbled "Thank you," then "Yuk!" and began wiping the ribbon off on her jeans. Dr. Augustin grinned at her, and she giggled.

When we were finally back on the main road, I thought about Detective Hummer's assessment of the power-line controversy.

"These people up here really don't like the electric company, do they?" I asked.

"I don't think they dislike the electric company exactly. I think it's more a case of disliking progress. And I can't say I blame them." He turned left onto Sloan Avenue. "That transmission corridor means more reliable service for all those new houses and shopping malls littering the countryside, which means a bigger flood from up north moving here. All of which results in less open space for the locals. The power company fencing off the corridor hasn't done much to engender goodwill, either."

"But would one of them actually murder somebody just to keep the project from happening? I mean, we're talking about horseback riding here, aren't we?"

He turned his head, and despite the darkness, I could tell he was glaring at me.

"Samantha, these people are not high-priced lawyers and surgeons who play polo on the weekends. People who have never cleaned out a stall in their lives. Most of those folks back there are fighting a losing battle and they know it. Ranching isn't a sport for men like Lester Jordan. It's their livelihood."

It was the first time Dr. Augustin had ever shown any disdain for the wealthy lifestyle I'd left behind in Connecticut. Was this the *real* reason he disliked Michael Halsey? Was he jealous of Michael's money? No, I told myself. Dr. Augustin is perfectly content with his life just the way it is. And then I caught myself smiling. Dr. Augustin in his jeans and hiking boots mingling with the gentry across the bay at the local tennis and polo club. Ridiculous! I shook the image aside.

"I thought you didn't like the good ole boy way of doing things."

"I never said I liked Les Jordan," he snapped. "I'm simply making a point about the importance to these people of this power-line issue. That's all."

Dr. Augustin took a sudden detour down North Lincoln. I was glad he had decided not to go through the project at night, but he was exceeding the speed limit. The Jeep's tires squealed, and I had to hold on to the door handle to keep from being thrown against him. He was clearly angry. However, I got the impression it wasn't because of anything I'd said or done. So, I risked opening my mouth again.

"That yellow Lab back there. He looked like he had tar on his feet. Could that have killed him?"

We passed the Municipal Services Building. Yellow police tape still encircled a portion of the property, even though it was back to business as usual. On the bottom two floors, anyway. And then, I shuddered. "Charred" was the detective's description of Jack Lanier.

"Maybe," said Dr. Augustin. "If he ingested a sufficient amount, although I can't imagine any well-adjusted dog eating tar voluntarily. Certainly, just that little bit on his feet wouldn't kill him. If it *was* tar."

He suddenly slammed on the brakes and smacked his hand on the steering wheel. I jumped and grabbed the armrest.

"Tar!" he shouted. "Someone used paint thinner to clean tar off that dog's feet and legs." He looked over at me. "The terrier that John Deland brought in."

A car behind us honked, and Dr. Augustin glanced in the rearview mirror, then started up again.

"No one is purposely poisoning those dogs," he said. "They're getting into the stuff all by themselves."

He couldn't have been more excited if he'd won the lottery. I let go of the armrest.

"I'll bet there's an illegal dump site someplace near Carriage Hill," he continued. "More than one, probably. Roofing tar, waste oil, grease trap pumpage. Pesticide residue. They're called 'Midnight Dumpers'—people who can't or won't pay for proper disposal of the stuff, so they sneak out late at night and spread it on the ground. Orange groves are popular spots I'm told. The ground is sandy, and the mess filters down pretty rapidly."

"But that chow didn't have any tar on her feet," I said.

"True. But that chow died from some toxic substance. Maybe something dumped in the general vicinity of the tar." He paused. "I told you, tar, in and of itself, probably didn't kill that Lab. I wish we'd been able to look at a sample of its bone marrow."

He spotted a McDonald's and turned into it, then stopped alongside the drive-through's little speaker box.

"Two small coffees," he said, after the garbled "Welcome to McDonald's, may I take your order?" greeting. Then he looked over at me. "You want cream and sugar?"

I didn't even want coffee, but I nodded anyway. He proceeded to the pickup window and paid the girl.

"We should cruise down that power-line corridor behind Maraldee Manor," he said after we were under way again. "Seems to me that would make a good dump site."

From the smell of the coffee, I knew it was way past its prime. The fact that it looked like something a midnight dumper might pour in an open pit didn't help. I snapped the lid back on my cup without drinking any.

"Who knows," said Dr. Augustin, "maybe the Kenney child and his friends have somehow gotten into hazardous waste out there. Maybe we've got another Love Canal on our hands."

I had finally gotten used to his childlike glee at discussing morbid and revolting topics, but it wasn't like him to overlook the obvious.

"Maraldee Manor is six or seven miles from Carriage Hill," I said. "Surely those feral dogs don't travel every day back and forth between the two developments."

Dr. Augustin was silent for several minutes, gripping and releasing the steering wheel, a sure sign that he was frustrated. I waited for him to defend his point—tell me how wrong I was. That pack dogs travel great distances in the wild. Of course, that's when food is scarce, and we'd already established that Carriage Hill was a cornucopia of edible delights.

"You're right," he said, his voice surprisingly calm, considering.

He turned down Sabal Palm Court and stopped in front of my apartment building. "That dump site, if there *is* one, must be somewhere out in the woods behind Carriage Hill. It's possible that surveyor—what was his name?—Trexler, saw whoever was doing the dumping and got himself killed as a result."

I picked up my purse and, still holding my cup of hazardous waste, opened the door. "Thanks for taking me along tonight," I said, ignoring his reference to the dead man. "I really enjoyed it."

Dr. Augustin grinned. "I take it you're not game for another trip into the woods?"

I got out and closed the door. "See you Monday," I said, still ignoring him. Then I dashed across the parking lot, coffee sloshing out around the lid of the cup and onto my nice clean sweater.

CHAPTER 20

•

Monday, October 18

The candy corn was back on Cynthia's desk. She had dispensed with the cauldron in favor of a cut-glass candy dish from home. I hoped it wasn't irreplaceable. While Cynthia talked to a client on the phone, I watched Charlie put his paw in the dish and scoop out one of the orange and yellow kernels. He sniffed it, pushed it over to the edge of the desk and watched it fall to the floor. Then he went after another one.

"Scat!" said Cynthia, hanging up the phone.

Charlie gazed at her with his emerald eyes, then stuck his paw back in the candy dish.

"I'm warning you," she said, shaking a finger at him.

I walked across the room and picked the cat up. He squirmed and protested, until I put him on the floor. Then he gave Cynthia and me a parting glare and huffed off down the hall, tail in the air like a staff.

I gathered up the candy and threw it in Cynthia's trash can. "You wanted to see me?" I asked. She'd been trying to get me alone since eight o'clock. I checked the clock over her desk. It said 11:10.

Cynthia looked over at Dr. Augustin's door, then at the empty parking lot.

"I went out Saturday night," she whispered.

You'd have thought she had committed a lewd and lascivious act in public, the way she said it. I tried not to look too amused.

"You did?" I whispered back. "Alone or with someone?"

Cynthia frowned at me. "*With* someone, of course."

Of course, I thought.

"Remember that gentleman I told you I met at my support group?" she asked. "The one with the beard?"

"I thought one of the group's rules was you weren't supposed to date another member until you'd been divorced for at least six months. That you'd be preying on each other's loneliness."

Cynthia pouted up her face. "It's been over a *year!*" she whined. "Thirteen months and three days, to be exact."

How many hours? I wanted to ask her, but didn't. I, on the other hand, was trying to forget how long it had been since David abandoned me at the church on my wedding day. That certainly constituted a divorce, didn't it?

"Sorry," I said. I smiled. "So how did it go? Where did he take you?"

Cynthia replaced the frown with a child-in-awe look. The one she usually reserved for Mr. Halsey. "We went to a fancy Italian place over in Tampa and then we went dancing. Until midnight. And afterward, he took me out for coffee." She was becoming a little flushed and breathless. "I didn't get home until two." Like this was the sin of the century.

"Good for you," I told her.

A car drove up and stopped.

"That's our eleven-thirty," said Cynthia, suddenly very businesslike.

I watched an elderly woman struggle out of the car, cat carrier in hand. The woman's normally silver-blue hair looked like gun metal in the overcast.

"I'll tell Dr. Augustin," I said and walked across the room toward the hallway. I stopped and turned around. "Take it slow, Cynthia," I warned. "Remember your resolve to never let another man hurt you the way Mr. Caswell did."

She pretended not to hear me.

Dr. Augustin spent the morning calling around, trying to find out if any midnight dumpers had been working the Carriage Hill area. At noon, he was short-tempered and quick to point out every little thing that Tracey and I failed to do exactly right, so I knew he hadn't been successful. I breathed a sigh of relief when he left for lunch.

I was eating my cottage cheese in one of the exam rooms and finishing up *Last of the Mohicans* when Cynthia tapped on the door.

"Yes?" I said.

She opened the door a crack and stuck her head in. "Sorry to bother you, but there's a Mrs. Knowles out front. Says we have her dog. A mixed terrier named Sinbad. John Deland sent her here."

I stared at her for a couple of seconds, while my brain tried to deal with this unforeseen and, what I considered very serendipitous, occurrence. Maybe now we'll get some answers, I told myself.

"Put her in Room Two, would you?" I stood up. "I'll get her dog."

Cynthia nodded and was about to leave when I stopped her.

"Did she pay?" I asked, my voice low. Dr. Augustin would skin me alive if I let the dog go without getting at least partial payment.

Cynthia nodded. "All of it," she said. "She was so happy to find we hadn't euthanized her dog, she didn't even blink at the bill."

"Good," I said. "And make sure we have her address and phone number, in case I don't ask the right questions." God forbid.

Cynthia said okay and went back to the reception room. I went to the kennel to get Sinbad.

Randy and Katie were awake. When he saw me, Randy dribbled the little rubber ball over to the cage door and began working it through the bars. I hadn't heard from Michael in a week, which wasn't like him. And I had no way to get in touch with him. The longer he took to contact me, the more convinced I became that Mary's son wasn't the only reason he went to New York.

"Sinbad?" I said to the dog in the cage beneath the kittens.

The terrier perked his ears and got up. He came over to the door, tail wagging.

"Your mom is here to take you home," I told him.

I opened the door, and Sinbad let me pick him up. Frank had given him another bath. He smelled like flea shampoo.

"I sure hope she can tell us how you got that paint thinner on your legs."

Sinbad licked my face and breathed his doggie breath on me.

Mrs. Knowles started crying the moment she saw her dog. It was a reunion Walt Disney would have gleefully rubbed his hands over. One of those tearjerker movie moments. Sinbad practically jumped out of my arms and into the arms of Mrs. Knowles, then began washing her face. I left them alone and went for a box of Kleenex.

When I got back, Mrs. Knowles had composed herself and was sitting down. Sinbad was in her lap.

"I'm sorry for acting like such a sentimental old fool," she said, sniffing, "but I've been so worried about Sinbad."

The dog looked up at her and wagged his tail.

"You see, I took off his collar so I could give him a bath— he got tar all over his feet and legs from that parking lot again, and I had to use turpentine to get it off. Anyway, I left him in the backyard for just a minute, while I went to get the shampoo and a towel." She scratched Sinbad on the head. "He ran off with the boy next door. He likes to play with the neighborhood children, you see."

"You might consider having him tattooed," I said. "In case he and his collar are ever separated again."

I smiled at her. She was a plump but nicely dressed woman in her early fifties, with auburn hair that probably wasn't entirely natural, since there wasn't even a trace of grey in it. But it was far from cheap, either.

"You mentioned he got tar on his feet from a parking lot. Where exactly was that?"

She put Sinbad on the floor and brushed off her skirt. "The recreation center on Sloan Avenue," she said. "The City has been resurfacing that lot for what seems like ages and ages.

"I've asked Billy's mother to please not take Sinbad with them when they go down there, but it's hard, I know. Sinbad does love children." She paused and looked at the wall behind me. "George and I never had any of our own, and we dote on the neighborhood kids, especially Billy and Joey and their sister Grace."

I thought she was going to cry, again, but she busied herself securing Sinbad's collar around his neck. She took a leash out of her purse and snapped it on the collar.

"I really do appreciate everything you and . . . the doctor have done for Sinbad," she said.

"Dr. Augustin and I are just glad he's okay," I said, "and that you and he have found each other."

I walked them up to the reception room, where Mrs. Knowles thanked me again. Then she and Sinbad left. I watched them drive off.

"By the way," said Cynthia as I was headed back to my cottage cheese, "have you heard from Michael?"

Without looking directly at her, I shook my head. "No. Not yet. He's probably busy with Mary's son. You know, trying to find a private school that will take him. Transferring his records. That sort of thing. He'll call the first chance he gets."

"Of course he will," said Cynthia.

Neither of us sounded very convinced.

Dr. Augustin returned at 1:30, still in a rotten mood. He came in the back way and went directly into his office, slamming the door behind him.

I was at the front desk working on our weekly supply order. I chewed on my pencil. It was a toss-up as to which course of action I took regarding Sinbad. I could knock on the door and risk having him snarl at me, or I could wait for his mood to change before telling him and risk his discovering that the terrier was gone and then snarl at me.

Dr. Augustin opened his door and went into the lab. I hesitated, then got up and followed him.

"I have good news," I said, praying fervently that it was.

He put the coffeepot down and looked at me.

"That terrier's owner finally surfaced. John Deland sent her over." I paused, swallowed, and went on. "She paid her bill. All of it. She was thrilled you didn't euthanize the dog. His name is Sinbad, by the way."

He took a sip of coffee and continued to look at me, his features expressionless, his eyes flat black.

"You were right about the tar."

At that, a tiny smile nudged up the corners of his mouth. "Glad to hear it," he said. "Tell me more."

We went into his office. He sat down at his desk and propped his feet up. I leaned against the bookcase. I couldn't be sure his mood wouldn't change again, and I wanted to be close to the door.

"It wasn't the first time Sinbad had come home covered in tar," I told him. "Mrs. Knowles said the dog goes down to the Northeast Recreation Complex regularly with the kids next door. Apparently they're resurfacing the parking lot, and Sinbad goes where he shouldn't."

Dr. Augustin frowned. "That parking lot is asphalt. I can't imagine a dog getting more than a little stuck to the bottoms of his feet by walking on it. Hardly enough to warrant soaking his legs in paint remover. And if that yellow Lab got into the same thing Sinbad did, it wasn't asphalt. That dog was up to his knees in tar. Like the stuff they use on roofs." He didn't say anything for a while. Then he took his feet off the desk and turned his chair around. His back was to me.

"We should drive up there anyway and take a look

around," he said. "I'll swing by your place around seven o'-clock."

His presumptuousness was more than I could handle. "I have a life outside this clinic, you know," I snapped. I backed up a few feet.

I couldn't see his face, but his tone was calm. "Of course you do, Samantha," he said. "Make that seven-thirty."

CHAPTER 21

•

It was dark by the time we got to the rec center. There were only six cars in the parking lot, all of them along the street side of the building. I figured Monday must be a slow night, because most parents are trying to recover from a weekend filled with soccer and football games and piano recitals.

Dr. Augustin drove slowly across the empty pavement. Suddenly the Jeep's headlights picked up a row of wooden barricades. He pulled in front of them and stopped. He turned off the engine but left the headlights on, then got out. I followed him.

"I can't believe this lot needs repairing after only five years," he said. "Even the lousy contractors the City hires aren't that bad."

He pushed one of the barricades aside so we could pass through. I expected us to leave footprints for all eternity, like the ones birds and dogs and mischievous children leave in newly poured sidewalks. But the asphalt was dry and unyielding.

Dr. Augustin stood still for a minute and looked around. Then he walked to the edge of the pavement.

"They aren't repairing this parking lot, Samantha. They're enlarging it. This is new asphalt." He paused. "And it looks like they've been adding on little by little for some time." He pointed to the closest light pole, which was quite some distance away. "See how this part of the lot doesn't have any security lighting? They probably haven't gotten around to putting up any new poles. I guess the planning department underestimated the popularity of this place just a bit."

"So you think Sinbad walked in the new asphalt and got the stuff on his feet?" I asked.

Dr. Augustin frowned. His eyebrows almost touched, throwing unnatural shadows over the rest of his face. In the Jeep's headlights, he looked positively ghoulish. "I thought Mrs. Knowles said her dog had tar on him. On his legs. And the goo on the Lab wasn't asphalt. Asphalt, the kind used for paving, is moist and crumbly, not liquid. Not like tar. At least not normally." He sounded disappointed. We were back where we'd started.

At that moment, an enormous form appeared out of the darkness only a couple of yards to our left. We hadn't seen him coming, because the glare from the Jeep's headlights had blinded us. I jumped behind Dr. Augustin.

"What exactly are you guys doin' out here?" the man asked, suspiciously, his right hand resting on the head of a nightstick hanging from his belt.

He wore a security guard's uniform. Either he'd gained weight since signing on or he'd borrowed the uniform. His belly strained against the bottom two buttons on his shirt. I could see white peeking through the gaps. And his pants, slung under his gut and several inches below his presumed waist, were threatening to fall down.

"Evening," said Dr. Augustin. He held out his hand, but the guard didn't budge. "We're with Animal Control," he added, almost truthfully. "We're looking for those wild dogs who've been bothering the folks in Carriage Hill. Can't have a bunch of potentially rabid animals running loose can we?" He smiled.

The guard relaxed and took his hand off the nightstick. "Those damned dogs have been prowling around here, too."

He pointed out into the darkness. "Turn over the garbage cans in the picnic area, before the maintenance guys can empty 'em. And leave their shit all over the place." He looked quickly at me to see if I'd been offended.

"I know what you mean," said Dr. Augustin.

"Hey," said the guard, "there goes a couple of them hounds now." He pointed a finger toward the woods.

The headlights barely reached that far, but I caught a glimpse of four luminous orbs shining out of the trees like bicycle reflectors. Then they winked off and were gone.

"Right," said Dr. Augustin. "We'll just see what's what. Samantha, would you get the flashlight out of the glove box?" He offered the guard his hand again. "Thank you for your help, Officer," he said, emphasizing the "Officer" part.

The man puffed out his chest, adding further strain to the buttons, and shook Dr. Augustin's hand. "I'm just a lowly security guard," he said, as if nothing could be further from the truth, "but I do try to keep track of things around here."

"And you're doing a mighty fine job, too," said Dr. Augustin.

I bolted for the Jeep, glad for the excuse to get away. They were making me ill with all their phony posturing.

The flashlight wasn't in the glove compartment. After a quick search through the wadded-up McDonald's bags on the floor behind the passenger seat, I found it and, crossing my fingers, switched it on. It worked, at least for the moment.

When I rejoined Dr. Augustin, the guard had left for more important duties. Like dinner.

"Animal Control, huh?" I said, handing him the flashlight.

"Hey, John Deland is the reason we're out here, prowling around in the dark." He stepped into the grass and headed for the woods.

"You're not seriously intending to look for those dogs tonight, are you?" I asked from the security of the parking lot.

"I'm just going to check around the picnic area. You can stay by the Jeep if you like." He vanished into the darkness, then suddenly reappeared, more or less, in the glow of his flashlight.

I watched him and the flashlight bob along for a minute or so, then dashed after him. "Wait up," I said.

The picnic area looked different at night. The security lighting around the picnic tables gave everything a pinkish Cristo-like tone, as if the whole scene, including the paper cups on the ground, had been put together by some Miami artist with a hangover.

Dr. Augustin aimed the flashlight into each trash can, then walked down to the retention pond, startling a flock of water birds that shrieked and flapped off into the woods. I kept glancing around, half expecting to see Cujo headed our way, fangs dripping rabies virus. But all I saw was a marsh rabbit that looked more terrified than I was.

"That's kind of stupid," said Dr. Augustin. He was standing at the edge of the pond.

"What is?"

"They've let this drainage swale erode away." He aimed the flashlight along a shallow ditch that led back toward the parking lot. "All the grass is dead."

The swale was taking on the appearance of a small canyon, at the end of which was a delta that fanned out into the pond for several feet.

"They probably intend to put a pipe here, eventually," I said. "About the time they install the extra light poles on the parking lot addition. You know, cart before the horse."

Dr. Augustin shook his head and began walking back along the left-hand side of the swale. I took the right side. We were almost to the parking lot, when I stumbled, then felt myself sinking into the ground.

"Ack!" I said, trying to keep my balance. I struggled to pull my foot out of whatever I'd sunk into, but the earth was swallowing me up like quicksand. I tried not to panic. "Help!"

Dr. Augustin came back and pointed the flashlight at me, then at the ground. He offered me his hand. With some difficulty, I managed to extricate myself and quickly jumped to his side of the swale.

"Geez," I said in disgust. "Just look at me."

We stared at the black ooze covering my sneakers and my jeans halfway up my calves. Dr. Augustin leaned over and dredged a finger through the stuff. He sniffed it.

"I think we've found out how Sinbad and that yellow Lab got tar on their legs. Or whatever this is. It looks and smells like tar. Or at least some kind of petroleum product. Take a whiff." He stuck out his finger.

I sniffed and jerked my head back. "Yuck," I said. "I guess we've also found out where your midnight dumper has been operating."

Dr. Augustin scanned the area immediately across the swale from us and then slowly began working his way up the swale, shining the flashlight along the right bank, periodically stopping to look out toward the woods. I followed him, noticing with every step that my jeans and socks were becoming stickier and less pliable. I began to worry about how difficult it was going to be to get them off. I was also concerned that whatever had killed the Lab and at least two of John's pack dogs might do me in as well.

"I don't think so," said Dr. Augustin. "This doesn't strike me as a dump site. At least, not a recent one."

"Maybe this mess is left over from the parking lot addition," I offered.

We made it back to the Jeep, and Dr. Augustin turned off the flashlight. Then he went around to the rear of the vehicle and lifted the hatchback.

"I told you, Samantha, road asphalt is not runny." He

BEWARE SLEEPING DOGS   171

found his medical bag and took out two specimen jars. "I'll send a sample of that stuff you're wearing to Bob up in Gainesville. He can tell us what it is. And I'll get a sample of water from the retention pond, to see how contaminated it is. Whatever's flowing down that drainage swale can't be doing the aquatic life in the pond any good, that's for damn sure."

He took a tongue depressor out of his medical bag and scraped a healthy slug of the black goo off my sneaker and transferred it to one of the specimen jars. He screwed the cap on and handed it to me, along with the tongue depressor. Then he picked up the flashlight and headed back across the parking lot.

I sat down in the rear of the Jeep and dangled my legs over the bumper. It was obvious my sneakers were a lost cause. My jeans were pretty well trashed, too, although soaking the bottom six inches in paint remover might resurrect them. "I suppose I can always turn them into cutoffs," I said, aloud. They weren't my best jeans, but that was hardly the point, was it?

I heard Dr. Augustin call my name. I hopped down and followed the Jeep's headlights across the parking lot. Dr. Augustin was standing by a large oak tree. He handed me the specimen jar, filled with water, then leaned over and carefully picked up the body of a white egret.

"This is the fourth corpse I've come across, all of them waterbirds of one sort or another. Two moorhens, a little blue heron, and this snowy egret. And there are several dead fish at the edge of the pond. Nothing big or obvious. But it is an indication that something is contaminating the water here." He was still holding the egret. "Let's go," he said. "We need to get you cleaned up."

I pointed to the dead bird. "What are you going to do with that?"

"I thought I'd send it along to Bob with the water sample and the tar."

I swallowed and thought about the yellow Lab and the

chow mix John had brought us. Environmentally sensitive creatures like birds and fish were one thing. Dogs were another entirely. "You don't think this stuff will make me sick or anything, do you?"

Dr. Augustin laughed. "Just don't lick your feet."

CHAPTER 22

•

Tuesday, October 19

"So, what do you hear from our good friend Mr. Halsey?" asked Dr. Augustin.

I finished prepping the last surgery of the morning—a schnauzer named Roxie—and opened the spay pack. Dr. Augustin eyed me over his mask.

"I didn't know you considered Michael a 'good friend,' " I said, cautiously.

Dr. Augustin had gone from hostile to depressed to Mr. Congeniality in the space of two hours, and I wasn't sure what was next. His moods could fill a chapter in a psychiatric manual.

"Of course, I consider him a friend, Samantha. Any friend of yours is a friend of mine." He pulled a glove on, snapping it up over the cuff of his gown sleeve. "So, have you heard from him?"

He wanted something, I was certain of that. Some piece of information he couldn't dig up himself.

"Not in the last couple of days," I said, not looking at him. Not in the last week, I reminded myself. Not since he left. It was beginning to eat at me.

"Too bad," said Dr. Augustin.

He positioned the drape over Roxie's belly and secured it. Then he reached for the scalpel.

"Why?" I asked.

"Because I need to find out about the rec center site. What was there before the city built that parking lot. Who owned the land originally."

"Isn't that public information? I mean, couldn't you find all that out by going to City Hall and searching the records?"

He threw a bloody sponge in the general direction of the trash pail. "If I had the time, I could, yes. But as you can see, I'm a little busy just now."

Grumpy was back. I reached over and picked the sponge up off the floor. "I'll tell Michael you miss him," I said. If he ever calls me, that is.

Dr. Augustin snorted into his mask.

Dr. Augustin left at noon. He told Cynthia he wasn't sure when he'd be back, and could she please reschedule our two o'clock? He didn't wait to see if she was successful or even if there was an appointment open later in the day, assuming the client agreed to the switch.

He took the box containing the sample of tar, the bottle of pond water, and some selected internal organs from the dead bird, fixed in preservative, with him. He said rather than wait for the courier to come pick it up, he would drop it off at the FedEx office himself on the way to City Hall. He asked me to call his chemist buddy up in Gainesville and tell him to expect it. That he owed him a beer.

"He's going to owe Bob a whole case of beer pretty soon," I told Cynthia as she dialed Mrs. Winter's number.

Cynthia frowned. "He's going to owe *me* a lot more than a case of beer, if he pulls this little stunt again. Hello, Mrs. Winter? This is Cynthia at Paradise Cay Animal Hospital. Fine, and you?"

I left her to do Dr. Augustin's dirty work and went into the treatment room. Tracey was back in the kennel with Frank. She was supposedly helping him finish his chores so he could leave early to practice. In actual fact, they were probably necking. It *was* lunchtime, after all. One day, Dr. Augustin is going to catch them, I thought, and then they'll be sorry. He won't fire them. That would be the humane thing to do. No, he'll probably make Tracey eat Big Macs for a week and take the scissors to Frank's hair. Or, worse, play Barry Manilow tapes over the intercom.

I checked my watch, then the treatment schedule to see if anyone was due for anything. We had four patients in Isolation and eight boarders, two of whom were on medication. I saw a note made by Frank to examine Randy's eye. That he'd been squinting. I suspected Katie had swatted him. He was a little pistol and probably deserved it. Hopefully she hadn't scratched his cornea. I knew Michael would want Dr. Augustin to do whatever was necessary for the kittens if there was a problem, but it would be better if he was informed beforehand. Which gave me an idea.

I went into the lab and, after staring at the phone for a minute or so, dialed Michael's number at the *Times*. He wouldn't answer, of course, but presumably someone would.

"Michael Halsey's office," said a pleasant-sounding young woman. "May I help you?" She was chewing gum.

"Yes," I said. "This is . . . Cynthia Caswell, at Paradise Cay Animal Hospital. Mr. Halsey is boarding his cats here, and we need to contact him about one of them. It isn't anything serious, but we do need his permission to treat the cat for an eye problem." I paused. "The New York number he left us isn't a working number. I assume one of our staff copied it down incorrectly."

I was keeping my voice as low as practical for fear of being overheard. Not only was I impersonating Cynthia, though I didn't know why, I was also lying. And doing a pretty damned good job at it, too, evidently.

"Let me see," said the woman. "I think this is it." She read off an area code and number, then gave me a second number. "In case he can't be reached at the first one," she said.

"Thank you," I told her. "You've been most helpful."

"Not at all, Ms. Caswell. Gee, I didn't even know Mr. Halsey had any pets."

So why are you giving me his number? I asked silently. But I certainly wasn't going to educate her in proper office etiquette.

After I'd hung up, I put the piece of paper with the numbers on it in my purse. It was ridiculous, really, but I felt a lot better.

Mrs. Winter was more than happy to reschedule Frosty's appointment. She had no desire to see me, certainly, and I felt sure Frosty's ailment, if indeed there actually was one, could wait.

Unfortunately, Dr. Augustin was still missing at 2:30, when Mrs. Westphall arrived with Princess.

"She's having trouble walking," Mrs. Westphall told me.

She was a handsome woman in a severe sort of way. Like she was perpetually irritated at something. Her clothes tended to fit her moods. I had never seen her in anything particularly feminine. That day she was wearing a long-sleeved white cotton blouse with a tiny black bow tie, a black pleated cotton skirt, and one-inch black pumps. She had on very little makeup and no jewelry. Her stomach was just beginning to protrude. If I hadn't known she was pregnant, I'd have assumed it was a case of early middle-aged spread. According to Dr. Augustin, Mr. Westphall was forty-six, and I assumed Mrs. Westphall wasn't far behind.

"She staggers and jerks her head like she's been drugged or something," said Mrs. Westphall. "I left work early for a doctor's appointment and stopped off at the house. I found her like this."

I looked down at the dog. She was lying on the reception-room floor, splay-legged. Her head rocked drunkenly back and forth, and she was panting to beat the band. She reminded me of Sinbad, when John Deland first brought him to the clinic.

"You haven't put anything on her, have you?" I asked. "Flea dip or paint thinner?"

Mrs. Westphall looked at me. "Paint thinner? Why on earth would I put paint thinner on her?"

I knelt down next to Princess and touched her gently on the neck. She jerked her head dizzily backward. "We had a dog in here a week or so ago with these same symptoms. The owner had used paint thinner to clean tar off the animal's feet."

Mrs. Westphall shook her head. "I haven't put anything on her. In fact, she hasn't even had a bath yet this week, and you can see how filthy she is. It's from running around in the woods behind the rec center and swimming in that nasty retention pond." She wrinkled her nose.

"Was she out there today?"

Mrs. Westphall shrugged. "Timmy only had a half day of school. One of those in-service training days for the teachers. I expect he went to the rec center to play basketball, even though I told him to come home and clean up the garage. Dick probably went to watch him and took Princess. He hauls that dog around with him most of the time. Why do you ask?"

"I don't know, really. Except Dr. Augustin will probably want to know what Princess was doing just before she got sick."

That rec center retention pond needs a sign with a skull and crossbones on it, I said to myself. Or the skeletal remains of a cow lying on the shore.

"Why don't you leave Princess with us, Mrs. Westphall? Dr. Augustin has stepped out for a minute. But he's going to want to run a few tests, anyway. We'll give you a call around five."

She agreed and, without telling Princess good-bye or giving the dog a farewell pat on the head, left. I buzzed Frank on the intercom.

"Give me a break, Sam," he whined when I asked him to come get Princess. "I'm late as it is. You know we practice on Tuesday afternoons."

"Can it, Frank. Dr. Augustin pays you to work six hours a day, and I don't think he considers fooling around with

Tracey work." I heard him smack the wall with his hand, and Cynthia flinched. Me and my big mouth, I thought.

Frank turned off the intercom. I looked over at Cynthia, but she was busy punching keys on the computer terminal. She had a faint grin on her lips.

Suddenly Frank appeared in the doorway to the reception room. "That was a cheap shot, Samantha," he said, scowling at me. He walked over to Princess and lifted her up.

"You're right," I conceded. "I'm sorry. It's Dr. Augustin's fault. He's AWOL again." I followed Frank down the hall and was glad to see Tracey sitting on her stool in the lab gazing through the microscope. Maybe she hadn't heard me.

"Please give Princess a bath," I told Frank, "but don't put her in a dryer cage. Just towel her off, then put her on a blanket in a cage in Isolation."

Frank eased the dog down into the sink. Then, without saying anything, he reached for his rubber apron.

"Thanks," I said to his back.

He continued to ignore me. I shrugged and went back to the reception room.

Dr. Augustin had entered his manic phase when he finally rolled in at 3:15. The waiting room was full, but even that didn't seem to daunt him. I suspected that instead of spending his lunch hour (and then some) at City Hall, he had been in an alley someplace injecting himself with laudanum, or whatever.

"Okay," I began, after he had treated Princess and we were back on schedule, "why are you in such a good mood? And does it have anything to do with what you discovered at City Hall?"

He finished washing his hands, pulled a paper towel off the roll, and walked across the hall to his office.

"I had Melody do a little digging for me, and she came up with something very interesting about the Northeast Recreation Complex site."

He tossed the towel in the trash can by his desk and sat down.

So, I thought, it wasn't Demerol. It was a redhead. I went over to the daybed.

Dr. Augustin picked up a small notebook and flipped it open. "From 1910 to 1952, the land the rec center is on was the site of the city's gas plant."

I blinked. "Gas plant?"

"For streetlights and various industrial purposes, the City generated gas from coal. Coke, actually. Now they use electricity and natural gas."

"So?"

Dr. Augustin frowned. "Sooo, the process of generating gas from coke results in numerous waste by-products, not the least of which is coal tar."

"But you said the plant was in operation until 1952. That's almost fifty years ago. Why is tar showing up on the site now?"

He tossed the notebook back on his desk. "Possibly because of the construction of that parking lot. I expect there was quite a mess left over when the site was closed down. Back then, nobody gave a damn about the environment or proper waste disposal. They probably just covered everything over, tar and all."

"I thought you said a little tar on their feet wouldn't cause those dogs to develop aplastic anemia."

"That's not what I said, Samantha. What I said was, a single run-in with a bone marrow-suppressing chemical probably wouldn't cause aplastic anemia. That it was more likely due to chronic exposure."

I chewed on a fingernail. "So what do we do now?"

"Wait for the results of those samples I sent to Bob. And see what additional information we can dredge up on the rec center site." He smiled suddenly. " 'Dredge up.' Good choice of words, don't you think?"

I grimaced. "You need to look at Randy. Frank says he's been squinting. I think Katie may have nailed him."

Dr. Augustin looked over at me. "Listen, I'm sorry I left you here alone until three."

"Three-fifteen," I corrected.

"Okay, I'm sorry I left you alone until three-fifteen. I got involved with this gas plant thing and lost track of the time."

Yeah, I thought, I'll bet you got involved.

He stood up. "Bring Randy to the treatment room, and I'll check his eye." He was all business again.

CHAPTER 23

•

Thursday, October 21

Randy had conjunctivitis, exact cause unknown, although by the time we got around to examining him Tuesday afternoon, the kitten had started to sneeze. Sneezing cats and coughing dogs terrify Dr. Augustin. The last thing we need in the clinic is an outbreak of some highly contagious upper respiratory infection. So Dr. Augustin had me give all of our feline boarders a booster vaccination. And I moved Randy and Katie into Isolation.

By Thursday, Randy was worse. His nose was runny, and his eyes were weepy. Katie looked fine. She seemed pleased that her brother was feeling a little "under the weather." She had taken possession of the rubber ball. I could see it peeking out from between her front legs.

At 12:45 Bob called from Gainesville. Dr. Augustin immediately went into his office and closed the door. He was still in there when Mrs. Westphall came to get Princess. She said she was on her lunch hour, so I brought her dog up to Room 1 and knocked on Dr. Augustin's door.

"Tell her I'll call her this evening," he said. He had his hand over the mouthpiece.

I went back to the exam room. "As you can see, Mrs. Westphall," I said, "Princess is a lot better. Dr. Augustin wants you to keep her inside for a few days, though."

181

The dog was sitting on the exam-room floor, looking up at her mistress with what I interpreted as faint suspicion.

"Did you find out anything from those blood tests?" Mrs. Westphall asked.

She was staring back at Princess, with the same suspicious look in her eyes, as though the dog was going to give her something. Typhoid or plague, maybe.

"The results came back late yesterday," I said. "Dr. Augustin and I have been too busy today to discuss them. He said to tell you he'll give you a call this evening and go over them with you then."

I opened the exam-room door, and Princess stood up.

"Please have him speak with Dick," Mrs. Westphall said. "It's *his* dog. Anyway, all that technical business—I'm afraid I wouldn't understand a word of it." She took the dog's leash from me, and the two of them went out into the hall. "Thank you, again, Miss Holt."

I nodded. "Don't forget, now," I said, "keep Princess indoors."

She looked briefly at the dog, then at me. "If you feel it's absolutely necessary," she said.

"For now, yes."

I could tell the thought of having a dog in the house did not appeal to the woman. She raised and lowered her shoulders in a kind of wistful shrug, then continued on into the reception area.

I put our two o'clock client in Room 2 and went into the lab. Tracey was bent over her microscope. A tidy little row of brown paper lunch bags and margarine tubs and aspirin bottles sat on the counter. Cynthia had written "Bobbi" and "Spanky" and "Squeaky" on the containers. I noticed the exhaust fan was running, and the room reeked of citrus air freshener mingled with doggie doo.

Tracey turned around on her stool. She wasn't smiling. "Frank told me what you said to him Tuesday."

I was in the process of pouring myself a cup of coffee. I

stopped and put the coffeepot back on the burner. "I was out of line, Tracey. I told him I was sorry."

"You're just jealous, Sam, because your boyfriend is in New York. That doesn't mean you have to pick on Frank and me." She spun back around and pulled the slide she'd been studying from under the microscope. She paused, wrote something in her log, then tossed the slide into the container by the sink.

"I am not jealous," I snapped. "And Michael is not my boyfriend. He's just a friend. I don't have a boyfriend!"

"All the more reason to be jealous," Tracey said, almost jubilantly.

"Oh, for crying out loud!"

Just then, Dr. Augustin's door opened, and he looked in. "Knock it off, you two." He pointed his right index finger at me and waggled it. "Come in here for a minute, Samantha."

I went into his office.

"Close the door," he said. He sat down at his desk and picked up a sheet of notepaper.

I did as he asked. I expected him to yell at me for engaging in mudslinging with the help, but he apparently had more important things on his mind.

"Bob analyzed those samples we sent him." He let his words hang in the air like a carrot on a stick.

"And . . . ?"

"And I think I know why John Deland's dogs are developing aplastic anemia."

I sat down in the chair next to his desk.

"Bob found several polynuclear aromatic hydrocarbons— naphthalene, mainly."

"As in mothballs?" I asked.

"He nodded.

"Those dogs are getting sick from wading in mothballs?"

Dr. Augustin looked at me and rolled his eyes. "No, Samantha," he said, feigning patience. "Please let me finish."

I leaned back in my chair. "We have clients," I said.

He glanced at his watch. "In a minute." He flapped a sheet of paper at me. "Bob also found benzopyrene, which is a chemical in coal tar related to naphthalene, but unlike naphthalene, in small quantities can cause cancer and birth defects. But what's *really* important, here, is he detected a trace of benzene in that glop you unearthed." His pupils were dilated, like a cat's eyes just before it pounces. "As you know, benzene is a highly volatile organic solvent and evaporates rapidly in air. The little bit he found in our sample means there's probably a lot of it under the soil in that tar residue.

"My guess is that the tar was disturbed when they excavated for that rec center and, after the paving addition, started seeping up and running into the retention pond. Which explains the dead fish and birds. The dogs up there are probably ingesting benzene and God knows what all when they dig around next to that picnic area."

He put the sheet of paper in his top drawer. "Short-term exposure to benzene causes neurological disturbances. Dizziness, headache, shortness of breath, staggering, and tremors. It can also cause cardiac irregularities. Long-term exposure to benzene can cause aplastic anemia and leukemia."

"Why didn't somebody do a little research before that rec center was constructed?" I asked. "You know—find out about the gas plant and dig all that junk out of there?"

"Chances are, nobody thought about it. You weren't here when construction started on the Thunderdome down in St. Petersburg. They had the same problem there—the site had been a coal gasification plant. Construction had to be halted, while crews dug out a lot of contaminated soil. Nobody foresaw that one either."

Cynthia knocked on the door, then opened it a crack. "It's almost two-thirty," she said. "We're running out of chairs here."

Unless someone had put a sign up out front advertising

free rabies shots, Cynthia was exaggerating just a wee bit. But she got her point across. Dr. Augustin stood up.

"I'd like to look at some of the data the City took at the rec center site prior to construction. Core borings in particular. See if the tar was evident back then."

Oh, great, I thought. In Michael's absence, Dr. Augustin will want me to search through the files in City Hall. Then I remembered Melody, and pouring over engineering drawings and tables didn't seem like such a bad idea after all.

"Let's talk about this later," he said.

Sergeant Robinson dropped by at five. He was alone, unfortunately. It would have been fun to see Tom again.

"Thought I'd bring you folks up-to-date on our investigation," he said.

Again I wondered why he was being so chummy with a lay person. Dr. Augustin looked pleased, though, and indicated his office. The detective went with him.

The waiting room was empty, and Cynthia was at her desk. She raised her eyebrows a notch, then turned back to her computer terminal. I could feel the chill her silence was generating. I knew it would quickly become an arctic blast if I didn't fill her in before the day was out. I sighed, went into Dr. Augustin's office, and closed the door.

"Our forensics people analyzed the powder residue on Trexler's body," Robinson said. "It matches the powder residue on Lanier perfectly." He loosened his tie.

He'd elected to sit on the daybed, so I sat down in the chair next to Dr. Augustin's desk.

"They were killed with the same gun?" I asked.

"Not necessarily," said Robinson. "The gunpowder is the same, which means the ammunition came from the same source. The bullets could have been fired from the same rifle. Or from different rifles. Without the bullet that killed Trexler, though, we can't be sure."

Dr. Augustin was fiddling with the handle on his gumball machine. He switched to a loose screw on the arm of his

chair. Worry stones and pet rocks were invented for people
like him.

"Did you find anything out about those wood shavings?"
he asked. Apparently aware that I was looking at his hands,
he clasped them over his stomach.

"Poplar," said Robinson. "Eastern poplar, to be exact.
Grows all over the eastern U.S. I found out building contractors use a lot of it. We've checked with area lumber
yards. There's a surge of new home construction going on
right now, especially in the northeastern section of the
county. So there's no easy way to trace those shavings to a
particular contractor, let alone some do-it-yourselfer. No,
whoever built Trexler's coffin, assuming there was a coffin,
won't be ID'd from the type of wood he used."

A dog barked out in the waiting room.

Dr. Augustin checked his watch. "Looks like our last
client of the day is here, Samantha."

I got up and headed for the door.

"By the way, Miss Holt," Robinson began, "Detective
Hummer said to tell you hello."

Dr. Augustin's reaction was swift. He stood up, drew his
eyebrows together, then looked at me and dipped his head in
the direction of the reception room. "You'll have to excuse
us, Pete, but duty calls."

"Of course," the sergeant said. Then, as I was about to
open the door, he cleared his throat. "You realize, the press
doesn't know about the wood shavings," he said. "We'd like
to keep it that way. At least for now." He waited.

Dr. Augustin nodded. "No problem," he said. "Right,
Samantha?"

"Right," I said.

Sergeant Robinson did not appear totally convinced, but
he smiled anyway and followed me out into the reception
room.

At six I went into Isolation to check on Randy. Katie
was curled up next to him. She opened her eyes. They

looked so cute—Randy all puffed up and squinty-eyed, his sister still healthy but lending whatever comfort cats are capable of.

"Give it a week, Samantha," said Dr. Augustin from the doorway. "He'll be fine. He was vaccinated. Really, it looks worse than it is."

I knew that, I said to myself. I picked up Randy's rubber ball and stuffed it back in the cage. Katie watched me but stayed where she was.

"Let's assume," I said, turning around, "that both men were shot by the same person. I can see why Lanier might be dangerous to have around. He probably found the contamination in that retention pond. Maybe he saw some of those dead fish or a dead bird lying nearby. Or he took some water samples and had them analyzed. I mean, that was his job, right? But how does Billy Trexler fit into all this? A surveyor for the power company. What could he possibly know or do that might incriminate the killer?"

Dr. Augustin looked at me, his face registering mild surprise. Like only he was capable of deductive reasoning.

"Well?" I asked, my voice unintentionally brusque.

He went over to one of the top cages, opened it, and extracted a little Pekingese who'd gotten into some rat poison the previous week and almost bled to death. She was looking a lot better, thanks to numerous blood transfusions and multiple injections of vitamin K.

"I haven't a clue," he said.

Now *I* was surprised. Lack of data had never stopped him from jumping to conclusions before. At least not where criminal activity was concerned.

"It's possible that we're dealing with two different and unrelated cases here," he said. "Pete did say that the police haven't been able to prove the same rifle was used to kill both men."

He took his stethoscope off the wall and listened to the dog's chest. Then he peered in her mouth and eyes. "Have Tracey run another PCV on her," he said.

He put the Pekingese back in her cage and shut the door.
Then he leaned against the wall and smiled at me. His eyes
were piercing. I could feel the color start to rise in my neck,
so I went over to the sink and began washing my hands.

"I think we should notify Mr. Halsey about Randy's condition, don't you?" he asked.

"You told me he was going to be fine," I said. "That it
looked worse than it really was."

"Yes, that's true. But I would certainly want to know if
my pet were sick, wouldn't you?"

"Never trust a smiling cat." Now where had I heard that
expression? It certainly fit Dr. Augustin to a tee. At that moment Randy and Michael were the furthest things from his
mind.

I turned around. "He's busy up there in New York, dealing with some urgent family matters," I said quickly. "I
don't want to bother him, if it isn't absolutely necessary."
My voice was giving me away.

Dr. Augustin's smile broadened. "You haven't heard from
him since he left, have you? And I'll bet he didn't leave you
a number where he can be reached, either."

"I certainly *do* have his number," I snapped.

"Good," said Dr. Augustin. "You can call him and ask him
to get one of his reporter buddies at the *Times* to help us. I
need to know as much as possible about William Trexler.
Who his friends were, where he spent his free time, who his
ex-wife was."

He hung his stethoscope back on its peg and went out into
the hall. He stopped and looked over his shoulder.

"Oh, and Samantha," he said, his voice low, "I don't need
to remind you that all of this is hush-hush. See if Halsey can
come up with someone who knows the meaning of 'Off the
record.' "

He didn't even wait for me to snap my heels together.

CHAPTER 24

•

I sat on my bed and stared at the phone. Tiny tooth marks dotted the cord. The handset had a hairline crack in it. During her early adolescence, Tina had evidently found the phone fascinating. She'd done in my other extension. Lately, though, she and Miss Priss had taken an interest in the pull cord on my vertical blinds. I could hear clanking noises coming from the living room.

I stared at the phone some more and thought about what I would say and how I would say it. I prayed Michael wouldn't ask me how I came to have his number. If he called his office and spoke to the girl who'd given it to me and if he talked to Cynthia . . . That's the trouble with lying, I thought. You have to cover all your bases.

I unfolded the scrap of paper I'd written Michael's telephone numbers on, then picked up the receiver. The time had come. I dialed the first number.

After several agonizing seconds, a child's voice answered.

"Hello?" he asked. At least, I was pretty sure it was a "he."

"Hello," I said. "My name is Samantha Holt. Is Michael Halsey there?"

"Who?"

"Michael Halsey. He's visiting from Florida. You know, where Disneyworld is." Maybe I had the wrong number.

"Minute," said the child.

A loud clunk was followed closely by "*Mom! Phone!*" I could hear Bugs Bunny talking in the background.

Tina ambled into the room and hopped up on the bed. She began eyeing the telephone cord.

Cobwebs were forming over my hand and the telephone, and my ear was growing numb. "I'll have to take out a loan to pay my phone bill after this," I told Tina. I could almost see the little digital readout, or whatever the phone company used, whizzing along, the seconds turning into minutes, the minutes into hours. The kid's mother obviously hadn't heard him or she was indisposed. And the child, having done his duty, was back watching cartoons, the phone, and me, forgotten. I should hang up, I thought.

Then I heard a woman's voice, Dorothy's voice, I was pretty sure, and another clunk as she picked up the receiver.

"Christopher!" she said sternly. "How many times have I told you not to play with this phone? What if someone needed to reach me?"

The line went dead.

I waited for a short time, as if the connection might suddenly, miraculously, reestablish itself. Then I hung up. "Damn!" I said. Tina put her ears down and arched her back.

I picked up the phone and tried again, this time dialing the second number.

"Yes?"

It was Michael. The sound of his voice and the suddenness of it rendered me temporarily mute.

"Hello?"

"Michael," I said, "it's Samantha."

He drew in a sharp breath. "Samantha! What a wonderful surprise! I was beginning to worry that something had happened to my favorite veterinary technician."

Well, I said to myself, you have a strange way of showing it. "I thought you were going to call me," I said to him.

"I tried. Believe me. Saturday night, Sunday afternoon, Monday night. You always seem to be out."

My my, do I detect a note of irritation? I asked myself. Perhaps even a little jealousy?

"You need an answering machine, Samantha," he said. "I thought about calling the hospital, but you people are always so busy there. Although I would have enjoyed a nice chat with Cynthia." His thyroid was in high gear.

"So," he continued, "how are my kittens?"

"Randy has a cold," I said. "It's nothing to worry about, at least not right now. But I thought you should be aware of it."

"Thank you. But I'm not worried, because I'm sure he's getting the very best possible care." When I didn't say anything, he went on. "And how are you doing, Samantha? Working too hard, I'll wager. And skipping meals." He paused. "I promise to take you to Tuttles as soon as I get back."

"When *are* you coming home?"

"I plan to be here another week, ten days at the most. I'm trying to wrap up a few things. Financial obligations, mostly. Why? Do you miss me?"

"Of course, Michael. We all do."

I knew it wasn't exactly what he'd wanted to hear. He was silent.

"Do you remember that dead guy Dr. Augustin and I stumbled across out in the woods east of Carriage Hill?" I asked.

"Yes."

There was no doubt about it. Michael was disappointed, even more so now that he knew the real reason for my call.

"William Trexler," I said. "A surveyor for the power company. He was shot with a hunting rifle, just like Jack Lanier—you remember, that man the police found in the fire at the Municipal Services Building?"

"I remember."

"Well, there's a chance the same gun was used to kill both of them. The problem is, Dr. Augustin can't figure out what the connection between the two men was, if there was a connection. He wants to know if you would be willing to suggest somebody down here who can help us dig up some information on Trexler."

"Let me see what I can find out and I'll call you."

He didn't sound very happy about being involved in another one of Dr. Augustin's investigations, which surprised me. He usually jumped at the chance.

"Wouldn't it be better if one of your coworkers at the *Times* did the digging?" I asked. "I mean, you'll have to make a bunch of long-distance calls, won't you?"

"I said I'll do it, Samantha."

It was the first time Michael had ever been short with me. In fact, I couldn't remember ever seeing or hearing him angry at anyone. Well, except for the inept *Times* staff, and that was more a case of frustration than anger.

"I'll call you tomorrow night," he said. "Around seven-thirty."

"I'll be home." I tried to sound cheery. "And I'm going to hold you to that dinner invitation."

"It's a date, then," he said halfheartedly. Then he cleared his throat. "Listen, I have to go. I'll talk to you tomorrow, Samantha."

"All right," I said. "Till tomorrow."

He didn't say good-bye or tell me he loved me or ask me to give Cynthia and the kittens a hug for him. So why did I feel let down? Wouldn't it be better if he didn't love me? I asked myself. Then we could be friends without any strings. Right?

I sat on my bed and watched Tina chew on the telephone cord.

CHAPTER 25

•

Friday, October 22

At 8:05 the phone rang. I was in the surgery, so Cynthia got it. Almost immediately she called me on the intercom.

"Samantha," she said, "it's Dr. Augustin. For you."

I shut the door to the autoclave and picked up the extension. "Hello?"

"Sam, I won't be in until ten. What have we got this morning? Anything that can't wait until lunch?"

"No, I guess not," I said. "A spay/declaw. A tumor removal on that twenty-year-old Pomeranian. Both of them will be staying the night, anyway. Oh, and a tooth extraction."

"Good. We'll do them at noon. I'm going to see if I can locate the results of those core borings and any other useful data on that rec center site."

"I kind of figured you'd ask *me* to do that," I said. Was I actually disappointed?

"And I figured you'd grind your teeth and act huffy if I did. Besides, why should you have all the fun?"

I ground my teeth.

"Hold the fort down, Samantha. And if Sergeant Robinson happens to call before I get back, ask him if poplar is used for interior moldings and staircases."

"Why?"

"Just ask him. I'll see you at ten." He hung up.

193

Moldings and staircases. Dick Westphall specializes in interior woodwork, I thought. Surely Dr. Augustin doesn't suspect Dick. And even if the Horseman's Association is somehow involved in Trexler's death, what possible reason would they (and Mr. Westphall, in particular) have for killing Lanier?

I put the surgical supplies back in the cabinet and went to tell Cynthia and Tracey about the change in schedule.

At 9:30 Tanya Cummings drove up in her white Ford pickup (complete with pink neon lights under the chassis and around her license plate) and got out.

"Looky who's here," I said to Cynthia. "Won't Dr. Augustin be sorry he missed her?"

Cynthia took one look at Tanya and went back to her filing.

Tanya was dressed, as usual, in skintight jeans—the kind you have to zip up while lying flat on your back. Or possibly, she put them on wet, then walked around for a couple of hours while they dried. In any event, they so severely restricted her abdomen that her chest had to do all the work of breathing. Which was probably intentional, anyway.

Her T-shirt (extra small) said HOT DOG VENDORS DO IT STANDING UP. Tanya was one of those infamous roadside wiener peddlers the City Commission had unsuccessfully tried to put out of business by requiring them to cover their buttocks. The law, in effect, says that to expose one's "anal cleft" is a no-no. It is clearly discriminatory, since at every football game and in a lot of suburban front yards in the summer, overweight men are regularly exposing their "anal clefts," no matter how unintentional the action is.

So Tanya and her buddies starting wearing flesh-colored tights under their T-backs. From ten feet away—the distance between Tanya's rear end and the nearest motorist zipping down the highway—you couldn't tell the difference.

There weren't any statistics regarding the number of accidents caused by gawking drivers (male or female). But all the free publicity in the newspaper had increased sales considerably, according to Tanya. Even straightlaced conservatives like Cynthia had to give the girls credit for their perseverance.

Tanya went around to the passenger side and helped her rottweiler, Oscar (for Oscar Mayer, presumably), out of the truck. The dog was obviously not feeling well. He could barely walk, and he hung his head glumly.

I hurried over to the door and opened it. Tanya, with some effort and a lot of encouraging words, finally made it into the reception room with her dog. Oscar collapsed in front of Cynthia's desk.

Cynthia handed me the Cummings file.

"What happened to him?" I asked Tanya. I couldn't see any tar on his legs or smell any paint thinner. Besides, Tanya lived on the beach, not up near the Northeast Recreation Complex.

"He stopped eating a couple of days ago," Tanya said. "I figured he was punishing me for leaving him cooped up in my apartment." She smiled at me. "I've been pretty busy lately." She looked back at Oscar. "Yesterday, he started vomiting. I thought all he had was an upset tummy. But he should have gotten over it by now, and he hasn't. And he's had a little diarrhea. Not much."

"Do you think he might have gotten into something?" I asked. "Eaten something he shouldn't have?" I checked his vaccination record. He was up-to-date on all his shots.

Tanya frowned. "He chews a lot. When he gets bored. Shoes, mostly. And he tore up one of my stuffed animals a couple of months ago."

"So, it's possible he swallowed something," I said. "Is anything missing? Jewelry? Sewing stuff? Yarn, maybe?"

She shook her head. "He's going to be all right, isn't he?"

She attempted to kneel down beside her dog, but gave it up. Cynthia, I noticed, made no effort to hide her amusement. Fortunately, Tanya wasn't facing her.

"Dr. Augustin had to step out for a short time, but he'll be back. I'm going to move Oscar to one of our treatment rooms, where he'll be more comfortable." I looked over at Cynthia, and she buzzed Frank on the intercom.

"Why don't you go on home," I said. "I'll have Dr. Augustin give you a call as soon as he examines Oscar."

After Tanya had undulated her buttocks out to her truck and driven off, Frank and I muscled Oscar's ninety-odd pounds into Isolation. We put him on a cage pad on the floor. He wasn't going anywhere, that was pretty apparent. And I didn't want to risk infecting the boarders in the kennel, in case Oscar did have something contagious. Like parvo. Frank used half a bottle of antiseptic soap on his arms and hands and threw his T-shirt into the trash.

At ten our first appointment of the morning arrived. It was a suture removal, so I took care of it, and the client left. Our 10:15 was an eye recheck, something Dr. Augustin would have to see personally, so I put the dog and her owner in a room and crossed my fingers.

Oscar was holding his own. I'd hooked him up to an IV and was administering fluids, but could do little else until Dr. Augustin arrived. If the dog started to go downhill, I would have to get help from someplace.

At 10:30 I went up to the reception room.

"If he's not here in fifteen minutes," I told Cynthia, "call Dr. Wilson. See if he'll come over and fill in."

Cynthia looked up from her computer screen. "You really want to do that?" she asked. "Dr. Augustin will not be pleased."

"To hell with Dr. Augustin!" I shouted. "*I'm* not pleased. He has obligations *here,* not at City Hall or wherever. *Here!*"

Cynthia stared at me like I had suddenly been beset by demons. I smoothed down the collar on my uniform top and stuck out my chin.

"In fact," I said, a little more calmly, "let's not wait. Let's call Larry right now."

She didn't move.

"*Now*, Cynthia." I turned and stomped out of the room, nearly running over Tracey. "What are *you* staring at?" I snapped and then, before she could respond, hurried into the bathroom and slammed the door.

Larry Wilson had been in charge of the local emergency clinic for a little over a year. The E-clinic is open at night and on weekends. They see hit-by-cars, mostly, and ailing or injured pets who have suddenly shown up at their homes after being lost or missing for several days.

A lot of veterinarians fresh out of school get stuck working at emergency clinics. It's like making medical residents and interns do a stint or two in a hospital emergency room. Trial by fire, I call it. You learn a lot, and they say you develop a tolerance for stress. Which is what I was counting on.

When Larry drove up at eleven, our 10:15 and 10:30 clients were in the process of leaving. The eye recheck was particularly put-out that Dr. Augustin was in absentia. And Larry agreed that Dr. Augustin should probably look at her poodle, since he'd done the surgery. So the woman left in a huff.

Our 10:30 was an elderly gentleman who didn't care who treated his dog, at long as someone did. I was relieved. One for two wasn't bad. Of course, the day was young.

At 11:30 we had a few minutes, so I told Larry about Oscar.

"I'll take a look at him," said Larry. "If it is an obstruction, we'll need a couple of radiographs to pinpoint it. How cooperative is this wiener dog of yours?"

I smiled. Dr. Wilson is a little guy, about five-six, one hundred thirty pounds. He employees a very husky male technician at the E-clinic to deal with large dogs.

"If you're thinking Oscar is a dachshund," I said, "I hate to disappoint you. He's a ninety-pound rottweiler."

Dr. Wilson was at the sink washing his hands. He looked

over his shoulder at me and frowned. "Terrific," he said. "So how cooperative is this ninety-pound rottweiler?"

We took two radiographs of Oscar's abdomen. Even without contrast media, they showed a blockage low in his small intestine.

"It may be a foreign body," said Dr. Wilson. "Hard to tell."

He peered up at the view box on the wall in X-ray. It was at eye level—Dr. Augustin's eyes.

"I don't think it's a tumor," he said. "And there doesn't appear to be any perforation. No free gas or fluid. We need to get in there, though." He removed the radiograph and turned off the light. "Starting him on fluids as soon as he came in was exactly right, Sam. Good job."

Dr. Augustin is not a strong advocate of "attaboys." If I *hadn't* started Oscar on fluids, I'd have heard about it. I smiled gratefully at Larry.

We saw one more client, a woman who I knew for a fact came to our clinic to ogle Dr. Augustin. She looked extremely disappointed when Cynthia told her Dr. Wilson, instead of Dr. Augustin, would be examining her cat. Her makeup and hair clearly indicated a lengthy preparation time. But the cat was evidently important to her. And she was obviously flexible. I heard her ask Cynthia if Dr. Wilson was married.

Later, as Larry and I were getting ready for Oscar's surgery, Dr. Augustin walked into the surgery.

"Well, now," he said. "What have we here?"

It was hard to tell his mood from his voice, but his eyes were smoldering. I continued to lay out supplies and equipment, undaunted by the prospect of unemployment.

"Greetings Lou," said Larry.

Either he hadn't noticed the sudden fall in the room's barometric pressure or it didn't concern him. After all, it wasn't *his* job at stake.

"Samantha tends to overreact at times," said Dr. Augustin. "I'm sorry she got you out of bed."

"No problem, Lou. I was already up, anyway."

He stuck the radiograph in the view box next to the refrigerator and flipped on the light."

"Oscar, here, has a probable foreign body obstruction," said Larry. "I was about to go in there and check it out. I assume you'd like to do the honors."

Dr. Augustin joined Larry at the view box and together they studied the radiograph. I retreated, once again, into the bathroom.

When I came out, Dr. Augustin was on his way down the hall. He stopped.

"Larry is going to assist me, Samantha," he said. He hesitated. "I'm sorry I was late getting back." Then he smiled— a crooked half smile I couldn't interpret. "Gee, I seem to remember saying that earlier this week. Anyway, you were smart to call Larry." He turned back around and quickly disappeared into Isolation.

Wow, I thought. An "attaboy" and an apology both in the same day. Aren't I the lucky one?

The surgery on Oscar was going well, apparently. Since Larry was assisting, I was free to do other things. Like stay out of Dr. Augustin's way. I could hear them laughing and carrying on, though, like a couple of adolescent males with a dog-eared copy of *Playboy*. Curiosity finally overcame me, and I stepped into the doorway between the surgery and Isolation.

"What's so funny?" I asked.

Dr. Augustin and Larry locked eyes briefly. I knew they were grinning under their masks.

"We'll need to show Ms. Cummings the cause of her dog's illness, Samantha," said Dr. Augustin. "Would you be so kind as to clean it up and drop it into a specimen jar?"

He indicated the sink. I went over to it, expecting to see the remains of a shoe or teddy bear. Instead, I found several little square packages, most of them empty or riddled with tooth marks, and a small pile of condoms, apparently unused.

"Don't you agree that Ms. Cummings should be informed about the hazards of leaving small objects lying around?"

Larry giggled, and I quickly turned on the water.

Larry stuck around for the tumor removal, then left. It was almost two. Our first client of the afternoon was Glynnis Winter. Frosty was still scratching, despite the fact that the carpet had been cleaned. At least that's what Mrs. Winter claimed.

"We'll have to do that spay/declaw tonight," said Dr. Augustin. He threw his dental instruments into the sink and began washing his hands.

I carried the Yorkie to a recovery cage. "Did you locate any of the data collected out at the rec center site?" I asked. "I mean, you were certainly gone long enough." He was gone long enough, I told myself, to take the damned borings himself.

"Give it a rest, Samantha. I said I was sorry. Again. What do you want? An apology written in blood?"

Well, I thought, that's a start.

He dried his hands, then went over to the corner of the room, where Oscar lay on a cage pad. The dog was awake, but groggy. He rolled an eye up at Dr. Augustin and halfheartedly wagged his stump of a tail.

"All the physical and chemical data Jack collected were in the files on the third floor of the Municipal Services Building," said Dr. Augustin. "Needless to say, everything was lost in the fire. Convenient, huh?"

He checked the Yorkie's mouth. "I did find out that the original core borings were taken and analyzed by Sand Lake Testing Laboratory. It's located in St. Petersburg. I have the address on my desk." He closed the Yorkie's cage. "I'd like you to go down there and see if you can get a copy of the original test results. Surely Sand Lake keeps that information around. For a few years, at least. It's probably on disk."

"They're not going to release that information voluntarily, are they?"

He shook his head. "No, probably not. But I'm counting on you to sweet-talk it out of somebody. Go during lunch Monday."

I sighed. "Sure," I said.

"By the way, Samantha, did you talk to Mr. Halsey last night?"

"*Mister* Halsey? I thought you considered Michael a friend. Mr. Halsey sounds like a client, not a friend."

Dr. Augustin moistened a paper towel and began to scrub the top of the autoclave, which was already one step away from sterile, it was so clean.

"Yes," I admitted, finally, "he said he'd see what he could find out about Trexler and call me."

Dr. Augustin switched his attention to the countertop next to the sink. That really ticked me off, since he'd watched me clean it only moments earlier.

"Good," he said. "This case is really starting to bug me."

Gosh, I thought, I never would have guessed.

CHAPTER 26

•

I didn't get home until 8:15. We had a couple of walk-ins who put us even more behind than normal, and then there was the spay/declaw. In the rush to get everything done and all the animals medicated, I completely forgot about Michael. It wasn't until I put my key in the door that I remembered his 7:30 call.

I threw some food at Tina and Miss Priss, mostly to shut them up so I could use the phone, then quickly dialed Michael's number. I let it ring a good ten times, then slammed the receiver down in disgust.

I had fallen asleep in front of the TV. The volume was low, fortunately, or I wouldn't have heard the phone at all. I ran into the bedroom.

"Hello?"

"Samantha," Michael said. "I was about to give up on you."

I sat down and rubbed my eyes. The clock on my end table read 11:20.

"I didn't get off work until eight," I said. "I'm sorry. I called you as soon as I got home, but you were out someplace."

"I had a dinner engagement." He paused. "Listen, how would you like to join me up here for a couple of days? The weather is beautiful, and a lot of the trees still have their color. Just say the word, and I'll have a ticket waiting for you at the airport."

"I can't, Michael. I work tomorrow. I can't just take off and leave Dr. Augustin without a technician. You know that." No matter how much Dr. Augustin deserved it, and never mind the fact that Tracey could cover for me.

Michael didn't say anything.

"Thanks, though. It would be nice to visit New York, again. Maybe do a little shopping."

Truth was, I longed to see rolling hills, smell the smoke from a wood-burning stove, hear the melancholy loons on Tapestry Pond. But most of all, I needed a vacation from Louis Augustin, PI.

"Think of all the restaurants we could visit," he added.

"Michael . . ."

"Sorry," he said. Then he cleared his throat. "I did some calling around today and found out that William Trexler worked for Peninsular Power Company for five years prior to his unfortunate end. As a surveyor.

"He'd been married twice. The first time to Shirley Rhoades. She was killed in 1989 in an automobile accident. Mr. Trexler was driving, but the police determined that he wasn't at fault.

"His second marriage ended last year in divorce. No children by either woman.

"Other than that, I couldn't find out much about his personal life. He was a sport fisherman and had a twenty-three-foot Proline moored at the Brightwater Beach Marina. No criminal record, other than a couple of traffic tickets. Interestingly, he had a thirty-thirty Winchester, registered in his name."

"Where is it?" I asked.

"The rifle? No one knows. Or the police aren't saying."

I opened the drawer to my end table and took out a notepad and pencil. "First wife died in 1989. Divorced second wife last year. Owned a boat and thirty-thirty Winchester rifle. Anything else? Where did he work before the electric company hired him?"

"Brightwater Beach Engineering Department. Again, as a surveyor. They hired him right out of school. He graduated from Gaither High, in Tampa, by the way. I couldn't find out why he left the City's employ and went to work for the power company. Better pay, possibly. His personnel file at the City was unavailable. I did discover that he'd been promoted to crew chief a year before he quit."

I made a few more notes. "Anything else?"

"No. Sorry. I'm hampered a bit by having to do my poking around over the phone."

"Hey, this is great, Michael. Really. Dr. Augustin had better be pleased or he'll hear about it from me." I chose my next words carefully. "If he has any additional questions, though, would it be all right if I called your friend Chip?"

Michael was silent. I could hear him breathing.

"Michael?"

"I'd really rather you didn't, Samantha. I don't want to involve anyone else in this. And besides, Chip doesn't have access to my resources, so it probably wouldn't do you any good to contact him, anyway."

"Okay," I said. It continued to dog me—the feeling that Michael didn't want his coworkers at the *Times* to know about me. Or, in Chip's case, to speak with me in his absence. What was Michael so afraid of?

"Listen, it's late, Samantha. I'll let you go. But would you do something for me?"

"Sure, Michael. What is it?"

"Think about my offer. The hospital is closed Wednesday. You could fly up Tuesday night and fly back late Wednesday. Maybe Dr. Augustin would be willing to let you take Thursday off, which would be even better."

"I'll think about it," I said. "But you're coming home next weekend, aren't you? I'll see you then."

"Hopefully," he said. "But I'd like to show you around

here. Take you upstate to see some property I'm thinking
about buying. As an investment. I'd like your opinion."

"I'll think about it."

"Good. I'll call you Sunday evening. Say eight o'clock?"

Later, as I was eating leftovers from Freddy's, I thought
about Michael's invitation. Clearly there was more to it than
the fact that he missed me or wanted my opinion on a potential investment opportunity.

"As I see it, he wants my opinion on that piece of property," I told Miss Priss, who was sitting at my feet, making
little chirping noises and drooling lightly, "because he has
plans for it, and those plans involve me. He is thinking about
moving back to New York and he wants me to go with him."

Priss squinted and pawed my knee.

"Well," I told her, "there isn't any question is there? Dr.
Augustin needs me here to help him solve this case. Right?"

Miss Priss opened her mouth and let out a tiny "Mew."

"Okay, okay," I said. "So maybe Michael doesn't have a
corner on the scaredy-cat market."

CHAPTER 27

•

Saturday, October 23

I heard Cynthia click her tongue disapprovingly and stuck my head out of the supply closet.

Tanya Cummings was on her way across the parking lot. She was dressed for the second leg of a triathlon—black spandex bicycle shorts, white Fuji T-shirt, helmet, gloves, and bicycle shoes. The T-shirt was a couple of sizes too large, but she had solved that problem by tying the lower edge in a knot. This allowed her freedom of movement and us a chance to admire her perfectly toned tummy.

She propped the bike up against the wall and took off her gloves and helmet, tossing her shoulder-length beach-bunny blond hair into the wind.

"She's here to visit Oscar," I said to Cynthia. "Have her wait, and I'll make certain he's presentable."

Cynthia looked down her nose at the trim muscular body in black and white, but didn't say anything. I wasn't sure if she'd heard about the condoms. It *was* possible jealousy had colored Cynthia's opinion of Tanya just a bit. I hated to admit it, but I found her physique a little irritating myself. When she goes to the Moon, she probably orders steamed veggies and seltzer water, I thought, while everyone else is ordering curly fries and beer.

I smiled through the glass at Tanya. "At least in those shorts, she'll be able to kneel down beside Oscar," I said.

Cynthia frowned, and I left her to polish up her friendly receptionist skills alone.

"Well, it's obvious Trexler didn't commit suicide," said Dr. Augustin. "It's tough to shoot yourself in the back, particularly with a rifle. The question is, did he kill Jack Lanier and then get himself popped in retaliation? Or did someone take Trexler's gun and use it to kill both of them?"

We were in X-ray, doing a chest shot of a poodle with a chronic cough and a positive heartworm test. I went into the darkroom with the film cassette.

"You're assuming the same rifle was used on the two men and it was Trexler's rifle," I said through the door. I put the film in the automatic processor, reloaded the cassette, then opened the door.

"True," said Dr. Augustin. But the cops can't find the gun, which seems awfully suspicious to me."

The poodle was back on the floor, panting and coughing.

"Why do you suppose Sergeant Robinson failed to tell us about Trexler owning a thirty-caliber rifle? And why didn't he tell us the guy worked for the city?"

"Probably didn't know at the time."

Sure, I thought. If Michael can find it out in one day, all the way from New York, then the cops should be able to do it in a matter of minutes. At least the gun registration part. No—Sergeant Robinson is being very selective in what he tells Dr. Augustin. Enough to keep him happy, but not enough to undermine their investigation. Now, armed with what Michael has given us, Dr. Augustin is going to get the poor sergeant fired.

I took the finished radiograph out of the processor and handed it to Dr. Augustin. He stuck it under the clips on the viewing box.

"Nasty, nasty," he said, pointing to the heart's enlarged right ventricle and the bulging pulmonary arteries. He switched off the light and removed the radiograph. "Stick her in a cage in the kennel," he said, indicating the poodle. "I'll go tell the owner."

He met me in the hallway a few minutes later, and we went into his office.

"Have Tracey get a blood sample from that dog before lunch. The usual—CBC, chemical profile. And let's do a urinalysis and ECG. If everything looks more or less acceptable, we'll start treatment Monday or Tuesday."

"Do you still want me to pay Sand Lake Testing Laboratory a visit?" I asked.

Dr. Augustin glanced up from the notes he'd been making in the Wrylie file. "Naturally. We still need to find out if the City knew about that tar before the rec center was built. My guess is, they did. Or at least somebody did. Trexler probably discovered it when the site was being surveyed. Maybe he disapproved of the cover-up and that's why he quit."

Dr. Augustin took a penny out of his desk drawer and put it in the gumball machine. He turned the crank and a shiny green sphere dropped out. He popped it into his mouth and chewed thoughtfully for several seconds. His jaw muscles bulged. A pit bull should be so lucky, I thought.

"I wonder why Trexler was killed now," he said, "five years after the fact."

I heard Cynthia show our 11:30 client into an exam room. I turned to go.

"I wish I could remember what went on at the commission meeting when the plans for the rec center were first discussed. I can't believe I missed it."

I couldn't either.

"It must have come up when I was on vacation," he continued. "Anyway, at lunch I'll go request a transcript from that meeting. Or meetings. See who opposed the site or who might have had something to lose if the rec center was moved to an alternate location."

"This is Saturday," I said. "City Hall isn't open on Saturday."

"Oh, I'm confident I can find someone who's willing to put in a little overtime on the weekend," he said.

"No doubt," I replied sarcastically, "but Dr. Wilson isn't available to fill in for you."

Instead of snapping at me, however, he smiled, which surprised me.

"I've been thinking, Samantha," he said. "Larry told me he's tired of the emergency clinic. He wants to work normal hours and see more than half-dead creatures scraped up off the pavement." He paused. "How would you feel if Larry came to work here Tuesdays and Thursdays? In the afternoon. He wants to continue at the E-clinic for a few more months. That way he can ease into our routine and not lose any pay in the process."

And you can run around looking for clues, I thought, and be on time for commission meetings and soccer games.

"That would be nice," I said. "We all like Larry a lot." What I didn't say was it would be nice to work in a relaxed atmosphere, if only for a couple of afternoons a week.

"Great!" said Dr. Augustin. "I'll call and tell him he can start the beginning of November." He went back to his note writing.

I didn't move. "What about today?" I asked. "We have clients all afternoon."

He didn't even bother to look up. "No problem. I'll be back by two."

"Sure you will," I muttered and went through the lab and across the hall.

He was back at 1:30. I followed him into his office.

"What did you find out?"

Dr. Augustin sat down at his desk and opened the McDonald's bag he'd brought with him. I felt saliva begin to collect in my mouth. There is something Pavlovian about the sight of those golden arches, even on the side of a paper sack.

"Not exactly what I'd hoped for," he said. He opened his top drawer and took out a salt shaker. "Melody ran off a copy of the minutes from the meeting for me, but couldn't find the supporting documents. I'll have to go back Monday, I guess, if I feel it's necessary." He lifted a large order of fries out of the bag and shook the contents of the Dead Sea over them.

"The commissioners were aware that the land had been the site of the city's old gas plant. Core borings hadn't been taken, though. All they had were the preliminary surveys and the architect's renderings of the building and grounds."

He put a fry in his mouth, then took a Big Mac out of the bag. I swallowed. The odor of well-used cooking oil and special sauce was making me weak.

"The Parks Department guy pitched the rec center as a sort of land reclamation project," he said. "Turning something old and ugly into something beautiful. In actual fact, that land was the only piece the City owned up there. To buy private land would have been prohibitively expensive, given the Parks and Recreation Department's budget." He took a bite of the Big Mac and chewed.

"Why didn't someone mention the Thunderdome?" I asked. "Seems to me the risk of expensive clean-up would have worried those cost-conscious commissioners."

"The mayor did ask if there was a chance of finding toxic chemicals underground," he said, wiping his mouth. "But the City's engineering people assured her core borings would locate any contamination that might exist. And that all the data would be collected before final plans were drawn up."

"So, what did they do—approve the thing contingent on further study?" I asked.

He nodded. "Obviously, the borings didn't turn up anything. Or—someone made sure they didn't."

"The Parks Department would have had a lot to lose if the rec center couldn't be built there, don't you think?"

"I expect they'd have built it anyway," he said. "But not in that part of the county, where it was needed the most."

He took another bite of his sandwich, stuffed another fry

in his mouth, then wadded everything up and threw it in his trash can. It was almost two. I needed to finish midday treatments and get ready for the afternoon clients. I walked over to the door.

"Something else, Samantha," said Dr. Augustin suddenly. I stopped.

"I figure the tar started coming to the surface when they first excavated for the rec center. It was covered up again, and now the grading and drainage work they're doing for that parking lot extension has disturbed it a second time."

"Which means?"

"Which means that other than our killer, a few more people than just Jack Lanier and William Trexler know, or knew, about the tar and the runoff into the retention pond."

"Like the guy who took the core borings?"

"Yes," he said. "And the contractor doing the site excavation. And now the paving contractor. To name a few."

"So where do we go from here?" I asked. "Aside from my visit to Sand Lake Testing Laboratory, of course."

Dr. Augustin looked at his watch, then stood up. "I'm going to see what I can find out about that paving contractor." He grinned. "Don't you think our parking lot could do with a little resurfacing?"

CHAPTER 28

•

Jeffrey was leaning against the second-floor railing drinking a beer when I got home.

"I thought you were working, Jeffrey," I said. I opened my door and went inside. Jeffrey followed me.

"They hired a new guy who can't work Fridays, because he goes to a marriage counselor or something. So I volunteered to switch days off with him."

He turned on my TV and sat down on my recliner. I felt a tiny prickle of irritation. Jeffrey considers my apartment an extension of his apartment. Which is better than it used to be, I guess. Before he got a steady job, Jeffrey didn't have enough money to buy food, so my food was his food. Now he brings home leftovers from Freddy's, sometimes enough for the entire apartment building.

I fed the cats and changed my clothes. Then I went into the living room and sat down on the sofa. "I feel like going out for a beer, Jeffrey," I said. "Care to join me?"

He smiled. "Are you buying?"

"Yes, Jeffrey, I'm buying."

We took my car, because I value my life too much to ride in his. When Jeffrey first starts up, it sounds like a horse with a bad case of heaves and periodically belches giant clouds of noxious fumes out the tailpipe. The brakes work, but the bench seat isn't securely fastened to the floor and slides back and forth like a rowing machine.

"But it's a *classic,* Samantha," Jeffrey said to me when I told him I would rather walk over a bed of hot coals.

"Then it belongs in a museum, Jeffrey, not out on the road."

He didn't talk to me for a whole week. It was like I had slighted his best friend.

Woody's is a popular little café seated on the edge of an inlet known as Blind Pass, because from the Gulf you can't see it clearly. You have to know where it is and once you enter it, you have to make a sharp ninety-degree turn to the north. The current is swift and treacherous, and I am amazed more people returning from a day of fishing and drinking don't crash their boats against the rocks. I'm also amazed that the proprietor of Woody's hasn't incorporated this potential for marine disaster in his advertising campaign. Everybody loves a good disaster. To serve it up with a cold beer and a grouper sandwich would be paradise for sure.

The parking lot was full, so we left my car a block south of the place. It is a narrow street with very little room to pass even when there aren't any cars parked along the curb, and I am always afraid for my paint job. Of course, the parking lot at a beach bar probably isn't a whole lot safer.

Jeffrey disappeared inside to use the rest room, and I got us a table for two right next to the seawall. It was breezy and cool, and I was glad I had worn a sweatshirt. Several obvious northerners sat at a table across from me. They were wearing swimsuits and that boiled lobster look that is popular with tourists from Iowa and Michigan. I could almost feel the heat radiating from their bodies, and the smell of Noxzema was hard to miss.

The waitress came by and took my order. I wanted jalapeño poppers. I settled on u-peel-em shrimp, instead. An image of Tanya Cummings in her bicycle shorts was making me very calorie-conscious. But I drew the line at seltzer water.

Jeffrey came over and sat down, just as our beer arrived.
To keep it frosty, the bartender had dropped a Ziploc bag
filled with ice cubes into the pitcher.

"Those Canadians over there are going to be sorry tomorrow," Jeffrey said, pouring beer into two glasses.

"Why?"

"The guy with the Mickey Mouse ears was in the men's
room. His neck and arms are blistered," he said. "He told me
they were from Ontario. Attending some conference at the
Holiday Inn. He wanted to go back home with a tan. I told
him he shouldn't have tried to do it all in one day."

"He probably doesn't have more than a day or so," I said.
"Only executive types and rich retirees can afford to keep
houses here and up north."

"Speaking of which," said Jeffrey. "How's Michael? I
haven't seen him lately."

Jeffrey, bless his heart, had spared me from having to
bring the subject up myself. "He's still in New York. Taking
care of a personal matter."

I paused while our waitress delivered the shrimp, a couple of plates, and two little containers of drawn butter. Out
over the water, six pelicans in perfect formation, their wings
outstretched, their huge beaks tucked neatly in, floated
silently along like a border patrol on maneuvers. Whenever
their leader flapped, the rest of the troops flapped. When he
glided, they glided.

"He wants me to fly up there for a day or so," I said. "He
says he'll buy my ticket."

Jeffrey dug a handful of shrimp out of the basket and
dumped them on his plate. Then he slid over one of the butter dishes.

"You're going, of course," he said, expertly peeling a
shrimp.

"No, I'm not."

Jeffrey had the shrimp halfway to his mouth. His hand
stopped in midair, but his mouth remained open. He reminded me of a huge fish about to strike a lure.

"No? Why not?" He put the shrimp in his mouth and chewed. "If he's buying the ticket, where's the problem?"

It must be nice, I thought, to live in such a tidy world.

"It's not as simple as that, Jeffrey. The man has an ulterior motive."

Jeffrey winked, flashed his pearly whites at me, and reached for another shrimp.

"Not sex, Jeffrey," I said. "At least that's not his primary objective at the moment."

The Canadians were leaving. They had purchased Woody's caps made of gaudy Hawaiian print fabric with Woody's logo screen printed on the front, and everyone except the man with the Mickey Mouse ears was wearing theirs. I vowed never to buy another souvenir. At least nothing wearable.

"And what might that be?"

I refilled my beer glass. "I'm relatively certain he's going to move back to New York and wants me to join him."

"How do you know that?" Jeffrey asked.

I told him about Mary's son and the land purchase and about Michael wanting me to see it beforehand. While I was talking, a bunch of runners appeared and took the table vacated by the Canadians. Our waitress obviously knew them because she came over with a pitcher of ice water and a stack of paper cups without being asked.

Jeffrey waved at a couple of the runners. "Are we talking marriage, here, Samantha?"

"He hasn't asked me yet, but I keep getting the feeling he'd going to."

"And what are you going to say?"

I peeled a shrimp, started to dunk it in the butter, then remembered Tanya. I looked around for some cocktail sauce. There wasn't any.

"I don't know," I said. "I don't want to hurt Michael, believe me. But I figure if I have to argue with myself about it, then it isn't meant to be. I mean, if I'm not absolutely positively in love with him, then I ought to say 'No.' " I looked at Jeffrey. "Right?"

Just then, in perfect unison, everyone turned toward the horizon, where the sun was setting and the sky was the color of a ripe pumpkin. It was almost as if we had fallen under some sort of spell, which wasn't far from the truth. And then it was over.

"I guess," said Jeffrey, coming to suddenly. "It isn't like I have a lot of experience in that area, Sam, but it seems to me you should definitely love the guy if you're going to marry him." Then he grinned. "Unless he's loaded, of course, and very, very old."

I kicked him under the table.

A band, complete with enormous amplifiers, was setting up inside. The windows were open, and I knew that very shortly, my private conversation with Jeffrey would either end or become somewhat less private, as shouting was the only way we would hear each other.

"But how am I going to tell him, Jeffrey? He's the kindest, sweetest man I have ever met, and I simply cannot bring myself to hurt him."

Jeffrey put his hand over mine. "If you marry him without loving him and move to New York when you really don't want to, won't that hurt him? I mean, in the long run?"

I decided then and there that Jeffrey could watch my television and raid my refrigerator anytime he wanted.

"Let's go inside," I said. "I'll treat you to an order of jalapeño poppers." And then I remembered Tanya. Oh, what the heck, I thought. Tomorrow is another day.

CHAPTER 29

•

Sunday, October 24

When the phone finally rang, I felt like I was in the waiting room at the dentist's, and they'd just called my name. Or the priest had just arrived at my jail cell. But the long speech I'd prepared about not wanting to leave Dr. Augustin on such short notice, particularly in light of his "investigation," was wasted.

"Hello, Samantha," Michael said. "I've got some more information for you about William Trexler." He sounded a little out of breath. "I gave a friend of mine over at the marina a call. Seems Mr. Trexler was planning to leave the country. He had his boat up for sale and he was getting ready to quit his job with the power company. Ron said he thought Trexler had come into a large sum of money or was expecting to very soon. I asked Ron if Trexler seemed nervous or scared, but he said not that he could tell."

"Where was he planning to go? Did your friend say?"

"Trexler was vague about that, but Ron seems to think he was going to South America. Brazil, probably, since Trexler spoke Portuguese."

"Portuguese?"

"His second wife is Portuguese."

"I thought they were divorced."

Michael gave a little chuckle. "Here's the interesting thing, Samantha—wife number two disappeared a couple of months ago."

"What do you mean, 'disappeared'?" I asked.

"Disappeared. Vanished. Left without a trace, lock, stock, and barrel. Quit her job at the bank and didn't give a forwarding address. She put her furniture in storage, canceled her credit cards, and withdrew all of her money—it wasn't much—and shoved off, as they say."

Michael was positively amazing at times. "How did you find all of this out on a weekend?" I asked.

He laughed. "A good reporter never divulges his source, Samantha. Suffice it to say, I had to call in a lot of favors."

And now, I owe *you* one, is that it? I thought, a little angrily. But Michael had never asked for or expected "payment" for helping Dr. Augustin and me before.

"Other than the fact that both Lanier and Trexler worked for the City, and spent a lot of their time in the field, were you able to uncover any connection between the two?" I asked. "Common friends, or maybe Lanier had a boat there at the marina."

"I didn't ask Ron about Jack Lanier," Michael said. "It didn't seem relevant at the time. But other than that remote possibility, I didn't find out anything that ties the two men together. Except their employment history. And, of course, the bullets that killed them. Where is Dr. Augustin going with this thing, anyway? I presume he feels there is something tying the murders to that proposed transmission corridor."

I kept quiet.

"Off the record, Samantha."

"He isn't sure," I said hesitantly.

Old habits die hard, and listening to Dr. Augustin blaspheme reporters for a couple of years certainly makes an impression on one. In spite of Michael's proven integrity.

"But he seems to think that some hazardous waste near the Northeast Recreation Complex may be the *real* reason the two men were killed."

"Oh, really?"

His tone was more than I could handle. I decided I'd better not say anything more.

"Go on," he said.

"I really don't know anything else. Honest." I hoped he believed me. If we'd been face-to-face, I wouldn't have stood a chance.

"Dr. Augustin is keeping you pretty busy, Samantha," he said, suddenly changing directions. "I can see that."

If I hadn't known better, I'd have sworn he wasn't even remotely interested in hazardous waste.

"I can understand why you don't want to leave right now," he continued. "So I won't push you. No matter how much I'd like to have you here with me."

I felt greatly relieved. "So. You'll be home . . . when? Sunday?"

"Possibly sooner. If I can manage it. I'll let you know. By the way, how is Randy doing?"

"The same, pretty much. But he's still eating, so there isn't anything to worry about. And Katie hasn't come down with it. Dr. Augustin doesn't think she's going to, either."

"That's good news," he said. He took a deep breath. "I'll let you go, Samantha, for now. But I'll call again, maybe Wednesday. In the meantime, give Cynthia my best." He laughed. "And please, stay out of trouble. Tell Dr. Augustin to do his own detective work."

"I will," I said. Yeah, and pigs can fly.

CHAPTER 30

•

Tuesday, October 26

Monday had been one of those god-awful days where all you can do is take a lot of deep breaths, keep your mind on the matter at hand, and pray it will end soon. You'd like to blame it on the moon but can't because the moon isn't full, or on a temperature inversion, even though the air is squeaky clean and sixty-eight degrees. It was one of those days that makes you wish you had a healthy case of food poisoning just so you could go home.

Two emergencies and a full surgical schedule kept me from visiting Sand Lake Testing Laboratory over lunch, which only added to Dr. Augustin's foul mood. He is an equal opportunity employer; he has no favorites when it comes to verbal abuse. At three, I overheard Tracey on the phone in the lab. She was requesting information about the junior college's dental hygienist program. I asked her to get two copies.

The next morning was so quiet and peaceful by comparison, I decided I must have imagined the whole thing.

"What does DWPM mean?" Cynthia asked. She squinted down at the paper on her desk. "DWPM, 60, semiretired, excellent SOH, enjoys classical music and dining out. ISO S/DWF, 40–60 looking for lasting relationship. What is ISO S/DWF?"

I closed the file drawer and turned around. "What on earth are you reading, Cynthia?" I asked.

She held up a copy of *Creative Loafing*. "It's one of those free newspapers. Most of the restaurants around here have them. I picked up a copy over the weekend." She blushed.

"DWPM means 'divorced white professional male,' " I said. "SOH probably means 'sense of humor.' And ISO S/DWF means 'in search of single or divorced white female.' " I leaned on Cynthia's desk. "Why are you browsing through the personal ads, anyway? I thought you were seeing the guy from your support group."

Cynthia quickly closed the paper, folded it in half, and stuffed it in the trash can. Then she kicked the trash can as far under her desk as possible, like a cat trying to cover up something disagreeable.

"I was just curious," she said defensively.

She swiveled her chair away from me and touched her computer mouse. Tanya Cumming's account popped up on the screen. Cynthia turned back around. There were tears in her eyes.

"He lied to me, Samantha. Lied to the whole group. He said his wife left him for another man." She opened a desk drawer and took out a box of Kleenex. "We believed him," she said, pulling loose a tissue. She dabbed at her eyes. "And felt sorry for him. He was really convincing."

I waited.

Cynthia blew her nose. "*He* left *her.* But not for a woman."

I held my breath and waited some more. But Cynthia wasn't going to make it easy for me.

"He left her for a man, is that it?" I asked.

Cynthia sat bolt upright and frowned at me. "Of course not," she said. "He left her in Ohio so he could take a job down here. When she wouldn't move away from her mother —she's in a nursing home, apparently—he told her good-bye and took off in their car. She *had* to divorce him."

"Well, Cynthia, obviously the marriage wasn't working or she'd have agreed to move. I mean, unless she also had a career. And I don't think her mother qualifies as a career, do you? Besides, they could have moved the woman to a facility down here."

"But he *lied,* Samantha."

"Cynthia, people lie. Men lie, women lie. Believe me, I know." Like the time I said you looked nice in that yellow and lime-green sundress, I thought. "You have to look at the circumstances."

"No, I don't," she said. "I simply cannot allow someone like that into my life. How could I ever trust him?"

Pearl wandered into the room and hopped up on Cynthia's desk. She stared at the candy corn. Cynthia reached over and scratched her on the head.

"Why can't people be more like animals?" she asked.

"People *are* animals," I said.

"You know what I mean. Honest about the way they feel."

"Cats lie, too," I said. "So do dogs. It's just harder for us to know when they're doing it, because we don't speak their language."

Suddenly Cynthia woke up. "How do *you* know so much about D/SWFs?" she asked, her eyebrows arched unevenly. She was stroking Pearl's back, unaware that the cat was edging closer and closer to the candy corn.

"I read those personal ads occasionally. Out of curiosity. The same as you."

"I do not read them, Samantha! I just happened to run across one when I opened that silly newspaper."

"Okay, okay," I said.

The candy dish slid off the desk. I grabbed it before it hit the floor but not before it dumped its contents everywhere.

"Bad girl!" said Cynthia to the cat.

Pearl jumped down and dribbled a kernel across the linoleum.

"I'll get the broom," I said.

* * *

"Greed got William Trexler killed," said Dr. Augustin. He checked his watch and made a note of the time in the poodle's file.

I slipped a rubber cap over the catheter in the dog's leg and carried the animal to her cage. "I beg your pardon," I said.

"He was obviously blackmailing somebody. Presumably the man responsible for killing Jack Lanier. Probably the same man who tried to hide the contamination at the rec center site."

"How do you know it's a man?" I asked, determined to get equal consideration for women, even if we were talking about murder and mayhem.

He looked down his nose at me. "How many female contractors and land developers do you know around here?"

"Okay," I said. "So it's probably a man. But why now? If Trexler knew about the contamination five years ago, why resort to blackmail now?"

We stared into the cage at the poodle. It was her first heartworm treatment, and considering her condition, Dr. Augustin was understandably concerned.

"The stakes went up just a tad, don't you think," he said, "when the guy killed Jack?"

"The stakes may have gone up," I said, "but so did the likelihood that Trexler would be killed, as well."

"I didn't say he was smart, Samantha, just greedy."

"What about Trexler's wife?" I asked.

"What about her?"

"Do you think she's involved in the murders? I mean, it seems awfully coincidental for her to disappear right now."

He shrugged. "Maybe she and Billy Boy made up and were planning to take off together. Go to Brazil with the loot. Or maybe she got scared. Who knows. In any case, I doubt she's our murderer."

We went into the surgery.

"What we need to do now," he continued, "is find out what data were gathered out at the site prior to construction,

and who had access to those data. Even if you can't get a
copy of the core boring results, at least find out who reviewed them, both at the testing lab and at the City."

I opened the cabinet and took out a spay pack. "I wish
you'd tell me how I'm going to get this information without
making somebody suspicious," I said. "Asking a lot of questions about that stupid rec center is bound to alert someone.
If William Trexler was an idiot to blackmail the killer, then
what does that make us?"

Dr. Augustin gave me his best imitation of the Cheshire
cat. "We're curious, that's all. Samantha, you need to learn
to relax."

There certainly are a lot of curious people around here
today, I thought.

"Sure," I said. "But please remember what being curious
got the cat."

Dr. Augustin didn't say anything, but I noticed his smile
was fading.

John Deland drove up at five minutes to twelve with two
more presumed victims of benzene intoxication. The first, a
mangy-looking mutt with a lot of German shepherd in him
and a lot of tar on him, took his last breath before John could
drag him out of the carrier. It is hard to get terribly emotional over a strange dog who's already dead, especially if it
was old and ugly to begin with. But the second victim was
none of those things, and I felt a tightening in my throat
when John pulled her out of the carrier.

"It's just a puppy!" I said. "What is she, twelve weeks,
maybe?"

"That's about right," said John.

We were in an exam room. The puppy, a mixture of chow
and shepherd, was a furry little brown creature with a mot-
tled blue and pink tongue. She was terrified, but wasn't
making any effort to bite John, so I risked touching her with
my bare hand. Her reflexes were off, and her head jerked
around in a motion that lately was becoming all too familiar.

"I sure wish I knew what was making these dogs sick," said John. He took off his gloves and put them and the puppy's carrier on the floor. "The City has been pretty sloppy with its paving job over at the recreation complex. I figure that's what the other one got into. But all this puppy has on her is mud."

I started to tell John about the buried coal tar when Dr. Augustin came in the room. He glanced down at the corpse on the floor, then took his stethoscope off the wall.

"Where did you find them?" he asked.

"In the woods just west of the Northeast Recreation Complex," said John. "The security guard called my office this morning at seven-thirty to complain about wild dogs digging through the garbage cans in the picnic area. He was going on and on about rabies. Apparently some idiot told him the dogs were rabid."

I looked up at Dr. Augustin, but he kept his eyes glued to the puppy.

"I told him none of the dead ones we'd sent to Tampa had rabies," John continued. "And I assured him we were doing everything we could to catch them, but we've been saying that for months. Geez . . . all we need is another rabies scare."

He held the puppy down so Dr. Augustin could listen to its heart. I opened a drawer and got out a syringe and a couple of blood collection tubes.

John went on. "The guard wanted to know if the two people we sent out last week caught any of the lousy mutts—his words. When I told him I wasn't sure who he meant, he described you guys perfectly." He chuckled. "What *were* you doing out there, anyway?"

Dr. Augustin prodded the dog's belly. "Looking for a source of that tar," he said, pointing to the limp body in the corner. "The owner of the terrier you brought us a couple of weeks ago—the one with the strange solvent smell on him—said she used paint thinner to clean tar off her dog's legs. She said he got the stuff on him over at the rec center."

I held the puppy, while Dr. Augustin drew a blood sample. Then he picked up the dog's carrier and gently shoved the animal inside.

"Samantha," he said, "you need to leave. It's already past noon." He tapped the carrier with his hand. "Drop this little guy off with Frank on your way out. Tell him to give her a bath but not to stress her out too much. And use a muzzle." He picked up the two blood vials. "Have Tracey do a CBC. Hold on to the serum. I think we already know what's wrong."

I waited while John put on his gloves and eased the dead dog back into its carrier.

"I think I'll give the Parks and Recreation Department a call," he said. "If the stuff is killing these dogs, think what it's doing to the wildlife out there."

Dr. Augustin rubbed his right temple with his index finger. "Hold off on that call, John," he said. "I'd like to do some checking around first. I think there's more to this than just a sloppy paving job."

He looked perfectly innocent, but John wasn't stupid and he'd known Dr. Augustin far too long.

"You're working on another case, aren't you?" John asked. "Does this have anything to do with that dead man you and Sam found out in the woods?"

John and I stared at Dr. Augustin.

"I thought you were leaving, Samantha," he said, not looking directly at either one of us.

I winked at John, picked up the carrier and the tubes of blood, and left.

CHAPTER 31

•

Sand Lake Testing Laboratory was located in an industrial area of St. Petersburg just off I-275. In fact, the parking lot was *under* the northbound lanes of the interstate. Traffic rumbled overhead, and the support columns hummed. When a particularly heavy vehicle thundered by, a flock of pigeons flew out of the shadows. I looked up and saw a couple of those fake plastic great-horned owls bolted to one of the I-beams. They are supposed to discourage pigeons from setting up housekeeping. From the large pile of droppings on the pavement beneath the owls, I gathered the pigeons weren't impressed. I ducked, as one of the offending birds flew by, and hurried out into the safety of the sunlight.

The building itself was a rectangular concrete block structure painted white. The trim was dark green. There wasn't anything really remarkable about the place except the landscaping out front, which was new. I could see where the strips of sod hadn't grown together yet, and the cypress mulch around the shrubs was still light reddish-brown, instead of stale coffee-colored.

An eight-foot chain-link fence encircled the rear of the property. Behind it, a dusty white van with a dented front bumper was parked next to an old Chevy Camaro and a motor scooter. Imprinted on the van's side panel in dark green was the company's name, address, and phone number, along with their logo—a tall palm tree on a beach with several generic vee-shaped objects superimposed over a giant sun. I decided the vee-shaped objects were seagulls, although they could have been arithmetic symbols. They didn't look fat enough to be pigeons.

The sign next to the entrance read SAND LAKE TESTING COMPANY, INC.—MATERIALS TESTING, WATER ANALYSES, COMPLIANCE TESTING. It was probably all the references to "testing," but I felt my stomach start to churn the way it always did in school when I was handed an exam I hadn't studied for. This "test" wasn't a whole lot different. The trip down from Paradise Cay had taken exactly forty minutes, and I still hadn't come up with a reasonable explanation for wanting the data from the recreation complex site. I would have to "wing it," as Dr. Augustin said. I hoped I could do a better job than the owls.

A police car, sirens blaring, whizzed by, and I pushed open the front door.

The reception area was small but nice. The walls were covered with 8x10 framed color photographs of what I guessed were past job sites. I recognized the entrance road to Carriage Hill. Little nameplates beneath the photos identified an aerial view of Maraldee Manor, minus the houses, the eighteenth hole at one of the golf courses in Fox Meadows, minus the grass, the City's garbage handling facility, and the Northeast Recreation Complex. Oddly, the photo of the rec center site was the only one taken following construction. The grass was fresh and green, the crepe myrtles were in full bloom, and the retention pond, with its picnic area, looked like it belonged in an English garden.

There was no one sitting at the reception desk and no other visitors. I checked out the magazines on the table by the door. There were copies of various engineering and material testing journals, but nothing of interest to me. Not even a *Newsweek*. I yawned.

"Yes?" said a voice behind me.

I turned around. A man about forty-five, in a dirty white

lab coat and half glasses stood in the doorway. He was hold-ing a carrot stick in one hand and a beaker filled with tea in the other. I knew it was tea, because the bag was still in it.

"Well?" He was tapping the floor with his foot. It seemed more the result of taut nerves than rudeness.

"I'm looking for some information," I said. "About a job you . . ."

"Everyone is out," he said. "Come back at two." He turned to go.

"I can't," I said. "I'm on my lunch break. If I'm late get-ting back, I could get fired."

He hesitated, as if he, too, was at risk of losing his job and understood my predicament. He looked longingly at his car-rot stick, then threw it in the trash can by the reception desk.

"If we could please keep this brief," he said, "I'll give you whatever help I can." He pointed to the hallway. "Follow me."

We went past a room crammed with a lot of fancy and ex-pensive instruments. One, in particular, caught my eye, and I stopped at the doorway for a moment to watch it. The gad-get looked like a sequential analyzer of some kind. A carousel tray filled with small, fluid-filled vials rotated until one of the vials was beneath an inlet pipette. After a couple of seconds, some of the fluid was sucked up and carried into the bowels of the instrument, presumably mixed with reagent, and passed through the beam of a spectrophotome-ter. The results of the analysis would be recorded some-where, although I didn't see a printer.

The analyzer rotated a vial of rinse solution around to the pipette, in preparation for the next sample. Suddenly my laboratory guide stuck his head out of a room farther up the hall.

"Please, Miss . . . ? I really haven't got all day."

I hurried down the hall. "My name is Holt," I said. "Samantha Holt."

He didn't say anything. He turned left into a room that had SOILS LAB on the door, and I followed him inside.

This room was vastly different from the high-tech, sterile conditions of the chemistry lab I had just left. All of the instruments and gadgets in the Soils Lab seemed to be designed to handle very large-sized samples of rock and dirt. There was a fine dusting of what appeared to be limestone or cement or, possibly, gypsum on the floor and several of the tables. Brass sieves, most of them stacked one on top of the other, a heavy-duty balance, and some sort of lab oven sat on the largest of the tables.

My host put his beaker of tea on a cluttered desk in the corner of the room. The desk was big and dark gray and resembled something I had seen once in an Army-Navy store. A photo on the desk showed two middle school-aged children—a girl and a boy—beneath a Christmas tree.

"Adorable children," I said. "Are they yours?"

The man's furrowed brow smoothed out a little, and a very faint smile bent the corners of his mouth. "Yes," he said. "Ashley and Ray, Junior."

"You're Ray, then?" I stuck out my hand.

"Yes," he said, leaving my hand and his first name hanging naked in the air. "Now what do you want to know?"

"I'm doing a little environmental study with some middle school children out at the Northeast Recreation Complex ," I said, putting my hand down. "We're looking at various native plant communities and the kinds of soil they grow best in." As I improvised, I mentally thanked Justin Blaize for his contribution to my education.

Ray pulled at his chin. He looked a lot like Vincent van Gogh, or at least the portrait of the artist I remembered studying in art history class. Ray still had both of his ears, but his expression clearly indicated a troubled man.

"So what exactly did you want from us?" he asked, tapping his foot again. If he knew about the contamination and was suspicious of my interest, he didn't show it.

I glanced around the room and spotted a narrow table against the wall, in the center of which were three sausage-shaped objects about eighteen inches in length. The first was sliced open lengthwise, the two halves laid out on plastic wrap. I could see bands of light and dark, layered like a vanilla torte iced with fudge frosting. Several empty glass jars bearing tiny white labels were lined up along the wall behind the sausages.

"Are those core borings?" I asked, pointing to the table.

Ray nodded. He was still tapping his foot.

"What do you do with them?"

"Analyze the various layers to determine the type of soil components at a particular site," said Ray. "We establish grain sizes and do compression and consolidation tests." When I didn't say anything, he added, "To find out how much settling might occur under a building."

"Oh," I said stupidly.

"You were asking about some environmental study?"

"Yes," I said. "At the Northeast Recreation Complex ."

A buzzer sounded somewhere down the hall. Ray looked at his watch.

"I've got to catch that," he said. "Wait here, and I'll see if someone else can help you." He left before I could open my mouth.

I walked slowly around the room, keeping my hands in my pockets. There was a shallow pool to the left of the door, above the floor, constructed out of cinder blocks and mortar and, presumably, some type of sealant. The pool was filled with water. It contained five four-by-eighteen-inch concrete cylinders. The water just covered them.

I heard a noise and turned around.

"Hi," said a young man dressed in jeans and a long-sleeved denim shirt. "Ray told me to give you whatever help I can." He smiled broadly. "I'm Bob Fields."

"I'm Samantha Holt. I appreciate this. I'm doing a school project. It involves looking at some core borings and other 'boring' stuff." I laughed lightly.

"Oh, core borings can be really fascinating," said Bob. "It's like being an archaeologist, in a way. Seeing what's in a site's past."

I suddenly realized that I might get more information out of Bob than I bargained for.

"I'm interested in the Northeast Recreation Complex site," I said. "My class is studying the geology of the area. I guess what I need is data from any core borings you guys took there."

Bob thought for a minute. "When was that?"

"I think about six years ago. Seven, maybe."

He nodded. "Before my time. But all the data should still be in the files." He pointed to the door. "Come with me, and I'll check."

We went out into the hall. I could hear Ray talking to someone in the chemistry lab. He didn't sound happy. He was trying to explain why he was behind schedule.

"In here," said Bob, opening a door next to the Soils Lab.

I went in. One side of the room was a jumble of file cabinets and cardboard file boxes, piled floor to ceiling, and cartons of glass jars like the ones I'd seen with the sausage rolls next door. Except these contained soil samples and, with their rusted lids, looked old enough to be, themselves, ancient artifacts. On the other side of the room, positioned on a low table, were two computer terminals, a couple of printers, several boxes of disks, and two chairs. Both computers were on, their screen-saver programs running. One depicted the USS *Enterprise* cruising slowly past comets and asteroids and the occasional Klingon warship. The other had a flock of winged toasters flapping silently by.

"Have a seat," said Bob. He sat down in front of the *Enterprise* and pulled over a spiral-bound notebook. He flipped through it. "Let's see, the rec center site would be listed how? Ah, here it is."

He typed in a series of numbers and letters, hit "Enter," and waited. After a few seconds, a long list came up on the screen. Bob scrolled down the list, then stopped and copied another series of numbers down on a small tablet lying next to the computer. He pulled over one of the disk boxes and started thumbing through the diskettes.

"We don't keep much information about the sites we work on in the computer, because if we did, the hard drive would fill up pretty fast. A lot of space is already occupied by programs that we need to analyze the data we collect. We put all of the detailed information about each site—the survey, the owner of the property, any easements and rights-of-way that might have been granted, construction details, and, of course, the soils and water quality analyses—on diskettes. Only the file names and codes are kept in the computer. Sort of like the card catalogue at the library."

He continued to flip through the box. "Here it is," he said. He pulled out a diskette and slipped it in the B drive of the computer. Then he directed the computer to retrieve the rec center files.

"That's strange," he said. He was hitting the "Page Up" and "Page Down" keys.

"What is?" I asked.

"There's hardly anything here from the Northeast Recreation Complex site. No soils data that I can find. Let me start over." He began retracing his steps, starting with the spiral-bound notebook.

I was beginning to get a bad feeling about what had started out so well, with Ray telling Bob to give me whatever I wanted, if just to get me out of his hair. Of course, it shouldn't have come as any great shock—the fact that the files had been purged. The question was, who had done the purging?

"It isn't here," said Bob. His shoulders drooped. "I don't know how, but most of the field data for the rec center site has been deleted. Or else, it was never entered in the file, which isn't very likely." He got up. "I'll ask Ray what happened to it. He's been here forever. If anybody knows, he will."

"No," I said quickly. "Don't bother him." I didn't want to draw any more attention to me or the rec center than I already had. I pointed to the file cabinets. "What about there?

Maybe we can find a hard copy of the data in one of those cabinets or boxes."

The possibility, however remote, that he might still be able to help me lifted Bob's spirits as well as his shoulders. He reminded me of Frank, in a way, except he didn't look like a vagrant and he hadn't attempted to undress me visually.

We searched through the file cabinets, looking under every file name Bob could think of. Then we went through about half of the file boxes. There was no sign, whatever, of the rec center site core borings.

"We keep data in these dead files for ten years," said Bob. "Longer if there was any kind of legal problem with the land or the project. It should be here." He scratched the side of his face.

"You know, Stuart Webster might have a copy of the boring logs. He usually keeps a copy of everything he does. For résumé purposes, according to him. He was the materials tester back then. At least I'm pretty sure he was. He would have analyzed the borings and filled out the logs." He smiled. "Wait here, and I'll see if I can find him. I'll be right back."

I wailed a full ten minutes, twiddling my thumbs and browsing through the file cabinet, just in case we had missed something the first time through. We hadn't. I dug into the boxes of glass jars. I found samples from Maraldee Manor and the Fox Meadows golf courses. I unearthed stuff from 1982 that had shriveled up in tiny marble mummies that rattled around in their containers. I even ran across samples taken at the dog track. It was as if Sand Lake Testing was the only lab of its kind in the county. Unfortunately, I didn't find anything from the old gas plant site.

I had gone back over to the computer table and was about to sit down when Bob appeared in the doorway holding a single sheet of paper that looked like Mad Max had been chewing on it.

"Stuart is out of town," said Bob, "so I helped myself to his files. He didn't have anything on your site. I mean, nothing substantial. I found this by accident in the back of his

drawer. It was caught under the metal file folder supports."
He put the sheet of paper down on the table in front of me
and smoothed it out. "It's a diagram of the site, showing the
location of each core boring that was taken. See?"

He put his finger on one of the six small back circles labeled B1–B6. They were scattered around areas outlined in
black and labeled "Building" and "Parking."

"Sorry I couldn't locate anything else," said Bob. "You
might want to check with the Brightwater Beach Engineering Department. The boring logs and soils analyses would
have been sent there."

"Do you know who I should ask for?"

Bob shook his head. "Sorry."

"Well, you've certainly been a big help, anyway," I said.
I touched the mangled sheet of paper. "May I keep this?"

"I'll get Celeste to make you a copy," said Bob, picking it
up.

I followed him up to the reception area, where a woman
about Cynthia's age, but without Cynthia's charm, sat at the
desk smoking a cigarette. Bob asked her if she would mind
photocopying the site diagram. His tone of voice was extremely submissive, like Celeste was the alpha dog, and Bob
was the runt of the litter, begging for scraps. Celeste took
her time answering him. Through several lengthy drags on
her cigarette and a dramatic pause while she searched
through the papers in her in-box for some reason to tell him
she had more important things to do, Bob waited patiently. I
would have done the copying myself, rather than be humil-
iated in front of a visitor, but the Xerox machine, like first
crack at a freshly killed rabbit, was probably off-limits to the
likes of poor Bob.

"Give it to me," the woman said. She snatched the paper
out of his hand, looked at it like perhaps he had just dug it
out of the garbage, and left the room.

Bob turned to me and shrugged. I studied the photos on
the wall. Pretty soon, Celeste was back. She handed the
copy and the original back to Bob.

"Don't forget to collect for that copy," she said. "Ten cents."

Before Bob could say anything, I dug into my purse and came up with a quarter. I gave it to the woman.

"Keep the change," I said.

Grinning, Bob handed me the copy.

"Thanks again," I told him.

Without batting an eye, Celeste put the quarter in her top drawer and reached for her cigarettes.

I sat in my car and watched the pigeons snuggle up to the plastic owls. It was 1:45. If I played Russian roulette with the St. Petersburg and Brightwater Beach police, I still wouldn't make it back to the clinic before 2:15. And Dr. Augustin would promptly ask me why I hadn't gone to the Brightwater Beach Engineering Department in search of the core boring data. Which would mean Wednesday, my day off, would be spent there instead of at the beach.

I started the car, scaring up a couple of the pigeons, and headed for the Municipal Technical Services Building.

CHAPTER 32

•

The area ringed in yellow tape had shrunk to the southwest portion of the building, where chunks of brick, concrete, and broken glass lay in a heap on the ground. But the
fire that had gutted the top two floors of the Municipal Technical Services Building was still evident from as far away as
City Hall. The structure looked like a giant chocolate Drum-
stick in the process of melting.

I parked on the street and put enough money in the meter
for two hours. I figured if I was there any longer, a fifteen-
dollar parking ticket would be the least of my worries.

The Engineering Department was located on the second
floor, according to the directory next to the elevator. The elevator, however, was out of service, so I took the stairs. I
had to hold my breath most of the way up, because the odor
of wet, charred wood and plastic was nauseating, and it naturally got worse the higher up you went in the stairwell.

On the second floor I followed the signs down the hall to
the Engineering Department. The reception area was painted
pale pink, which seemed a little odd for a sewage, drainage,
and paving department. And there was a large watercolor on
one of the walls, depicting a scene in the Everglades, complete with cypress trees veiled in Spanish moss, and a
Florida panther. That I also found a little incongruous, since
I always thought the Brightwater Beach Engineering De-

partment was only interested in filling the swamp, not admiring it.

The receptionist, Mina Tobias, according to her little nameplate, was young and very thin, with a long neck and short blond hair. She was wearing a fluffy pink sweater that seemed much too large for her. It made her neck look even skinnier, and the more I studied her, the more she began to resemble a flamingo. I wanted her to stand up so I could see if her knees bent backward. But she continued to sit. She was pecking, birdlike, on an electric typewriter.

"Excuse me," I said gently.

Mina jumped, striking a key she obviously hadn't intended to strike. She frowned at the paper in the carriage, then looked up at me with an exasperated expression on her face.

"I'd like to speak to one of the engineers," I said, "about the Northeast Recreation Complex ."

"You need to go to the Parks and Recreation Department," she said. "It's on Piedmont Street. 522 Piedmont." She turned back to her typewriter.

I tried again. "I'm interested in the site studies you people did before construction. Bob down at Sand Lake Testing told me to speak to one of the engineers."

Mina frowned, mostly at her typing, then turned around in her chair and attempted to smile. Her front teeth were crooked.

"Sorry," she said. "I'm a little rusty."

To be rusty, I thought rather uncharitably, you must first have been proficient.

Mina pulled the phone over and lifted the receiver. "Anyone in particular?"

"Whoever worked on the rec center project," I said. "That would be about six or seven years ago, I think."

Mina punched in a four-digit number, waited a couple of seconds, then purred into the receiver like a cat in heat. "Hi, Conrad, it's Mina. Just fine." She giggled. "Listen, there's a lady up here who wants to talk to you about the Northeast

Recreation Complex. She says Bob at Sand Lake sent her to us."

She was holding the receiver lovingly to her mouth, the way some singers do their microphones. "Sure, Conrad. Bye." She hung up.

Honey dripped from the handset.

"Conrad Miller will be up in a sec," she said. "Have a seat."

She returned to her typing, but I noticed she did a little quick preening of her hair and sweater in anticipation of Conrad's visit.

I hadn't even settled myself when a man in his early fifties, with greying auburn hair and a neat steely mustache, appeared in the doorway. He was tall and fit and well-dressed in trousers and a sport shirt, open to the neck. I could see Mina trying to control herself. She wet her lips.

"Miss . . . ?" asked Conrad, ignoring Mina.

"Holt," I said, getting up. "Samantha Holt." I walked over to him and held out my hand.

He shook it. "Please come this way, Miss Holt, and I'll see if I can help you."

I could tell from Mina's expression that Conrad could help *her* anytime. We left her staring absently at the water-color.

The Engineering Department had either taken over someone else's quarters and made do, or had outgrown their original digs. The main room was a maze of desks and file cabinets. The majority of the desk's occupants appeared to be clerical staff. Off the main room were several tiny office cubicles, most of them housing at least two people. Their names were on the wall next to their doors. I presumed they were the engineers. A glance in one of the offices showed three desks jammed together in the center of the room and a long narrow worktable pushed up against one wall. A three-drawer file cabinet occupied the rest of the space.

A second large room connected to the first was obviously the drafting area. Six people, two of them women, were bent over drafting tables working diligently.

Conrad had a corner office all to himself. It was tiny but neat. Pictures of hunting dogs, retrievers mostly, some of them with dead ducks clamped between their jaws, hung on two of the walls. A third wall had several diplomas and certificates of appreciation on it. One of them was from Ducks, Unlimited. I assumed the ducks hadn't been the appreciative parties.

"Please sit down, Miss Holt," said Conrad, indicating the chair next to his desk. He sat in his own chair, leaned back, and crossed his legs. "You wanted to know about the Northeast Recreation Complex ?"

"Yes," I said. "I'm taking an archaeology class at the university. We're learning about Indian settlements and such. And our teacher told each of us to select an area where subsurface studies had been done and see if we could get the core boring data. He's going to show us how archaeologists use the information to pinpoint possible ancient human activity."

I smiled. If Conrad Miller knew anything about archaeology or had ever taken an archaeology class at the university, I was dead.

"I can assure you, Miss Holt, that the Northeast Recreation Complex was never used by Indians. There aren't any burial mounds or kitchen middens on the site. In fact, the land was used by the City for industrial purposes, and very little of it is in its natural state. Sorry."

He ran a finger over his mustache and rocked slowly back and forth in his chair. The spring under the cushion squeaked.

I frowned. "I don't think it matters if Indians ever lived there," I said. "My instructor just wants to show us how you can tell certain things about an area's past by studying the soils under the surface." I tried to look like Shirley Temple.

"Why did you select the recreation complex land?" he asked. He picked up a paperweight—a piece of marble with some kind of seal cast in bronze on it—and studied it briefly.

Then he put it back on his desk and looked at me. His eyes were grey.

"I used to play soccer there," I said, "and one time a couple of my teammates found some bones in the woods nearby—of a possum, I think—and I just thought it would be a good study area for an archaeology class."

Suddenly I realized there was no way I could have played soccer at the Northeast Recreation Complex. Not while in high school, anyway. People tell me I look young for my age, but not that young.

Conrad smiled ever so slightly, which made me all the more nervous. But he didn't accuse me of lying, at least not to my face. He got up and walked over to his file cabinet.

"I'll make you a copy of the boring logs," he said, "and the soils data. That's about all I've got that might be useful to you."

"I'd appreciate whatever you can give me, Mr. Miller," I said. "I'm under the gun on this thing." Bad choice of words, Samantha, dear, I thought, but appropriate.

Conrad pulled a file folder out of the top drawer and thumbed through its contents. He extracted several sheets and put the folder down on top of the file cabinet. He pushed the drawer closed.

"Follow me, Miss Holt," he said. "I'll have Mina copy this for you."

We went back out to the reception area, and Conrad gave the sheets to Mina.

"Miss Holt needs a copy of these, Mina. No charge." He nodded at me and smiled, then started to leave. He stopped. "Good luck with your archaeology class," he said. Then he disappeared around the corner.

Mina got up, puffed out her rosy breast, and went in the direction of the drafting room. I watched her walk. Her knees bent normally.

Ten minutes later I was sitting in my car, Conrad's boring logs spread out on the seat next to me. There was something odd about them. I reached into my purse and got out the copy of the site layout Bob had given me. Then I put it next to the one I'd gotten from Conrad. It took me a couple of seconds to see why I'd been confused and I felt a tingle of excitement.

Bob's drawing showed six boring sites, four under the proposed building and two under the proposed parking lot. Conrad's drawing showed four boring locations, two under the building and two under the parking lot. And I knew, without looking, that the soils data Conrad had given me would be free of any tar residue.

So, I thought, someone purged the files at Sand Lake Testing *and* made certain the core borings and soils analyses sent to the City did not indicate any contamination. But was it the same person, someone at Sand Lake, who altered the data, or are we dealing with somebody at the City, as well? Conrad Miller, perhaps?

I looked at my watch. It was 3:20. I shoved all the papers into my purse and started my car. If I was lucky, Cynthia hadn't started calling the police or the hospitals yet.

CHAPTER 33

•

"Don't you *ever* leave me alone with him again!" Tracey said through clenched teeth. She sounded like she had a wad of cotton in her mouth.

I had gone in the bathroom to change out of my jeans and back into my uniform, but before I could shut the door, Tracey joined me. There is no "bath" in the hall bathroom, only a toilet and sink, and it is a tight fit for one person, let alone two. Tracey and I were practically nose-to-nose or, rather, nose-to-throat, since Tracey is several inches shorter than I am.

"I assume we're talking about Dr. Augustin," I said.

"Who else would we be talking about?" she asked, her jaws working again. She put the toilet lid down and sat on it, drawing her feet up off the floor to give me more room.

"Frank, for one," I said. "I certainly wouldn't want to be caught alone with him." I took off my jeans and slipped my uniform pants off the hanger on the back of the door.

Tracey ignored the jab at her Prince Charming. "How have you managed to stay here as long as you have?" she asked, her voice low. "That man is, well . . ."

"I think the word you're looking for is deranged," I said, pulling on my pants.

Tracey hesitated, then nodded. "I mean, one minute, he complains about me not being in the exam room to help him,

243

and the next minute he wants to know why I'm behind on the lab work. I finally told him to make up his mind, and he looked at me with those eyes of his until I said I was sorry."

"You didn't."

"What, tell him to make up his mind?"

"No," I said, "say you were sorry. I thought you were tired of letting men control you."

"I couldn't help it. But I wasn't sorry, not one bit. I should have told him to grow up. He acts like such a baby sometimes."

I folded my jeans and T-shirt, looked around for a place to put them, then plunked them down in Tracey's lap. I turned on the water and squirted soap into my hand.

"I was alone with him for over a month this summer before you came along," I said. "Trust me, he isn't singling you out."

I finished washing my hands and was pulling a paper towel off the roll under the mirror when a loud knock on the door caused Tracey and me to jump. I grabbed the edge of the sink.

"Whenever you two are finished with your little chat," said Dr. Augustin through the woodwork, "I'd appreciate some help out here." His voice was muffled, but the irritation in it was undeniable."

Tracey put her hand over her mouth. "Oh, my God," she whispered. "You don't think he heard us, do you?"

I threw the paper towel in the trash and took my clothes from her. "Probably," I said. "But don't worry. It's a chemical imbalance in his brain that makes him act irrationally. Undoubtedly the result of all the meat he eats. It, too, will pass."

Tracey didn't look the least bit amused. She hurried into the lab, giving Dr. Augustin as wide a berth as possible.

"I want you to call your buddy Michael," said Dr. Augustin, "and have him look into the ownership of Sand Lake Testing Laboratory."

We were in the kennel examining a boarder who wasn't eating.

"My guess is," he continued, "Justin Blaize owns it, which would explain a lot. Unfortunately, privately held companies are tough to investigate. It's not like you can go to your local Merrill Lynch office and ask for a prospectus."

"What about the paving company?" I asked.

Dr. Augustin stared at me.

"You were going to check out the paving contractor who's been extending that rec center parking lot."

He closed the cage door and leaned against the wall. "I never had a chance. But I did get the company's name from Melody—Textite Paving Contractors. It's a local outfit. Have Michael look into them, too, while he's at it."

He and I went down the hall to his office. It was almost six.

"You're going to be late for your soccer game," I said.

"I can't go tonight. I've got to give that poodle another heartworm treatment." He sat down at his desk, pulled out a bottom drawer, and put his feet up on it. "Care to join me?" He was smiling.

Just as predicted, Dr. Augustin's mood had improved over the course of the afternoon. Needless to say, the obvious disparity between the core boring location diagrams I'd given him hadn't hurt.

"No, I think you can handle it all by yourself," I said. Then I pointed to his desk, where the site diagrams were lying side by side. "It is possible, isn't it, that the changes to the soils analyses were made at Sand Lake, and the doctored reports transmitted to the Engineering Department without their knowledge? Maybe the City doesn't know about the contamination."

"Don't kid yourself," he said. "Somebody knows. Let's assume for the sake of argument that Sand Lake Testing and Textite Paving, as well as Blaize Excavating, are owned by Justin Blaize. Don't you find it a little coincidental that Mr. Blaize gets as many city contracts as he does. Brightwater

Beach always, without exception—which is half their problem, you understand—goes with the low bid. How do you think Mr. Blaize manages to undercut the low bid every time without help from the inside?"

"Dumb luck?"

He frowned. "Have Michael check out this Conrad Miller. See how long he's been working for the City, and if his bank account has undergone any abnormal growth over the last few years."

"What if Textite Paving isn't owned by Justin Blaize? What if they didn't know about the tar?"

Dr. Augustin slipped a penny into his gumball machine and turned the crank. A small red sphere dropped into view. Dr. Augustin lifted the flap, and the sphere rolled into his hand. I gulped. It was as if the gumball machine was bleeding.

"Then I guess we can expect a few more bodies to surface," said Dr. Augustin, "as our killer continues to clean up after himself."

"Gee," I said, "what a pleasant thought."

Dr. Augustin grinned sadistically and eased the drop of blood between his lips.

CHAPTER 34

•

Thursday, October 28

Instead of spending my day off at the beach, I spent it in the library, thanks to Dr. Augustin. Since I had no intention whatever of calling Michael for any reason for fear he might bring up the matter of my visit again, I really had no choice.

My high school English teacher used to tell us when seeking information, ask a librarian. Or the mailman. My mailman periodically gets confused and leaves my stuff with the old lady downstairs. Her name is Roberta Stiles, which is nowhere close to Samantha Holt. So I settled on the man behind the reference desk at the Brightwater Beach Public Library. He was in his seventies, a tiny bit stoop-shouldered, but had a smile worthy of a Polident commercial and a card catalogue for a brain.

I had exhausted my supply of good cover stories, so I told the man I was doing a research project on Blaize Excavating, Inc., which was more or less the truth. I did say the purpose of my research was to show how a small company grows and diversifies over time, which was stretching it some, but not actually a lie. In any case, it didn't take us long to dig up the required information. We did a quick search of the *Florida Business Directory* and *Contacts Influential*. In the process, I learned what a Standard Industrial Classification code is. Blaize Excavating, Inc., was 1794, for what it's worth.

None of the listings for Sand Lake Testing Laboratory or Textite Paving Contractors gave an owner's name or a company president. However, they both had the same mailing address—a P.O. box—which, fortunately for me, was the same P.O. box listed for Blaize Excavating, Inc.

I thanked the gentleman at the reference desk and went to the post office. There I was informed in no uncertain terms that giving out the name of the person renting a P.O. box is illegal. So much for using the postal service for investigative purposes, I thought, as I headed home.

The next morning I decided to get it over with early. When Dr. Augustin is right about something, he makes no effort to hide his jubilation. And he had been right about Sand Lake Testing and Textite Paving. So I was prepared for his cocky "I told you so" smile and his irritating habit of constantly bringing up the subject just to rub it in. But Dr. Augustin can also be unpredictable.

"What about that engineer who reviewed the core boring?" he asked me, over a Bedlington terrier with an abscessed tooth. Like the connection between Textite Paving and Blaize Excavating was of minor consequence. "What did Halsey find out about him?"

I had forgotten all about Mr. Miller, not that remembering him would have done me any good. I didn't have Michael's contacts and I doubted the little man at the reference desk was *that* resourceful.

"I . . . Michael wasn't able to find out anything yet," I said.

"Why not?"

He was concentrating on the dog's jaw, so the evil eye I gave him was wasted.

"You can't expect miracles," I said. "He's in New York, not Brightwater Beach. Besides, he's busy with his own problems, which, you may be shocked to discover, are probably more important to him than finding out who killed Jack

Lanier." I sometimes surprise even myself. "You should be glad he's helped us as much as he has."

Dr. Augustin looked up. He was smiling. "I *am* glad, Samantha. It's fortunate for us Mr. Halsey is still enamored with you."

That's a matter of opinion, I thought.

"Anyway, keep after him, will you? Someone in the Engineering Department is involved in this thing, and I am going to find out who it is."

Not if they find you first, I said to myself. And then I remembered *I* was the one poking around, asking the questions.

At 10:30 Tanya Cummings arrived to pick up Oscar. She was wearing her shrink-wrap jeans, but instead of her HOT DOG VENDORS DO IT T-shirt, she had opted for one bearing a giant rottweiler on the front. The dog's face was nestled between her breasts, and every time she breathed, the rottie looked like he was smiling.

I put Tanya in Room 1, then went to the kennel to get Oscar. Dr. Augustin met me at the door.

"Where is that specimen jar containing the condoms?" he asked me.

"I have no idea," I said. "Try your office." I headed for the exam room. Oscar trotted along behind me.

"Uh, Samantha," Dr. Augustin said, catching up with me, "I'll take him." He reached out for Oscar's leash. "You go ahead and finish doing treatments."

"I'm done," I said. He knew that.

"Then find something else to do!" He frowned, snatched the leash out of my hand, and led Oscar into Room 1.

At 11:30 Dr. Augustin came out of the exam room, followed by Ms. Cummings and her dog. Dr. Augustin was clearly amused. He handed me the Cummings file, winked, then hurried into Room 2. He was humming to himself.

I followed Tanya up to the reception room. She smiled at me and Cynthia like nothing out of the ordinary had transpired in the exam room. I guess it is tough for someone who works half-naked on the shoulder of a six-lane highway to get embarrassed about anything.

"Mommy is sooo glad her baby is all better," crooned Tanya. Since she couldn't lean over without causing an intestinal obstruction of her own, she bent her knees slightly and patted Oscar on the head. "But you were such a bad boy to get into Mommy's things."

Oscar and his T-shirt look-alike smiled.

Cynthia evidently had heard about the condoms, because she wouldn't look directly at Tanya and she handled Tanya's check like it had cooties on it.

The chow-shepherd puppy was doing much better. Frank had given her a squeaky toy, and the chirping noises it made were driving Randy and Katie nuts. Randy was finally able to look at me without squinting and he was breathing through his nose.

"I want to keep this puppy here for a while," said Dr. Augustin. He opened the cage door and scratched the dog's neck. "Very young, actively growing animals are more likely than adults to develop problems following exposure to toxic substances like benzene. We need to monitor her blood and liver enzymes."

"You're not going to send her back to Animal Control?" I asked, amazed he was willing to spend the extra money knowing Animal Control wouldn't reimburse him.

He shook his head. "Not right now."

Suddenly I thought about Daniel Kenney and his son, Joey. "Those kids in Maraldee Manor," I said. "The ones with cancer. You don't suppose they got sick from playing at the rec center, do you?"

Dr. Augustin shut the door to the puppy's cage and looked at me. "Not unless that tar has been coming to the surface all along," he said. "Leukemia doesn't happen overnight. And that's assuming some environmental factor has caused the Kenney child to develop it in the first place, which I doubt will ever be determined." He went over to the sink and began washing his hands. "Besides, somebody would have noticed the tar before now—on their kid's clothes or their pet's feet. If we go with what John is telling us, those feral dogs only started dying off a month or two ago. Probably about the time they started extending that parking lot."

"So what are we going to do now?"

Dr. Augustin dried his hands. "I don't know about you," he said, "but I'm going to lunch."

I was in the lab, filling a prescription when the phone rang. Without thinking, I picked it up.

"Samantha," the voice said, "it's Mike. I was out until late last night and didn't want to wake you." He paused briefly. "I hope I'm not catching you at a bad time."

I peeled the label off the roll in the printer and stuck it on the bottle. "No," I said. "We're between clients." I frowned. I had spelled "teaspoon" wrong. It read "tespoon."

"I have good news," Michael said. "I'm coming home Saturday. Late. How about dinner Sunday?"

"That would be nice," I said, surprised at how much I wanted to see him. Or was it the offer of a fancy meal and the chance to wear nice clothes for a change that excited me?

"Great! And how would you like to accompany me to an art exhibition Sunday afternoon? I'm doing a feature on it. Photos and paintings of animals—wildlife, mostly. It's a fund-raiser. You'll enjoy it, I promise."

"Sounds like fun."

"Good. I'll pick you up at three-thirty." He cleared his throat nervously. "Samantha, I . . . I'll see you Sunday, then."

"Sunday it is."

And then before I could ask him about Conrad Miller, he hung up.

CHAPTER 35

•

Friday, October 29

"Damn!" shouted Dr. Augustin.

I heard a loud thud as he tossed a hemostat onto the draped surgical tray, and risked a glance at the dog on the table. No blood pulsed into the air from a severed artery. All of Dr. Augustin's fingers appeared to be intact. And the heart monitor was still broadcasting a nice steady rhythm from the speaker on the wall. So I waited.

"I should have seen that," he said.

He put his right hand into the dog's abdomen and probed around. Had he lost something in there?"

"Is there a problem?" I asked cautiously. "Is she okay?"

It wasn't like Dr. Augustin to make a mistake in the surgery, much less admit it. And for me to highlight the error was asking for trouble. Especially when even talking to him that morning was risky. Things hadn't gone his way at the commission meeting. Something about downtown redevelopment.

Dr. Augustin's pupils constricted suddenly as he focused on my face. "Who?"

"The patient," I said, pointing to the shar-pei. "Mrs. Long's dog."

He gave me one of his milk-curdling glares. "What on earth are you talking about?"

"Well, you seemed upset. I thought there was something wrong with Mei Ling."

"Of course there's something wrong with her," he said caustically. "Why the hell do you think I'm wading around in her belly?"

I adjusted the flow rate on the IV. The silent drip, drip, dripping was like a slowly melting icicle. I thought about the waterfall in Mrs. Treckle's great room. Which brought the Tarot to mind. And the Prince of Wands. And the Death card.

"I was talking about Lester Jordan," said Dr. Augustin. He reached for the spay hook, then changed his mind. He put his hand back in the dog's abdomen.

"The county commission chairman? Why?"

"Because Lester Jordan was the City's public works director before he decided to go into politics. Because the public works director oversees the Engineering, Utilities, and Highway departments. Because, as director, Lester Jordan would be able to bring Justin Blaize on board as the department's principal contractor for the Northeast Recreation Complex project."

He paused while he worked the dog's grossly enlarged uterus out of the abdominal cavity. "This animal should have been spayed six years ago," he muttered. "If she's lucky, this tumor is benign."

I didn't say anything. Mrs. Long wasn't one of Dr. Augustin's favorite clients. To her, Mei Ling was a source of income, nothing more. The poor dog had produced countless puppies, had countless more aborted when Mrs. Long failed to keep her confined during her estrus cycles. And now the animal had a tumor the size of an orange in her uterus. It was Dr. Augustin's contention that the growth was the result of whatever drugs the dog had been given to artificially control her reproductive system. Needless to say, Mrs. Long had not gotten the drugs from Dr. Augustin.

"Okay," I said. "So it's possible Mr. Jordan and Mr. Blaize conspired to hide the contamination at the rec center site. But why would they want to? I mean, what motive could they possibly have? Seems to me, Justin Blaize would stand to make a lot of money removing that coal tar from underground. Why hide the fact that it's there?"

"If the problem was discovered early enough—like at the core boring stage—I assume the Parks and Recreation Department would have moved the complex," said Dr. Augustin. "Put it on another piece of city property, which would mean no recreation center for the Maraldee Manor, Carriage Hill, and Fox Meadows folks."

He put the uterus and ovaries in the stainless-steel bowl on the surgical tray. Then he went back into the dog. Pretty soon, he took his hand out and began to close the incision.

"I didn't feel anything else in there, nothing obvious anyway. I'll dissect that uterus after we're through here, and you can send off some tissue samples."

"Not to change the subject," I said, "but why would locating the rec center up there be important enough to hide something as dangerous as hazardous waste?"

"Good question," he said. "Money, undoubtedly. That rec center was the draw for a lot of very expensive homes."

"But you said that part of the county was due to be developed eventually, anyway."

He snipped off a piece of suture material. "Yes, but the rec center and the high school that went in shortly thereafter had a lot to do with the type of housing the developers elected to build. Families versus retirees. Three-hundred-thousand-dollar and up ranchettes versus condos and manufactured housing. Someone stood to make a small fortune selling off pastureland at those kinds of prices."

"Like Lester Jordan?"

He nodded. "Like Lester Jordan."

I shut off the anesthesia. "And his buddy Justin Blaize would be assured of getting all the city site work up there if he went along."

"Exactly."

"What about Dick Westphall?" I asked. "You seemed to think he might have had a hand in Trexler's murder."

Dr. Augustin stared at me. "Why do you say that?"

"Because you wanted to know if poplar was used for interior woodwork. Mr. Westphall does interior woodwork, right?"

"Very good, Samantha," he said. He went back to stitching. "But I've decided Dick Westphall stood to make money either way. The per-square-foot price might be higher for homes like those in Carriage Hill, but the number of jobs would go up if developers were to put in four houses to the acre or condos. Besides, I've known Dick Westphall for years. Dick doesn't impress me as a murderer."

"All right," I said, "Jordan and Blaize were in this cover-up together. But why worry about it now? Jordan has made his money, hasn't he? Why murder two men and burn down the Technical Services Building now?"

"What do you think would happen to Lester Jordan's political career if this cover-up became public?"

"Good point," I conceded. "But doesn't there have to be someone else involved? Someone actually employed by the City now? The person who is continuing to hide the mess at the rec center and continuing to hire Justin Blaize?"

"Most likely," said Dr. Augustin.

I waited for him to elaborate, but he didn't.

"So what are you going to do now?" I asked. "How do you plan to finger Trexler's killer?" God, I thought, I'm starting to found like Sam Spade.

Dr. Augustin was quiet for several seconds. Then he took a deep breath and shook his head. "Samantha, I hate to admit this, but I have no idea."

"You're not serious?"

He dabbed a gauze sponge over his neat little knots, then threw it at the garbage pail, as usual missing it. He peeled off his gloves and pulled down his mask.

"Yes, I am," he said. "The current public works director was Jordan's second in command. But he's a typically inflexible bureaucrat who sweats at the mention of anything the least bit controversial. He couldn't possibly be our city connection. Unless Jordan is still controlling him, which is possible, I guess. Still, I wouldn't imagine he'd be particularly trustworthy." He took off his gown and balled it up.

"You could always break into Jordan's house," I said, "and look for Trexler's rifle."

Dr. Augustin was about to toss the gown onto the pile of dirty instruments. He stopped and looked at me. A glimmer of a smile passed over his face. "Why, Samantha, I'm surprised at you. Breaking and entering is against the law. How many times have you told me that?"

"Several," I said. "Besides, I was just kidding." At least I hoped I was kidding.

Dr. Augustin lifted the dog off the table and, with me holding up the IV, carried her to a recovery cage.

"We could always go to Sergeant Robinson with what we know," he said, standing by the cage, his hand idly scratching the shar-pei's head. "Let the cops find the killer."

I laughed. "Yeah, right. Now look who's kidding?"

Nothing more was said about the rec center drama or any of the players. At noon, Cynthia left on an errand for Dr. Augustin—something about the dry cleaners. I couldn't imagine what Dr. Augustin owned that might need dry cleaning but figured it wasn't any of my business. Since we were almost out of computer paper, I asked Cynthia to pick some up on her way back to the clinic. I agreed to cover for her up front.

At 1:30 Tracey appeared in the doorway to the reception room. She had the stray puppy—tentatively named Lucky by Dr. Augustin—on a leash. The animal was bouncing around like a freshly landed fish on the deck of a boat.

"I don't think she likes that leash and collar," I said.

Tracey leaned over and picked the puppy up. The fish act continued. Tracey finally gave up and put the dog back on the floor.

"I'm trying to housebreak her," she said. "It'll make finding her a home a lot easier."

"Does Dr. Augustin know you have her out of her cage?"

Tracey shrugged.

We watched the puppy investigate one of the reception-room chairs. Suddenly she squatted and began to urinate.

"No!" shouted Tracey.

She ran toward the puppy but only succeeded in driving the animal backward through the puddle of urine and out of her collar. Then, before Tracey could grab her, the dog spun around and dashed off down the hall, leaving a trail of wet paw prints in her wake. Tracey put her hands on her hips, and stared at the puddle.

"Good luck," I said, smiling.

She headed after the puppy but stopped in the doorway. "What are you doing tonight?" she asked me, turning around.

"Nothing that I know of."

"Want to go to the Seafood Festival?"

I started to ask her why she wasn't shadowing Frank to whatever low-rent beer joint had hired him that night, but caught myself. Tracey and I were, thankfully, back on speaking terms, and I figured the invitation was her way of making amends.

"Sure," I said. "I went last year and enjoyed myself."

"I'll drive," she said. "Let's leave about . . ."

She was interrupted by a loud racket back in the kennel. She stuck her head around the corner, then withdrew it again. She stepped out of the way just as a large orange cat, its hair wet and standing out in tufts like porcupine quills, came flying into the reception room. Close behind it was the puppy, barking gleefully.

The cat jumped up on Cynthia's desk, sending a shower of water droplets and the front section of the newspaper into my lap. Tracey continued to stand with her backside pressed up against the wall. Her expression was one of tempered amusement. "Uh-oh," she said.

At that moment Frank appeared. He was soaking wet, which was nothing unusual. But his T-shirt looked like it had been through a paper shredder. And there were tiny, but ever increasing lines of blood on his left arm.

He pointed to the cat, who was sitting hunched up on the edge of the desk, its ears very low, its throat rumbling like a slowly approaching freight train.

"Thanks a lot, Tracey," he said. He frowned at the puppy. "Why is that animal out of its cage, anyway? What if he's got rabies?"

"*He* is a *she*," said Tracey. "And does she look rabid to you?"

The three of us watched as the puppy growled and snapped at imaginary flies.

"Yes," said Frank. Then he pointed to the cat. "He needs to go into a dryer cage, Tracey. Maybe you would like to put him there." He left.

Tracey grinned. "I guess I'll hold off on the housebreaking for a while."

She walked over to the desk and, before I could suggest a carrier might be in order, picked the animal up. The rumbling became a bansheelike scream, which started the puppy barking again. Tracey dropped the cat, and it took off down the hall, followed closely by Lucky.

"I'll pick you up at seven," Tracey said, hopscotching over the wet spots on the floor.

I wiped the water off Cynthia's desk with a tissue and started gathering up the paper.

At 5:30 Dr. Augustin called me into his office. "I've decided to take you up on your suggestion, Samantha," he said.

His back was to me. He was lining the books up on his bookcase—making certain that they were all the same distance from the edge. And he was dusting the shelves and books as he went, which I interpreted as a sure sign of trouble.

"What suggestion?" I asked, trying to remember when I had been so foolish as to put ideas in his head.

"You said I could always break into Lester Jordan's house and look for Trexler's rifle. Well, I think that's an excellent idea."

"I also said I was kidding."

He began sorting through the mess on his desk. "If I'm not mistaken, Jordan's farmhouse is located fairly close to that horse barn and arena," he said. "We'll go there tomorrow night. During the team penning, I'll do a little reconnaissance of the area."

"And what am I supposed to be doing while you get yourself arrested for burglary?" I asked. Or shot, I thought.

"Follow Lester Jordan around. Ask him to explain the finer points of team penning to you. Or ask him what he thinks of that transmission corridor. Be inventive, Samantha."

"What about his wife?" I asked. "What if she decides to stay home tomorrow night?"

Dr. Augustin looked over at me. His eyes were very dark. "Jordan isn't married. He's a rich, eligible bachelor. The fact that he's sixty years old shouldn't matter to you."

I could feel the anger rise up in me like Old Faithful. Why did I continually let him get to me? "I have plans for tomorrow night," I said, as calmly as possible. "I'm afraid you'll have to do your breaking and entering all by yourself."

I turned around and walked slowly and purposefully out of the room.

CHAPTER 36

•

The huge hammerhead hung by its tail from a boat davit. Maroon liquid dripped occasionally from its mouth into a bucket on the ground beneath it, as flies jockeyed for position around the animal's lower jaw. A sign on the davit said GUESS THE SHARK'S WEIGHT AND WIN A TRIP FOR TWO TO THE BAHAMAS. PROCEEDS BENEFIT THE MARINE RESEARCH CENTER.

Tracey and I stood next to three other people who, like us, were trying to come up with the winning number. The creature's lifeless eyes, stuck like pearl buttons on either end of its fleshy snout, were staring at us.

"What do you think?" Tracey asked me. "Five hundred pounds?"

"At least," I said.

The wind shifted suddenly, and the aroma of charbroiled fish and hamburgers was temporarily masked by a distinct odor of decomposition. An image of the late William Trexler popped into my head.

"Come on," I said, dragging Tracey by the arm.

"Wait a minute," she countered, "what about the shark?"

"You'll just be throwing your money away." I steered her upwind of the hammerhead.

"It goes to charity, Sam."

"Right," I said.

I stopped at the small welcome booth and picked up one of the festival's little brochures. It had a map giving the location of each vendor and display. I began searching for the nearest beer wagon.

"What's gotten into you?" Tracey asked.

I didn't say anything. We started walking down the street. It was slow going because of the crowd.

"I heard you arguing with Dr. Augustin," she continued. "Why does he try to get you involved all the time in stuff he ought to be leaving to the cops to do?"

"He likes to have company when he breaks the law," I said. "I think the real issue here is why I *let* him get me involved."

"Why do you?"

We stopped at a booth selling beverages, and I bought us each a draft. At three bucks a pop, there was very little danger of us becoming inebriated.

"I don't know," I said. The beer tasted fishy. I drank it anyway.

"Well," Tracey said, "I'm sure not going to let him drag me into anything crooked or dangerous."

Just wait, I thought. He'll suck you in eventually.

"So, Tracey," I said as we browsed through the T-shirts hanging on a rack along the boardwalk, "why aren't you with Frank tonight? Isn't his band performing somewhere?" I pulled out a shirt with a great blue heron and a roseate spoonbill on it. The price tag said twenty dollars. I put the shirt back.

"Yes," she said.

"What?" I asked, in response to her grin.

"You'll see."

I spotted a pottery booth and headed for it. Tracey left for the beer vendor and a couple of refills. When she got back, and we were being pushed along by the crowd again, I offered to buy her an order of fried veggies. I hadn't had any supper, and the beer was making me dizzy. But Tracey declined, mumbling something about beef lard. I drooled over the charbroiled grouper. The great slabs of fish were being tended to by a deeply tanned and well-muscled type with tattoos over most of his body—at least the part I could see. A dragon peered out at me from beneath his T-shirt, which didn't quite cover his belly. The guy looked questioningly at me and pointed to one particularly juicy piece of fish smoking over the coals, but I shook my head. I wasn't willing to shell out seven dollars for a sandwich. Fries and cole slaw were extra.

It was nearly eight. The crowd and the noise were continuing to grow. It was a rowdy bunch. From the amount of beer the Anheuser-Busch people were selling at the half-a-dozen booths set up along the boardwalk, I feared the lines at the Port-O-Lets would soon challenge the Great Wall of China in length.

"I have to make a pit stop," I said to Tracey. "Before the crowd gets any worse."

We started wending our way across what had been a parking lot a day or two before. Now it was a conglomeration of trinket vendors and craftspeople and honest-to-goodness artists, each trying to capture the attention and money of the festival-goers.

I was more interested in my final destination than in the people milling around me and didn't recognize Detective Hummer until I was right next to him. I reached out and touched him on the arm. He looked over at me.

"Samantha!" he said. "What a surprise!"

He was wearing jeans, his Horseman's Association T-shirt, and cowboy boots. He had his arm around an extremely attractive brunette—a little thing wearing enormous silver earrings and a heavily fringed leather jacket. She looked familiar.

"You remember Susan Ferenzi," he said to me, "from the barrel racing?"

I smiled at her, and we shook hands. I introduced Tracey.

"Are you two here with Dr. Augustin?" Tom asked.

"Good Lord, no," said Tracey, much too quickly and ardently.

Tom laughed. "No, I guess you guys get enough of him during the day, don't you?" He looked behind me. "Dick, over here."

I turned around. Dick Westphall and a small boy of about nine or ten, who I took to be Westphall's son, Timmy, approached us from the direction of the Port-O-Lets.

"Dick and Timmy came with us," said Tom, after the Westphalls had joined us and I had introduced Tracey. "And I'm afraid Tim is already bored, aren't you, Timmy?"

The boy frowned.

Susan made a face. "All he wants to do is hang around that shark."

"Where is Darlene?" I asked Dick.

Dick looked away. "She isn't big on these things," he said. "And her condition makes her nauseated whenever she smells fish, or so she claims. Anyway, she had to work late."

A band started up somewhere, and Tracey tugged at my arm.

"If we want to get a seat," she said, "we need to head in that direction."

I told her to go ahead, that I'd join her. So she left with Tom and the others, and I took my place in line at the Port-O-Lets. A shaggy dog, wet and sandy, trotted by. He stopped to lift his leg on a trash can next to one of the portable toilets, then continued on across the parking lot. Several of us watched him with what I felt certain was mutual envy.

When I finally made it to the temporary stage set up on the waterfront, I realized why Tracey had been so insistent on us getting seats. And why she had come to the festival in the first place. Frank was part of the entertainment. Or, rather, his band was. "Death Watch" had finally landed a big one.

Frank looked different. For one thing, his hair was pulled back in a ponytail, rather than free-flowing. And instead of worn-out jeans, he was wearing pants made out of some shiny, satiny material. All of the band members had them on. Black, naturally. And the creases and wrinkles in the fabric caught the light so that your eyes had trouble focusing on anything except those pants. Elvis Presley could have benefited from a pair of those, I thought.

I sat down between Tom and Tracey. We were packed in like sardines. Timmy was sitting on Dick's knee.

Frank pounded on his drums and worked up quite a sweat, and the lead guitar wore a rut in the stage prancing back and forth. But all in all, the music was pretty good. Even Timmy found Frank's band entertaining.

At the break, Dick offered to go get beer and Cokes for everyone. He said he needed to walk around, that Timmy was getting a little large to sit on his knee. Susan went with him. Tracey took off to visit with Frank.

"Are you coming to team penning tomorrow night?" Tom asked me.

I watched Frank mop the sweat off his face and neck with a towel. I wondered if he was going to make it to work the next morning.

"I don't know," I said, remembering my conversation with Dr. Augustin.

"Oh, come on, Samantha. It's the Horseman's Association Halloween party. Everyone dresses up in costumes. Even the horses." He laughed. "Last year, I went as a horse, and my horse, Cherokee, was a cowboy. I rented my costume but had to make his—blue canvas jeans and a checkered tablecloth for a shirt. I put a cowboy hat on him and tied a red bandanna around his neck. We won first place for 'Most Humorous Horse and Rider.' "

"I'll bet Cherokee really enjoyed that."

"Well, probably not. But everyone had a pretty good time, anyway."

"I went as a Ninja Turtle," said Timmy. He'd been so quiet, I'd forgotten about him.

"And what are you going as this year?" I asked.

Timmy grinned. "Not telling."

I turned back to Tom. "I'll consider it," I said. "But I refuse to wear a costume."

Tom leaned forward and rested his elbows on his knees. "What do you think about Susan?" he asked, glancing around me at Timmy. Like Timmy really cared about anything other than Ninja Turtles and dead sharks.

"She's lovely," I said. "And very nice. I thought I saw you admiring her at team penning a couple of weeks ago."

He had something stuck to the back of his T-shirt. I reached over and plucked it off. It felt like a shaving of wood.

"I couldn't believe my luck when Dick told me she'd broken up with her boyfriend. I thought they were going to get married."

I examined the shaving. It felt fresh. Moist. I smelled it. Pine.

"What is this?" I asked Tom, holding out the shaving. "It was stuck to your shirt."

Tom took it from me. "I stopped off at the barn," he said, "to clean out Cherokee's stall and feed him. Les got in a load of shavings today." He began brushing himself off. "They stick to everything."

"Where does he get the shavings?"

"He picks them up from various lumber yards. We have to be choosy, though. A few trees are poisonous to horses if they eat the wood or chew on it."

I wondered if poplar was poisonous. I hoped not. I also wondered why Tom hadn't mentioned Sergeant Robinson or the case they were working on. Why he hadn't seen the possible connection between the shavings on Trexler's body and the shavings at the barn. Or maybe he had.

"I just might drop by tomorrow night," I said.

Tom looked at me and smiled. "You won't regret it, I promise."

Let's hope not, I thought.

CHAPTER 37

•

Saturday, October 30

The dew point and the air temperature clashed head-on somewhere between the clinic and Lester Jordan's ranch. And the farther we traveled from town, the thicker the ground fog got. Dr. Augustin slowed the Jeep almost to the speed limit. The moon was a day or two short of full, but bright enough to make the fog look like a blanket of snow. Trees, their bottom halves submerged in it, seemed to be floating. On either side of the road, cows ruminating in the pastures looked like figureheads on Viking ships or very fat Loch Ness monsters.

When I told Dr. Augustin I had changed my mind about going with him to the team penning, he acted like it was no big deal whether I went or not. But I knew he was pleased, because he offered to do treatments for me, so I could go home and change clothes. More importantly, however, he asked me which fast-food place I'd like him to stop at for supper. He can be such a gentleman when he wants to.

"Once we locate Jordan," said Dr. Augustin as he turned down County Road 72, "you keep an eye on him, while I whip over to his house. If the rifle isn't there, I'm not sure where else to look for it, short of breaking into Justin Blaize's house. And that could prove next to impossible, considering he has a family, and those homes in Carriage Hill have security systems to beat all security systems."

"Seems to me, Jordan wouldn't want that rifle on his property," I said. "Or Blaize, for that matter. It would seem more intelligent to get rid of it, don't you think?"

"Yes and no," said Dr. Augustin. "It *is* evidence, granted. But since the gun presumably was Trexler's and not Jordan's, there might be some advantage to hanging on to it."

"Like what?"

"Like being able to plant it somewhere else. Placing the blame on one of those Wiccans, for example."

"So maybe Jordan already did that," I said. "And we're wasting our time looking for it at Jordan's Place."

He tapped the steering wheel with his right palm. "Maybe. So maybe I'll get lucky and find an empty coffin in Jordan's garage." He sounded like he was serious.

Then I remembered the wood shavings on Tom's T-shirt. "I think I know where Trexler's body was stored," I said.

Dr. Augustin turned his head around. I could feel his eyes glowing like tiny charcoal briquettes.

"Oh, really?"

"Tracey and I went to the Seafood Festival last night," I said. "Detective Hummer was there. He had some wood shavings on his T-shirt. When I asked him about them, he said Jordan had just gotten in a new load of shavings for the horses' stalls. I think that corpse was stored someplace in or around the barn area. You know, where there are shavings."

Dr. Augustin was silent for a couple of minutes. He slowed the Jeep to a crawl and peered into the fog.

"Well?" I asked. His lack of enthusiasm at my discovery was aggravating. "What do you think? Could he have kept Trexler's body at the barn?"

Dr. Augustin spotted the sign to Jordan's place a second after we passed it. He came to a stop, then backed up. "It's as good a lead as we've had so far," he said, turning down the washboard road.

I wasn't sure it was actually a compliment, but it was probably the best I could expect from him.

"I'm glad to see you're finally using your head, Samantha," he added suddenly.

Well, I thought, at least he didn't throw in one of his "blond jokes."

He parked the Jeep in the shadows beside a huge silver horse trailer, and we headed on foot across the pasture toward the arena.

"Let's avoid the bleachers," said Dr. Augustin. "We'll be less conspicuous on the ground and should still be able to spot Jordan."

The barrel racing was evidently over, because the calf pen was being set up by a werewolf and two clowns. Tom had been right. Most of the spectators and a lot of the people on horseback were wearing costumes. Some of the horses were more elaborately decorated than their owners.

I almost didn't recognize Susan Ferenzi. She was dressed like an Indian maiden, with a beaded leather tunic and pants, and moccasins. Her hair was parted in the middle and braided. Danforth's Dandy was sporting enormous white spots on his bay coat and turkey feathers in his mane.

I looked around for Tom Hummer but didn't see him. Dick Westphall, it turned out, was one of the clowns putting the pen together. He passed us on the way out of the arena.

"Howdy, folks," he said. He had one of those big red balls on his nose and an orange wig.

Dr. Augustin stared at him, then laughed. "Quite the disguise, Dick."

"Yeah, thanks. Rodeo clowns are popular tonight. I don't expect to win anything." He caught sight of another clown—his twin—signaling him from the foot of the announcer's booth. "Gotta run," he said. "Catch you later."

I feared Dr. Augustin and I were going to be conspicuous no matter where we hung out. Even the guy selling T-shirts had on a costume—a white toga with a gold belt and a plastic helmet and sword.

Dr. Augustin bought us each a Coke, and we started walking back toward the barn area. Over the PA system, Darlene announced the first team—City Slickers Two (or Too). This was followed by the usual yelling and whistling as the riders tried to move their assigned calves toward the pen.

There weren't a lot of people working around the barn that night, presumably due to the costume competition, which was either fortunate or unfortunate, depending on your point of view. More people would have made our presence less obvious. Of course, it would also have made it harder for us to snoop around unobserved.

"If Jordan did hide Trexler's body here," whispered Dr. Augustin, "he'd want someplace secure—a shed with a lock on it."

"I expect all the tack rooms have padlocks on them," I said. I hoped he wasn't planning on breaking into every locked room we came across. For one thing, he didn't have his bolt cutters with him.

I heard Darlene say, "No time. Riders, please bunch your cattle." A young girl dressed like a ballerina suddenly emerged from one of the stalls. She smiled at us, then ran off toward the arena. She was wearing pale pink tights, and they had fresh wood shavings on them.

"I wonder what Jordan uses to transport those shavings," said Dr. Augustin. "Maybe our corpse got shavings on him when the killer moved him into the woods."

"A pickup truck?" I asked, peering into a stall with no nameplate on the door. "Or maybe a dump truck—the kind excavation companies use to haul dirt and debris. The ones with the roll-out canvas covers."

"You mean like Blaize Excavating uses?"

I nodded. "The cover would have hidden the body." I looked into another stall. A large commercial mower and a chain saw were occupying it.

We heard voices, and Dr. Augustin pulled me over to a stall housing a palomino and a Nubian goat. The goat put his front feet up on the edge of the stall door, stretched his head over, and began to lick my Coke can. Dr. Augustin scratched the horse's neck. Just a couple of city folk communing with nature.

The voices faded away. Darlene announced the next team—the Rough Riders—and a horse whinnied from an adjoining wing of the barn. The palomino answered. We checked out the rest of the stalls in that section, then went outside. Suddenly the crowd cheered. Obviously the Rough Riders had managed to pen one of the calves. And in record time, too. I thought about the woman and the two small boys. What costumes had they chosen for the event?

Dr. Augustin threw his Coke can in a large plastic barrel marked CANS, and looked around. The fog was getting thicker. And it was no longer confined to the ground. It closed in around us like mosquito netting. I could feel its damp weight in my nose and mouth when I breathed.

"That certainly has possibilities," said Dr. Augustin, pointing toward an outbuilding to our left, barely visible in the mist.

I added my can to the collection, and we walked slowly across an expanse of bare, well-packed earth. Several times we came close to stepping in piles of horse droppings, some of them still fresh and producing their own fragrant fog. I nearly collided with a set of cross-ties. Two eight-foot sections of power pole had been sunk into the ground. They each had a moth-eaten rope secured around it, with a snap hook on the free end. The piles of dung were more numerous in the vicinity of the cross-ties, and of course I managed to step in one of them.

The building turned out to be a true barn, very weathered and in need of paint and clearly much older than the rambling rows of stalls and tack rooms we had just left. It was also not locked, and the light was still on. Dr. Augustin pulled open the huge wooden door and went inside. I hesitated. Although there was very little chance we would run across another body, especially in such a public place, with Dr. Augustin you never know. Then I heard voices, again, and I reluctantly stepped inside and closed the door.

The aroma that greeted me was a heady mixture of alfalfa, molasses, and licorice. It was a welcome relief after the dank gamy odor of urine and horse sweat that hung in the still night air back at the stalls. Bales of hay and feed bags were stacked up against the walls and down the center of the room, creating two narrow walkways just wide enough for a forklift to operate in. A small orange cat sat on top of one of the hay bales, his tail curled tightly around his front feet. He was watching something on the floor, something I couldn't see, with great interest. His ears rotated around on his head like tiny direction finders.

Dr. Augustin was in a far corner of the barn, inspecting an enormous pile of wood shavings. I joined him.

"It's a mixture, apparently," he said. "Mostly pine." He leaned over and scooped up a handful of flakes, then held them under my nose.

I took a whiff. "Smells like a hamster cage," I said.

He let the shavings flutter back to the pile, then brushed his hand off on his jeans. "This doesn't tell us anything," he said. "One thing's for sure. I'm not going to find that rifle here." He looked around.

"Why does Lester Jordan have to be involved, anyway?" I asked. "Justin Blaize could be working with someone at the City and has been all along with Jordan's knowledge." I shoved the toe of my sneaker, the one with the horse dung on it, into the pile of shavings. "Those core boring logs bother me. What if the soils people at Sand Lake Testing made a mistake and failed to identify the coal tar? You know, back when the City was first considering the site. Then, after the tar showed up and it was too late to move the rec center, Blaize and company tried to hide it. Maybe they were afraid they'd be sued by the City."

Dr. Augustin walked over to a set of stairs that led up to the loft. He started climbing.

"I've considered that," he said. "And you could be right. About the error, anyway."

Boards creaked as he made his way across the loft. I sat

down on a bag of sweet feed and tracked his progress from the tiny strings of dust that floated down with each step.

"But I still think Jordan is somehow involved," he continued. "Don't forget, he *was* the public works director at the time. And he's entirely too shrewd to let a thing like that get by without his knowing it. Besides, I don't trust him."

A mouse scurried across the floor and vanished behind a wall of hay. The cat broad-jumped off its perch, hit the floor lightly, and ran after the mouse. It was as if Dr. Augustin and I weren't even there. Presently, I heard the mouse squeal.

"You don't trust Michael, either," I said, waiting for the cat to reappear carrying its dinner. "And he hasn't killed anybody." And then I thought, at least nobody I know of.

Dr. Augustin came down the steps. He ran his hand over his hair and face. "That's different," he said, shaking his hand. Cobwebs clung to his fingers. He rubbed them over his shirt. "Come on, let's see if we can locate Mr. Jordan. I still need to get into his house."

We left the barn and headed for the arena, retracing our steps through the mist and the horse dung. The floodlights now had halos of various colors around them, and the bright light bouncing around in the fog made it hard to see clearly. I thought how terrible it must be to have cataracts, since I'd always heard it was like looking through milk glass.

We reached the concession area just as Darlene announced the break. Riders began converging on the gate and, one by one, entered the arena. It was a chance for everyone to show off their costumes and socialize. The calves, for their part, stood in a tight knot at the far end of the arena and waited. Their faces were devoid of expression, not that cows ever have much expression to begin with.

"There he is," whispered Dr. Augustin. "Standing by the stairs to the announcer's booth. He isn't wearing a costume."

I looked that way and saw Jordan in his cowboy hat talking to Justin Blaize. Blaize's hair was unmistakable, and like

Jordan, he was dressed in jeans and a long-sleeved shirt, rather than a costume.

"You keep track of Jordan," said Dr. Augustin. "I'll be back as quickly as I can." He started walking.

I ran after him. "What am I supposed to do, if he decides to go home?"

Dr. Augustin stopped and looked at me. "Just make damn sure he doesn't." He pointed at the Roman soldier selling T-shirts. "I'll meet you over there in about thirty minutes."

I bought a cup of coffee and walked around to the foot of the bleachers, where I figured I could watch the people in the arena as well as Lester Jordan. There was still no sign of Detective Hummer, although I doubted I would recognize him, under the circumstances. I'd seen Susan Ferenzi in the company of a rodeo clown, Batman, and the werewolf. Tom could have been anyone of them. Or he might have been called away on some urgent police matter.

I chewed on the edge of my coffee cup. Tom just didn't seem like the type to be chasing after crooks. He didn't even look the part, although I had to admit, television characters probably weren't the best examples of what a police detective looked like. And why didn't he talk about his job? There had to be something about it that wasn't "classified." I poured out the rest of my coffee. I was getting a headache.

A male voice interrupted the country music being broadcast over the PA system to announce the winners of the costume competition. One of the clowns and a scarecrow, each carrying an armload of ribbons and trophies, entered the arena. I looked over at the announcer's booth. Justin Blaize was leaning against the fence watching the awards presentation. He was alone.

"Damn!" I said under my breath.

I threw my coffee cup in a nearby trash can and started walking. Dr. Augustin hadn't told me where Jordan's house was, and in the fog I knew it would be difficult to spot from the arena.

When I reached the announcer's booth, I stopped and scanned the area for some sign of Jordan. The male voice was talking again. It said that Susan Ferenzi on Danforth's Dandy had won first place in the Most Attractive Horse and Rider category. Big surprise, I thought. The audience began to cheer and clap. I watched Susan trot her horse over to the gate. Turkey feathers flapped in the breeze. I took a step, then looked down. I was standing on the shoulder of a deeply rutted gravel drive that led east, away from the arena.

With my luck, I told myself, this will probably dump out on CR 72, miles from Jordan's house. But I started down it, anyway. I couldn't decide which scenario terrified me more—Jordan catching Dr. Augustin sneaking around in his garage, or Dr. Augustin finding out I'd let Jordan give me the slip.

The gravel was loose, and my sneakers wobbled and floated over it. Once or twice I nearly fell. My right hand still hurt from my encounter with the late William "Billy" Trexler, and I wasn't about to risk injuring my other hand. A lot of good I'd be at the clinic with two wrists out of commission, I thought. So I slowed down.

"This is nuts," I muttered. "It would serve Dr. Augustin right if he got caught breaking into Jordan's house."

I was about to turn around and go back to the arena when up ahead through the haze I saw someone in a clown costume. Or, rather, I saw a batch of blue, red, and green polka dots floating like Lucky Charms in the milky fog. And then I lost him. I picked up the pace a little, but the clown failed to materialize. So I stopped and stood in the middle of the drive, hands on my hips, trying to decide what to do next. I figured I had gone a half a mile, maybe more, and still hadn't located Jordan's house.

By now, Dr. Augustin has either found what he was looking for, I thought, or Jordan has got him staked out over a fire ant mound. And then I heard faint voices to my right. A man and a woman. I couldn't be sure, but the man sounded like Lester Jordan.

I stepped off the gravel and walked slowly and quietly through the trees toward them. It was so dark, I couldn't distinguish one shadowy form from another, but knew they probably couldn't either. I stopped about fifteen feet away and listened. The man was talking. It was Jordan.

"Blaize is coming over," he said. "Some business matter. You wouldn't be interested. Besides, won't Dick start looking for you, if you're not back in time for the second half? He's not stupid."

The woman moved away from Jordan, and I saw she was wearing a witch's costume—long cape and tall conical hat with a wide brim. And she appeared to be holding a broom. I couldn't see her face or any other distinguishing features.

"Please, Les, I won't stay," she said. "I need to be with you right now. Even if it's only for a few minutes."

I couldn't believe my ears. It was Darlene Westphall. Needless to say, I was relieved to have located Jordan, but this sudden turn of events had me puzzled. Darlene Westphall and Lester Jordan, lovers? Won't Dr. Augustin be amused, I thought.

Jordan and Darlene embraced, their black forms melding into one. Then they parted and headed together down the drive, cowboy and witch making a rather curious couple. I followed them, carefully avoiding the crunch of the gravel.

And then the outline of a two-story house appeared through the haze. To the left of the house, at the end of the gravel drive, was a small barn, or an enormous garage made to look like a barn. A thin line of light seeped out from beneath the double doors. I held my breath and waited for Jordan to notice the light, but he and Darlene had other things on their minds. After they were safely in the house and a light had come on in one of the downstairs rooms, I took off for the barn.

CHAPTER 38

•

When I got to the barn, I stopped and put my ear to the
door. I heard what sounded like a ventilation fan running but
nothing else, so I pulled the door open and slipped inside.

The left half of the building apparently served as Jordan's
private stable. There were three stalls. Two were occupied—
one by a buckskin and one by a bay. The third was filled
with wood shavings.

The right half of the building was a garage. A new black
Ford Bronco, its windows heavily tinted, gleamed menac-
ingly. I have read enough Stephen King to be suspicious of
all inanimate objects, particularly automobiles, and quickly
stepped away from the front bumper. The Bronco's neighbor, a white Ford pickup truck, looked pretty harmless. It
needed a bath and a few coats of Rust-Oleum.

Yard maintenance tools and other assorted hardware hung
on the wall to the right of the door. To the left was a set of
metal shelves containing miscellaneous horse grooming
aids, various insecticides, and several cans of paint.

One of the horses whinnied, and I looked behind me. Dr.
Augustin was coming around the Bronco.

"What are you doing here, Samantha?" he asked. He was
frowning.

"Jordan came back to the house," I told him. But I didn't
add "just like I said he might." "I wanted to warn you."

"Terrific," said Dr. Augustin. "I suggest we get the hell out of here."

"I take it you haven't found anything useful."

He shook his head. "Wood shavings. But then he has a horse."

"No rifle?"

"No rifle."

He pushed the door open and stuck his head out. Then he motioned for me to follow him. Outside, we both glanced across the yard. There was movement in the house. A figure passed in front of the light.

"There's something else," I whispered. "Darlene Westphall is with him. I think they're having an affair."

Dr. Augustin stared at me, then looked back toward the house. "Really," he said. He didn't sound amused. Of course, he and Dick Westphall are friends, I reminded myself.

Dr. Augustin pointed to the south side of the barn, and we made our way slowly over the gravel, trying to minimize the noise our shoes made. The scrunching seemed louder in the fog, as if the sound waves were being reflected back at us. It was like being in a large empty room with no carpeting. At that particular moment, I'd have sworn my heart rate was being broadcast over the PA system down at the arena.

Once we were out of the moonlight, such as it was, Dr. Augustin stopped and leaned against the barn. We could still see the house and the window.

"I guess this means we can go back to the arena, right?" I whispered. It never hurts to ask, I always say.

Dr. Augustin didn't move. He was watching the house. Suddenly he backed up and pulled me with him. I looked across the driveway. Dick Westphall was approaching the front porch. He had taken off his red nose and wig but was still swaddled in polka dots. After pausing briefly, presumably to listen to the conversation inside, he walked over to the front door, opened it, and went in.

"What is the point of hanging around?" I asked. "You can't search the house now. It's gotten a little crowded in there for that, don't you think?"

Dr. Augustin chewed his gum and continued to watch the house. I sighed and slid down the wall to a sitting position. The second half of the team penning was obviously under way. I could hear the crowd off in the distance and a male voice calling the teams, except I couldn't tell exactly what he was saying.

"Well?" I asked.

Dr. Augustin blew a bubble and caught it before it popped. "Any guesses as to where Mrs. Westphall works?" he asked. He was smiling. At least it sounded like he was smiling.

"Of course," I said. "She's our city connection, isn't she? The one who sees to it that Justin Blaize gets all the rec center contracts. I'll bet she worked for Jordan back when he was public works director."

Dr. Augustin chuckled softly. "Highly likely." He grabbed my arm. "Come on," he said. "Let's go find out what they're saying in there."

I went with him, and we crossed the gravel again. The party inside was heating up. I heard Darlene shout something unladylike, and then Dick responded with a couple of choice words.

Dr. Augustin stopped at the corner of the house and crouched down behind the shrubbery. I joined him, my knees sinking into the moist soil. I tried not to think about the creatures I knew were napping there. A tomcat had evidently been by fairly recently. He'd left his mark on the wall. I could smell it. Which meant Jordan probably had a cat. And I found myself wondering how anybody with a cat could murder someone. Two someones. Didn't people like that torture animals when they were children?

We were only a few feet from the window, which was open partway. And I heard Dick call Jordan an impotent son of a bitch.

"My my," responded Jordan in his folksy twang, "look who's calling who impotent."

Nobody said anything right away. Then Darlene made a little gasping noise.

"I should kill you both," said Dick. "Nobody would blame me if I did."

"You don't have it in you," said Jordan. Then he laughed.

I heard gravel crunch and looked over the hedge. I felt Dr. Augustin freeze. Justin Blaize was headed for the house, apparently unaware of the confrontation that was taking place inside. Clearly, he was also unaware of our presence in the bushes. He walked over to the porch and climbed the steps.

"Put the gun down, Dick," said Darlene. "Let's not do anything stupid."

Blaize stopped.

"And I should listen to someone who gets herself knocked up by a sleazeball like him?"

Blaize backed away from the door and went down the steps. He stood there for a second, then crossed the gravel again, this time slowly and carefully, and headed for the barn.

"So what are you going to do," asked Jordan, "stand there pointing that gun at us all night? At least let Darlene sit down." For a sleazeball, he sounded pretty sensitive.

"I think we should all sit down," said Dick. "And discuss our options."

From the tone of his voice, I doubted there were more than a couple of options open. And I didn't figure Mr. Jordan was going to like either of them.

Blaize had gone in the barn.

"Face it, Dick," said Darlene. "Our marriage was over years ago. Timmy was the only thing holding us together and you know it."

"And Timmy is such a bright little boy," said Jordan. "It would be a shame if you lost him, Dick, wouldn't it? I mean, if Darlene were to get sole custody. And if you're in jail, well . . ."

"Yes," said Dick, "Timmy is bright, isn't he? And I think he deserves a good college education, don't you, Lester? Not at any old school, either. Someplace up north. Duke maybe."

"Are you suggesting a deal, Dick?" asked Jordan. "Just exactly what are you offering in trade? Darlene?"

He laughed again, that time heartily. And Dick probably would have shot him then—I would have—except Darlene started to cry.

I reached over and touched Dr. Augustin's arm. I wanted to "get the hell out of there," as he had put it earlier, but all I got in return was a slight twitch of irritation. Obviously, he didn't intend to leave yet. Not without the rifle or, lacking that, something else in the way of evidence to give the police.

I stood up. If he wasn't going to get help, I would. I prayed Tom Hummer was back at the arena. I didn't remember seeing a pay phone anywhere, and since I didn't have the keys to the Jeep, I couldn't use the cell phone.

I gave Dr. Augustin a parting scowl, then stepped out of the shrubbery. The fact that he never even acknowledged my leaving really ticked me off, although it shouldn't have. It was typical, really.

I managed to steer clear of the gravel between the house and the barn and pretty soon was jogging down the drive toward the arena. I was concentrating on my footing and didn't see the werewolf until it was only a few feet in front of me. In the fog-diluted moonlight, it almost looked real. I stumbled, and the werewolf grabbed my arm.

"Samantha!" the creature said. "What are you doing out here?" He pulled off his mask. It was Tom Hummer.

I almost hugged him. "Looking for you," I said, somewhat out of breath.

He wiped his face with the mask, then smiled. "Well, here I am. A bit sweaty, but at your service. By the way, have you seen the Westphalls? Gus is having to call the teams and he's never done it before."

"That's why I was looking for you," I said quickly. "Dick Westphall is back at Jordan's place. Darlene is there. I think she and Mr. Jordan have been having an affair, and Dick found out." I took a deep breath. "He has a gun. Dick, I mean. I left Dr. Augustin hiding in the bushes outside the house. But I don't know what he thinks he can do alone. I was hoping you might be able to talk Dick into handing over the gun before somebody gets hurt."

Tom began ripping off the rest of his costume. He was wearing jeans and a T-shirt under his fake hair and rubber. And a pistol. It was in a holster clipped to his belt.

"My horse is in his stall," he said, pointing over his shoulder toward the main barn area. "You remember where that is?"

I nodded.

"He still has his saddle on," Tom continued. "There's a cell phone in one of the pommel bags. I want you to get it and dial 911. Have them send me some backup. Just explain that I'm here. Give them my name and badge number—766—and tell them it's a domestic dispute. That weapons are involved. In the meantime, I'm going to Jordan's place to calm everyone down."

He left his costume in a heap on the ground and raced toward the house. I took off in the opposite direction. As I entered the barn where Tom kept his horse, I remembered Justin Blaize and felt a wave of panic. What if Tom didn't see him. What if Blaize had a gun, too? Maybe he was the one who'd done-in Lanier and Trexler and wouldn't hesitate to kill a cop, as well.

I opened the stall door and cautiously approached Cherokee. But the animal was obviously one of those bombproof horses riding instructors and dude-ranch wranglers love. He didn't even look around at me when I began digging through the saddlebags for Tom's cellular phone.

After I'd dialed 911 and given the woman on the other

end of the line the required information, I ran back to Jordan's place. I took the phone with me, just in case. You never know.

Dr. Augustin was standing at the edge of the drive next to the barn watching the house when I got there.

"So, Samantha," he said, "what took you so long?"

Dr. Augustin and I waited next to the barn for Tom's backup to arrive. No shots were fired, although Justin Blaize had shown up with a gun, as I had feared. A rifle. Dr. Augustin told me Blaize had come out of the barn with it, which I felt certain didn't sit too well with Dr. Augustin, considering he'd searched the barn thoroughly, or so he claimed.

They took Dick Westphall away in a patrol car, but only as a precaution. Jordan wanted to press charges. Darlene, however, managed to talk him out of it. Apparently, she wasn't all bad.

Once again, it didn't seem like the time to bring up the matter of the coal tar, even for Dr. Augustin. Nevertheless, I was greatly relieved when one of the officers took Blaize's rifle. Another precaution, Blaize was told. He could claim it in the morning.

Dr. Augustin and I were standing with Tom outside the house while the cops did their thing.

"I suggest you check that rifle before you give it back to Mr. Blaize," Dr. Augustin said, so matter-of-factly I wasn't really paying attention. "I think you'll find it's a Winchester thirty-thirty."

Tom and I stared at Dr. Augustin.

"You're not suggesting . . ." Tom began.

"Just check it," Dr. Augustin said. The Cheshire cat was back.

CHAPTER 39

•

Sunday, October 31

My reunion with Michael wasn't exactly what I'd expected—what either of us had expected, I'm sure. When I opened the door at 3:30, he looked very much like he had on our first date—nervous, his tie too tight, his face a little flushed. And I had that butterfly stomach feeling I always got as a teenager whenever I went out with somebody for the first time. You saw them at school every day, but you never really knew them until the two of you were alone in a car. I feared Michael and I would have to get acquainted all over again. Two weeks might as well have been two years.

During the drive, he babbled on about his trip, his wife's son, all the restaurants he'd visited. By the time we reached the Brightwater Beach Art League Building, I was worn out. But it was a happy fatigue. He'd played my favorite music, opened the car door for me, and offered me his arm. And, as usual, he smelled terrific.

The art exhibit, a fund-raiser for the area's humane organizations, was being sponsored by the Bay Area Veterinary Medical Association. They'd chosen Halloween to increase public awareness about animal cruelty.

If I'd known ahead of time who the sponsor was, I wouldn't have gone. Dr. Augustin obviously hadn't seen fit to mention it to me. But he was there. I hardly recognized him. With his cream linen trousers and silk shirt, tieless and buttoned all the way up, and his Italian loafers, he looked like Yanni at the Acropolis—more muscles and less hair, but close enough to give every female in the place heart palpitations.

Melody What's-Her-Name, a bigwig in the Art League, as it turned out, was shepherding him around like he was a prized stallion, instead of a man. I did notice that most of the checkwriting was being undertaken by women, so maybe Melody knew what she was doing.

Michael got me a glass of champagne from the bar, then excused himself to call his office. I looked at a few of the photos and paintings, then hung around the hors d'oeuvres table, trying to avoid running into anyone I knew. The canapés, as befitted a humane organization benefit, were meatless, with lots of fruits and veggies—not something that would appeal to the average veterinarian—so I felt pretty safe. I wished Tracey had come. She, at least, would have enjoyed the food.

I was studying the little toast squares topped with some leafy concoction when a familiar voice said, "Wouldn't a Quarter Pounder with cheese taste good right about now?"

I turned around. Dr. Augustin's teeth glistened in the simulated north light of the gallery.

"I hate to admit it," I said, "but, yes, a hamburger and fries would hit the spot."

Dr. Augustin sipped his champagne, made a face, and put the glass down on a passing tray. The waiter grinned.

"So," I said. "Why didn't you mention this little gala? Or is it just for veterinarians and other big shots?"

He shook his head and frowned. "I was trying not to think about it, to tell you the truth. This whole affair was Melody's idea. Trust me, I wouldn't be here, if they hadn't agreed to push the county's spay/neuter program in their advertising." He looked around. "Where's Mr. Halsey? I saw you come in together."

"He went to make a phone call. By the way, have you

heard from Sergeant Robinson or Detective Hummer? About the rifle, I mean."

"No, not yet. I'm surprised your buddy Halsey hasn't sniffed out the contamination at the gas plant. It would make a great story." He smiled again. "Or have you guys been too busy 'catching up' to discuss it?"

I knew he was baiting me. I could feel his eyes working overtime. I picked up one of the toast squares and took a bite. The leafy green stuff tasted like some kind of seaweed. I tried not to gag as I tossed the remains in one of the trash receptacles conveniently positioned nearby. There were already several other toast squares in the can, along with some of the little rice cakes slathered with brownish goo.

I was looking around for something unhealthy to drink, when Michael came across the room carrying a full bottle of champagne.

"You look like you could use a refill, Samantha," he said. "Greetings, Lou." He smiled at Dr. Augustin, then poured champagne in my glass. "I hear from my sources in the police department that you two have been busy," he said.

Dr. Augustin and I exchanged glances.

Michael put the bottle on the table and picked up a stuffed mushroom. "When Samantha asked me to check up on one William 'Billy' Trexler—that you were interested in knowing if his death and the death of Jack Lanier might be related—I naturally became interested."

He put the mushroom in his mouth and chewed. I sipped my champagne. How much had I told Michael? I couldn't remember.

Michael dabbed at his mouth with a paper napkin. "Then when she told me about the hazardous waste at the recreation complex, I'm afraid my curiosity got the better of me."

Dr. Augustin examined his right thumbnail. He was scowling.

"Anyway," continued Michael, "I just got off the phone with my contact in the Homicide Division. Apparently, they've arrested Justin Blaize for murder—Trexler's and

Lanier's—and, in all probability, they'll charge Lester Jordan with conspiracy to commit murder, although I understand he is trying to make a deal. I imagine the City and the County will be reeling from the effects of that recreation complex fiasco for years. And a lot of lawyers are going to be able to retire when it's all over. They have you to thank for that, Lou."

Dr. Augustin quit scowling. "How many people knew about the coal tar and the cover-up?" he asked.

Michael shook his head. "That I can't tell you. The police are still trying to sort it all out. But I shouldn't think too many. Outside of the contractors doing the site work and the paving, that is. And they were all loyal to Justin Blaize or, more accurately, to his money. Lanier and Trexler weren't part of the inner circle, and they paid dearly for it.

"Blaize and Jordan go way back, evidently. Jordan and the elder Mr. Blaize were in the military together. After law school, Blaize's son, Justin, took care of both his dad's business affairs and those of Lester Jordan. Then when his father died, Justin gave up the law to run Blaize Excavating and help Jordan with his real estate dealings. Obviously, there is a lot more money to be had in real estate and land development here in Florida than in the law."

Dr. Augustin laughed. "Obviously." Then he grew more somber. "What about Darlene Westphall?" he asked. "How does she fit into all of this? Other than her infidelity, of course."

Michael shook his head. "I haven't heard. I do know she's been the administrative assistant to the public works director for about ten years."

He used a toothpick to spear a slice of carambola.

"Why did Mr. Blaize decide to dump that body out in the woods?" I asked. "He's obviously already buried it somewhere else. Why dig it up? And why put that pentacle symbol on the guy's forehead?"

Michael looked at the slice of star fruit as if it had suddenly taken on satanic properties. He pitched it in the trash.

"You remember that piece we did several weeks ago about the Wiccans up in the Carriage Hill area? I hate to admit this, but it was my idea to run that story. Anyway, my guess is, Blaize and Jordan decided to capitalize on superstition, as well as the power-line issue. Your door decoration was additional camouflage. Jordan admitted directing a couple of his men to do the work. It was chicken blood, by the way."

He looked at his watch. "We should be going, Samantha. Our reservation is for six." Strangely, he looked as if he'd lost his appetite.

He and Dr. Augustin shook hands. Then Michael and I walked toward the door. Before we could get out, however, Michael was nabbed by a woman from the Art League who wanted her name in the paper. While I listened to her talk about her plans for a showing of driftwood sculpture, I glanced back at Dr. Augustin. He had Melody on his arm, and they were headed for the bar.

EPILOGUE

•

Monday, November 1

The rain woke me a half hour before my alarm was due to go off. I rolled over and tried to go back to sleep, but it was too late. Priss had seen me open my eyes. She started to purr, and pretty soon she and Tina were on either side of my head, waiting. Then Priss touched my nose with her paw.

"Go away," I said.

But it is difficult to intimidate an empty stomach. The purring got louder.

I expected to find black crepe paper and balloons strung up in the lab. And Tracey telling unfunny over-the-hill jokes. She and Frank can get away with such things, being the children.

But nobody said a word about my birthday, even though I could see the big red asterisk on Cynthia's desk calendar and the words "Sam's B-day" written beneath it. Whatever they're planning, I told myself, will undoubtedly include something intended for the aged and infirm.

So I tried not to think about it, as Dr. Augustin and I did two spays and a neuter, tried not to dwell on the fact that I was thirty-three and had absolutely nothing to show for it. And, to top it all off, it was raining—hardly an auspicious beginning to my thirty-fourth year.

At eleven o'clock, Katrina Treckle came into the clinic

288

with an attractive wicker basket containing an orchid plant in full bloom. The two large white blossoms were incredibly fragrant, and soon all traces of rainy day wet dog had been erased from the reception area.

Mrs. Treckle was, of course, wearing black, but her expression was a bit brighter than it had been lately, probably owing to the fact that Halloween was finally over. Cynthia had pulled out the decorations box and was doing a little repair work on our paper turkey. Obviously, in Katrina's eyes at least, turkeys did not fall into the same category as black cats and witch's cauldrons.

"This plant is for you, Miss Holt," said Katrina, handing me the basket. "Happy birthday."

I took the orchid. "It's beautiful, Mrs. Treckle," I said. "You'll have to tell me how to care for it, though. I've never owned an orchid before." Then I eyed her suspiciously. "How did you know it was my birthday?"

"Oh, I have my ways," she said, as if the stars and planets spoke to her at regular intervals, which, in Katrina's case, was a distinct possibility. Then she gave me a quick course in orchid culture and said she was late for an appointment across town.

At the door she turned and pointed a finger at me. "Don't forget the Tarot, Miss Holt," she said. "When the question is posed, let your heart show you the way." She smiled her smile and left.

"What was that all about?" Cynthia asked, her interest naturally peaked by Mrs. Treckle's mention of the word "heart."

I put the orchid on her desk. "Did you know that vanilla beans are actually seed pods from certain species of orchids?" I said, looking everywhere but at her.

The party was in Dr. Augustin's office. There was the traditional pizza, one with pepperoni and Italian sausage and one without. And Cynthia's famous mandarin orange cake. I ate one piece of pizza and two pieces of cake.

Tracey gave me a book entitled *Eating to Stay Young,* which, mercifully, was the only overt reference to the aging process made that day. I thanked her, then ate my second piece of cake.

At 1:30 Michael arrived carrying a single white rose in a silver bud vase. I took him into Dr. Augustin's office, where the pizza and cake were still lurking. Dr. Augustin had stepped out for a few minutes.

"Won't you at least have a piece of cake?" I asked. He'd declined my offer of cold pizza.

"Well," he said, "if Cynthia made it, how can I possibly refuse?" He clearly had something on his mind. He was perspiring lightly, and he was pacing back and forth.

I cut the cake, put it on one of Cynthia's little dessert dishes, and handed it and a fork to him.

"Please, Michael, sit down," I said. "You look like you're about to fly out of here."

He went over to the daybed. "Sit with me, Samantha," he said, putting the cake on one of the bookcase shelves. "I have something I need to say to you."

We sat down, side by side. The daybed creaked.

"I can't think of a better way to put this," he started, "except . . ." He reached into his jacket pocket and took out a small black velvet box. "Will you marry me, Samantha?" He opened the box.

I stared numbly at the ring. It was an emerald set in white gold and surrounded by diamonds. Exquisite, yet tasteful, I thought with what little of my brain was still functioning.

Undaunted with my apparent paralysis, Michael pulled the ring free of the box, took my left hand in his, and slipped the ring on my finger. For the first time in the nine months I had known him, Michael's hand was like day-old fish—cool and clammy.

"Please say you will, Samantha," he begged.

I admired the ring under the overhead lights, watched the kaleidoscope of color blink on and off around the emerald with each twist and turn of my hand. The ring fit perfectly, of course.

"I don't know what to say, Michael." I kept hearing Katrina telling me . . . telling me what? Her ability to see into the future—*my* future—was unnerving to say the least.

He put his right hand on my arm. "Say yes."

I looked into his kind blue eyes and realized how much I really had missed him. I took a deep breath, and thought about the Tarot.

"Yes," I said.